THE VILLAGE IDIOT

ALSO BY STEVE STERN

Fiction:

The Pinch, a novel

The Book of Mischief, stories

The Frozen Rabbi, a novel

The North of God, novella

The Angel of Forgetfulness, a novel

The Wedding Jester, stories

A Plague of Dreamers, 3 novellas

Harry Kaplan's Adventures Underground, a novel

Lazar Malkin Enters Heaven, stories

The Moon & Ruben Shein, a novel

Isaac and the Undertaker's Daughter, stories

For Children:

Hershel and the Beast

Mickey & the Golem

STEVE STERN

THE VILLAGE IDIOT

A NOVEL

MELVILLE HOUSE
BROOKLYN · LONDON

First published in 2022 by Melville House
Copyright © Steve Stern, 2022
All rights reserved
First Melville House Printing: July 2022

Melville House Publishing
46 John Street
Brooklyn, NY 11201
and
Melville House UK
Suite 2000
16/18 Woodford Road
London E7 0HA

mhpbooks.com
@melvillehouse

ISBN: 978-1-61219-982-5
ISBN: 978-1-61219-983-2 (eBook)

Library of Congress Control Number: 2022938730

Designed by Patrice Sheridan

Printed in the United States of America

1 3 5 7 9 10 8 6 4 2

A catalog record for this book is available from the Library of Congress

For Bob Dickerson, friend of a lifetime,

and Sabrina, naturally

1

THERE ARE MANY TALES, mostly untrue, about the friendship between the artists Chaim Soutine and Amedeo Modigliani. My favorite involves a boat race. This was in 1917, when you could stand in the streets of Paris and feel the muffled percussion from the guns on the Western Front. German zeppelins were often seen overhead. The black-market price of a pack of Caporals or a couple of kilos of coal was extortionate; a pot-au-feu cost fifteen sous. At night the streetlamps were dimmed, the avenues empty, the shop windows X'd over with bomb tape. The cafés were closed before curfew and the galleries shuttered. What remittances the impoverished artists may have received from abroad were no longer crossing the border. They ate, when they ate, thin gruel at fly-by-night canteens. In the face of such general dreariness, the irrepressible Tuscan Modigliani, convinced that he knew just the thing to lift the spirits of the bohemian quarter, proposed a regatta.

The artists would construct their own vessels from scrounged materials, then race them in the Seine between the pont Louis-Philippe and the viaduc d'Austerlitz. The winner would receive the prize—a bottle of Château Lafite Rothschild filched from the cellar of the Café du Dôme—from the hands of the notorious Kiki, Queen of Montparnasse.

I can imagine the scene: painters and sculptors waiting to compete in their jerry-built boats on an afternoon the poet Max Jacob has declared the most glorious in the history of the world. The sunlight is unfiltered nectar; the soft-blowing April wind wears velvet gloves. The Fauves Vlaminck and Derain, however, are observing with disapproval the reflections of the Beaux Arts facades on the surface of the river: their prismatic shimmering is too much like an Impressionist palette. Moïse Kisling and Ossip Zadkine, both in uniform, are there on leave from the Front. Apollinaire is present as well, invalided with the injury to his outsized head that, along with the Spanish flu, will take his life on Armistice Day. Cyclists have abandoned their *velós* and booksellers closed their stalls along the quai des Célestins to watch the proceedings. Lovers on the banks disentwine and onlookers crowd the parapets of the pont Marie. The art dealer Zborowski, wishful as ever, is on the promenade collecting wagers and distributing receipts: the smart money is on Brancusi's hand-carved scull *The Flying Romanian*.

Picasso's contribution is *The Neversink*, a gaily painted Cubist contraption rocking dangerously in its berth, already on the verge of disproving its name. By contrast, the bark of Fernand Léger, on whose person you can still catch a whiff of the gas from Verdun, appears to be relatively seaworthy. So does Diego Rivera's rubber dinghy (dubbed *La Cacafuego*), despite the heavy freight of its passenger. Tsuguharu Foujita's *Vixen*, a flat-bottomed outrigger powered by a Singer sewing machine, rides the current with a tactical finesse. Maurice Utrillo has borrowed a porous coracle from a child. It founders directly upon launching so that the melancholy painter has to be fished out of the river with a grappling hook. A languid Raoul Dufy has entered a scow with a crenellated tower that will be truncated by the first bridge it passes under. Max Jacob has tarted up his punt to look like an argosy. There's the wallowing *Raft of the Medusa* haphazardly piloted by the potted Russians Kikoïne and

Krémègne. Modigliani himself is seated imperially in an enamel bathtub, his red cravat floating behind him in the breeze, the tub harnessed to a troika of canvasback ducks.

Utrillo's mama, Suzanne Valadon—ex-acrobat and former mistress of, among others, Toulouse-Lautrec—is wearing a hat like a hanging garden. She puts twin pinkies to the corners of her lips and lets loose the shrill whistle that is the signal for the race to begin. Predictably, Brancusi's scull shoots out ahead of the others, though for a time Foujita's *Vixen* keeps pace with it. The Russians and Rivera ply their oars for all they're worth, but it's clear from the outset they're no match for the front-runners. The sculptor Lipchitz relaxes in the stern of a barnacled fishing dory, while his wife shows herself remarkably adept at trimming the sail. But unfortunately, the wind offers little in the way of propulsion. The pug-faced writer Blaise Cendrars makes some headway in the driver's seat of a Fiat runabout mounted on twin pontoons, but his single arm—the other was blown off during the attack at Champagne—restricts him to rowing in circles. Meanwhile, having been thus far neck and neck with *The Flying Romanian*, Foujita begins to fall behind, and so decides to ram Brancusi amidships with the prow of his boat. It's at that point that Modigliani, making wonderfully steady progress in his duck-drawn tub, takes the lead. Cheers go up from the embankment as the handsome Italian, arms folded and smiling serenely, cruises upriver past the tip of the île Saint-Louis.

But Modi, as his friends call him, has a secret advantage. He's had a vision, as when has he not? Between his consumption of absinthe, opium, and hashish, his days are a series of hallucinations only occasionally tainted by reality. This particular pipe dream involved a Viking longboat towed by swans, outdistancing in competition the inferior vessels of all the other artists-turned-mariners-for-a-day. In the end it had been easier to corral ducks than swans, and a smut-blighted bathtub was more readily available than the longboat. Then he confided in his young friend, the Litvak painter Soutine, his plan for ensuring his victory: To assist the ducks in propelling his vessel, a length of rope attached to the tub would be fastened at the other end to a deep-sea diver, who would haul it faithfully forward from the bottom of the Seine.

The always anxious Soutine was not unaccustomed to the Italyaner's wild fancies, but this one took the knish. He'd yet to finish shaking his head over the absurdity of the scheme when Modi informed him that he would have the honor of being that diver harnessed to the tub.

"I can't swim!" was his despairing response.

It wasn't the first time he'd been inveigled by his friend into playing the part of his accomplice in some compromising circumstance. There was the night he'd accompanied Amedeo to a building site to steal blocks of limestone for his massive sculptures, the morning Modi had conscripted him into acting as his second in a farcical duel. And so on. Why, when Chaim wanted only to be left alone to paint his bruised fruit and dead animals, did he continue to allow the crazy Tuscan to entice him away from his easel? The answer was one he could not even admit to himself: that he adored his only friend this side of idolatry; and adoration, outside of art, was a thing that didn't come naturally to Chaim Soutine.

So, with grave misgivings, he went along with Modi to meet his acquaintance—Modi had many acquaintances—in his cobbled-together rescue cabin near the pont Mirabeau. This was Gaston Babineaux, salvage diver and unlikely art lover, who brought up suicides and murder victims from the river for the prefecture of police. The grizzly old water dog agreed to the loan of his *scaphandre de plongeur*, the ponderous rubber suit with its copper helmet and weighted boots, in exchange for an original Modigliani. He even volunteered to keep abreast of the diver's progress, following him along the embankment with the portable respirator. Then, seeing how Modi's companion had begun to tremble, he assured him there was nothing to worry about, except maybe a phenomenon known as "the squeeze."

"That's when your air hose is punctured and the negative pressure sucks your flesh and soft tissues up into the helmet. There was this diver I knew got so much of himself sucked into his helmet they buried the helmet instead of a coffin."

Seeing how Chaim had turned the green of moldy cheese, old Babineaux let go a guffaw that infected Modi as well. "Chaim," he said, trying to control his laughter, "think of a knight donning his armor to go into battle."

Thus did Chaim Soutine, late of the shtetl of Smilovitchi in the Russian Pale of Settlement, find himself toiling along the murky bed of the River Seine.

Many obstacles litter his path: wine bottles, suitcases, skeletal umbrellas, sculpted faces fallen from a bridge pier, artillery shells from previous centuries, a wheelchair—they come only briefly into focus in the turbid water, then fade away. The breathing gas pumped into his helmet from the surface supply tastes of disinfectant and smells like burnt hair. It's delivered through a valve operated by gnashing his teeth, which releases the flow of the oxygen-helium mixture until his aching jaw has to let go. Then he panics a breathless few moments until he's able to bite down again.

The diving costume to which he's confined weighs eighty-six kilos; the heavy boots kick up clouds of silt as he forges doggedly forward. The rope round his waist, looped at its other end through a hole in Modi's tub, further impedes his advance. The lead counterweight at his chest is shaped like a heart. How, wonders Chaim in his discomfiture, did I let the meshugah Italian talk me into this? Still, when not oppressed to near delirium by his immersion in this alien element, he experiences an occasional buoyancy that contradicts the fear. After all, Chaim is no stranger to claustrophobic confinement. Hadn't he spent days penned in a chicken coop or locked in a dank coal cellar back in Smilovitchi? His punishment for having broken the Second Commandment by making pictures.

The old leather-faced plongeur had called the air hose "your umbilical," and I like to think that, underwater, the painter might have entertained some unplumbed memory of being an infant again, suspended in amniotic impregnability. He might feel this despite the fierce dissent of his better instincts. Maybe he even remembers a tale he'd heard from his credulous mother about the Angel of Forgetfulness. He hates these *bubbeh maysehs*, these grandmother's tales, by which the shtetl folk increase the already overcrowded population of their rural ghetto with meddling demons and angels. In this fable the angel that watches over the child in the womb provides a light by which it can see from one end of the world to the other. The prospect includes the entirety of its life to come. But as soon as it's born the apprehensive angel tweaks the child under the nose so that it forgets everything.

What's the point? wonders Chaim.

But suppose that in the scaphandre the artist, like the child in the womb, has available to him the whole of his past and future. His life unfolds before the glass of his viewport, flickering amid a school of minnows that are swallowed up in turn by a big fish with a mouth like a bullhorn. Perhaps it's a function of the pressure on his brain of the tons of water above him and the artificial air in his helmet. Call it a species of rapture of the deep. But there it is now, the past—thinks Chaim, it should laugh with the lizards! What is there in the years that trailed behind him but hunger and ill use? And as for the future, he's had dire enough intimations of it while studying the subjects for his still lifes.

"Chaim," Amedeo once asked him, indicating the gutted hare hanging from a hook in his studio, "what do you see in its entrails?"

"What do you mean?" he replied.

"Can you read them like an oracle?"

Chaim harrumphed. "I see in them nothing but blood and kishkes," he lied, because he sometimes perceived in them more than he wished to see.

He wishes the past had begun no earlier than an afternoon four years ago when he departed the third-class car at the Gare de l'Est. His first encounter with the pandemonium of the Parisian streets had unnerved him and caused him to duck back into the station, though there was no comfort in its milling crowd. Seeking sanctuary, he ignored the address in his pocket and accosted passersby with the single French phrase he'd learned, "Où est le Louvre?" Their answers were incomprehensible. But following some homing instinct, he schlepped his rope-strung suitcase through passages and arcades; he stumbled past mannequins in emporium windows, along an avenue of ivory-white houses with wrought-iron balconies that might have lined a boulevard in paradise—and there it was.

Understand, Soutine had never before been face-to-face with a masterpiece. He'd only seen cheap reproductions and faded plates in the books of the small academy library in Vilna. Now, in those baroque, quarter-mile-long corridors, he came upon, unannounced, Titian's *Entombment* and El Greco's writhing, attenuated *Christ on the Cross*; he approached without fanfare Rembrandt's *Bathsheba at Her Bath* and—God help him!—the Dutchman's magisterial *Slaughtered Ox*. He viewed Corot's *Lady in Blue*, the cascading folds of whose gown made him forget even to look for the *Mona Lisa*; and a portrait in oil by Jean Fouquet of Charles VII, whose unhappy eyes penetrated his vitals like a cobbler's awl. He felt he might be close to a seizure and hugged the walls, frightened of the uniformed guards staring suspiciously at the threadbare Jew. He wanted to hide in the privy until the museum closed, then haunt the galleries by himself all night long, or for eternity.

It was only by virtue of some cosmic error, Chaim decided, that the likes of him was allowed to enter such a place. Shaken to his toes from a surfeit of bliss, his ulcer flared, his left eyelid fluttered like an insect's wing. He had upon him only the meager pin money donated by a sympathetic doctor in Vilna. Nevertheless, for the first time in his life he hailed a motor-cab and gave the driver the scrap of paper with the scrawled destination: 2 passage de Dantzig, Montparnasse. This was the address of la Ruche, the Beehive, the octagonal artists' phalanstery fabricated out of a disassembled pavilion from the 1889 Universal Exposition. The same world's fair for which the Eiffel Tower had been built. The eccentric structure, whose cupola towered above the surrounding rooftops, had been financed by the beneficent sculptor Alfred Boucher, who lived with his pet donkey in an outbuilding on the overgrown grounds. The Beehive itself housed a disorderly warren of studios thronged with a ragtag assortment of gifted immigrants who had swapped the poverty of inhospitable nations for the more romantic poverty of the City of Light.

No one there was especially happy to see Soutine. His reputation for being a temperamental *nudzhe* had preceded him among the Russians, some of whom had been his fellow students in Lithuania. They informed him that the swarming tenement was full up. The good-natured sculptor Miestchaninoff, however, agreed for some imaginary fee to share his studio, at least until the yokel from Smilovitchi was on his feet. A decade would pass before that was the case.

Fanatically private despite their close quarters, Chaim hung a burlap curtain over his designated corner of the wedge-shaped studio. It was a blind corner unilluminated by the tall windows that gave onto the roof of the Vaugirard slaughterhouse, whose stench pervaded the apartments night and day. (Its butchers, with an inherent disdain for artists, would raid the Beehive's garden at night, lopping off the heads of sculptures with brickbats.) He painted in his long johns to preserve his only suit of clothes, itself already much the worse for wear. As always he worked in fits and starts, attacking the canvas during the fits like a berserker. In Vilna his teachers had tried to wean him from his unschooled early efforts. They'd humbled him with the examples of the Old Masters, stunned him into an apoplexy with images from Dürer and della Francesca. They hampered him with the rules of symmetry and linear perspective. Housebroken, he'd settled for attempting sober *nature mortes* in the manner of the Dutch, or two-dimensional, tempura portraits like those preserved on the walls of Byzantium. Still tentative during those first months in Paris, he painted in muted pigments: burnt sienna, yellow ocher, Van Dyke brown, and on audacious days a tincture of Prussian blue. But that was before he met Modigliani.

He hadn't been looking for a friend. He had even avoided his compatriots Kikoïne and Krémègne, with whom he'd studied and starved in Vilna. The electrifying air of Paris was a shock to his system after the prevailing gloom of the Russian Pale. Reclusive by nature, since arriving in the city Chaim had gone virtually to ground. He might have attained some fluency in the language of his somber pigments, but with other people he could be inarticulate to the point of moronic. Moreover, when not painting he was occupied with the business of survival. He'd spent the remainder of the Vilna doctor's subsidy on a tutor who'd abandoned him with only the rudiments of a pidgin French he would never master. To assuage his lifelong hunger, he took odd jobs. He appeared for the sunrise shape-ups at the sites of public works, humped crates at the Gare Montparnasse, hoisted baskets of produce at les Halles. It was labor that aggravated the chronic inflammation of his intestines and left him disabled for days.

With the pittance he earned, he purchased the fruit, fish, and fowl that became the subjects of his compositions. He painted them with a watering mouth, convinced that his empty stomach heightened his concentration. Then ravenous, he would devour his subjects. On the evening he made the acquaintance of Modigliani, he was painting a brace of herrings dangling from a chianti bottle. He was involved in daubing a dollop of red to the neck of the sap-green bottle, a pale red the color of a robin's breast with which he was dissatisfied. That's when the curtain was yanked aside by Jacques Lipchitz, who whispered to Amedeo Modigliani, "The Litvak Soutine."

They hadn't known he was there. The two artists had come to visit Oscar Miestchaninoff, who was absent from his studio. They had poked about in the meantime, inspecting the sculptor's sleek marble heads. Curious to see more, Lipchitz drew aside the hanging burlap to reveal the immigrant in his paint-dappled *gatkes*.

As Chaim, in his absorption, was oblivious to their presence, they stood there watching his rapt activity. "The *shtot meshugenah,* 'the village idiot,' they called him back in Hotzeplotz or wherever he comes from," Lipchitz confided to the Italian. But when he started to drop the curtain, Modi grabbed it, still interested in observing the painter at work. Lipchitz looked from Modigliani to the grubby shtetl refugee, wondering what he was so fascinated by.

They might have turned and departed unnoticed had not the bluff Miestchaninoff hailed them upon entering his studio: *"Landsmen!"* At that Chaim turned from his easel and was outraged. He spat three times in anger at their trespass, and remembering his naked canvas, spun around to cover it with a sheet.

"We were just admiring your . . . offering?" said Modigliani, aiming a finger at the herrings, as if the fish rather than their rendering were the object of their espionage.

Chaim fumed. "You had no right!"

Modi stepped forward to introduce himself, calm in the face of the painter's vexation, but not yet ready to be pacified, Chaim was slow to take his hand. Though he nevertheless accepted the offer of a cigarette; it was his policy never to refuse a handout. Then even as he bent to let the Italyaner light his Gitanes, he was struck by the man's Sephardic beauty, which he seemed to recognize despite their never having met. Who hadn't heard tales of the penniless prince of the carrefour Vavin?

He was everything that Chaim wasn't. There was a thorough-bred elegance about him that the nap of his velvet jacket and the frayed edge of his cardinal-red scarf could not impugn. His dense shock of curling midnight hair was disheveled from having been tousled (one supposed) by a model or mistress. His faun's eyes were at once teasing and tender. In his presence Chaim was keenly aware of the heavy lids of his own sloe-black eyes, the left one given to a nervous tic, the right half-hidden by a fringe of oily hair. His nose was a bulbous beetroot, his lips what the goyim called "nigger." Hadn't he entitled the single self-portrait he'd bothered to execute *The Grotesque*?

Modigliani graciously invited Soutine to join them for aperitifs. "I've had a loan today from my rainy-day patron Guillaume. The drinks are on me."

Still reluctant to let go of his umbrage, Chaim couldn't help but feel flattered at being included. No one in recent memory had requested his company. Grudgingly he conceded that his work was in any case kaput for the night.

"I was going out anyway," he lied, and began to pull on his filthy pants over his filthy long johns. He snuffed out the spirit lamp and followed the rakish Italian through the little regiment of carved busts and torsos.

Lipchitz and Miestchaninoff, however, begged off. Jacques remembered that he had a wife and the pie-faced Oscar a rare commission to complete. So it was left to Modi to introduce the unfledged immigrant to the city after dark.

"Come, Soutine," he said, "without hope, we live in desire."

It was an enticement Chaim would hear various versions of in the coming months and years. But while he resolved each time to resist the Italian's calls to waywardness, he nearly always responded like one in thrall to some hypnotic suggestion.

Whereas Chaim was inclined to keep to the shadows, Modi strolled the evening streets as if, despite his insolvency, they belonged to him. Nothing belonged to Chaim and he disliked drawing attention to that fact. Modigliani, on the other hand, nodded to every shopkeeper sweeping a doorstep or sommelier raising a café awning. He blew a kiss to an aging streetwalker and merrily kicked a stray dog. He sniffed the air, discerned "an ill wind abroad in the soft night air, or is that your bouquet, Soutine?" Because Chaim had an aversion to bathing, fearing the science of municipal plumbing, primitive though it was at la Ruche. But before he could respond to the perceived insult, his companion had begun to recite a poem.

"'À l'aurore, armés d'une ardente patience, nous entrerons aux splendides villes!' Do you know Rimbaud, Soutine? I'll loan you a volume."

Nostalgic tonight, Modi had it in mind to revisit his former haunt of the Butte Montmartre. It was a long walk, since a hackney fare was out of the question, across the river and up the boulevard de Clichy past the gaudy shrine of the Moulin Rouge. Above Pigalle the steep streets narrowed and the storied quarter still retained pockets of rusticity: here a grape arbor, there a windmill, a lurid apache bar, an open-air *guinguette*. Along the way Modi played the part of cicerone, invoking the names of luminaries— Lautrec, Bruant, Jane Avril—who had consecrated the music halls and ateliers of the Belle Époque. He pointed out the caged window from which Gérard de Nerval had hanged himself and a condemned house Modi had himself once squatted in. He recalled the banquet for Henri Rousseau hosted by Picasso at the rambling folly of his Bateau Lavoir. There the Douanier, enthroned and wielding the scepter of his violin, presided over a bacchanal that included the entire roster of Bohemia. And Modigliani, late and uninvited, claimed to have crashed the affair just after his arrival in Paris.

"I personally intercepted the drops of wax dripping from a Japanese lantern onto the floppy cap of Monsieur Rousseau."

The two artists fetched up in a seamy tavern called le Lapin Blessé, a humbler cousin of the celebrated Lapin Agile farther up the hill. They took a table at the rear of the premises, its surface imprinted with rings from generations of overflowed cups. Above them hung a red-shaded lamp, behind them a wall plastered with sensational newspaper clippings from the previous century. Modi ordered a bottle of wine and, after swilling the lion's share, another. He continued regaling his companion with gleanings from his literary heroes, declaiming lines from Dante and D'Annunzio; he repeated Rimbaud's famous shibboleth, which he'd adopted as his own: "Le dérèglement de tous les sens!" and listed the ways he'd found to put that concept into practice.

"My senses are deregled already enough," Chaim had muttered. He hadn't meant to interrupt, but Modi paused long enough in his running monologue to chuckle, light a cigarette, and call attention to Chaim's runny nose.

Chaim duteously wiped the snot on the back of his hand. While gratified to have been taken up by the loquacious Italian, he was becoming eager to get back to his precious solitude. It was clear to him, despite the brief span of their acquaintance, that Modigliani had constant need of a gallery to play to; he must be always in the act of cultivating his legend: *le peintre maudit*, a homonym he set much store by. Even now, in the company of a soap-dodging greenhorn whom he had no call to impress, he was performing.

"I'm Apollo when I work," he declared, uncorking a small vial of ether that he poured into his wine, "Dionysus when I'm away from my chisels and paints," quaffing the glass and offering the dregs to his companion, who declined.

"Begging your pardon," submitted Chaim, amazed at his own presumption, "but it's a difference between to live and to work?"

Modi ignored him, rattling on about the sanctified enterprise of his art: that it was closer to *le vrai*, the real, than the world itself as it appeared to the unawakened soul. "When I make a portrait, it's more like the model than the model is like herself. Do you paint nudes, Soutine? Oh, the ladies, what a nuisance they can be with their false modesty! I have to throw a sheet over their cast-off underclothes so that my studio won't look like a boudoir. You know, Courbet claimed that he could give in his nudes all the character of Paris . . ."Coughing fruitily, he turned to gaze toward a window that overlooked the Hill of Martyrs, named for a decapitated saint whose severed head continued to preach. At the foot of the hill the lamplit city was spread out like a drunken spider's web.

Not wishing to disturb Amedeo's meditation, Chaim nevertheless made so bold as to murmur an ambition of his own. "I want to show all that is Paris in the carcass of an ox." But it wasn't true; he cared nothing for the essence of Paris. And when the day came that he could afford to bring a whole bovine carcass back to his studio, it wouldn't be Paris he painted but the ox itself: the ox *c'est lui*.

Having apparently heard him, Modi turned back toward Chaim and seemed to wait for him to continue. The immigrant squirmed in his seat, uncomfortable under anyone's stare; his flat features didn't bear close scrutiny. But Modigliani had fixed him with his vitreous, dun-brown eyes, and Chaim, who never gave freely of himself, felt called upon to contribute another two centimes.

"There was in Smilovitchi eleven of us children," he offered, "twelve if you counted my papa, who was himself a child. Like the rest of us he was always hungry, and would pick from our kasha the *gribenes*, the cracklings. My mama would see this and pass to him her plate, so she often went without. But"—he was thoughtful—"I don't remember I ever expressed to her gratitude."

Leaning forward, Modi placed his elbows on the table and propped his dimpled chin on his fists. "Where does it come from, Soutine?"

"Where comes from what?"

"The itch to paint. When did it infect you?" For Modi himself, born under the bright Tuscan sun, was an heir to cultural aristocracy, Spinoza an ancestor on his mother's side. The family had encouraged his artistic pursuit. But this lumpish Litvak had stumbled out of a howling wilderness that never heard of sfumato or Claude Monet.

"From bedbugs I get the itch," grumbled Chaim, actually reaching into his half-buttoned shirt to scratch his chest. He was becoming increasingly uncomfortable under the Italian's regard. It was as if Amedeo perceived something in him that Chaim preferred not to see in himself. Resenting this excess of consideration, he came to a conclusion of his own and suddenly blurted, "I don't need to make from your kind of murdering yourself a romance! My own art will murder me soon enough." Then he waited for Modigliani to get up and storm out of that flyblown joint, after which they would become estranged, as he'd estranged so many others.

But Modi, short-tempered as he so often was and likely to take offense at much less, only offered reflectively, "That's the difference between me and you, Chaim. May I call you Chaim?" Chaim marveled that he hadn't already. "I keep my torments out of my art. I save them for when I'm drunk or in love. Whereas you—I saw it at a glance—you smear them into your paintings like hot grease on an open sore."

The artist's earnestness was finally more than Chaim could endure. "What torments?" he exclaimed. "I am all the time a happy man!"

At that, though he tried to stifle it, Modi gave himself up to uproarious laughter. He took hold of one of Soutine's hands (as tapered and delicate as his face was coarse) as if grasping a lifeline. "Myself," he said when he'd caught his breath, "I'd rather be secure in my misery than risk being happy. Sans blague," he proclaimed, "happiness is an angel with a serious face." Then, always prepared to raise another glass at the slightest excuse, he added, "Let's drink to happiness!" and shouted for the barman to bring them *absinthe ordinaire*.

The burly taverner shambled forward from behind the bar carrying a tray containing a slender azure bottle of the clear elixir. The tray also held a pitcher of water along with two reservoir glasses, a bowl of sugar cubes, and a small slotted silver spoon.

Modi rubbed his hands in anticipation. "Have you had the grand wormwood, Chaim?"

Chaim's familiarity with spirits had been limited to the cheap bar mitzvah schnapps and vinegary wines of the Russian Pale; later on he'd learned to scarf a leftover eau-de-vie from the tables along the boulevard Raspail. But absinthe had so far remained a myth. Modi explained that it had been outlawed in the more respectable establishments, among which, judging from the sideways caps and wrist tattoos of its clientele, the Lapin Blessé was not. Then he began, with a precision that belied his advanced state of intoxication, to enact the ceremony of preparing "the green fairy."

"After the first glass you see things as you wish they were," he intoned, "after the second, things as they are not; then finally you see things as they are—a celestial nightmare!"

Modi uncapped the bottle and filled the two glasses, sliding one toward Chaim. He poured water from the porcelain pitcher into them both, turning the clear liquid to a misty jade. He placed a cube of sugar on the spatulate spoon, dipped the spoon into the drink, and lifted it out again. Then he took a match from his pocket, struck it on the table, and lit the sugar, which burned with a lambent blue-green flame. Once the sugar was caramelized, he again dipped the spoon into the absinthe, where the flame spread to engulf the surface of the drink. He poured more water into his glass, dousing the flames, and took a sip. He closed his eyes, opened them, startling Chaim with their incandescence, then passed him the spoon and said, "Now you."

His left eyelid in full flutter, Chaim attempted to follow suit. He managed despite shaky hands to ignite the sugar and dip it in his drink, which flared like a torch. Gasping, he reached for the pitcher to drown the blaze, knocking over the glass in the process. The flames traveled along with the spilled liquid across the width of the wooden tabletop, leaping from the table to touch off the old newspapers that covered the wall. The artists watched spellbound as a paper boasting the headline J'ACCUSE! shaded from coffee brown to chrome orange before curling into a gobbet of red combustion. In a matter of seconds, the entire wall of that spit-and-sawdust saloon was a billowing trellis of flame. The handful of rough customers were on their feet and making in a body for the door. Chaim and Modi were among them, though not before they'd witnessed the barman snap out of his paralysis and charge the conflagration. Furiously he attempted to smother the flames with his apron, but the apron itself caught fire. This sent the man into a Saint Vitus's dance whose frantic flapping only succeeded in fanning the blaze. So swiftly did the flames spread about the walls, dropping incendiary blossoms from the ceiling onto the tables below, that it seemed as if the boîte had been all along a tinderbox waiting to be lit. Windows shattered, labels on bottles blistered and peeled before the bottles themselves burst like shrapnel. The whole place had become an inferno and the barkeep, helpless to mitigate the disaster, fled into the street outside with the rest of his patrons.

It took the fire brigade the better part of an hour to negotiate the switchback lanes of the quarter. By the time they arrived— steam issuing from the brass pumper and the nostrils of the heavy horses that pulled it—le Lapin Blessé was a smoldering mound of cinders and ash. That the ruin was situated on its own barren parcel of ground, bounded by a now carbonized hedge, was all that had kept it from having incinerated the surrounding houses. Rubberneckers and tongue-lolling dogs swelled the ranks of those already gathered to watch the spectacle. Children jeered the tardy *pompiers* lurching among the embers and laughed at how their dribbling hoses caused the collapsed tin roof to sizzle.

Soutine and Modigliani had remained among the onlookers, standing under an arc lamp wreathed in smoke. They were joined there by the barkeep, whose disconsolate humor suggested he might also be the boîte's proprietor. Having ceased his quiet sobbing, he turned toward them, his fat face terrible with its singed eyebrows and beard.

"Ja sooey dezolay," said Chaim in his embryonic French. "I'm sorry."

The brokenhearted man sniffled, then brought down a hammy fist upon the crown of the Litvak's bare head. Chaim crumpled onto the cobbles from which Modi, himself unsteady on his pins, gently scooped him up. "Come, mon vieux," he said, "it's time we got back to work." Upheld by his friend's giddy grip on the back of his collar, Chaim needed no further persuasion.

2

THE ITCH. WHERE *DID* it come from?

Remember, the artist is underwater, the whole of his experience parading before him through a shaft of filmy sunlight penetrating the surface of the river. He needn't recollect or anticipate anything, but simply trudge forward through a consolidation of time, suffering the events that came before and those that followed after. Meanwhile, the rope attached to Modi's bathtub and tied round his waist, plus the hose connecting his helmet to Babineaux's much touted respirator, the Bracegirdle's Peerless, keep him tethered to the present.

What comes before he could do without, thanks all the same. *After* is better: after come the dancing houses of Cagnes-sur-Mer and the undulating trees of Céret, the dizzy verticality of the cathedral at Chartres, places that should have eclipsed forever the mud of Smilovitchi. There had been no pictures in the shtetl to stir an itch. Only a rank aggregation of hovels huddled about the rutted arena of the market *platz*. Art was barely a rumor, history only the binding of Isaac, the burning bush, the parting of the Red Sea. Or else it was an ill wind that blew rampaging Cossacks and the czar's latest edicts across the grassy landscape, and sentenced Jewish sons to decades in the Russian army from which they seldom returned. Oh, there were sepia photographs of fork-bearded patriarchs, and

perhaps an illustrated advertisement clipped from a *goyisheh* newspaper. But even the symbols and fantastic animals decorating the
ceiling of the old timber synagogue had faded to pastel stains. They
had been painted there in a time before the Second Commandment
had become incontrovertible.

"Thou shalt not make unto thee any graven image, or any likeness of anything that is in heaven above, or that is in the earth
beneath, or that is in the water under the earth."

His brothers laughed that Chaim's pictures resembled none
of those things, though they lustily participated in beating him
over them just the same. His father would have had the injunction
carved for a sign upon his brow. Once in a rage he went so far as
to begin an incision with his scissors in the boy's forehead, then
settled instead for beating him and locking him in the cellar. No
wonder he'd run away so often, only to return frostbitten and hungry from a night in the forest or fields. So why did Chaim persist
in making his pictures, drawing and painting on any available
scrap of fabric or paper whenever he could bargain for materials?
Why did the draft horse in the market stall or the rheumy-eyed
bagel peddler seem incomplete until he'd captured them with a
stick of colored wax on a cardboard panel? And why, when he'd
traced their likeness, did he feel so triumphant, as if—how to say
it—each image he made was some kind of intricate container for
his soul? Moreover, a funny thing: no matter how clubfooted or
pussle-gutted his subject, they all seemed somehow to be worthier
containers than his own.

It occurs to Chaim in his submarine element that he'd never
asked such questions of himself before Modi goaded him. After the
fire in Montmartre he returned to his still life, only to judge the
liver-brown tone describing the neck of the painted chianti bottle
as lacking in conviction. He took up another tube and squeezed a
glob of alizarin crimson onto his palette. *Crimson.* The word alone

thrilled him. He could taste it the way he'd once tasted the honey dripped over the letters of the Hebrew alphabet on his first day in cheder. And when he dipped his brush in the glossy pigment and touched its tip to the canvas with a flick, he felt his spine vibrate like a struck tuning fork. It was a color that expressed itself beyond texture; it had a meaning he understood with his growling belly and genitals, even if he couldn't quite apprehend it with his unquiet brain.

Colors have spoken to him from the cradle in a babel of languages, which he distinguishes, one from the other, by their peculiar sensations. Burnt ocher is the warmth of the shelf above a ceramic-tiled stove, ultramarine a breeze evoking a feeling of flight; yellow orpiment conjures the chanterelle or sometimes the livid flesh of a cholera victim, but even that has its own stunning heat. They are beautiful, those colors, though beauty was a suspect merchandise in Smilovitchi. Chaim has long since forgotten most of the Talmud portions he was made to recite in his childhood, but an admonition from the *Mekhilta de-Rabbi Ishmael* has stayed with him: "Anything made by man to represent the beautiful and sublime risks making an idol."

"So I'll make ugly," he had resolved with uncharacteristic defiance.

Amadeo has seen the shine in him. A mensch, he shares with Chaim the little he has, be it tokens from a dealer or mistress or the erratic allowance he receives from his mother in Livorno. He introduced Chaim as a prodigy to that dreamer Zborowski, who now endows him on occasion with the trifle he calls "a stipend."

"I can see through you, Soutine," Modigliani once asserted. He maintains that Chaim's fits of temper and fetor of body are a strategy to keep others at arm's length. That way he's left alone to focus exclusively on his fervid art. "We're geniuses together," Modi assured him—he's very liberal with the word; "but like Nietzsche says, 'A man who possesses genius is unbearable unless he possesses at least two other things: gratitude and cleanliness.' "

Toward the latter, he has tutored Chaim in the use of a knife and fork and in how to brush his mossy teeth. If Chaim sneezes at dinner in the home of a prospective patron, Modi whips off his cravat and, without interrupting the conversation with their hostess, hands it to the sniffling immigrant. He makes excuses for Chaim when, leery of the indoor facility, he's seen pissing against a tree in the back garden. When he secures an atelier among the glass and half-timbered cages of the cité Falguière, Modi invites Chaim to join him. They've slept there side by side on the cold stone floor, surrounded by a moat of pesticides intended to repel the fleas for which Chaim is a magnet. (Calling them "God's dandruff," Modi has tweezered a nest of them from Chaim's ear.)

What has he done to deserve the Italian's generosity, let alone his affection? Especially when he has nothing to give in return. The question still nags him in 1915 at the cité Falguière, where he paints his fruit and fish and broken-necked geese with a hectic aggression. He paints flowers in a spotted vase on an old canvas primed with rabbit-skin glue. What kind of flowers are they? How in hell should he know? All flowers are tchotchkes in the Yiddish vernacular; nature is the preserve of the goyim. The only thing Chaim knows about these flowers, plucked from a bed in the Jardin des Plantes, is that they have petals like little ballerina skirts the color of sapphire. And he must paint them or be overwhelmed by their clamorous existence. He paints the flowers over other flowers as is his custom. Seldom able to afford the cost of a fresh canvas, he buys antique paintings for next to nothing in the *marché aux puces*. Sometimes he doesn't even bother to scrape off the pastoral scene or the still life, painting over what's already there. The tepid former compositions challenge him to vanquish their mediocrity, and in this way his work is a palimpsest, the layers graduating—as Chaim sees it in his transports—from rubbish to truth.

He paints portraits as well of those he's able to lure into his studio with the promise of (if not material compensation) eternal life. Though he makes the offer tongue in cheek, there are those who consent, if only out of curiosity or boredom. There's the ragged clochard just shy of a cadaver, raptor-like in his beaky profile; the old woman, quite obviously mad, who refuses to remove a hat like a great upended basin. He never makes preliminary outlines of his sitters—he's no great shakes as a draftsman—but commences straightaway to slather the canvas with color. He stirs the brushes in his spectral palette until they're so loaded with paint he can feel their heft. Then he strokes with the bristle end, scratches with the handle, and scores the paint with the palette knife. Once he smeared the oils so hard with his thumb that he dislocated it. He chafes and furbishes the paint until it turns to flesh and the flesh assumes its original mystery. Fabrics glow in an extravagance of affection for the bodies they clothe, and Chaim wants to shout that he's the inventor of all that is human.

For such hubris he pays dearly. The guilt from his self-regard can leave him enervated for hours, and often, more often than not, he will take out his guilt on the paintings themselves. He slashes and cuts to bits many more than he preserves. A raised brow or a look askance from a fellow artist and he will remove the work from his easel and stomp on it like a fractious child. Let his countryman Pinchus Krémègne object to the length of a finger or the cast of an amethyst eye and he will slice an *X* across the canvas with a kitchen knife. It got back to him once that Jules Pascin, the quarter's de facto master of ceremonies, had called his paintings "schmiermalarei." "You get a lunatic like Soutine in every shtetl," he had allegedly said. After which Chaim splashed kerosene over

a dozen canvases and mauled them with steel wool. Overhearing
Modi quoting Baudelaire—"I hate the movement that destroys the
line" (and this not even in reference to Chaim's own work)—he
tossed portraits and still lifes alike into a bonfire in the courtyard
of the impasse Falguière.

Most of the time, however, he needs no one other than himself
to pass a terminal judgment. In truth, Chaim can glory in these or-
gies of destruction with an exuberance not so dissimilar from what
he feels when creating the paintings. To destroy them is a kind of
proxy suicide, which is satisfying just short of the real thing.

Sometimes his remorse comes full circle. Then he will gather up
the fragments of his canvases and stitch them back together with
the meticulousness he learned from his patch-tailor father. It's the
only skill he inherited from an otherwise worthless patriarch. He
patches his clothes—tattered garments gone practically pointillist
from spattered paint—with the same care, though they soon fall
to pieces anyway. Once, bereft of a single shirt, he cut his long
underwear into two parts; he poked his head through the crotch
of the pants and his arms through the legs, which he'd trimmed at
the knees. Later he appeared wearing the *schmatte* at the Café de la
Rotonde. Seeing him so clownishly attired, Modigliani howled with
laughter and asked whether he shouldn't be walking on his hands.
Then, realizing how he'd hurt his friend's feelings, Modi removed
his own shirt on the spot and insisted that Chaim take it for his own.

"Wear it in good health."

The gesture was perhaps motivated as much by exhibitionism as
by charity. In those days Modi was given to taking his clothes off in
public. He was proud of the milky pallor of his lean anatomy and
enjoyed taking every opportunity to show it off, circumcised manhood and all—at least until drink, drugs, and disease had begun to
take their toll. The cosmopolitan clientele of the Rotonde, however,
scarcely blinked at Modi's displays.

Located at the busy crossroads of the carrefour Vavin, the Rotonde is, from twilight on, headquarters of the 14th arrondissement's bohemian elite. Its beaten tin ceilings are five meters high, its zinc bar a U-shaped furlong; the walls are beveled mirrors, the banquettes full-grain red leather. There is a rack of journals scrolled around spindle-shaped wooden rods. In winter coal-burning braziers warm the terrace, which the Spaniards call *la playa Raspail*; there is a broad awning under which the patrons remain seated throughout the fiercest weather. The bullnecked proprietor, Père Libion, welcomes the influx of artists, who flock to the café after they've lost the light in their studios. He allows them to linger for hours for the price of a cognac or a café crème, and occasionally lets them repay their debts with the paintings that ornament the café's interior. He doesn't, however, tolerate prostitutes, drug dealers, or drunken brawls, which he settles himself with a bat he calls la Frappeuse. On any given night you can see gathered there an international assemblage of painters, writers, grifters, slumming socialites, and political exiles. Among them, hotly debating the virtues of Orphists versus Fauves, Fauves versus Futurists, and so on, there is always a healthy population of Jews.

They come from Cracow, Lvov, Drohobycz, Odessa, Vitebsk, Stare-Constantinovska, and Smilovitchi. All have been helplessly drawn by the gravitational pull of Paris, the lodestar of artistic experiment. To get there they have defied taboos, evaded bureaucracies, and scrapped the identities that had defined them for millennia. They have arrived in a metropolis roiling with subversive energies, where transgression is the order of the day. Lately it was the scatological skylarking of Alfred Jarry's *King Ubu*. Then Nijinsky horrified the balletomanes during a performance of *L'après-midi d'un faune* by making love to a swatch of crepe de chine. Erik Satie has recently reemerged from hibernation to shock the purists with his macabre humoresques, and from his table at le Restaurant Baty, in the city that declares itself the birthplace of reason, the poet Apollinaire champions every violation of reason and decency. When he isn't entertaining the bourgeoisie by some public knock-down, drag-out with his lover du jour, Amedeo Modigliani scandalizes them by garnishing his painted nudes with tufts of pubic hair. From the general response you'd think pubic hair was his very own perverse invention.

The aspiring Jewish artists who inhale this tonic atmosphere in 1910, 1911, and 1912 are jolted by its relentless vitality into manic activity. Those not stymied by the city's garish profusion are inflamed by it. They are young, poor, often reduced to beggary and suffering from neglect, but all are aware that the historical moment is nevertheless too good to be true. As a result, more painting is being done at this time in France by immigrants from the East European ghettos than the Jews have produced in all the centuries that have gone before.

Many of these *ostjuden* have brought along with them to Paris the heavy baggage of those centuries. Their habits of affliction dating back to the Covenant should have died hard, but in fact most have exchanged old habits for new with a breathtaking alacrity. They have swapped their gabardines and kippahs for sailors' jerseys and wide-awake hats, kosher wines for lemon mandarins and hashish. The gadfly Max Jacob has seen the face of Christ on the wall of his garret and converted to Catholicism, in the hope that it will curb his yen for little boys; Moïse Kisling has assumed a swashbuckling attitude and fought a duel. He and his fellow la Ruche alumnus Ossip Zadkine were among the first to volunteer for the French army when war was declared. Some, however, like Mané-Katz and the poseur Marc Chagall, have experienced a rare strain of homesickness. *Nostalgie de la boue*, they call it. They have conceived of the shtetl an exotic romance that they translate into their work, to the utter disgust of Chaim Soutine, who never looks back.

Feh on their dancing fiddlers, thinks Chaim, their doleful rabbis bundled in shawls and praying in midair! They're only pandering to the current craze of what the dealers like to call "folk art." As
if grinding poverty periodically interrupted by peasants slaughter-
ing *zhids* for sport is a spur to quaint reverie. Such airy conceits are
a criminal betrayal of the sovereignty of the genuine article. *The
whip hand of the actual*—isn't that Amedeo's battle cry? Though
even he, for all the classical harmony of his canvases, filters his vision through a kaleidoscope of artificial paradises. Trusting neither
memory nor imagination, Chaim must always have his subjects
in front of him. His eviscerated animals and joyless widows and
schoolboys owe nothing to dreams. He excises from his paintings
every last remnant of unreality. Just as, so often dissatisfied, he
lacerates the paintings themselves.

Let the whole *farblunget* immigrant crowd enjoy their shared
destitution. Chaim will keep his destitution to himself—though
his efforts to remain reclusive, the solitary prisoner of his work, are
ultimately in vain. He is never really alone. No one ever makes a
clean break from the shtetl. And personally, I believe there were
chimerical stowaways in that suitcase full of brushes and oils he'd
lugged onto the train from Vilna. They're with him now as he walks
through the years at the bottom of the Seine: the bogies bred from
the blind superstitions of his ancestors.

He thinks he may be growing accustomed to this subaquatic
realm. His "bonnet," as old Babineaux calls the helmet, has admitted only a small seepage of water where it's bolted to the diving suit.
The gas from the hand-cranked respirator, which the old salvage
diver trundles along the bank to keep pace with Chaim's movement, is no more impure than the putrid air of his studio. Sensitive
to his accomplice's occasional incontinence, Modigliani had advised Chaim to visit the WC before donning the cumbersome rig,
and for once his stomach is behaving itself. In some ways he finds

the world beneath the Seine less frightening than the one above, with its carnival of temptations and renegade Jews unshackled from the past. Their freedom is not his freedom, which is primarily the freedom to starve and go mad.

Ahead of him, however, the sunlight from above has created an aurora of watery draperies, and from their folds wave creatures out of his mother's cautionary tales. She had names for them, these runty household interlopers said to be demons and fallen angels—a fine distinction. They are *lantekh, shretelekh, kapelyushniklim,* and the child murderer Lilith, malign spirits against which one must be always on guard. They were as integrated into her religion and that of her tribe as the Old Testament God and his prophets. From his boyhood Chaim has resisted wasting an ounce of credulity on them; he scoffed at the amulets and occult conjurations the people employed to purge their wretched hovels of such figments. Aren't they harried enough by the laws of Jehovah and Czar Nicholas, that they have to concoct whole species of menacing beings to increase their misery?

But Chaim has not always been so dismissive of the *yenne velt,* the supermundane. Once, in his sixth year, enchanted by the tale of the wonder child Yoyzel Frandrik, he inscribed on a scrap of butcher paper the Hebrew characters (*Yod Heh Vov Heh*) that the rabbi said stood for the Unutterable Name of God. He made an incision in his foot with his mother's rusty carving knife, inserted the paper, and (terrific pain notwithstanding) stitched up the wound with his father's needle and thread. Then he waited to sprout wings like Yoyzel and fly from his dismal little town. Instead, the foot became severely infected, swelled to the size of a Sabbath loaf, and turned the brilliant green of a ripe honeydew. The speaker lady was called in to drain the ulceration and apply a resin and snail slime dressing. When the soiled holy name was extracted from the wound, Chaim was soundly throttled by his father, the punishment stingingly inten-sifying the agony he was already in. Afterward he swore off any dea-lings with magic forever, though it appears that the denizens of that domain are not yet done with him. For there they are, come all the way from their native habitat just to harass a poor artist and remind him of what he needs no reminding of: that Paris—even from seven and half meters underwater—is no distance at all from the past.

The past is as present in the river today as are the days yet to come. Here he is still in the meat locker in Smilovitchi, where the butcher Gdalye has dumped him after beating him senseless for painting a portrait of his father the rabbi. The meat locker is as immanent now as the stone shepherd's hut in Cagnes three years hence, where he will receive the telegram from Zborowski inform-ing him that Amedeo is dead. And the locker, the hut, the cloudy water—all are occupied by his own personal imps. They've attached themselves to his wits like limpets since his migration from the Pale. Of course they're nothing, insists Chaim, only hallucinations brought on by his incessant indigestion, though they've presumed to identify themselves by name: the triplets Snvy, Sansenoy, and Semangelof, who claim to have been exiled from *Olam ha Ba*, the Upper Eden; and Laila, a daughter of Lilith, who at this very mo-ment is doing a fair impersonation of a *rusalka*, a mermaid. Her coral-red hair floats like tentacles as she presses an alabaster breast against the glass of his faceplate. Then, with a flick of the iridescent tail she's developed for the occasion, she glides away.

To his shame Chaim has resorted to his mother's all-purpose incantations to try to rid himself of the lot of them. "Shabriri," he has intoned from the center of a Magen David chalked on the floor at la Ruche, "briri, riri, iri, ri," to no effect at all. If such hocus-pocus has any currency in the shtetl, it doesn't extend as far as the City of Light.

But why do these unbidden visitors persecute *him* instead of that midget Mané-Katz or the woolgatherer Chagall? Those bluffers could commit them directly to their canvases, in which demons and angels would be perfectly at home. Chaim will never paint anything in which he doesn't believe. "You don't exist," he assures Laila during her nocturnal visits. She purrs in his ear that his savage manner of working excites her, then bites the buttons off his union suit and rides his hungry loins. In the mornings he finds himself polluted after a fashion for which the holy books sentence the guilty to impoverishment and delinquency if not death. Frankly, it's the least of what he feels guilty about. The awful truth is that, even though the succubus lacks a consistent corporeality, she provides a useful function. She takes care of Chaim's need for love so that he can reserve his authentic passion for his painting.

But in this Chaim is deliberately confusing desire with love. Love for a mortal woman is a thing he won't dare to contemplate, not until after Dr. Barnes has come and gone. He has come to Paris before, but by 1922 the advent of Albert C. Barnes is cause for a flurry of universal expectation. Viewed by the cynical as a glorified snake-oil salesman, to the penurious artists of Montparnasse he's a fairy godfather who can wave his wand and turn a pauper into a prince. Among the Semitic circle at the Rotonde, word of his arrival is greeted like the coming of Messiah, and they begin to conspire among themselves as to how they might secure his blessing.

He's a tall, portly man, Dr. Barnes, with a round head of thinning salt-and-pepper hair, and a chin he juts forward like a ship's prow to compensate for its weakness. His bushy brows rest like twin caterpillars atop a pair of rimless glasses, behind which his steel-gray eyes are in a perpetual squint. A squint that discourages all nonsense but his own. He is a vigorous, forthright Philadelphian with dogged opinions and a shrewd eye for the innovative in painting, though he still retains (and perhaps cherishes) some aspects of the rube. His confidence in himself is further emphasized by the clench of his teeth around the stem of his bulldog pipe. From his childhood friend William Glackens, a founding member of the Ashcan School, he has early on contracted a hankering after high art that verges on a covetous obsession. Glackens had educated him with regard to the modern European movements and later became his emissary, traveling at his friend's expense on purchasing missions to Paris. In recent years, however, Dr. Barnes has conceived a desire to visit the source of the art in person.

A self-made gentleman fond of pinstripes and spats, he has earned the right to be a blowhard. He was born into a poor family and put himself through medical school by boxing and playing catcher for a semiprofessional baseball team. He took degrees from the University of Pennsylvania and later Heidelberg but never practiced as a physician; his internship at the Pennsylvania Hospital for the Insane, where the patients were routinely force-fed and lobotomized, had thoroughly disabused him of that inclination. Instead, he went to work for a pharmaceutical research company, where he soon after invented the miracle drug Argyrol. This is a silver nitrate antiseptic marketed as a general panace, a cure for ear, eye, nose, and throat ailments, and gonorrhea. He patented the drug, formed his own company, and made a fortune. An educational zealot, he compels his laboratory workers to attend his daily seminars on Dewey, Santayana, and William James, and has since devoted the rest of his time to pursuing his passion for collecting art.

He's in Paris in '22 shopping for more Renoirs, Manets, Matisses, and Cézannes, but he's open to recent experiments. He's uninterested in the Cubists—"All that geometry gripes my can"— but likes the early Picasso, whose *Acrobat and Young Harlequin* he's already bought at a salon of Gertrude and Leo Stein's. (The Steins sneer at his boorishness but appreciate the color of his money.) There are more blue period Picassos in Paul Guillaume's gallery in the classy rue de la Boétie, along with others whom the dealer deems "cutting-edge." The dapper Guillaume, in his gold-rimmed pince-nez and felt gloves, has been designated Dr. Barnes's "foreign secretary." He's eager to introduce the rich American to some late procurements, such as the prurient nudes of Jules Pascin and Amedeo Modigliani. The latter's work resembles, in its sphinxlike simplicity, the African art for which Dr. Barnes has also developed an appetite. The doctor is viewing all with acquisitive intent when his eye lights on a painting leaning against a radiator, which the dealer has failed to call his attention to. It's the portrait of a young man in a white uniform and chef's hat with an ear the size of a cuspidor. The paint is laid on so thick that the man's prideful face, and the bloodred kerchief he clutches, are practically three-dimensional.

"That one's a peach!" exclaims the American.

Unfamiliar with the expression, Guillaume states the obvious. "It's a pastry cook."

"Who's the artist?"

Guillaume, who's taken the painting on consignment from the out-of-pocket agent Léopold Zborowski, tries to capitalize on Barnes's enthusiasm, albeit backhandedly. "Chaim Soutine. You should see the fellow, Monsieur Barnes. It's an article of faith with him that ablution is a heresy, a change of clothes a sacrilege."

Dr. Barnes appears gleeful. "Introduce me," he insists.

The gallery owner eventually facilitates a meeting, though not before driving the American in his Peugeot Bébé around to Zborowski's flat in the rue Joseph Bara, where there is a trove of Soutines. Zbo has arrayed them against the walls of the guestroom he once set aside for Modigliani to paint in. There are the older still lifes of dead fish, flesh, and fowl, and later landscapes from the south of France, in which the houses and trees all appear to be caught up in a hurricane. There is a troupe of misfits in hotel livery pictured in Olympian poses. Suffering their onslaught of colors and medley of tragicomic moods, Dr. Barnes experiences something like a whiplash of his rational faculty. The good doctor, for all his bluster, is a sensitive man. He perceives the paintings as so far beyond nightmarish as to come out the other side of fear.

"I'll take them all!" he declares.

Zborowski reports the windfall to the artist himself, whom he finds slumped over a table in the back of Marie Vassilieff's canteen. On the wall behind him hangs a drawing of a party during which Marie relieved a drunken Modigliani of a pistol and pushed him down the stairs. Abstemious since the death of his friend, Chaim is sipping the bottle of Perrier he's been nursing for hours. His coat is patched like a burlesque hobo's and his pungent aroma reaches Zbo's nostrils from across the table.

"There never was an unlikelier candidate for a Cinderella story than you, Soutine," says the spade-bearded dealer, between whom and the Litvak no love is lost. Chaim doesn't know Cinderella from Queen Esther, but even he must concede that the news is good.

The meeting with Dr. Barnes, however, does not go well. During the two years since Modigliani's death, Chaim has been adrift. He has returned to Paris from time to time, nosing about the quarter as if not quite convinced that his friend is still dead. He is—and the city appears hollowed out in all the places he once inhabited. So Chaim turns around and heads south again. Too restless to settle in either of his previous retreats for very long, he shuttles back and forth between the towns of Cagnes on the Mediterranean and Céret in the Pyrenees. The harder he tries to save himself from despair with his painting, the more his painting seems to reject his efforts, and he falls into periods of stagnation for months on end. A luftmensch, he dwells in a sty when in the mountains, in a windowless stone hut when near the sea. Frightened by the depredations that drink had wrought on Amedeo, Chaim tries to resist the need for alcohol his friend had abetted him in cultivating, but his gastric troubles persist all the same. He swallows gallons of bismuth to coat the lining of his stomach, though his guts are often more convulsed from hunger than ulcers. Whenever a rise in the stock market permits Zbo to send him a few shekels, he is liable to spend them on painting materials rather than food. Then he squanders the materials on works that he destroys.

Now and again he is seen in familiar Paris haunts. His acquaintances, only slightly less pinched than he, tend to avoid the schnorrer, nor is he inclined to seek them out. He loiters outside the brasseries, a stooped figure in a patched reefer as splattered with paint as a Joseph's coat, hoping to cadge the heel of a baguette or a café au lait.

"Give a look," the jocose Moïse Kisling remarks upon spotting him from a distance, "it's Soutine waiting for manna to fall."

By pure coincidence he happens to be in town when it falls.

Having informed him that he's hit the jackpot, Zbo—for whom Chaim has suddenly become his fair-haired boy—persuades him to come round to his apartment to meet the millionaire. Late the next morning, much later than the agreed-upon time, Chaim arrives. He has pressed his antediluvian suit by tucking it under his bug-ridden bedding overnight and combed the lice out of his greasy hair. In Zborowski's parlor the American bites down his annoyance and rises with the air of a superior greeting a prospective employee to extend a glad hand.

"Ah, Soutine. Good."

Which is all it takes to render Chaim speechless. Morbidly bashful at the best of times, he's tongue-tied in the presence of the formidable doctor. This is the man responsible for the reversal of his misfortune, an impossible turn of events. According to Zbo, Dr. Barnes has offered forty-three thousand francs for some fifty-two canvases, the works. Minus the dealer's commission, Chaim will still be left with what for him is a staggering amount. All his life he has distrusted *mazel*; good luck is a concept fraught with cruel ironies. He's longed for it of course. He has sat of an evening in the Luxembourg Gardens, gazing up at the high windows of the houses of the gentry that border the park. He's even imagined himself living in them, reading his journal in carpet slippers while ignoring his wife's pleasantries, perhaps mussing the hair of his children before handing them over to their governess. Sometimes the idea of complacency soothes his insides like a broth. But his steadfast habit of wanting precludes his knowing how to *have*. Longing is Chaim's true métier.

In response to the doctor's bone-crushing handshake, he manages a muttered how-do-you-do.

They're in the parlor whose door still features the slapdash portrait of Soutine that Modigliani had painted on it one night in a burst of after-dinner exuberance. (This by way of twitting Zborowski's wife, Hanka, who protested throughout, while her husband assured her the door would one day be invaluable.) Zbo invites all to sit, while the highborn Hanka, barely concealing her distaste for the slovenly artist, offers tea and boiled *teyglakh* on a tray. Chaim bolts a fistful of the knotted pastries and sucks his tea with adenoidal noises through a sugar cube wedged between his teeth. Dr. Barnes looks on in fascinated revulsion. Then, dismissing the painter's lack of engagement, he continues holding forth on his theories of art education, a disquisition apparently interrupted by the artist's arrival.

"You can't learn to appreciate masterpieces by wandering like a ding-dong around a gallery any more than you can learn surgery from visiting a hospital ward . . ." His conversation is a mixture of rudimentary French and a jargon-laced Americanese largely incomprehensible to Chaim. Moreover, there's a rehearsed quality to his opinions, which seem aimed at no particular audience. Growing animated, he chomps on his pipe, then empties its briar bowl in his saucer; he removes his eyeglasses from a vest pocket, puts them on, then takes them off again. He complains about the asinine preconceptions your rank-and-file philistine absorbs from birth in a society "which they don't give a good goddam about art."

"Light, line, color, and mass," he contends, folding his arms, "they're the whole ball o' wax. Forget your historical context and your chronology and genre or whatever your con-o-sewers call style; give me light, line, color, and mass and you can eighty-six all the rest . . ."

Chaim is only half listening. The half he does hear seems beyond presumptuous and he anyway resents being lectured to. At the same time, he feels himself shrinking in the face of the collector's brashness, keenly aware of how his Slavic features and *kartoffel* nose might appear to an American goy. Self-consciousness aside, however, he bristles when he hears the man starting to get personal: for the millionaire has begun to discuss Chaim's work and that of Vincent van Gogh in the same breath. Van Gogh, thinks Chaim, was a madman, whereas *he*, give or take the odd delusion, is remarkably straight-thinking and sane. Van Gogh slathered on his paint like some moonstruck mud dauber, while Chaim is a master of impasto. This last Chaim murmurs with satisfaction under his breath.

Insensible to the artist's failure to respond, the doctor continues, "Take the trees, Soutine. Van Gogh's and your own. There's that bunch in the street of your seaside town, where was it?"

When Chaim's answer is not immediately forthcoming, Zborowski, deferential to the point of groveling, offers, "Cagnes-sur-Mer." Then he darts out of the room and returns almost instantly with the painting in question. It's already wrapped and labeled for shipping, but Zbo rips off the paper to reveal a tortured chorus line of swaying trees.

Dr. Barnes leans forward and slips on the glasses again. "You and van Gogh, Soutine—ah, those harsh colors, the chaos and bold, shrieking lines! You and him can squeeze tragedy from the bark of a tree like . . . maple syrup. Grief and tragedy, tragedy and grief . . ." The man is practically crooning.

"They're elms," tenders Chaim aloud this time, his temples throbbing. But the collector, on a tear now, ignores him.

"Every tree is a Tree of Life; they're Yggdrasil, y'know, the cosmic tree the Norse god Odin hangs from; they nod and sway like—what's that thing you Jews do in your temples . . . ?"

No longer able to contain himself, Chaim interrupts in his broken French, "The peasants in Lithuania, they worshipped the trees. They would put for offerings at the foot of them plates of stinking goose liver and jars of kvass. They were all of them ignorant pigs."

Barnes blinks, disliking the artist's tone. Has he been insulted? If so—his quick temper is renowned—he will wring the sheeny's scrawny neck. But still basking in the glow of his self-content over the haul he's attained for a song, he remembers his egalitarian philosophy.

"Do you like Negroes, Soutine?" he inquires, with a slight tremor of his extra chin.

Chaim has never met a Negro. He's seen their exaggerated images high-stepping and playing horns on posters for a club in place Pigalle; he's seen the masks in the Trocadéro made by barbarous *schwartzes* that Modi was so enamored of. They'd always given him *shpilkes*, those masks.

"I love Negroes," declares Dr. Barnes, an earnest if crack-brained progressive. "Someday I'll build a museum that only admits darkies. Then, through my program of artistic enlightenment," he announces grandiloquently, "they will become the dynamic factor by means of which democracy will finally come of age . . ."

Chaim has had enough, and suspects from the doctor's demeanor that the feeling is mutual. He gets to his feet with a farewell
gesture, neglecting to make the apologies that Zborowski begins to
make for him. He lurches for the door, which mocks him with the
coarseness of his own painted effigy. Closing it behind him, he can
still hear the American observing acerbically, "There's no accounting for talent." Chaim thinks that talent doesn't begin to explain
what he has.

3

THE ITCH. SCRATCH IT and a flame bursts forth. The flame surrounds and engulfs, tickles and scalds, but does not consume. From where does it come, the itch? Nobody but Modi has ever asked him. Nobody, least of all Chaim himself. Can it be ignited, he wonders, by another—like maybe a lady . . . ?

The mermaid, grown bored with the diver, has given his helmet a final coquettish slap with her tail and disappeared in a perturbation of bubbles. Chaim doesn't miss her. He has enough to contend with from the clunky boots and his labored rebreathing, let alone the strain of towing Modi's bathtub. Then there are the events transpiring fore and aft. Chaim marvels that he can be both a spectator of and participant in all he passes through. He steps over what appears to be the spine of a serpent, circumvents a one-wheeled hansom cab streaming willow moss. In 1918 he rides in a jolting Daimler omnibus that Zborowski has hired with funds borrowed from his sometime benefactor Jonas Netter. This is not long after the boat race and Modigliani's disastrous exhibition, his only one-man show, at the Berthe Weill Gallery in rue Victor-Massé. (The gendarme that ordered its closing was forced to pronounce his reason as the presence of "female f-f-fur" on the nude in the window.) The gun the Germans call Big Bertha is rocking the foundation of Napoleon's tomb, the Spanish influenza is making its bid to rival the Black Death, and Zbo wants to protect his investments. So he packs Amedeo Modigliani, Maurice Utrillo, Tsuguharu and Madame Foujita, and a peevish Chaim Soutine into the backfiring bus and drives toward the salubrious Côte d'Azur.

They install themselves in a farmhouse Zbo has rented in a vineyard just outside the town of Cagnes-sur-Mer. The town sits on a hill above the Bay of Angels, the hill itself crowned by a congeries of tile-roofed houses and sequestered squares besieging a medieval château. There is a port with a fleet of painted fishing boats and a park with tropical foliage where flamingos and iguanas range free. There is the wine-dark Mediterranean Sea. Sun-baked Cagnes is the jewel of the Alpes-Maritimes department, but Zborowski's household is not a happy one.

For one thing, Modigliani's health is precarious. He furtively coughs up blood and phlegm, and complains of the unavailability of the poisonous canary *mominette* with which he medicates himself. At breakfast he is seen not so discreetly dissolving hashish pellets in his coffee, their smell of rancid butter pervading the air. Moreover, he has sent for his mistress Jeanne Hébuterne, a waifish, ethereal, tallow-pale girl with braided whorls of strawberry-blond hair at her temples. She is nine months pregnant with their child. Her worried mother, Eudoxie, who despises Modi, has followed her daughter to the coast and taken rooms in the nearby town. She keeps the submissive girl with her and out of reach of the dissolute artist as much as possible. Driven to distraction, Modi alternates between fawning over his enceinte lover and excoriating both mother and daughter for their heartless mistreatment of him. Much of the time, pining for his Paris watering holes, he steals off to Nice to exploit the vinous hospitality of the artists Sauvage and Archipenko, who are in residence there.

Utrillo, an erstwhile partner in crime of Modi's, has tagged along with him once or twice, but mostly he staggers alone about

the harum-scarum alleys of the Haut-de-Cagnes district in the upper town. He is not long for this holiday. Recently discharged from
the Picpus asylum and escaped from his mother's strict supervision, the maundering Utrillo is ill-equipped for freedom. He has
neglected to bring with him the tintype postcards from which he
copies the views of Montmartre that are his only subject, and the
out-of-doors is a milieu he's experienced only during transits from
his bed to some local dram shop. That is, when his mother hasn't
kept him locked in his room. Left to his own devices, he becomes a
public nuisance. He frightens children with his bug-eyed stare and
assaults a young woman who resembles—he later claims—Joan
of Arc, whom he is fixated upon. Zborowski cables his mother,
Suzanne Valadon, circus acrobat turned model turned painter herself, to post his bail and send his ticket home.

Zbo tries his best to play peacemaker. Beyond the tensions between the artists, which he attempts to mediate, there is his wife's
prickly disposition to appease. The starchy Hanka has no patience
with the moods and tantrums of these prima donnas and bedlam-
ites, and has never been able to abide the loathsome Soutine. She's
appalled by Modi's behavior with regard to his pregnant lover
and cool toward the only other woman in their mènage, Foujita's
wife, Fernande, who was formerly a prostitute—though she has
since become a model spouse. Fou-Fou, as the wiry Nipponese
artist is called by his friends, is congenial enough. But his singular appearance—the black bangs, goggle-like spectacles, earrings,
and brush mustache—gives him a look the hybrid of an Eskimo
and an owl, which only calls more unwanted attention to their
caravansary. In addition, he wears baggy pajamas and sandals,
practices the dances he learned from Isadora Duncan in the street,
and has a habit of bringing stray cats back to their domicile.

"Their stench," remarks Hanka for all to hear, "is worse than
Soutine's."

Fou-Fou's presence further irritates an increasingly volatile Modigliani, as it was rumored that he may have deflowered Jeanne in her student days. Nor is there much goodwill between Soutine and Foujita, who has taken to calling Chaim "the Lizard." The pet name is inspired by the inordinate amount of time the Lithuanian spends lying supine in the sun on the town's stone parapets. It's true that Chaim is largely idle. The explosive colors and riotous vegetation of the Provence landscape have stunned his conscious-ness as jarringly as the bombings in Paris; the bottomless indigo immensity of the Mediterranean bludgeons his sensibility with awe and cripples him with inertia. The picturesque has never really agreed with him. He cannot work in such an environment, and un-able to work, he can't sleep. He complains of acute heartburn from Hanka's Polish dishes, the *placki* and duck-blood soup, complains of the unchanging perfection of the balmy climate. He wonders, though he mentions this to no one, how the shretelekh have dis-covered him even here. And too, he worries about Amedeo, who seems to be coming apart.

The Italian's fabled allure is much diminished. He has lately lost both weight and teeth, and his marmoreal pallor is tinged with a glaucous yellow. His raven curls lie flat as if pasted to his brow and he shivers even as he sweats buckets in the warm weather. When not glazed over from inebriants, his eyes are possessed of a basilisk intensity. His cough boils and bubbles in his chest and his breath-ing sounds like a rustling of dry leaves. Chaim can't bear to watch the feverish to-and-fro of his intemperance and dissipation. When he isn't trying to entice Jeanne from the clutches of her terma-gant mother with the promise of marriage, a union that will le-gitimize the birth of their child, Modi is warning her to keep away from him. It's for her own good, he tells her, quoting his revered Lautréamont: "Wolves and lambs look on one another with ungen-tle eyes." At other times, summoning a bygone vivacity, he might invoke apropos of nothing the doomed poet's more risible sayings: "My anus has been penetrated by a crab!" It's during one of these antic moods that he proposes an excursion to visit the Impressionist master Auguste Renoir, whose house is in the vicinity.

He has wangled an invitation through friends who live in the neighborhood of Renoir's palatial villa, les Collettes. Chaim asks him why he wants to visit a mothballed old *fortz* whose cloying work neither of them has any use for. "Think of it as a tour to an anthropological site," replies Modi, with a smile that suggests an ulterior motive. Chaim winces. He has no wish to accompany his capricious friend on such a questionable pilgrimage, but as so often before, he's cajoled into providing what Modi calls "moral support." On the seven-kilometer slog to the villa, they might have been mistaken for a pair of hapless vagabonds. Along the road Amedeo reviews the arc of the master's career: his early embrace of Impressionism, his rejection of it in favor of a classicism "that who can distinguish from Impressionism?," his fence-sitting during the Dreyfus affair. This last item Modi relates in an ominous tone.

"He never had the strength of his convictions," he adds, taking a swig from his pocket flask.

"What are his convictions?" wonders Chaim.

"That if the Jews have been kicked out of so many countries, there must be a good reason for it. France, beware!"

Chaim feels the familiar cramp in his gut. He's witnessed it before, how his friend is compelled to wear his Jewishness like a badge, while Chaim would rather erase all vestiges of his if he could. Especially the map of Jerusalem that is his face. Modi's attitude does not bode well for the visit.

But once they arrive at the imposing red-roofed stone pile rising out of its grove of olive trees, even Amedeo seems humbled. From the estate's hilltop situation, shaded by chestnuts, carpeted in lavender, dappled with sunflowers and purple thyme, you can see all the way to the beach at Cap d'Antibes. They're admitted to the house by an attractive young maidservant in a white pinafore, whom Modi informs that they're expected. The maid withdraws and a comfortably plump, florid-cheeked woman in her middle years comes forward (thinks Chaim) to eject them forthwith. Instead she greets them pleasantly. She introduces herself as Madame Renoir and cautions the artists that they must make their interview brief, as her husband's health is frail. She escorts them through bright, high-ceilinged rooms as lush with flora—potted bougainvillea, sprays of hyacinth, lemon trees—as the garden outside. A museum-worthy collection of paintings, gifts (Madame vaunts) from her husband's peers, adorn the walls. Other housemaids are seen bus-tling about, all of them shapely and blond and wearing pinafores. At the threshold of a solarium-like annex that Madame Renoir calls the *petit atelier*, yet another zaftig blond, this one wearing nothing at all, is making her exit. The silk shawl she pulls hurriedly over her shoulders hides only her shoulders. Scarcely seeming to notice, Madame Renoir announces the two artists to a bent figure in a rattan wheelchair.

Chaim is more shocked at his first sight of the decrepit master than by the naked lady; he's ready to pay his respects and beat a swift retreat when he feels the Italian's hand gripping his sleeve. He's tugged forward into the studio where Modi introduces them both to Pierre-Auguste Renoir.

The old artist is wearing a large flat cap trimmed in mos-quito netting, which he lifts over his face with a hand like a claw. Streamers of colored ribbon hang from the hand, ribbons used—as legend has it—to bind the brushes to his gnarled fingers.

"The price of leaving the windows unshuttered," he says in refer-ence to the veil of netting. His voice is reedy as a panpipe.

Indeed, the ferns and flowers that border the glass-roofed enclo-sure are orbited by midges and butterflies. Leaning against the clay pots are a number of paintings featuring voluptuous female nudes. Behind the wheelchair, instead of an easel, a large linen canvas revealing yet another fleshly form—no doubt the one that has just absconded—is stretched upon a pulleyed contraption attached to a bicycle chain. This mechanism presumably enables the canvas to be raised and lowered to compensate for the artist's lack of mobility. The jerry-rigged device and the disfigured artist himself appear as eyesores in that otherwise luxuriant studio.

There are no chairs, ensuring that any audience with the far-famed master will be short-lived. Modi and Chaim stand awkwardly on the slate tiles.

"So you're painters too," says Monsieur Renoir. He's slumped almost double in his chair, one shoulder raised to an ear in a permanent shrug. His cheeks are hollow grottoes, his beard a goatish tuft, the ice-blue eyes fixed in a moist stare.

Aware of his companion's having blanched at the artist's princely condescension, Chaim's heart sinks. But Modi is all charm.

"Maestro," he says, "remembering the poverty of your own youth, please forgive us for coming empty-handed. Allow our admiration to be our gift."

The old man closes and opens his red-rimmed eyes by way of expressing noblesse; he's clearly accustomed to receiving the homage of pilgrims. Then suddenly his face is contorted in a hideous grimace, a spasm having apparently convulsed his entire body. But just as quickly as it's seized him, the pain seems to let him go.

He lifts his wizened head. "The suffering passes and the beauty remains," he says, eyes shifting left to right to indicate the evidence of his paintings. A marmalade cat leaps onto his blanket-covered lap and settles there.

Chaim feels embarrassed for the old artist, while at the same time ashamed at having intruded upon him in his sapless decline. Modi, on the other hand, expresses concern, stating his readiness to offer any assistance he might. Chaim wonders whether the old man can detect the insincerity in his tone.

"Thank you," says Renoir, "but I want for nothing here." His thin smile is that of a personage accustomed to being venerated as a martyr to his art, an exemplar of fortitude overcoming adversity. Once again he raises his chin in a gesture of tenacity, but the effect is of a turtle extending its head from its shell. The tilt of the head is contemplative. "Now where were we?" he asks, alluding perhaps to a conversation that has yet to take place. "Oh yes—there are two qualities of art," he opines unsolicited; "the first is indescribable, the second inimitable." The cat purrs like a motor.

Chaim suppresses an acid belch while Modi wags his head enthusiastically.

"Work lovingly done is the secret of all order and happiness," the artist continues. "But first you must learn the laws of nature. Copy nothing but nature."

Chaim recalls Kisling's adage: "Nature, my friend, is anti-Semitic."

The warmed-over bromides keep coming, having doubtless served to satisfy the scores of aspirants who've beaten a path to the master's door. Modi persists in making noises of encouragement, which goad the old man into near animation.

"There's something in painting that can't be explained," he confides, struggling but failing to sit erect, "and that something is essential." Then, as if responding to an imaginary challenge, "Why shouldn't art be pretty?" Attempting another glance toward his canvases. "There are enough unpleasant things in this world."

"Tout à fait d'accord!" Amedeo full-throatedly concurs. Chaim rolls his eyes toward the tempered glass ceiling.

"Paint with joy," declares the old artist, approaching a possibly dangerous excitement, "with the same joy with which you make love!"

"Sans blague!" exclaims Modi, then launches straightaway into a somewhat revised verse of Baudelaire's, while Chaim fears the *alter kucker* will discern in it the parody of his own ardor. "It is the hour to be drunken!" shouts the Italian. "To escape the lot of the persecuted slave of time, be ceaselessly drunk—on wine, on painting, and on virtue!"

The master sinks back into his chair, obviously shaken by Modi's outburst. He appears nevertheless serene, like one who, having made his point, rests his case. In a voice ragged now with fatigue, he asks his impetuous guest, "Do you paint nudes, monsieur?" Mercifully ignored, Chaim wonders where he's heard this question before. It's tantamount to asking Amedeo whether he ever has intercourse.

"On occasion," simpers Modigliani.

The old artist heaves a sigh that seems to leave him visibly deflated. "I paint them as if they were some splendid fruit. I never think I've finished a nude until I want to pinch it. I stroke the buttocks for days before completing a painting." The misshapen fingers trace contours in the air. "Do you like buttocks, monsieur?"

The sun-drenched studio is fulsome with sensuality, and unable to censor the image, Chaim pictures the master's manhood as a shriveled horseradish root. Amedeo coughs his rattling cough, and Chaim can't decide which of them, the maestro or Modi, is closer to death.

"I prefer cunts," replies Modigliani, the connoisseur of buttocks, then lets loose, "For me the female torso is not a mass of flesh covered with green and purple spots signifying putrefaction. Not these doxies fit only to be hung on the walls of a brothel. I'm talking about your women, Monsieur le Maître, you Jew-hating bastardo!"

Bowing, he abruptly exits the studio, leaving Chaim alone with the sputtering old man. In the ringing silence Chaim attempts an apology: "They are an excitable people, I'm told," clearing his throat, "the Tuscans." He stands there marveling at how little the old artist's assured immortality has in common with the papery homunculus in the wheelchair, and is nauseous with pity. Then he's contrite at having dared to pity such an eminence. Respectfully he inquires, "Can I come back sometime and paint for you your portrait?"

The cat howls and frees itself from the artist's talon-like hand. When he finds his voice again, the great Renoir shrieks, *"Fous le camp!"* Get the fuck out of here!

✦

SHORTLY THEREAFTER, MODI'S MISTRESS Jeanne gives birth to a baby girl. A girl herself, the wraithlike Jeanne is for the most part uninterested in caring for the child. Overjoyed nonetheless, Modigliani trumpets his paternity and sets out from the hospital in the direction of the *mairie* to register the birth, illegitimate or no. He stops at a shady *estaminet* along the way to augment his celebration and commences an epic bender during which mother and child are entirely forgotten. Days later, having recovered some version of sobriety, the artist finds Jeanne reinstalled in her mother's apartment. She's on the verge of acquiescing to the hateful woman, who suggests placing the infant in the hands of a wet nurse who will dutifully starve it to death. In a scene worthy of tabloid melodrama, an incensed Modi matches his mother-in-law curse for curse, then gathers up his common-law wife and their newborn daughter and carries them away from Provence. Zborowski and Hanka have already preceded him back to Paris. Zbo has given his motive for abandoning his stable of artists as the need to sell more paintings, though when has he sold any paintings in the past? But the rent money for their communal hearth is overdue, and besides, Hanka is fed up with the company. This leaves only Foujita, the complaisant Fernande, and Chaim in the house at Cagnes.

Fou-Fou, who has been peddling his feline portraits to rich tourists, has also received an advance on a commission from a generous patron. All the same, he's not eager to foot the bill for the freeloading Litvak. The advance is soon spent in any case, and the landlord, irate over their thoughtless abuse of his property, engages the local gendarmerie to evict them and confiscate their belongings. (This includes their canvases, which he later uses to roof a henhouse.) Chaim is now left alone and strapped for funds in the far-off Midi, which suits him fine. While he has no reason for being there, he's reluctant to depart. For one thing, he's afraid of the suspicions the Parisians harbor toward the foreigners in their midst since the start of the war. Hasn't he already been the object of a neighbor's slanderous report? Then there's the still-raging epidemic and the bombs. But most of all Chaim has no wish to return to the forum of his friend's further disintegration. For Amedeo's behavior since the birth of his child has been unsettled in the extreme. When not in a protracted fever of elation over his fatherhood, he's in desperate flight from all responsibility. In either case the result is the same: his pulmonary consumption, aggravated by drink and drugs, shows every evidence of having entered its final stage, and he can no longer conceal its ravages with his signature whimsy. Any attempt to intervene on his behalf by friends, however, is met with angry disdain.

"I am the skipper at the helm of Rimbaud's drunken boat!" he'd vaingloriously declared before leaving Cagnes. It was the same declaration Chaim remembered him making on that luminous afternoon of the artists' regatta. Only now, thinks Chaim, the boat is not in the Seine but in that underworld river from the poem by another Italyaner that Modi is so fond of quoting.

Zbo, at Hanka's behest, has promised to send Chaim a few sous from time to time, if only to keep him out of Paris. So much does his wife revile the artist's presence. With this mean subsidy Chaim

lets a stone shepherd's hut in a pasture just outside the town of
Cagnes. At night animals bleat, bray, and howl; the wind whistles
through the cracks in the walls, making an eerie music, like the
diabolical humming of the she-devil when she takes her pleasure.
But in the mornings something else happens. The light of the south,
which had initially beleaguered him, takes Chaim by surprise: the
landscape bleeds light. This is not to say that the natural world had
never invaded the shtetl. There were meadows and forests abound-
ing in mushrooms and wildflowers all over the Pale. Hadn't he
chosen to spend nights alone in the forest, his hair on end at the
sounds of unseen animals, over facing his father's wrath? But nature was generally perceived by the pious as just another class of oppressor. As if the oxygen required by the woodland that ringed the
ramshackle town were requisitioned from the Jews, leaving them
short of breath. To admire a tree in favor of, say, a page of scripture
was a kind of heresy. But here in the Alpes-Maritimes the landscape
has assumed a familiarity that begs to be possessed. Though not in
the sense of ownership; Chaim has never been the acquisitive type.
Rather, the trunks of the plane trees and the oleander blossoms, the
yellow broom and scarlet gladioluses, invite the painter to inhabit
them the way a ghost takes possession of a living soul. Such a ghost
is known in the Old Country lore as a *dybbuk*, a notion Chaim
roundly rejects.

He rises at dawn after the usual insomniac night, chews a stale
crust with a schmear of some noxious paté. He shaves when he
shaves without water, wipes the blood with a paint-stippled rag, and
tries to reheat yesterday's coffee over a paraffin lamp whose oil has
burned away to vapor. Then he sets out with paint box and easel to
locate a vantage reserved for his eyes alone. He trudges over a dozen
rugged kilometers in his quest, finds a pine sprung like an opened
umbrella from a rocky outcrop, a stream spilling out of a beard of
feather moss, but has the feeling God has been there before him.

Cowed, he settles on sites—a quarry, a sheepfold, an abandoned sawmill—already altered by the hands of men. He paints them, then scrapes the paint from the unfinished canvas. He comes full-circle at dusk to find that the town itself remains undiscovered, at least from his peculiar angle of vision.

He mounts a vigil until the first morning light. Looking left and right to make sure no one is watching, he begins to paint an avenue of cypresses winding up the hill toward the château at the top of the town. He paints the crenellated ramparts and a sliver of the baie des Anges, the zinc yellow houses with green shutters and rust-red roofs, a ladder of red stairs climbing a steep street to the very pinnacle of Haut-de-Cagnes. He paints a breeze like a bridal veil wreathing a steeple. But the breeze under his rapid stroke increases in velocity, becoming a whirlwind that threatens to sweep up the town and uproot it from its aerial perch above the sea. In its turbulence the spinning environment strips the colors of their residual drabness to reveal the shrillest of aniline blues underneath, the cadmium reds that can stop Chaim's heart. In the end, having tapped the violent charge inherent in the town's deceptive tranquility, he has made the scene his own. He goes to sleep unwashed and hungry, which is nothing new.

He stacks his canvases with care, stuffing newspaper in the larger fissures of his hut to ensure a stuffiness that nearly precludes his breathing. The air-tightness of his abode will keep the work safe from the harmful effects of the climate. For the paintings themselves Chaim feels an uncategorizable affection. The sumptuous terrors and terrible passions contained in these paysages inspire in him a sensation beyond language that makes him want to fall to his knees and weep vinegar tears. But after having executed several score of such landscapes, he grows fretful. He decides he's leeched the town of Cagnes-sur-Mer and its environs of all drama and urgency. He recalls the crackpot campaign of Vincent van Gogh to make holy the light of Provence and begins to abhor the Côte d'Azur. In a letter to Zborowski Chaim expresses his discontent and asks for the means to travel elsewhere. Anywhere but Paris. Zbo, whose wife is a constant flea in his ear, heartily agrees: not Paris. So why not try perhaps the unspoiled Moorish village of Céret at the foot of the Pyrenees? This is the former haven of the Cubisters and their disciples, who had years ago used it up for their purposes and since decamped. Chaim will have the place all to himself.

He arrives in time for the *féria* on Bastille Day. The heat is infernal as the horsemen in their blue and white outfits run the young bulls across the great stone arch of the Devil's Bridge. The herd is pursued by roistering, half-naked youths, who grab hold of the tails of bulls and are pulled through the streets on their heels. Caught up in the fervor, Chaim follows the crowd to the *corrida de toros*, where he too buys a ticket and becomes transfixed by the brutal spectacle. He thrills at the surgical skill of the pig-tailed matador in his suit of lights, even applauds the aerodynamic passes of his magenta cape; then he can barely keep from losing the lunch he hasn't had as the bull is impaled by the matador's hidden sword. The animal, in its quivering death throes, may as well have received its coup de grâce from the butcher of Smilovitchi. (Chaim sees the man dragging out the carcass by its filed horn and hanging it alongside others in his meat locker.) But the town of Céret itself, with its jumble of terra-cotta roofs floating on a raft of cherry blossoms and asphodel, is inviting. Its history, as is touted everywhere, is as much Catalan as French: there were many sieges; there were plagues, during one of which an infamous doctor ordained that untold victims be buried before they were entirely dead. There is the bridge the Devil helped build in exchange for the soul of the first person to cross it. There are tall mountains and deep gorges, white water and dark green forests.

The intoxication that Chaim had exhausted in realizing the landscapes of the Midi he soon recovers in the hills around Céret. In fact, he is fairly besotted with all he surveys. But where the cliffs and cascades and the houses nesting on their wooded heights might have represented to another an idyllic repose, Chaim cannot leave well enough alone. Why does he feel compelled to transform that repose into chaos? The question is moot, and Chaim never asks it. All he knows is that when he paints, he is battered and tumbled about—heart, head, and kishkes—by an inner turmoil he wrestles with like Jacob with his angel. He exults in the conflict. He struggles to subdue a vision that will fling him into the void if he can't manage to pin it first to the gessoed canvas. A vision he must secure as if battening a sail in a storm. It's a task that can only be accomplished through the medium of oils. Watercolor is much too anemic, egg tempera (such as preferred by Chagall) too effete, gouache and encaustic too arid and opaque. Only oil lends an image that tactile dimension. With it you can trouble a placid surface into the crest of a wave or the furor of a maelstrom. You can, with the aid of a palette knife, prize the bark from a slow-drying oak tree or the mud from the sole of a sun-thickened shoe. With your thumb you can place a gout of blood in the yolk of an egg.

After completing a painting—not that Chaim has ever judged a painting complete—he's spent to the point of prostration. But unlike in the Midi, when long days of lassitude followed his exertions, no sooner does he finish a piece in Céret than his energies begin to gather again. The work will not let him rest, nor does he wish it to. The afflatus he'd acquired and lost in Cagnes has returned with a breakneck momentum. But while he feels, on the one hand, carried away by its current, on the other he credits himself with generating the flood. He is a demiurge—a word he's learned from Modi—and he no longer takes the time to turn around and destroy

his imperfections. He's enthralled by his own daring and by his
hand's swift complicity with his eye. The paintings accumulate by
the dozens. Often they seem more a by-product than the fruit of
his labors, like the sparks in the wake of a knife sharpener's emery
wheel. Then months pass and the time comes when he has viewed
the plane trees and crooked streets from every possible (and impossible) perspective, until the trees and streets survive for him only as
incrustations of pigment. That's when Chaim does what had been
so nearly unthinkable in Paris. Pathologically shy, he nevertheless
summons the chutzpah to buttonhole various citizens and offer
them the coppers he might have spent on his sustenance to pose
for him.

Of course, even when he's able to overcome his bashfulness,
there's his self-absorption and general disagreeableness to contend
with. Such traits are a poor advertisement for potential sitters.
Moreover, he has no studio but the "converted" cowshed he's leased
from a farmer, so he must paint the few subjects who are willing
wherever he finds them. He finds an ossified old man on a bench
in the Jardin d'Enfants, with half-closed sea-green eyes and folded
hands. A gallery owner will dub the portrait (and its variations)
The Praying Man, though Chaim, who seldom bothers with titles,
deems prayer as useless as a chocolate samovar. By the same token,
the dementia that is later attributed to the reptilian old woman
in pink, and the piggy little boy a merchant will label *The Village
Idiot*, may or may not be accurate. All Chaim knows is that whatever misery or dread holds them in its grip also keeps them frozen
in place. Not so the staff of the Hôtel Garetta, where Chaim has
briefly taken a room till he can't pay the bill. (It was the first in a
descending order of increasingly sordid rented rooms.) The irregular duties of the hotel page boys, waiters, valets, and chambermaids
allow them the leisure to volunteer as models. But their restlessness
must be forever placated by the artist, who can hardly control his

own impatience with their fidgeting complaints. He has repeatedly to promise them further recompense (which they will never receive) rather than berate them for their lack of forbearance.

Those who endure the lengthy sittings are invariably displeased if not appalled by the end results: the supposed artist has exaggerated their worst features, aged them by decades. None are unhappier with the outcome than the pastry chef Rémi Zocchatto. Having reluctantly agreed to a session on a terrace behind the hotel, he immediately has second thoughts. He stands with head cocked and arms akimbo, watching in bewilderment the painter's pitched skirmish with the canvas, questioning his intentions throughout. "Why paint us rather than our betters?" he asks, with a sneer suggesting that he of course has no betters.

Chaim's answer, while honest, is impolitic. "I like your uniforms." Naturally the artist is aware of the time-honored tradition in which innocent, cherubic bakers' apprentices are depicted in sentimental genre scenes. You see such cards in every *boutique de souvenirs*. But Chaim is genuinely attracted to the titanium white and scarlet lake of their livery. More than that, however, he's drawn to the contrast between the uniforms that would reduce them to types and the faces that declare their particularity. Their faces reveal a kind of molten identity just this side of caricature, while at the same time remaining distinct with arrogance, humility, aggression, cluelessness, and cunning in their several combinations: in short, the many aspects of themselves that plead for the painter to save them from oblivion. Chaim mixes their humors along with his colors, reserving the right to add a soupçon of oblivion. Still, when the pâtissier steps forward prematurely to glimpse his portrait, he's outraged.

"It took you all this time to make me look like a cretin?" he shouts.

Chaim refuses to understand his objection.

"You've made a jester's cap of my chef's toque—and what have you done to my ear!"

It is the elephantine ear that will catch the eye of the snake oil tycoon from America.

In the interim, what has become of Chaim's adherents, that cavalcade of imps and hobgoblins who, if for no other reason than curiosity, have followed him to Paris and on to Cagnes? If anything, they've multiplied here in Céret. Ignored by a younger generation whose messiah is Karl Marx, these creatures out of the household tales of Chaim's childhood have fled west along with the legions of immigrants. Perhaps intimidated by these goyisheh parts, they have suspended the mischievous roles they played in the Pale; they've ceased stealing babies and tying elf-knots in the beards of holy men. What holy men? They've even gone so far as to pretend to have gotten religion. The humbugs, they crowd Chaim's cowshed studio, where he's lately taken to sleeping, and lobby for his greater piety.

"Hayim Solomonovitch," exhorts Semangelof, the talkative one, "go already back in shul. You'll remember there from where you are coming."

As if Chaim could forget the last time he was in the old timber synagogue in Smilovitchi, when he made the sketch of the rabbi with his nimbus of beard, his nose like a dorsal fin, that precipitated his undoing?

"*Zakhor!*" intones the frog-faced spirit. "Remember! which it's from the ancient Hebrews their watchword. Or as the Yids say, '*Zolstu krenken un gedenken.*' You should sicken and not forget."

As if memory itself, thinks Chaim, who refuses to dignify this pipsqueak nothing by speaking with it, is the symptom of a disease. The pests, they're more annoying than the *punaises* that bedeviled him and Modi at the Falguière. If they encourage him in anything, it's to retreat even further into his work. Still he realizes, when he returns from the trance of his creative mania, that he's all alone but for them. Then he wonders whether it's by dint of his own demonic activity that they perhaps regard him as a distant relation? Am I *banim shovav* like my mama called me, a wicked son?

Not that Chaim doesn't cherish his solitude. He seldom initiates conversation with his models and avoids the popular Grand Café, where a remnant of the vanished artistic community still holds court. There are newcomers as well, drawn to the picture-postcard hilltown consecrated by the trinity of Picasso, Braque, and Gris. Chaim's old Vilna classmate and fellow veteran of la Ruche, Pinchus Krémègne, is one of them. He has preceded Chaim by a year and, having had word of the Litvak's coming, looked forward to receiving his old landsman: they would be habitués of le Grand, where they'd revive their former arguments over schnapps and café crèmes; they would perhaps go on landscape-painting rambles together. But if Soutine was aloof in Paris, in Céret he is virtually untouchable.

At their initial meeting Pinchus greets him in a companionable *mameloshen*, "Vos macht a yid?" And later, under the eucalyptus that shades the terrace of the Grand Café, he proposes a good-humored toast: "As Rabban Gamaliel says in *Pirkei Avot*, 'Either friendship or death.' "

Then right away Chaim pours cold water on his welcome. "Don't start please with your Torah thumping, Krémègne."

Stung, Pinchus nevertheless tries to sustain his bonhomie. To make conversation, he recalls a problem of aesthetics that he and Chaim had used to bandy about, but Chaim's testiness turns the issue into a heated argument. In hopes of improving the mood Pinchus invites his old friend back to his orchid-and-wisteria-bowered studio to view his new work, which Chaim judges tersely as "serviceable." He concludes that the Cubists have had a perverse influence on Pinchus's paintings: he has borrowed the fundamentals of their technique while keeping a firm foothold in the figurative, lacking the courage to embrace either wholeheartedly. "I don't like it you should straddle the fence," pronounces Chaim. Pinchus reminds him that his particular brand of fence straddling has proven quite marketable and goes so far as to accuse his guest of jealousy. Chaim harrumphs like he's beyond the influence of anyone living or dead. And maybe, thinks Pinchus, suddenly heedful of his own ebbing hair and trades-man's face, he is.

Which perhaps accounts for the regard he holds, despite himself, for such an ill-mannered vulgarian. When next they meet, Pinchus makes yet another effort to remind Chaim of their mutual history, recalling their academy days in Vilna.

"Krémègne," replies Chaim, ever incorrigible, "don't you know it can poison you, the nostalgia."

After that his old schoolfellow tends to keep clear of Chaim Soutine.

The population of Céret avoids him as well. Some, encounter-ing the unkempt recluse in a woodsy blind where he's set up his easel, brushes clutched in a fist and clenched between his teeth, have come to take him for granted; others, stumbling across him napping in a patch of purple woodruff or under a rosemary bush, recoil as if from some ghoulish anomaly. Old women cross themselves when they pass him on the pont du Diable or in the Plaza of the Fountain of Nine Jets; children taunt him with catcalls. Chaim pays them scant attention, just as he scarcely acknowledges the news that the war has ended. History happens back there in the world where he's only a tourist. He's no more concerned about the armistice than he was about the tidings of a revolution in Russia. Although he had taken a moment to won-der how his family may have fared, and to gloat over the fact that Chagall and Mané-Katz were stuck in the mother country they'd foolishly returned to. He'd also recalled the pair of conspiring celebrity emigrés Modi had pointed out at the Dôme.

"Note how their heads are practically hydrocephalic," he'd remarked of the one with the lustrous bald pate and his comrade with the sharp nose and round spectacles, "which will one day readily lend themselves to monuments."

A year passes in and out of his cowshed, and Chaim starts to feel that he's plundered the Pyrénées-Orientales of its treasures. He has begun predictably to tire of the region and makes plans to head back to (where else?) the Mediterranean and Cagnes-sur-Mer. Once there he finds that its panorama has ripened again in his absence. As before he's undeceived by the apparent calm of the place, which he portrays in the midst of a seismic disturbance that seems to rattle no one's bones but his own. The Provençale sun incites a searing lucidity, and again Chaim feels his work as a wound that can only be cauterized by the application of the Venetian red or ultramarine oils to his canvas. His enduring rapture, however, is abruptly terminated by a telegram from Zborowski informing him of the death of Modigliani. It's the first telegram Chaim has ever received, and the bicycle messenger who delivers it, as he waits for the tip that is not forthcoming, is horrified by the cry that the message has caused to issue from the recipient's throat.

The cable is naturally short on details, citing only the day and time of Amedeo's demise and the date of a funeral Chaim has already missed. The rest he learns over the coming months: that the final diagnosis, made after the fact, was tubercular meningitis. Modi had languished for weeks in a squalid flat at the top of 8 rue de la Grande Chaumière, where Gauguin had once resided before him. Blood bubbled from his lips like—said Moïse Kisling, who witnessed his extremity—"boiled borscht." Jeanne, nine months pregnant with their second child, never left his side, not even to fetch a doctor who might have forestalled his end. She was apparently too dazed and disabled from grief to do anything but try to feed him sardines from a tin and watch him die. When he received no answer from inside the studio to his repeated knocking, the artist and neighbor Ortiz de Zárate broke down the door. A bumbling physician was called in, who insisted that the patient not be moved until his hemorrhaging stopped. The hemorrhaging never stopped. By the time Modi was transferred to the Hôpital de la Charité, a clinic for the poverty-stricken and homeless, he had fallen into a coma from which he never emerged. His drinking companion Kisling attempted to make a plaster impression for a death mask but botched the job. The plaster fell apart, tearing the eyebrows and strips of his skin from Modi's once beautiful face. His mother wired from Livorno that he be "buried like a prince."

Jeanne Hébuterne, when she'd ceased her desolate keening over the corpse, told Zárate, "I know he is dead but I know too that he will soon live again for me." She did not, however, wait for his resurrection. The very next day she stepped like a sleepwalker out of a fifth-floor window in her family's apartment, shattering to splinters herself and her unborn child on the stones below. Because Monsieur Hébuterne and his harridan wife refused to accept her broken body, she was taken in a handcart back to the rubbishy studio she had shared with her lover. There she was watched over by hired mourners who shooed away the rats that would have gnawed her flesh.

Chaim, who has expected the end for some time, nevertheless finds himself incapable of absorbing its finality. He has all his life fortified himself against attachment. It was easy in the case of his family. His father was a *momzer*, a pietistic brute, his mother benign but ground down by the tyranny of her husband. His brothers were bullies who invoked their father's sanctimony to justify their partaking in the punishment of an errant son. He remembers feeling some sympathy for his unhinged sister, Ertl, a rubbery-faced little girl who claimed to have witnessed her own funeral while looking through the eye of a needle. But, in her reasonable moments, even she was ashamed of him. There were Krémègne and Kikoïne, the companions of his apprentice years, who had sacrificed to him space they could ill afford in the broken-down carousel of la Ruche. But rivalry had since compromised their friendship. Only Modi had retained Chaim's unconditional gratitude and admiration, and—how do you say it?—his love.

"Dédo!" he cries out to the echoing hills. It's the nickname by which the Italian was known to his family and closest intimates. And although Chaim had also been invited to address him as such, he has somehow never deemed himself worthy of speaking the name. He isn't worthy now, but who is there to discourage him? "Dédo!" he shouts as if to summon Modi's spirit, but the only spirits that visit him are the unclean ones come to remind him of his apostate heart.

"Say after me," nudges Semangelof, "*yit-ga-dal v'yit-ka-dash sh'mei-raba . . .*"

Chaim repeats, but the words of the Kaddish, the prayer for the dead, uttered half in jest by a bogey, leave a sour taste in his mouth.

Rather than muddy his perception, though, grief tends for a time to enhance it. Or at least to give it, if possible, an added delirium. The tempestuousness of his landscapes swells to biblical extremes; the soul of the sitter or the flicked chicken is laid ruthlessly bare. Chaim's own self-portrait, with its blubber lips and nose like a stuffed wurst, is monstrous. Then the tempest subsides. As in Céret, the townspeople have grown used to seeing the bedraggled *peintre* clattering about with his materials, erecting his easel in covert places where he believes he won't be spied on. But the sight of a wretched outcast (does he ever change his clothes?) wandering aimlessly about the streets and the waterfront is alarming to them. *"Il refile le comète,"* they say: he retraces the path of the comet. He walks about all night. Banished from his vision, Chaim is lost. He contemplates taking his life as he's often done but dismisses the act for a shameful cliché. He's malnourished, his ribs as pronounced as plowed furrows; his rotten teeth are easily dislodged by his tongue; his ulcers have made a furnace of his guts.

This is the state in which Léopold Zborowski finds him. The dealer has kept Chaim in bread and herring all these months primarily as a favor to Modigliani. The crazy Litvak's obsessive paintings have never been to his taste. Then there's his churlish disposition and the fetid odor that has so offended his wife. But among Modi's deathbed ravings ("*Cara Italia! Cara Livorno! Sans blague!*") had been this: "I'm finished, Zbo, but I leave you a virtuoso; I leave you Soutine!" A dubious bequest, but the dealer feels it nonetheless incumbent upon him to travel south to assess his legacy. He finds the painter half-deranged and living in ungodly filth surrounded by a mob of stretched and rolled-up canvases. The paintings themselves rival in their distortions the most outré compositions of Goya and van Gogh. But when the dealer offers, albeit halfheartedly, to take them back to Paris to try and sell them, Soutine is seized with an unaccountable agitation.

"My work is drek!" he declares, gathering up an armload of canvases and rushing out of the hut, where he tosses them in a heap before starting a bonfire. Zborowski, however, is able to salvage the bulk of the paintings, which he manages to spirit back to the capital. He persuades Paul Guillaume to hang one or two in his rue de la Boétie gallery, and the rest is history.

4

AFTER HE RECEIVES HIS portion from the sale of his paintings to Dr.
Barnes, Chaim hails a taxi and asks to be driven to the sea. When
he returns to Paris, he decides to go shopping. Chaim has never in
his life shopped for new clothes, having always worn his brothers'
hand-me-downs or schmattes off the street market racks. Suddenly,
with cash in hand, he's discovered a desire to have himself decked
out à la mode, and so asks Zbo's advice as to how he should proceed.
The newly flush dealer of works now in demand—Modigliani's
since his passing and Soutine's since receiving the imprimatur of
Dr. Barnes—has become quite the clotheshorse himself: he wears
double-breasted waistcoats, silk neckties with Prince Albert knots,
Italian-leather shoes polished to shine like obsidian. Too busy with
buying and selling, however, to indulge the uncouth artist's whims,
he assigns Paulette Jourdain, his girl-of-all-work, to accompany
Chaim on his spending spree. But Paulette is a country girl, as
unacquainted with Parisian haute couture as is Chaim. She's skittish to boot, having been warned of the Russian's unpredictable
moods. They nevertheless make their way together to the only department store either has heard of, the Galeries Lafayette on the
high-toned boulevard Haussmann. It's the first time Chaim has
been on the ritzy right bank of the river since the burning of the
boîte in Montmartre.

The immense fin de siècle emporium is a cathedral of the
choicest merchandise. The facade is resplendent with scrolls and
festoons; its interior contains a world. There are four stories of
men's clothing alone, each floor connected by a series of sweeping Art Nouveau staircases. The galleries surrounding the atrium
appear to float beneath the lofty blue glass and steel dome. The
clientele—fashionable, affluent, poised—appear to have stepped
from the pages of *La vie parisienne*. Awed and weak-kneed in these
uncharted parts, Chaim has an urge to grab the hand of Paulette,
who is equal parts pretty and plain, but fears her startled response.
Observing the pair in their mutual stupor, an employee glides
toward them, his hair embrocated in the manner of the film star
Valentino. Chaim has the frantic sense that he's about to be asked
for papers to prove his legitimacy.

"Can I help you?" inquires the sales clerk. His oily tone seems to
assume that the unglamorous couple are in the wrong place, while
his smugness implies he will gladly steer them toward precincts
better suited to their class.

In lieu of documentation the artist produces from his pocket,
along with some stray flakes of tobacco, a thick roll of bills. The
clerk draws a priggish breath over the gaucherie of the gesture,
then makes a slight bow and readjusts his attitude. With a courtly
wave of the hand, he bids Chaim follow him into the labyrinthine
aisles of racks and displays. The very colors and textures of such
rich apparel could cause an immigrant Litvak's mouth to water.
At the head of every aisle stands a stylish male mannequin outfitted in an ensemble costume that the sales clerk identifies by
name: "The Longchamps, the Kenwood, the Wimbledon—as you
must know, the British look is *in* this season." He shows Chaim
a dinner jacket by Hugo Boss, a yachting suit from Savile Row;
he presents a houndstooth "jazz suit" draped over his arms like,
thinks Chaim, a pietà. There are broadcloth shirts with round-edge

detachable collars, poplin pinstripes, tweed plus-fours, two-tone oxford brogues. His eyes on stems, Chaim appeals to Paulette to help him choose, but the girl is as nonplussed as he. Meanwhile the salesman discharges a salvo of practiced platitudes.

"To achieve the necessary nonchalance," he effuses, holding up an incongruous pair of socks and striped trousers, "at least one article must not match." Then glib: "Never wear anything that panics the cat." And provocative: "A well-tailored suit is to a woman what lingerie is to a man." Which prompts Chaim and Paulette to share an erubescent blush.

Confounded by the man's relentless spiel and wishing him to *far gots tsulib* shut up, Chaim selects a wardrobe's worth of items almost at random, paying little regard to their size or price. A tape measure has materialized around the salesman's neck, but Chaim dismisses his counsel that he first try on the garments before buying them. Nor does he balk when his purchases, once they're rung up, have depleted the bulk of his bankroll. Distrustful of banks and anxious at having such weighty sums on hand, he's more comfortable reverting to his natural state of having none at all.

With Paulette's help Chaim manages the balancing act of conveying his armloads of parcels onto the Métro back to Montparnasse. He has rented a commodious studio on the rue du Mont Saint-Gothard in a quiet neighborhood near the Parc Montsouris, the prior scene of Modigliani's preposterous duel. The apartment remains largely unfurnished but for a barge-sized antique sleigh bed that Chaim has proudly imported from the Clignancourt flea market. There is the inevitable havoc of canvas boards and easels, the parqueted floor parti-colored from spilled oils. Despite the open windows the air is thick with astringent odors. There is no art on the walls. Still giddy from such conspicuous consumption, Chaim has the extraordinary idea of asking Paulette to watch while he exhibits himself in his finery. Then no sooner has he asked than he apologizes for the untoward request. Paulette, however, is under Monsieur Zborowski's mandate to make herself available to the artist throughout the afternoon. She seats herself on the unmade bed in its shallow niche in the posture of an astute audience.

Chaim smiles at her, which the girl finds unexpectedly winning. Witnesses have maintained that Soutine's seldom-seen smile (notwithstanding his taupe-brown teeth) had the power to banish all traces of the sullen and irascible from his features. It could make you forget that sullenness and irascibility were his stock expressions.

He ducks with his parcels behind the muslin modesty screen he's erected as a changing area for the models he now has the gelt to hire. Long-drawn minutes elapse before he reappears dressed to the nines. He's wearing the three-piece Yorkshire tweed, the foulard four-in-hand, the raquette collar with the gold bar, and the felt fedora. He's still smiling. Clearly called upon to give a verdict, Paulette tells him he looks very nice. She sees he's dissatisfied with the lukewarm assessment and tries again, this time recalling, somewhat inaptly, one of the salesman's tired proverbs.

"Clothes don't mean nothing till somebody lives in them."

Chaim's new clothes might have been lived in for ages, so poorly do they hang on his round-shouldered frame. The knot in the tie is lopsided, the pant cuffs overlap his wing tips, and the outsized hat makes his ears fold like wilting petals. The suit itself, thinks the girl, looks rumpled and unhappy at having been fastened upon such an ill-favored specimen. But the smile . . .

Chaim seems not to register the left-handedness of Paulette's comment. He's looking aside from the girl on the bed to the pier glass over the brick fireplace. What he sees is himself transformed, the new togs showing him ready to take possession of all he's been denied in his gloomy life. He's a thirty-year-old man who has lately become something of a commodity, the sole resident of a roomy atelier, alone—he suddenly realizes—with an obliging young woman. He hasn't frankly thought of Paulette as a woman so much as a neutral accessory of his agent Zborowski. But there she sits, a simple girl with a rosy complexion in a sensible walking suit, her biscuit-brown hair tied in a seemly bun.

"May I," he begins with all the mettle of his newfound confidence, "paint you?"

The girl might be uneducated but she hails from Brittany and recognizes a euphemism when she hears one. She has already been introduced by her boss to the auxiliary duties her job entails, about which she has only minimal qualms. Also, she feels sorry for the inelegant artist masquerading as a boulevardier. "Should I . . . ?" she asks artlessly, beginning to unbutton her cardigan. Chaim swallows but doesn't say no. Then she has shed her blouse and skirt and kicked off the Mary Janes. She leans back on the dirty sheets, a callow odalisque, wearing only her stockings and nainsook underwear. Her small breasts peek sheepishly from her unlaced bodice; her thighs above the mulberry stockings are slender and pale.

Chaim is not a complete stranger to the female anatomy. There were naked models in Vilna and at Fernand Cormon's École des Beaux-Arts, which he'd dropped out of after some months for lack of interest—and tuition. (Only one of his nudes from that period has survived, and that one a lady far beyond her tender years.) He has a brief fainthearted impulse to tell the girl this is not what he meant, but Paulette, having read what she's assumed is the real intent of his request, has called his bluff. So, in spite of a rioting heart, he begins to remove his new trappings piece by piece, with what he imagines is a semblance of devil-may-care. Then he's standing in front of Paulette in his gartered socks and drawers. But while the girl's expression remains for the most part impassive, the artist, sans raiment, can't help but see himself through her eyes: the flat face, the body amorphous and codfish-belly white. He is Hayim Sütin once again, the pariah of Smilovitchi.

Paulette leans forward to untie the drawstring on his shorts, which drop to his ankles. Her eyes grow wide, ogling how his thing appears exposed beyond mere nakedness.

"I've never seen a Jewish zizi," she says, reaching to stroke it.

"It's a schwantz," replies Chaim with self-loathing.

As the artist seems incapable of coming closer, the girl pulls him amiably forward by his organ. When it fails to grow hard in her hand, she gives it another tug, like a child yanking the cord on a pull-string puppet, but still it refuses to stand. Chaim has closed his eyes, trying to summon his sightly demoness, but Laila is as always a slippery and jealous illusion. Not an especially experienced girl, Paulette nevertheless leans close enough to put her chapped lips around his flaccid member. Groaning, Chaim takes a sudden hobbled step backward, nearly tripping over his drawers. The girl looks up to see his eyes still shut tight, a tear squeezed from the corner of one of them trailing like quicksilver down his cheek.

✦

WHEN HE OPENS HIS eyes, his vision remains blurred due to a mist of condensation on his faceplate.

"To reduce condensation," old Babineaux has told him, "just open the spitcock, suck in some water, and spit it out on your viewport."

"What's a spitcock?" Chaim had asked, but was ignored by the veteran plongeur busy making a last-minute check of his rebreathing apparatus. Adjusting gauges on the pump and paying out the air hose, he mumbled warnings: "Escaping gas can inflate the diving costume and result in a runaway ascent that causes internal pressure to burst the seal on your corselet and flood the suit . . ." But by then Chaim is more or less resigned to martyring himself for his friend, and no longer listening.

He steps over God knows what (a leather ball? a duckweed-entwined head discarded after the guillotine?) and sees above him the bottoms of a fleet of houseboats, their hulls knocking from a breeze on the water. They are the markers, he's been told, that he's nearing the viaduc d'Austerlitz, which signals the end of the race. But Chaim realizes to his astonishment that he's in no hurry. "I have become a creature of the deep," he gabbles around his mouthpiece, then chuckles. Since when does Chaim Soutine chuckle? But thanks to him, Modi has left behind all the other scuttled vessels. His victory is assured. The rubberized suit is cold, Chaim's head aches, and the supply of artificial air that singes the hairs of his nostrils and chafes his lungs may be close to running out. But passing through the detritus of his life down here, he has lost his sense of the life taking place above. Up above in 1917, where the zeppelins hover like a school of Leviathans, his *schwantz* has thus far been remiss in the presence of mortal women—while down here he has immediate access to the times his schwantz served him well.

Though it didn't until long after he's disgraced himself with Paulette, which, as it turns out, is no impediment to their friendship. Or what passes for friendship in Chaim's frame of reference. At any rate the girl continues to put herself at his disposal. This is due in part to her boss's bidding. The postwar art market is flourishing and Zbo is getting handsome prices at auction for the paintings of what is becoming known as the School of Paris. Soutine's works, since their election by Dr. Barnes, are chief among them. So it's in the dealer's best interests to keep the moody Russian as content and productive as possible. Toward this end he has placed Paulette, along with his recently hired chauffeur Daneyrolle, at Chaim's beck and call.

The girl doesn't need much encouraging; she's conceived a fascination for the changeable artist. She indulges his tics and tantrums and is amused by his late obsession with buying expensive hats and fancy neckties, though he's been known to stay in bed until a worn-out pair of shoes has been repaired. He has a morbid fear of losing his hair and will sometimes crack an egg over his scalp before donning one of his many hats. He keeps large amounts of cash in cooking pots and a toolbox hidden in his closet. Scorning the foods that he likes (sauerbraten, stuffed cabbage, chopped liver) as *treyf*, he favors instead a flavorless diet of skinless fruit, overcooked vegetables, and weak tea. He claims that such austerity is for the sake of his delicate stomach, but Paulette thinks otherwise: she suspects he may be punishing himself for the crime of at last being able to afford to eat what he wants. He's that depraved. He smacks his lips when he talks so that flecks of foam fly from his mouth and his teeth and gums are stained from tobacco, but his hands are swan-white and soft as a child's.

Frightened by the Italian's example, Chaim hasn't touched alcohol since Modigliani's death. Nor does he frequent the cafés of the carrefour Vavin, into which he regularly rode Modi's coattails in their wastrel days. Since the armistice the Rotonde, despite Père Libion's retirement, has roared back to life. (Moïse Kisling has appointed himself a kind of sergeant at arms there, in charge of seeing that the former proprietor's code of behavior is still adhered to—though he's often responsible for the most flagrant violations of that code.) Meanwhile rowdy new brasseries such as the Dingo, where the American expatriates gather, are cropping up around the quarter. There are outliers like the Boeuf sur le Toit across the river, where Cocteau and Francis Picabia have joined forces with the Dadaists to create a circus-like cabaret. There is the masked saturnalia of the Bal des Quat'z'Arts at which nude models exhibit themselves as living paintings. (In his day Modi had painted trompe l'oeil apparel on their naked bodies.) The city is in the throes of continuous ecstatic misrule, but Chaim prefers to keep to his studio in the evenings, reading his plebeian *Paris-soir*. He has dutifully tried Dostoyevsky—devoured him in fact—and the other authors Amadeo deemed essential, but they leave him discomposed to a troubling degree. Then he returns to the more anodyne entertainments of *Cartouche, King of the Bandits* and *Fantômas*. He has a turntable Victrola on which he plays a scratchy record of the *Brandenburg Concertos*.

"I listen now to Bach," he boasts to Paulette. Silent for hours on end, he utters these occasional confidences to the girl. "In Russia I didn't know even what was a piano."

If he goes out after dark, it's to the cinema, to which Paulette sometimes accompanies him; or he attends the boxing matches at the Hippodrome, where he dismays the girl by loudly cheering at the moments of utmost bloodshed. During idle periods between paintings, he might tour the galleries along the rue de la Boétie in search of examples of his early work. When he finds a canvas, he buys it back from the gallery owner and perhaps retouches it, but usually he hacks it to bits. (The chauffeur Daneyrolle has been instructed by Zbo to rescue the fragments when he can and take them to the restorer to be reassembled and refaced.) Chaim has judged the Céret paintings in particular as representative of a time when his talent had run amok.

The girl thinks that time is far from over. He dispatches her to les Halles to buy poultry, but when the merchant has her finger his birds to prove their plumpness, Paulette explains that it's the color of their feathers that matters. She returns with her purchases to his studio, where the artist is all in a flap to begin his still life. But rather than arrange the half-plucked birds on a table alongside pewter jugs and violins à la Jan Weenix or Chardin, he nails them by the beak or their outspread wings to the wall. He allows the girl to remain in the studio while he paints, provided she keep her head turned. Then she might hear him speaking to her or himself over the slap of his brushes. He uses one brush for vermilion, another for zinc white, another for emerald green, and so on, discarding each on the floor after a stroke or two.

"You had in Smilovitchi more butchers than chickens," she hears him say. "I saw when I was a boy a butcher cut the throat of a goose and bleed it out. I wanted to scream but the look of joy on the face of the butcher made to catch in my throat the cry. I feel it there always. It's the cry I am trying always to set free, but"—he pauses, and she pictures his look of perplexity—"I never can."

It is the longest speech the girl will ever hear him make.

Chaim sends her to the Vaugirard slaughterhouse to fetch "a calf's head of distinction," but when he's ready to acquire the carcass of an entire steer, he's obliged to go along in person to the abattoir. Some of the workers can remember chasing the mendicant artist from their midst in his la Ruche days, but now his pockets are deep. He chooses an animal whose sawed-open torso has only this day been despoiled of its lights and lungs. He has it delivered to 8 rue du Mont Saint-Gothard, where the neighbors watch aghast as the butcher boys stagger up the stairs with their ungainly burden. Chaim gives the knackered boys a few extra centimes to help him hoist the beast into the air by means of a block and tackle he's attached to a hook in the ceiling. Its hind legs are spread and bound to a wooden bar called a singletree, which Chaim has scavenged from an antique market in the marché des Patriarches. Its headless shoulders drag the floor. After innumerable trips to the Louvre, where he's stood in reverence for hours before Rembrandt's masterful *Flayed Ox*, it's finally his turn. He dismisses the girl so he can be alone with his prize. He admires the gristle and the graceful lapis tracery of its veins, the yolk-yellow globules of fat, the deep sepulchral cavern of the rib cage, the blood. He realizes that the animal has been slaughtered in violation of the laws of *kashrus*, which somehow piques his anticipation.

Chaim has deliberately refrained from eating in hopes that the hunger—once his native condition—will sharpen his senses. Then, when he's unable to restrain himself any longer, he scrapes the village idyll from some tacky eighteenth-century canvas and hurls himself into a debauch of creation. He breaks brushes in the fury of his rendering, mixes his oils as if stirring a cauldron; he will not rest until he's found the perfect shade of pink for the loins, purple for the bruised shanks, gold for the ore-like deposits of suet in its spine. He mixes carmine and lampblack to give the curved ribs the majesty of a church nave stained with gore, then leaves the awesome beast suspended in a cobalt emptiness. By dusk he has completed his first homage to the Dutch master. By midnight he has a second version on a larger canvas, by dawn a third on an even larger. In truth his carcass owes little to Rembrandt's, which is dead as a doornail, an effigy, whereas Chaim's is more vital in death than it ever was in its docile bovine existence. Which perhaps accounts for Paulette's horror when she reenters the studio in the late morning. It's as if she's blundered upon the scene of a barbaric crucifixion, while at the same time she feels in some way implicated in the victim's disemboweling.

Her fright is compounded by the savage countenance of the painter himself. In the frenzy of his labor he's rubbed his face with the heel of a pigment-smeared hand, so that he appears to be wearing a kind of aboriginal war paint. When he finally becomes aware of her presence, he shouts at her, "Don't look!" She claps her hands over her eyes, grateful for the warning even if too late; for she believes his caveat comes less from an impulse to conceal his work than to protect her from the petrifaction that might result from the sight of it. But in a moment she hears him appealing: "Paulette, I think I bled from the beef all its color." Because the meat, no longer fresh from the slaughter, has begun to dry out and turn gray. It is also starting to stink. "I need to make it again to shine."

She lowers her hands to gaze in bewilderment at the sleepless
artist as he explains what it is he's proposing. Then she's sent forth
on the strangest errand he's yet required of her. An hour later she
returns looking frazzled and teetering awkwardly from the weight
of a tin pail sloshing to the brim with thick blood from the abattoir.
(She had told the mystified butchers, implausibly, that the blood
was prescribed for a sick relation.) Chaim takes his place again behind his easel and enjoins the girl to splash the contents of the pail
over the dangling carcass. With the meat restored to its previous
burnish, its brisket and flank gleaming once again, the painter allows himself a cigarette. He takes a moment to gloat: "When I had
nothing, I painted only the limp mackerel and the nebbish hare; I
got now the fatted calf," then recommences his impetuous rite.

But it's summer and the studio is sweltering; the artist in his
dirty singlet is drenched in sweat as he works. For once his own
odor is no match for that of his subject, which, for all its radiance,
has begun to rot. The windows are open and bluebottles as big
as hailstones have started to swarm. They blanket the carcass and
encircle the painter, who remains as insensible to the flies as he is
to the smell. His neighbors, however, are not so indifferent to the
sickly sweet fetor permeating their apartments and seasoning their
ratatouille. Some have gathered outside his door and begun forcefully to knock. Paulette alerts Chaim to their racket but he refuses
to be disturbed. The knocking ceases only to be renewed some minutes later by an even more aggressive pounding and the voice of the
bearish Monsieur Kersausie, the landlord, demanding to be let in.

"Soutine, *sale connard*, I'll have you in the street!"

But Chaim is absorbed in limning an intricate fretwork of sin-
ews and flesh, and despite Paulette's vocal anxiety cannot leave off.
There is another interlude in the noise from the landing, then the
voices begin to swell again and the knocking assumes an authoritative staccato.

"Open in the name of the prefecture of police!"

"Chaim," cries Paulette, "les flics!" But when she turns from the door to summon the artist, he's nowhere in sight. She cracks open the front door with a sinking heart, then steps back as two officers in blue capes and képis barge in. Behind them shuffle a pair of uniformed workers from the sanitation brigade and behind them the head bobbing of the landlord and the gaggle of neighbors in the stairwell. All are momentarily thunderstruck by the sanguinary shambles that is the studio.

"Please," implores the girl, "be kind."

The younger gendarme covers his mouth, his cheeks bulging as he tries not to gag. The older buries his nose in the collar of his tunic and orders the public health workers to "remove this filth." But just as the workers step forward to perform their duty, an imperious voice is heard to call out, "Wait!" and yet another officer shoulders his way through the knot of onlookers. This one has a pencil mustache and monocle; he wears a leather-billed cap and a uniform sporting an array of ribbons and braids that signify his superior rank. He shows no apparent disgust upon viewing the ghastly tableau but instead approaches the incomplete painting on the easel. Nodding his head meditatively as he examines it, he exclaims:

"Formidable!"

At that word the closet door creaks open and out slinks Chaim, cautiously, his left eyelid aflutter. *Hab rachmones*, he wants to cry—Have mercy!—but controls himself enough to plead instead, "Your Honor, I am an artist. It is necessary, the carrion, for my work." He's prepared to fall to his knees in supplication when the officer pats his shoulder with a reassuring hand, then wipes the hand discreetly on his sleeve.

"But of course, Maestro Soutine," he says.

"You know me?" gasps Chaim, and stifles a sob. He draws a breath and straightens, actually expanding his shallow chest.

The officer introduces himself: "I am Lieutenant Zamaron," as
if his name is one to conjure with. "Léon Zamaron." He is, he affirms, the commissioner in charge of, among other things, renew-
ing the papers of foreigners residing in Paris. In this capacity he has
met a number of Chaim's compatriots. In fact, a discerning devotee
of modern art, he has acquired several paintings by members of the
so-called School of Paris. This includes the work of Modigliani and
Max Jacob, both of whom he has personally released on occasion
from the la Santé drunk tank. Chaim has heard of the fellow from
Kikoïne and others, how he appears out of the blue like a good
angel to aid immigrant artists in difficulty. "Antennae the man's
got!" Which is all well and good, but Chaim, ever single-minded,
petitions him again to be allowed to keep his steer.

Monsieur Zamaron removes his monocle, wrinkles his brow. He
confers with one of the white-jacketed sanitation men and there's
a deal of reciprocal muttering before the commissioner turns back
toward the artist, grinning broadly. "We have arrived at a solution,"
he announces. "You may keep your animal provided you agree to
treat it with injections of the preservative agent formaldehyde."

Chaim is moved to such gratitude that he insists the commissioner accept the gift of a painting. Zamaron makes a curt bow
of assent and steps forward to take possession of one of the beef
carcass oils he assumes the artist intended. But Chaim deters him
from his choice, pressing upon him instead a still life with pheasants. The commissioner sighs but graciously accepts the painting.
He gives a little salute and exits with his swag, leaving Chaim with
the impression that he had come expecting to receive a painting all
along. He's followed from the studio by the rest of the official reti-
nue. Unappeased, the neighbors remain grumbling on the landing,
even as Paulette closes the door.

By the time the team of municipal health workers arrive to
disinfect the studio in the morning, the smell has considerably

dissipated. Chaim had sent the girl out to a pharmacy the night before to buy syringes, hypodermic needles, and a four-liter bottle of the chemical solution. Once the artist had stabbed the gamy meat and pressed the plunger—an activity he relished perhaps more than he should—the miasma began to subside and the flies to lose interest in flesh whose decomposition had been postponed.

Thereafter, Chaim is never without his syringes and formaldehyde. He injects generations of dead animals, always with the feeling that he's performing a kindness along the lines of a postmortem triage. He buries his animals as well after the ox carcass, which he had deposited in an alley dustbin where it was nibbled at by a dog that died in agonies from the poison.

✦

A PERSON COULD BE forgiven for dismissing Soutine's simultaneous fore- and hindsight as an illusory effect of his vertigo. Not to mention his disorientation and motion sickness owing to an ambient pressure from the volumes of river water over his head. He has after all been down there a long time. But I know better. His sloweddown heartbeat plus the toxic influence of oxygen at high pressure, the buildup of carbon dioxide in his helmet, the distortion of scale and distance, have nothing to do with the consolidation of his past and future. Chaim's is an experience engendered by the womb-like impermeability he feels inside the diving costume. By now he has come to believe that the suit has the same supernatural properties he's attributed, with a willing suspension of disbelief, to his tweeds, spats, and fedoras. When he dons them, his glad rags, ill-fitting as they are, he is proof against the character (himself) who has dogged him all his days. What's more (and notwithstanding his initial setback with Paulette), he's begun to regard himself as ready for love.

That his immigrant acquaintances often fail to recognize him in his new protective coloring is evidence, he believes, that he has

eluded his former self. Or if one of his fellow artists suspects that
it's the old Soutine beneath his fine feathers and greets him in a
brotherly mameloshen, he pretends not to know the language anymore. Once, he's discovered by a cavalier-hatted André Salmon ru-
minating over a tasteless pap of milky potatoes at Chez Rosalie's.
"Is that you, Soutine?" inquires the raffish poet. "We thought you
were dead." When the artist shows no special signs to the contrary,
Salmon remarks, "If I'm not mistaken, doesn't *chaim* mean 'life' in
Hebrew?" "I don't remember," says a petulant Chaim. His loneliness is a cult of which he is the only member. At the same time he
feels that, having never had a proper sweetheart, he is finally worthy
of one.

The problem remains that he's still unsure about what consti-
tutes the love of a man for a woman, or vice versa. He knows it's
very different from what he felt in the past for Amedeo, and he's
sometimes embarrassed when recalling the degree of affection he'd
conceived for his dead friend. Hadn't the reckless Tuscan led him
so often astray? Though sometimes he dearly misses being led astray.
But now, a man with a reputation and a new suit of clothes, he
judges himself a prime candidate for entering into intimate relations with a lady of the opposite sex. For that, he thinks, it will of
course be necessary to free himself from the incursions of Laila,
that descendent of serpents, who continues to interfere with his
sleep. Ever since his long-ago bar mitzvah—a sorry affair with
days-old poppy seed cake—she's come at night to induce in him
the pollution so condemned in the pages of the *Shulchan Arukh*.
Chaim discounts the *Shulchan Arukh* and all the outworn texts he
was made to pay lip service to in his cheder days. But when asleep,
he's unable to resist the succubus's ministrations. So most nights he
lies awake to discourage her visits.

One result of this sleep deprivation is naturally an unbalanced
mind. Without the regular siphoning off of his seed, he is afflicted

by an aching and rampant schlong. Often, rather than stroke the beast, he wants to wring its neck like the lifeless fowl he continues to paint. In this way he comes to understand the true meaning of *shlogn kapores*. This is the ritual when, on Yom Kippur Eve, people swing roosters over their heads to transfer their sins to the bird. "You for death, me for life," they recite three times. Then the strangled bird is cooked for the meal that ends their New Year's fast.

He finds himself again looking sidelong at Paulette, with whom any physical involvement would now seem incestuous. Sensing his flaming rut, the girl, while not unsympathetic, nevertheless makes herself scarce. As always Chaim channels his anguish into his painting. But his unrest gets the better of him and he prevails upon Daneyrolle to drive him to the Mediterranean, where he contemplates a seascape, rejects it, and asks to be taken back again. The ordinarily compliant chauffeur informs Zborowski he will resign unless relieved of the artist's charge. By then it has anyway occurred to the artist that, unless he stays in one place, he will have little opportunity of meeting a helpmate. (For even though it's 1923 and in the cafés and cabarets of Paris all the old values are overthrown, Chaim still holds, for good or ill, a traditional view of a woman's role.)

During Paulette's truancy "the impudent ones," as they're called in the shtetl, infest the atelier and have a laugh at the artist's expense. What does love have to do with his travail? If he's honest, Chaim admits he doesn't know. So far he's only known the thing by its absence. Is it love they're after when the young and not-so-young men of Smilovitchi visit Hadassah the Cistern in her bark-roofed hovel beyond the tannery? She's said to be the *agunah*, the grass widow, of a long-absconded klezmer musician, once a beauty before falling prey to drink and wantonness in her abandonment. Despised by the women of the town, both Jew and gentile, she is maintained in her squalor by the men she services, who bring her firewood and jars of potato vodka. Hiding in the ditch near her abode, Chaim, in his ninth or tenth year, tries to sketch her with his charcoal pencil when she squats in her doorway. This is the pencil he bought with the kopecks he received from selling the Sabbath spoons he stole from his mother. For that theft he will be unmercifully thrashed and confined to the coal cellar for an indefinite period.

It's impossible to determine her age. Her hair, where it isn't sulfur yellow, is iron gray, her face and puffy limbs as blotched and lesioned as blue cheese. Her large breasts stir like nestling animals beneath her loose smock. In her muddy eyes, there is a serenity born of ignorance or a fathomless resignation, the boy doesn't know which. He doesn't even understand that such distinctions can't be reconciled, because the sketch he's made on his fragment of brown paper has done precisely that. He refrains, however, from drawing the men who warily come and go with their offerings, their expressions before and after uniform in their abiding shame. Besides, they are all too familiar to Chaim: Kalman the scissors grinder, Shloymke the rope spinner, the bull-necked Borukh and the fish-faced Gershon, his big brothers. Departing, they tighten the woven *gartels* about their waists, thus obeying the prescription to separate the heart from the genitals on your way to prayers. Later on they will offer their brides the end of that same belt to hold during the mitzvah dance at their wedding.

But the woman herself is irresistible in her ruination. How he wishes he had pigments to give her the depth and density she deserves. Still, he loses himself in the drawing, while also becoming more than himself. He's more than the homely, sickly, perpetually hungry son of a clothes mender, which is only a rank above schnorrer in shtetl society. Then it's sundown and the last of Hadassah's callers has left for the *ma'ariv* service at the synagogue. Emerged again from her hovel, she stretches, hugs herself against the chill, and spies the young artist's scruffy head poking above the edge of his trench. She gives him a gap-toothed grin and hoists her smirched garment over her waist. Chaim is throttled by a mixture of dread and awe, not unlike what he'll experience years later when standing before Gustave Courbet's *Origin of the World*. There is a spasming of his extremities that he cannot control, the fit triggering in turn a cackling of insane laughter from his audience. The fits remain undiagnosed throughout his life. A conscientious reader of the Dostoyevsky that Modi has bequeathed him, Chaim identifies the tremors as a kind of saint's disease, albeit a minor strain. He counts them among the expanding constellation of symptoms that exalt his suffering. All of them—the fits, tics, and gastrointestinal pains—contribute to the challenge the woman must face who will one day overlook the wreckage of the man for the sake of the artist. But where can he find such a woman, her price beyond jewels? Certainly not in a *nafkeh bias*, a brothel, like the one Kikoïne and Krémègne persuade him to enter in Vilna. The art academy in that city is an oasis of sorts—this despite hostile *shkotzim* instructors who destroy any letters in Yiddish the students might receive. The Jews of the city in their millennium-old ghetto are generous, and an indigent student need only knock at a mezuzah'd door of an evening to receive a meal. The Jerusalem of the North, as it's called, Vilna has an abundance of yeshivas, synagogues, Jewish newspapers, cafés, shops, and whorehouses.

"This place is strictly kosher," Chaim's fellows assure him, "duly certified by the rabbinate."

They have taken it upon themselves to see to it that Soutine has a woman before his twentieth birthday. But what he assumes is an odor of gross venery suffusing the building's clammy, paint-peeling corridors is enough to give Chaim the shakes, and he flees with his chastity intact.

Modigliani's efforts to get him laid are more difficult to oppose. But then why should he want to oppose them? Still, on this particular starless night in 1915, Chaim tries to tell himself he doesn't know where they're going.

The cells of the cité Falguière are even more porous than the walls of la Ruche, and while Chaim has managed to discourage other visitors, the Italian bursts in on him at all hours. Occasionally he's in the company of one of his models. They will do anything for him, Amedeo's lovelies. Some pose for the mere recompense of being transfigured into one of his gorgeous, stylized portraits, and for the plum of his fickle embrace. They fight over him, threaten to kill each other (or themselves) over him; at a nod from him they would even sit (or lie) for his ill-bred friend and neighbor. To Chaim it seems that Modi is deliberately tantalizing him. The women vamp and giggle as the intemperate Italian tugs at a diaphanous wrapper to bare their charms.

It's cruel of Amedeo to torture his friend in this manner. To say nothing of the disrespect with which he treats the ladies (though some give as good as they get). And how, come to think of it, should one treat a lady? With a firm hand, or maybe with tenderness in the hope that they will return it in kind? But what does Chaim know from tenderness?

"D'accord," says Modi in response to the Litvak's latest refusal to borrow a model. "If you don't want to paint them, you can at least fuck them."

Chaim is livid. "I don't like with floozies to shtup!" Then he instantly begs the pardon of Thérèse or Fleur or whoever is the current offering for having given offense.

"So who *do* you like to shtup, *mio farfallone*? Are you a monk? Since when are the Jews so keen on celibacy?"

Modi retires but is back again the next night, fresh from a dustup with the Englishwoman he's been running around with.

Her name is Beatrice—the worshipper of Dante should have his Beatrice—a writer as addicted to her ravening passions as Modigliani is to his. The amalgamation of their appetites is a lethal blend. When they aren't abusing themselves with alcohol, cocaine, and debilitating carnal acrobatics, they're galling each other with accusations of infidelity. Accusations generally founded in truth and resulting in violence. Encountering them, Chaim suffers in silence the disdain of Amedeo's combustible companion. Whey-faced and imperially thin, she treats him with supreme condescension if she acknowledges him at all.

Modi is pressing a rag to his cheek where the woman has drawn blood. "Come, Soutine," he says, "I'm in need of your immoral support."

Chaim recommends to him other cronies who might better serve him in that capacity. There's the perpetually soused Utrillo, for instance, and Max Jacob when he's in a profligate rather than a priestly mood. But having noted the shadows under Modi's blood-shot eyes, he worries that his friend's late infatuation is causing irreparable damage to his health. Of course, there's Chaim's own health to consider, already so compromised by his association with the Tuscan. Still, he can't help it, he feels privileged that Modigliani seeks him out at such moments. He lays down his brushes, mutters a curse, and slouches behind his friend out into the blind alley of the impasse Falguière.

The early autumn night is crisp and Modi is as usual under-dressed in his worn corduroys and unraveling scarf. His shirtfront is debonair despite being cut from mattress ticking. Chaim has on the moth-eaten reefer he wears in all weather. Leaves blown from the lindens that line the avenues crunch underfoot. Light spills through the cracks in the paint coating the streetlamps like yolk from indigo eggs. Modi pauses to buy a spray of violets from the flower lady outside la Coupole. A few of his comrades hail him

from the terrace and he greets them in return, while making a show
of peeling a franc note from a roll of bills. He hands it to the wilted
young woman and tells her to keep the change. Apparently he has
money tonight beyond the paltry sum he receives from Zborowski.
It must be a gift, or a theft, from his mistress, who is a salaried
journalist and quite productive when not incapacitated from their
mutual debauchery.

Chaim knows better than to ask their destination but does
anyway, and receives from Modi a typically gnomic response: "Io
fúi del cielo, I lived in heaven and must surely return there soon . . ."
He turns into the dog-legged rue Delambre and stops before a
staid *hôtel particulier*. Its exterior is undistinguished from the other
houses but for its thick-paneled door and the modest enamel sign
on the wall beside it. Lit from above by a ruby-red gas lamp, the
sign reads CHEZ BABYLONE. Modi tugs the bellpull and Chaim
begins to make his excuses.

"I got now in my studio a fish with wings . . . ," he explains.
It's a ray fish beneath which he's arranged some pomegranates that
appear to be dropping like bloody giblets from its innards. The
still life is a salute to the painter Chardin, whose own beady-eyed
skate hangs in the Louvre. His is a precise and constrained composition, whose dormant energies Chaim has begun to release in
a copy that looks a bit like a kite flown by a fiend in hell. He has
lugged the trunks of a dozen families from the sleeping cars at the
Gare Montparnasse to earn enough to buy the fish. "I'm not going
in," he states definitively.

"All I ask is that you keep me company," says Modi, sniffing his
bouquet.

"I know what kind place this is."

"It's a convent," his friend assures him, "staffed by sisters of
mercy."

The door opens and a half-clad mademoiselle invites them in. Chaim backs away only to be jostled from behind by a trio of newly arrived patrons, and Modi takes advantage of his forward motion to shove him farther across the threshold. Then they're in a crowded estaminet appointed like a first-class railway carriage with plush benches and lamps with shell-pink shades. There's a painting above the bar of a Rubenesque nude astride a giant rooster. Women in corsets and peignoirs are coaxing the men, who need little encouragement, to take a dram of Dutch courage before being escorted upstairs. Chaim is still poised to bolt when Modi returns from the bar to hand him a brandy, which he has stealthily laced with some drops of a chemical cosh.

"Think of this as a second bar mitzvah," croons the Tuscan, stuffing the nosegay into Chaim's coat pocket.

"I didn't like it my bar mitzvah the first time," says Chaim, tossing back the elixir nonetheless. But after a second drink he begins to feel strangely stoic, even a touch acquiescent. He allows Modi to hustle him up the stairs into the salon on the *premier étage*.

The large room is a miscellany of fantasy decor—tall screens decorated with nymphs and fauns, smoky mirrors to soften the features of clients and *nafkehs* past their prime. There are equal nods to the seraglio and the beau monde drawing room. There is a life-sized plaster sculpture of an unresistant Leda ravished by a swan. Under a softly lit chandelier a full-bosomed woman in a tasteful black frock, her hennaed hair piled high, is dressing down a woozy young man for some infraction: "Just where do you think you are!"

Modi calls to her, "Madame Pearl, my friend brought you flowers." He pulls them from Chaim's pocket and presents them to the smiling *maitresse*.

"Monsieur!" she exclaims, dismissing the miscreant and coming forward to accept the bouquet, which she tosses into a woven hamper along with a bower's worth of others. "Girls, look who's here!"

The "girls"—the term is a stretch for some while others look barely pubescent—have already surrounded the handsome Italian. A couple tease his hair as he tries to introduce them to Chaim.

"One day you will boast that you foutou'd with the great Soutine."

Ordinarily Chaim would have shrunk at being made the object of such attention, but the effects of the adulterated potion have left him somewhat philosophical.

Amedeo discreetly presses some notes upon Madame Pearl and receives in exchange the paper chits allotting the time a client may spend with the *horizontale* of his choice. Then Madame claps her hands, signaling the ladies to fall in line for inspection by the paying customers. They come, the ladies, in an assortment of shapes and sizes, some blowsy, some slender as wands, one or two perhaps even genuinely fetching beneath their excess of powder. A few wear pastel wigs or tie their hair in chignons after Lautrec's la Goulue. Their costumes vary from lace chemises and rolled lisle stockings to a nun's habit and a bridal gown. One wears nothing but a metal chastity belt, the key to which she waves flirtatiously.

Madame introduces them: "Phèdre, Violette, Calliope, Belle-Cuisse, Magdalène . . ." All wink and strike poses that show their best assets to advantage.

From the paisley chaise longue to which a couple of ladies have led him, Modi bids his friend take his pick. Bemused as he is, Chaim is under no illusions. He knows that he's perceived as Modi's creature and deserves no better assessment, even from whores. There is one among them, however, a young *putain* standing slightly apart from the others on the column's left flank, who looks as misfit as Chaim feels himself to be. Her face is chinless, eyes stolid and downcast, hair a nest of unspooling snuff-brown yarn. Mealy flesh spills over the top of her corset like risen dough. With her one might feel safe from humiliation; so Chaim points to the slatternly girl, inciting snickers among the others. The girl herself only dips her head a little further between her drooping shoulders.

Madame leans over to confide in Modi, though her voice is raised enough for Chaim to hear: "Monsieur, your friend shows compassion. Bijou is our laundress. I've allowed her to try her luck with the others as a favor to her ailing mother." No longer feigning discretion. "For all we know she's never been touched. It's a kindness."

"You see that, Chaim," says Modi, "a good deed."

At a nod from Madame the girl plods forward to take the artist's hand with her sticky fingers. She leads him without speaking up yet another flight of stairs, this one with a twisting iron banister. He follows her down a dim hallway past doors behind which tittering and dolorous groans can be heard, then into an unoccupied room. The room is windowless, lit by a flickering gas sconce, the air heavy with a caustic perfume no doubt intended to hide the essence of a multitude of sins. The red wallpaper is patterned in Moorish arabesques, the bed covered in tasseled flannel, also red. The rack beside the sink holds a towel and a rubber device whose purpose Chaim thinks he would prefer not to know.

Having shut the door, the girl plunks herself down on the bed. Yet to glance even once at her client, she begins to remove the black stockings and release herself from her stays. Her body burgeons forth as formless as a *kreplach* dumpling. The corset leaves raw indentations beneath her negligible breasts, the flush of her cheeks perhaps more occasioned by fever than rouge. She peels off her ample knickers and stands again to fold back the bedspread, her buttocks jiggling like tapioca. Then she lays herself back down on the mattress with her arms at her sides, her eyes open and stark-staring at the ceiling.

Chaim wonders how he should proceed, or if in fact he should proceed at all. Without bothering to remove his coat, he lowers himself uncertainly onto the edge of the bed; he inhales the girl's sour-pickle musk and is oddly moved by the proximity of this defenseless shikse. She is after all a living human person, despite her credible imitation of a corpse. Experimentally, he places the flat of his hand on her cushiony abdomen. He marvels at the warmth of her flesh, slides the hand over a rib, and feels even more light-headed than is accounted for by the influence of the enhanced drink. A small avian sound escapes his throat. Running his hand further along her torso, he realizes that his organ is upstanding in his pants.

"Bijou?" he says. Perhaps speaking her name might have some galvanic effect.

She doesn't stir, though he thinks he detects a moistness in her unblinking eyes. With his fingertips he grazes the aureole of a nipple, then squeezes the nipple—upon which she sits abruptly upright.

"My name's not Bijou," she says, her voice surprisingly sweet.

As startled as if he has actually raised the dead, Chaim ventures to ask, "What is it?"

"Mortimère."

" . . . "

"Bijou is what Madame decided to call me." Then, squinting as she contemplates his unlovely features: "Are you some kind of a Mongol?"

Chaim considers. "Yes, a Mongol."

She shivers from what might be a frisson of excitation. "They say my papa was a Magyar." Tilting her head. "What's a Magyar?"

Chaim shrugs.

"I never met him, my papa. He left me and Maman in the shit. We live in the Zone now behind the knackers' yard. Our house has billboards for walls and a tin roof. Maman calls it Mon Bonheur. The doctors want to put her in la Salpêtrière, but she's not potty; she just sees things nobody else can."

Chaim nods sympathetically.

"She's also got the scabies." The girl's blunt face assumes a solemn demeanor, her glassy eyes gone entirely elsewhere. "Make me feel pretty," she appeals to Chaim or God.

"How?" he wonders in all sincerity.

The focus slowly returns to her eyes. "Tell me!"

"Tahkeh," says Chaim, his Adam's apple bobbing, "you're pretty."

She pooches her lower lip. "I don't believe you." Then she grabs his hand, pausing to admire its perfection, and places it again on her unripe breast.

He squeezes as before, with no more delicacy than he might have the rubber bulb of a bicycle horn, and feels deeply sorry for them both. Meanwhile his putz, seemingly independent of his will or lack thereof, remains poker-stiff and still straining against the inside of his trousers. All at once, with a strength he might have thought beyond her means, the girl shoves him onto his back. "Enough with the jeux preliminaires," she declares, pinning his arms to the mattress as she straddles his thighs. She tugs at the crotch of his pants, popping the buttons of his fly, and reaches in to set free his engorged member. Then she raises her pelvis to stuff him inside her and begins to thrust her hips.

His scrotum and spine are elevated as if by an electrical charge. Astonished at this development, Chaim cries out, "We're shtupping!" and, transported by her heat, further qualifies, "It's good!" His eyes are closed as he grips the girl by her adipose hips. But as she bounces and grinds with a resolute ferocity, a ululation emanating from her open mouth, he believes he can feel her pliant flesh begin to ebb. He discovers contours, the hipbones becoming pronounced and fluid in their motion, spare as a fawn's. Folds of flesh uncrease in advance of the upward movement of his hands, leaving her skin smooth and firm, her breasts swollen into fullness. Chaim opens his eyes in time to see her shake loose the clot of her hair. Its serpentine tresses, scintillant and coral-red in the light from the gas lamp, lash her face and shoulders.

"Laila?" he gasps, his putz retreating like a snail into its shell. In a panic to reclaim the remainder of himself, he bucks the girl violently from the bed, then leans over the other side of the mattress to retch. Having landed on the floor with a thud that rocks the house, the girl scrambles for her belongings and flees the room.

Sometime later, as Chaim lumbers unsteadily down the stairs, Modigliani, still on the sofa attended by whores, calls to him, "Mazel tov, amico mio, today you are a man."

✦

THEREAFTER, EXCEPTING HIS FECKLESS audition for Paulette, Chaim keeps his schwantz in his pants. At least until Dvoira (now Deborah) Melnick arrives on the scene. He knows her from his time in Vilna. Her family was one of those at whose home he was periodically given meals. There was a rotation of Jewish families who fed the poor art students after the tradition of providing yeshiva *bochers* with appointed "eating days." On the days when a host family received them, they ate; on others they fasted. Dr. Melnick and his wife and daughter were welcoming to the intense and brooding young man from Smilovitchi, who they'd heard had an original gift. (It was said he painted his fellows in funerary poses, as corpses with candles at their heads and feet.) They were willing to overlook his lack of manners as a side effect of his unusual talent. He sat at their bounteous table on Shabbos, silently enduring the doctor's homilies

and scarfing up Froy Melnick's *tcholent* like a famished wolf. But
after the meal, when Dvoira played traditional airs on her violin,
Chaim would shut his eyes and grip the arms of his chair as if to
keep himself from being carried aloft.

The Melnicks may have intuited some unspoken affinity between their wide-eyed daughter and the aspiring artist. Her disappointment at Chaim's departure for France seemed to confirm
that suspicion. They may even have supposed, perhaps with some
apprehension, that the girl's choice of Paris in which to pursue her
musical studies had something to do with the young Soutine's being in residence there. And they would have been correct. But by
the time she encounters Chaim at the Café Select (he steers clear of
the Rotonde since his success, owing to the jealousy he suspects his
fellow artists of harboring toward him), she is no longer the shrinking violet of the Lithuanian ghetto. In fact, it's rumored she's had
liaisons with other alumnae of the Vilna Fine Arts Academy. But
for the untidy monomaniac from the back of beyond, augmented
as he now is by good fortune (it's 1925), she has always had a soft
spot. He was after all the first boy unrelated to her by blood to have
come into her family's home.

For his part, Chaim is impressed by the sophisticated young
woman Dvoira has become. She wears her dark hair bobbed beneath a jaunty cloche hat, her knife-pleated skirt hemmed just below the knee. Her unguarded berry-brown eyes are outlined in kohl
to give them a tinge of mystery; her lips are painted pigeon's-blood
red. Her laughter is effervescent and she's au courant with respect
to all the latest cultural phenomena. She's seen Poulenc's "atmo-
spheric ballet" *Les biches* at the Théâtre Champs-Élysées; she's seen
Josephine Baker's *danse sauvage* at le Bal Nègre, which Miss Baker
performs while wearing a tutu made out of bananas and nothing
else. Deborah even lets it be known that, incidentally, the tutu
was designed by Jean Cocteau. Instead of the classical composers

Chaim assumes she must be studying at the Conservatoire, her talk
is all of Debussy, Ravel, and Darius Milhaud. She smokes Gauloises,
is conversant in the "serious" novels of Colette, and has danced the
Black Bottom with American Negroes at Bricktop's nightclub in
Montmartre. Swept up in the élan of Paris as she is, however, she
seems genuinely pleased to have reconnected with the retiring artist.

But Chaim is as wary as he is flattered by her compliments. In
point of fact, Deborah Melnick is not the first woman to have conceived a fondness for the rough-edged immigrant. It has happened,
and not just with Paulette. There was Kiki before she became the
Queen of Montparnasse, immortalized in Man Ray's photograph
portraying her naked back and butt as a violin. One winter's night,
when she was locked out of a lover's studio in the Falguière, Soutine
gave her shelter. On a chivalrous impulse he set fire to a couple of
chairs to provide some warmth in his frigid atelier, and asked nothing of her in return. Not even the friendly flesh that she freely offered. This endeared him to her ever after. Youki Desnos, who had
left Foujita to become a Surrealist muse, has actively flirted with
Chaim, and the notoriously promiscuous Marevna has painted his
portrait. In it she captured something of the same haunted innocence that Modigliani had accentuated in several paintings of his
friend (portraits in which Chaim hardly recognized himself). Once
the flighty Hastings woman, while fondling her sublime Amedeo,
speculated in the Litvak's hearing on what it might be like to be
mounted by a Jewish troll. Back then Chaim still wondered in his
heart whether one must be some kind of hero to deserve the attentions of an authentic woman. Yes, said his heart. But while he
might do for a hero's sidekick or mascot, all should understand
what he knew enough to realize himself: that he was finally not a
candidate for romance.

But that was then, back before he'd become a personage. Now
his work is sought after, his finances in order, his sartorial turnout

impeccable. Galleries prominently display his paintings and critics praise him in the journal *L'amour de l'art.* "From the ghetto of Vilna, a crucible where unsuspected powers are fermenting, where farce and drama, the comic and the painful, the droll and the ridiculous coalesce, Soutine has come to us . . ."He's Gothic, they say, a Fauve, an Expressionist, a naïf—all labels Chaim derides while allowing that they don't hurt the sales of his tableaux. The still lifes that once sold at auction for under a hundred francs now go for a cool twenty thousand in the galleries of Paul Guillaume and Adolphe Goupil. The zealous Zborowski imagines that the dealers will soon be speculating in Soutine "futures." *École de Paris* is no longer a pejorative rubric, and its formerly exotic proponents—Modigliani, Kisling, Pascin, Chagall, Lipchitz, Chaim Soutine—have become staples of the new radical art. A lady might want, for motives not entirely pure, to hitch her wagon to a rising star such as Chaim's. They might, he thinks, dance attendance on him not for himself but for his renown.

That said, Chaim is overly mistrustful. There have been women who want to mother him like the draggled foundling that in their eyes he still is, even though his stock is up and his larder full. They want to straighten his collar and brush the bird droppings from the shoulder of the suit that has rejected him despite his delusions of class. They want to run hot water in the claw-footed bathtub he continues to avoid and wash the nits from his hair, to tease him for his pathetic bourgeois pretensions and fumigate his studio. They want to feel what it's like to have his fanatical energy concentrated exclusively on them. And Deborah Melnick, for all her freshly minted urbanity, is one of these.

One late August morning she brings flowers to the rue du Mont Saint-Gothard and, without being asked, sets about restoring some order to the chaos. Chaim looks on in stunned passivity. On the one hand he's outraged at the unauthorized license the woman is taking with his quarters, while on the other he feels obliged to her for tidying up. He doesn't like feeling obliged. But she's unobtrusive and gingerly in her efforts, folding here a cast-off pullover, picking up there a dead rodent by the tail. The other animals— the dangling partridges and Corsican hares—she knows enough to leave alone; she knows instinctively to give a wide berth to the artist's work space, for which he's appropriated much of the spacious studio. She respectfully refrains from approaching the easel or uncovering the canvases Chaim so assiduously conceals from her view and keeps up a constant chatter about "Ragtime-itis" and the films of René Clair.

Her subsequent social calls are also unannounced, a thing Chaim has never tolerated, though he finds himself almost resentfully looking forward to her visits. At Rosh Hashanah, the Jewish New Year, she shows up to remind him of the holiday he's forgotten and serves him gefilte fish made from a coveted family recipe. "The round fish balls," she informs him with an oddly lascivious lilt, "signify a full and plentiful year." In violation of his austere diet Chaim tucks into the dish, along with a generous helping of the red-beet horseradish guaranteed to foment a pogrom in his belly.

With such domestic gestures, Deborah Melnick usurps the good offices of Paulette Jourdain, until the girl, judging herself largely redundant, surrenders the field to the newcomer. Even Chaim's elemental hangers-on have given the advantage to the Melnick. Outside, it's *les années folles,* the city's crazy years, and the bacchanalian atmosphere allows imps and fiends of all orders to mingle with impunity among the revelers. Their favorite venue is the art students' ball in the square-acre courtyard of the Beaux-Arts Academy. There a disembodied dybbuk can take ready possession of a dancer in the grip of a dervish-like Charleston; a demoness can interfere with the scantily attired attendees of either sex to her heart's delight. For a time, the phantasmal company feels secure in their abandonment of the skeptical artist; forgoing jealousy, they have left him safely in the care of the young woman from Vilna.

Having also developed a taste for the decadence that defines the quarter, Deborah Melnick announces to Chaim, "I will be your ambassadress to gaiety." She's determined to introduce him to Parisian nightlife.

"Gaiety?" Chaim contemplates the word as if it were some foreign concept.

"Yes, Chaim, like fun."

"I had a friend showed me fun already a long time ago."

But Deborah insists that things are different now: "The city," she exults, "is like a fair in heaven," borrowing an expression from the Yiddish, and Chaim, in one of his torpid periods between paintings, lacks the will to oppose her entreaties.

He accompanies her to one of the soirées hosted by Jules Pascin in his elaborate studio on the boulevard de Clichy. Everyone there is disguised as sailors, mimes, apaches, clowns, and toreadors. Foujita is dressed as a crutched ragpicker out of Hieronymus Bosch, with a cage on his back containing a naked girl. Pascin himself is a waggish Lord of Misrule in a domino and cap and bells. In his very hesitant mingling Chaim perhaps rubs shoulders unawares with Laila and her minions, indistinguishable from the costumed others. He would have preferred attending a prizefight or a Chaplin film at the Gaumont Palace, though he has to confess that the scandalous carryings-on at the fête offer their own brand of entertainment. Things are even livelier on another night at the Cabaret Perruche, where the intrusion of high society into the mix of jazz musicians and underworld dignitaries makes for rousing theater. Chaim is diverted by the public displays of intimacy and the punch-ups that erupt after a purse snatching or a spurned amorous overture. He's stirred by the band's raucous rhythms and bluesy improvisations. Induced against his principles into downing a sweet rum punch, he's even moved to attempt a few clumsy steps of a *flash tants*. This is a dance performed at traditional shtetl weddings, which might give a new woman such as the young Deborah Melnick old-fashioned ideas.

She invites herself up to his atelier after an evening out. She's tipsy and still shimmying a bit to the music they've heard in the clubs of Montmartre. The beads of her tiered chiffon evening dress coruscate from the light of the electric wall sconces, though not a hair of her lacquered blue-black bob is out of place. She mimics with her uptilted aquiline nose the gyrations of the ceiling fan until she becomes dizzy and nearly falls down. Chaim hovers about her, making as if to catch her when she stumbles. He's somewhat shikkered himself, having partaken again of the alcohol he'd sworn off since Modi's passing. So far, knock on wood, there seem to be no ill effects. The girl laughs at his solicitude and shoves him playfully back onto the sleigh bed, which occupies that portion of the room she herself has reclaimed from disorder. Then she begins to perform for him, kicking off her pumps, reaching to unfasten the hooks at the back of her dress, allowing it to slide from her shoulders. Her movements are a parody of a striptease, no less provocative for their comical exaggeration, and Chaim is so absorbed that he forgets to be alarmed. No woman has ever disported herself with such abandon in his presence. But while her burlesque has set his heart racing, his more diffident mind still limps awkwardly behind.

He thinks he should maybe play on his Victrola a recording to cool her contortions, though what does he have that's appropriate? Only his Bach and Berthe Sylva's schmaltzy "Les roses blanches." Besides, he's too spellbound by the young woman's exhibition to move from where he sits. She's dancing toward him now wearing only—*Gott im Himmel!*—her bandeau brassiere and step-ins, twirling a stocking over her head. Her thighs are buttery smooth, her midsection soft and delectable, the convex navel a tiny pink gem.

Then she nestles her silk-clad bottom in his lap while continuing to bounce to the syncopation in her head. She gives him a wet kiss and opens his shirt, removes the spool cuff links from his sleeves, then slips from his lap to pull off his cap-toe shoes. Her expressions alternate between temptress and naughty child as she unbuttons his flannel trousers and swiftly tugs them down along with his drawers. The manhood that has lain dormant so long is still in repose.

Aghast, Chaim scrambles to cover himself but Deborah grabs his wrists. "It's nineteen twenty-six, Soutine," she appeals. "All is permitted."

"Not for me!" he exclaims, thus rejecting the notion of unchecked freedom—or is it perhaps the year itself? Having pulled his pants back up, he waits to be overtaken by shame. When, in any case, has he ever been able to want a woman who wants him in return?

Deborah stands and appears to struggle with an embarrassment she quickly overcomes. Then, undiscouraged, she taps her temple with a forefinger in a pantomime of being struck with a bright idea. She pads across the room to the umbrella stand in which she's deposited the fiddle case she never travels without. Who knows when some impromptu cabaret orchestra might be in need of her assistance? She bends to unlatch the case, looking between her legs as if to assure Chaim's advantageous view of her backside. Then she rises and removes the varnished spruce heirloom, in her family since the expulsion from Spain, from its velvet nest. She has played for him before though never en déshabillé. Tucking the instrument under her chin, she begins to make music, continuing the sensual swaying of her hips to the melody. She waltzes toward him, playing an oriental-sounding piece, maybe something by one of the Russians—Scriabin? Stravinsky?—who've taken Paris by storm. Peering coquettishly over her bow, she looks to see whether the haunting chords have had an effect on the listener, but Chaim remains sitting rigidly at the edge of the bed. She ends the émigré composition and sighs, dropping the snake-charmer routine, then shifts to one of the traditional tunes she played for the unrefined art student back in her father's home.

"Oifn pripetshik brent a fayerl," she serenades him in a kind of torch song contralto, "un in shtub iz heys . . ."

The marriage of the maudlin cradle song and Deborah Melnick's rhythmic motions has evoked in her audience, she observes, the beginnings of a smile. For in spite of his rallied resistance to the comedy of her seduction, Chaim has begun again to relax. Amused, perhaps beguiled, he leans back on his elbows and closes his eyes, which immediately snap open again. The girl sees what he sees: that he's staring in astonished chagrin at the tented crotch of his pants. She sets the fiddle aside, approaches the bed, and once again sits astride his lap.

"Ven der putz shteht . . . ," she whispers in his ear, and to himself Chaim completes the old saw, ". . . ligt der sechel in drerd."

When the prick stands up, the conscience goes underground.

◆

THE *YENTZING* IS GOOD, thinks Chaim (though what does Chaim know from yentzing?), but the sleeping together not so much. He's too accustomed to sleeping, or lying awake, alone. But the yentzing, the fucking—it makes him want to crow. He wants to put on his club collar and plus-fours and stroll past the bistros and tabacs along the boulevard Raspail with the woman on his arm. "A vildeh moid Soutine's got!" he imagines his old comrades-in-destitution exclaiming. Though it turns out that, for all her sauciness and worldly airs, Deborah Melnick is not really so *vildeh*, not so wild. She is something of a homebody at heart. She enjoys café society, likes seeing and being seen among the cultural avant-garde. She likes the reflection on her skin from the neon of Montparnasse and the footlights of the Théâtre de l'Étoile; she likes her rose cocktails. But perhaps even more, she likes returning to what she regards as the homey love nest she now shares with the acclaimed Lithuanian artist.

The artist, for his part, tries his best to participate in Deborah Melnick's romantic fantasy, though he's torn from the outset with misgivings. Feeling threatened by her "improvements" to his studio, he hangs a curtain around his work space to hold off the encroaching domesticity. He defends his altar-sized easel and the scrap heap of used paint tubes and brushes against the girl's broom and the dust skirt she's adorned the bedframe with. At the same time, he looks forward eagerly to the yentzing and he savors the freshly brewed noisettes she serves him in the mornings, along with a brioche and butter. "This is all Bontshe Shveig asked for in heaven," she informs him, recalling the Yiddish tale of a simple Jew who asks no more of Paradise. Chaim is irritated by the taint of Yiddishkeit that still lingers about her, how it jars with her image of a chic young thing. He's irritated at being reminded of anything that preceded the coming of Dr. Barnes. Nevertheless, it seems that, for all intents and purposes, he and the young woman from Vilna are an item. And isn't this what he's been longing for? The answer is not readily available.

Chaim doesn't remember having asked her to move in with him or the precise moment when he realizes that they're living together. But at some point her drop-waist frocks and flowered dressing gown have begun to edge out his own quality apparel in the wardrobe; her toiletries crowd the shelf in his bathroom like an Arabian skyline. Pink peonies and stargazer lilies replace the goblins that perched on the mantel. Initially, he's more intrigued than dismayed by the changes this invasion of femininity has wrought upon his living quarters. It's as if an aromatic storm has swept away all evidence of past vicissitudes. He misses the vicissitudes. He breathes nameless fragrances, examines a laundered unmentionable hanging from a window crank to dry. He inspects the ornate label on a tin of albacore and the nooks in a wheel of Emmental cheese in the bountiful pantry, the cache of cleaning agents stored beneath the galley kitchen sink. He's fascinated at first by his altered digs, then appalled. His flat is no longer recognizable, and Chaim Soutine plus the adjunct of a female companion (a mistress?) is unrecognizable to himself.

But the yentzing is good—though there is of course no end to his naïveté. He's never sure where to put his hands or what effect it might have to touch the woman's this or her that. His instincts take him only so far, and his clumsiness often defeats his instincts. He even swallows his pride enough to ask Moïse Kisling's advice concerning the care and handling of the female. The wisecracking Moïse places a hand on Chaim's shoulder and says in mock earnestness, "Women need a reason to have sex, Soutine, but men"—he raises a thoughtful forefinger—"they just need a place."

"Very helpful," mutters Chaim.

Kisling tells him to buck up: "Sex is the most beautiful, natural thing that money can buy." Then he gives the disappointed Litvak the gift of a dog-eared deck of pornographic playing cards, but the attitudes in the photos involve a degree of athleticism Chaim would never attempt.

Deborah, however, is patient with him, and gentle, surprisingly gentle given her friskiness on the night of their original dalliance. No one has treated him so gently since the evening Modi picked him up from the pavement after the fire in Montmartre. Sometimes, though, he resents that she should bestow on him a tenderness he feels he hasn't earned. The idea prompts him to return her caresses with the occasional smack or rough thrust. He has pinched her nipples and slapped her behind, which only elicits her rhapsodic squeals, as if their coitus is all in the spirit of good fun. Then he's doubly annoyed by her failure to apprehend his aggression, and ashamed at the latent cruelty he's discovered in himself.

He neither laughs nor smiles during their canoodling and is irked that she hasn't noticed, or if she has noticed doesn't seem to care. He resents that, after his carnal appetite is assuaged, the question of love never arises in his mind. There is only the question of whether the woman is too great a distraction from his work. Because the lethargy that was upon him when they renewed their acquaintance has returned, and it has become increasingly clear to him that the occupancy of Deborah Melnick is to blame. He's unable to paint with her in the house. Then even though she's away much of the day, occupied with her musical studies and marketing, his nerves are on edge anticipating her return. Also, there's the distraction of the music itself, which is not to say that her music isn't enchanting. The girl is quite accomplished, and her playing has been further refined by her teacher Rabaud, who was himself schooled by Gabriel Fauré. She can alternate styles with a seemingly effortless versatility, interpreting Satie's *Gymnopédie No. 1* with the same vibrancy she lends to Mozart's *Divertimento in D*, and to the Yiddish lullaby "Yankele." All have the power to relieve and transport her audience. But Chaim resents that power, which should by all rights belong to nothing outside of his work—and who can work with so much commotion?

He tries tactfully to explain the situation: "When I paint, it's like in my person I'm not here, you see, and I don't trust that they won't monkey with my person, some kibbitzer, when I'm not at home."

The young woman snickers; he sounds like a lunatic. Then she suggests they take a day off, perhaps attend a matinee of *Phi-Phi* at the Gaîtié-Montparnasse. Chaim wants to howl from his desire to escape her into his art.

This he manages to do from time to time, but only fleetingly. He invites Miestchaninoff and Kisling, one after the other, to sit for their portraits in the evenings. At least he won't be alone with her for a while, and maybe their presence—Oscar's deadly habit of talking shop, Moïse's ribald jokes—might even drive Deborah Melnick from the studio. Neither of the men are happy with the artist's unflattering renderings—who has ever been pleased with a Soutine portrait? He's aged them considerably and, adding insult to injury, distorted their features as in a funfair mirror. They linger, however, despite their displeasure, curious at seeing Soutine domiciled with a woman. In fact they behave for a change like perfect gentlemen, while Deborah assumes in turn her role as a model hausfrau. She bids them return anytime. In his vexation Chaim begins again to bring a menagerie of dead animals into the atelier, which he deliberately neglects to inject with the ammonia solution. Deborah demonstrates an unprotesting tolerance for them. He has the Vaugirard butcher boys drag in the grisly carcass of a crowbait workhorse, which he hangs from the ceiling with its intact head dragging the floor. It begins to spoil and again the neighbors complain, but Deborah, like Paulette before her, defends its necessity for the artist's work. Genius makes uncommon demands.

Chaim reminds himself for the thousandth time of the distance he's traveled from his term as the demon-plagued scapegrace of Smilovitchi. His paintings have caused a stir in exhibitions at the Café Parnasse and the René Paul Gallery; they're sold alongside Courbet, Sisley, and Derain at auctions in the Hôtel Drouot. Reviewers struggle to describe his talent: "Soutine is perhaps the painter in whose work the lyrical quality of matter has most profoundly sprung forth from it." "Soutine shows us a hallucinatory skinned rabbit that, with its red stumps, seems to implore the stars to take action against its human assassins." This isn't right, but it isn't wrong either. He has money, a commodious Paris address, a measure of fame, and at last a woman. He has also an itch that must be scratched until he bleeds, the scab picked until the wound bleeds again. It's a process that will not suffer witnesses.

Lacking the spine to rid himself of Deborah Melnick, he makes excuses to leave the studio without her. He has business with Zborowski; he has an appointment to consult with yet another specialist about his stomach troubles. He needs another hat. He realizes that the Chaim Soutine who *has* (the woman, the notoriety, etc.) is incompatible with the more comfortably familiar Soutine who *wants*, and he wanders the boulevards in search of his former self. He hasn't far to look. His spiffed-up reflection in the windows of the boulangeries and *marchés aux vins* doesn't deceive him. He sees through it to last season's undesirable, whom he still holds in delicious contempt. How can one have nostalgia for self-loathing? And yet . . .

His fellow artists on the terraces of the cafés he's sworn to avoid see through his genteel affectations as well, and mercilessly mock him for them. Chagall, back from Russia, is the worst of the lot. He had returned to find his studio at la Ruche ransacked, his only surviving paintings used by the wartime concierge to roof a bunny hutch. Although his fortunes have since been reversed and his work become more lucrative than ever, his success doesn't annul his resentment of the Litvak's. Their frequent pairing by critics wanting to bracket together all artists of Hebrew extraction has exacerbated the bitterness of their rivalry. To say nothing of their mutual distaste for each other's work. His ribbing from the jovial terrace of the Dôme lacks the good humor of Kisling's or Léon Indenbaum's.

"So, Soutine," remarks Chagall—a breeze teases the locks of his leonine hair, ruffles the lapels of his striped blazer—"is your heart still tugging at your insides?" This is the stock phrase Chaim had been known to employ when borrowing money he never returned.

A nerve struck, Chaim feels his fists beginning to furl, his liver lips sputtering foam. Chagall rises with his elfin grin. The sculptor Indenbaum steps between the two shtetl refugees lest they come to blows. Chaim departs the café flinging a Yiddish curse behind him—"Leeches should drink you dry!"—then detests himself for having resorted to that déclassé vernacular.

He sulks in front of Rembrandt's holy *Ox* in the Louvre. Outside, unbeknownst to Chaim, Josephine Baker walks her pet leopard through a murmuration of leaves blown from the acacias along the Champs-Élysées. Joan Miró, whose head barely reaches her buoyant breasts, tangoes with Kiki at the Jockey Club. André Breton and his insurgent followers storm the banquet of a Symbolist poet at the Closerie des Lilas; they swing from the chandeliers and tear the windows from their hinges. Cubism mutates into Art Deco and Max Jacob welcomes an opium-addled Cocteau into the Catholic Church. Erik Satie dies (all the whores and pimps of Montparnasse marching in his funeral procession). Le Corbusier plans to turn Paris into a factory, Renoir's son begins filming *Nana* on the advice of Zola's daughter, and Citroën's name appears in lights on the Eiffel Tower. Fitzgerald meets Hemingway at the Dingo. Chaim broods in front of the *Ox*, which he dares to think his own compares favorably to. Heartened, he races back to his studio, and ignoring Deborah, who's busy making a bouillabaisse, paints a still life with lemons. Then he slashes the canvas to bits. He returns to the Louvre the next day and stands for hours in front of Courbet's many-colored *Trout*, then runs back to his studio to paint another still life, which he also destroys. Deborah informs him that her parents, having been notified that their daughter has become an artist's common-law wife, have ceased paying her tuition at the Conservatoire. In fact, they've cut her off without a sou. She seems somehow proud of the development, which elicits in Chaim a bout of diarrhea.

He takes a morning train from the Gare du Nord to Amsterdam just to view Rembrandt's *Jewish Bride* in the Rijksmuseum. The cynosure of light on her forehead, her ringed fingers, the folds of her red dress tinged with gold cause his chest to contract, squeezing his heart into his throat. He knocks about the streets of the old ghetto flanked by the workshops of book printers and diamond cutters; it's here the master sought his models for King David and Christ. He eats *frites* with mayonnaise and vomits in a canal, sleeps in the station and takes the first train back to Paris the following morning. Deborah has been worried sick about him. Has anyone, Modi included, ever worried so about him before? He has a grateful impulse to dash out and buy her that gemstone necklace she admired in a window on the rue de Rennes. At the same time, he observes how the girl's chin seems to have receded a centimeter or two, how her tight coif looks more like patent leather than real hair. Inclining his head as he confesses where he's been, he notices that her ankles appear to be thickening. Moreover, her pots of alkaline coffee and gluey macaroons are poisoning him.

She chaffs him that it's time he made an honest woman of her, and sees his teeth begin to chatter and his strabismus recur. "Chaim," she snickers, "you're a child!"

Despite his discomfort, he's warmed by her silvery laughter.

Nevertheless, he renews his contact with the chauffeur Daneyrolle, whom he asks to drive him to the spa town of Châtel-Guyon in the Auvergne. He's heard that the thermal baths there may relieve his peptic ulcers. When the decorous chauffeur demurs, Chaim offers to pay the man out of pocket. Remembering the aimless odysseys that Soutine has instigated in the past, Daneyrolle continues to drag his heels, until his boss Zborowski intercedes on the artist's behalf: the cash cow must be indulged. Chaim sits in the rear of the bottle-green roadster, driving the chauffeur half-mad with readings aloud in his fractured French from a translation of *Notes from Underground.* The book has lately become his Bible. At Châtel-Guyon he takes a room in the Hôtel Princesse Flore with its heavy-handed opulence. The lobby is arranged in clusters of lavish baroque furniture; mythological frescoes divide the cherrywood paneling; a red-carpeted marble staircase descends beneath the yellow-glass rotunda. The windows of his room open onto a balcony overlooking a formal garden enclosed by hedges trimmed in the shape of chess pieces. In the mirror-walled dining room a string quartet neutralizes the clicking and scraping of sterling utensils on bone china. The menu caters to intestinal sufferers. It features an abundance of fruits, vegetables, and varieties of skinless poultry, plus something called psyllium husk, which is said to promote digestive health and soften stools without increasing flatulence. After Deborah's rich dishes, Chaim finds the fare reassuringly insipid.

The next morning he forgets for a spell his hydrophobia; he floats beneath the rib-vaulted ceiling of the palatial bathhouse, buoyed like a champagne cork by the warm mineral waters. In the mosaic-floored drinking hall he tastes and spews from his mouth the sulfurous waters themselves. He endures a pummeling rub-down from a thickset masseur he suspects of being anti-Semitic. Never has he been so luxuriously pampered, and never felt so out of place. He buys a postcard with a view of the town to send to Deborah Melnick, writes her an innocuous message, and tears up the card. Back in his room he attempts a full-blown letter of apology for his vanishing act but is frustrated by his ham-fisted command of the French language, and damned if he will write to her in Yiddish. Then Chaim is awestruck by the magnitude of his guilt. His thoughts go where they haven't gone since the lean days at la Ruche, back when he'd contemplated replacing the cockerel he'd strung up for a still life with Soutine.

"Veyz mir!" he moans aloud, and, "Sans blague!" redirecting his anger from himself toward the woman who has inspired his guilt in the first place. On the strength of that anger Chaim vacates his room and stomps down the winding stairs to the lobby.

All about him the prosperous take their leisure on upholstered love seats; they relax behind newspapers in winged armchairs, their every need attended to by the bustling staff. A porter laden with luggage is seeing a couple of perhaps young newlyweds into the elevator's gilded cage. A desk clerk with a supercilious air rings a bell to summon a baby-faced bellhop whom he abruptly dispatches to page a guest with a telegram. Black-stockinged chambermaids carry drifts of garments on their way to the laundry to be pressed; a valet hugs to his chest the clump of shoes he's been delegated to shine. The ginger-haired, treble-chinned maître d'hôtel, at once self-effacing and haughty, greets diners at the open oak doors to the restaurant. They manage, the hotel personnel, to be somehow simultaneously absent and present, never intrusive but always on hand when required. By the same token, the guests rest assured that the capable staff remain fixed in their places according to a strict, age-old hierarchy, a chain of command designated by their uniforms: the doorman's top hat and military greatcoat; the bellboy's scarlet, brass-buttoned jacket and pillbox hat; the clerk's morning coat; the double-breasted white tunics and mushroom toques of the cooks and pastry chefs. Chaim has developed a regular fetish for their sundry costumes.

The well-to-do remain forbidding and unapproachable, not to say similar to one another in their sumptuous threads. Let that bootlicker van Dongen and his ilk paint their portraits; Chaim is cozier among the lower orders. Like Manet and van Gogh before him, he's fated to make visible those who are largely unseen by society. But that's the least of his motivations. As in Cagnes after the rigors of Céret, he is drawn to the tension between the livery that ranks the servant and the face that reveals a panoply of temperaments at odds with servitude. He likes to place them in settings that include no defining details. Often versicolored, sometimes a cerulean blue, Chaim's swirling backdrops make his subjects vital conductors of the energy that surrounds them. That's why a Soutine portrait—to borrow Modigliani's boast—resembles the sitter more than the sitter resembles himself, while the energy that inspirits the portrait belongs solely to Chaim. It's at this point that he remembers he brought with him his box of oils.

But the excessive luxury of the Princesse Flore weighs him down. "I can't paint where there are rugs!" he declares aloud. He rents an empty room above a tobacconist's in the old town center. Always stammering in his attempts to proposition the subject of a portrait, Chaim flashes his money along with his requests. Then he feels like the market wife in Smilovitchi who lured stray cats with poisoned fish heads. The hotel staff are leery in the beginning of the common-featured arriviste in his unseasonable boating outfit, but they're not above earning a few extra francs. The valet reports back to the cook, who reassures the head waiter that the gent is indeed an artist of sorts, though the paintings themselves are dreadful. The bell captain, who fancies himself a ladies' man, complains that his face has been turned into a carnival mask. "The fellow was more concerned with the red of my mess jacket than getting my high cheekbones right. I look like a gargoyle!" The pâtissier remarks that "he lays on the paint with such thick licks and curls that you'd think he was icing a cake." The chambermaid practically weeps when recalling the hours she suffered under his tyranny. "He insisted I hold the pose like a statue, and if I flinched, he ground his teeth and cursed me. I scratched an armpit and he slashed the canvas to ribbons and threw it on the floor, then started all over again on another."

Regardless of his fitful antics, all that fall the servants troop back and forth between the hotel and the drafty room above the tobacconist's shop. They never cease grousing about their portraits: the crooked noses and pumpkin heads, the prematurely sagging flesh of their jowls. Though at least one *femme de chambre* is shocked at how her face—despite the rampageous brushwork that threatens to overwhelm the likeness—divulges an aching vulnerability beneath her confrontational stance. By December Chaim's funds have nearly bottomed out. He notifies that *ganef* Zborowski that he's sending a new lot of paintings back to Paris and intends to follow them himself soon after. Before he leaves, however, another bellhop volunteers for his portrait. No one has yet volunteered without a preliminary promise of remuneration. In addition, this one is a dwarf, exciting to Chaim, who thinks of Velázquez, until he sees through his disguise that the volunteer is none other than the self-proclaimed fallen angel Semangelof. Chaim flees the tobacconist's.

✦

HE RETURNS TO THE rue du Mont Saint-Gothard hoping that Deborah Melnick, having realized that their connection is finished, has cleared out. But she's there, though gone is the high-spirited ingénue of their initial reunion. Gone the modern girl determined to draw him out of himself while civilizing him in the process. She's put on weight in his absence and is looking dowdy in her aproned housedress, a helix of hair over her forehead having escaped her shingled bob. Face powder has succeeded only in accenting the pastiness of her forehead and cheeks. Her bare arms are gooseflesh from the unheated studio, her languid eyes damp, but her jaw is set firm: she's been waiting a long time for this re-encounter. At first she merely states flatly that, since Chaim has ceased sending payments, the rent is months past due. The landlady is threatening eviction. Chaim shrugs; he's thinking of moving anyway. The tears stream down her cheeks, leaving snail tracks in the powder, but her voice is unwavering.

"I'm not fat, Chaim, if that's what you're thinking," she submits. "Shvengert, Chaim; I'm pregnant."

His reason foundering, he denies the possibility. Never has it occurred to Chaim that he might get a woman with child. As for contraception, he's always assumed she knew what to do. "The child is not mine!" he insists, and proceeds to accuse her of having slept with all of Montparnasse while he was away. He calls her every kind of putain, *kurveh*, slut, *la grue*. Deborah turns away from him to bend and stir a pot of potato soup in the brick fireplace, her stove since the gas has been cut off. There's something of the careworn balebosta in her pose. With her back still turned she weathers his fulminations, then rises with a little difficulty to deliver her ultimatum.

"You will have now to marry me."

The fluttering of his eyelids echoes the faltering of his heart. "But I don't love you!" he gasps through a constricted throat. Her weary expression confirms the irrelevancy of his admission.

Chaim feels as if his feet have been swept from under him by the irresistible current of fate. All subsequent arguments fizzle before they even reach his lips. When reason returns (along with its musty companion, conscience), Chaim admits defeat. The situation is indisputable. He agrees to accompany the woman the next day to the Pletzl, the Jewish quarter in the Marais that he has always made a point of avoiding.

Deborah has put herself stylishly back together for the occasion. She wears a violet tam-o'-shanter and a sequined tea dress beneath her shawl, the fabric gathered at the waist to hide her tumescence. But her efforts to reconstitute the erstwhile sophisticate have only increased her fiancé's bleak awareness of her condition. It doesn't help that this neighborhood of fallen splendor, with its crumbling hôtels particuliers and dingy vest-pocket shops, is populous with bearded men in funereal attire and women wearing wigs like pumpernickel loaves. They scurry in and out of the kosher butcher's, gather haggling round the carts of peddlers selling yard goods and fish. They have re-created a shtetl in the heart of Paris. Chaim is as derisive of them as of the demidemons that persist in hounding him. Aren't these the same self-righteous zealots who made of his childhood such a misery?

The taciturn couple walk along a block of plywood hoardings plastered with bills advertising a call to the faithful by the Vizhnitzer Rebbe, a performance by the visiting Moscow State Yiddish Theater. Intimidated by its anomalous pomp, the couple bypass the recently constructed Art Nouveau synagogue on the rue Passée. They choose instead a modest storefront *shtibl* nearby. A shop bell jingles as they enter and an old mossbacked sexton in a crumpled skullcap squints up at them over his broom. The dismal room is barren but for a few rows of straight-backed chairs, a potbelly stove, and a warped wooden cabinet that makes do as a holy ark. There's a lithograph of Moses parting the waters tacked to the mildewed wall. When Deborah announces their purpose—Chaim having lost his tongue—the *shamus* unbends his scarecrow frame to assume a ludicrously officious posture. He bids them wait and ducks behind the "ark" to knock at a door and inquire within. He returns to tell them in a whisper (why is he whispering?) that the rabbi will see them now.

The rabbi's dimly lit chamber is as cluttered as the prayer hall is austere. Thick tomes vie for space on the bowed shelves with various ritual accessories: menorahs, spice boxes, a ram's horn that Chaim, so estranged from tradition, briefly mistakes for a hearing trumpet. The rabbi himself is seated behind a broad desk strewn with opened volumes showing yellowed pages, some with columns of text, some with debits and credits. His hooded eyes and buzzard beak are overshadowed by a hat resembling a snare drum covered in fur. His sidelocks dangle, his meaty lips protruding polyp-like from his beard. In his way a majestic figure, thinks Chaim.

"So," he wheezes, "you want to wed."

Is he asking or telling? It's all Chaim can do to keep from saying no. He thinks he might smother from the room's dense venerable-ness. Closing his eyes, the rabbi has begun to itemize a laundry list of requisite preparations for the nuptials: there must of course be a ketubah, a marriage contract, signed by two witnesses. There's the hall to be booked, the chuppah erected, and so on. Chaim wonders whether the man, having perceived some hesitancy on the part of at least one of the parties involved, is trying to discourage them. He feels a pang of gratitude.

"The *nissuin*, the wedding, is a weighty undertaking—" the rabbi continues, when Deborah interrupts.

"But," she wants to know, "can you not marry us now?"

Finding his voice, Chaim answers for the rabbi that this is clearly impossible; they obviously have much yet to do prior to the ceremony. He apologizes to the old man for having imposed on his time and allows that the wedding will have to be postponed. Upon which the aspiring bride thrusts a hand into his inside coat pocket and snatches his wallet; the artist's jaw drops as if she's pulled his heart from his chest. The wallet is fat with the cash Zborowski has advanced him on what he expects to earn from the new paintings, and Deborah waves it like smelling salts under the rabbi's nose. He lifts a fibrous brow and rises slowly to his full four-foot-eight.

"Like it says in Talmud," he intones, "it is an even greater mitz-vah for the poor to accept tzedakah than the rich to give it." Then he sighs like a tin whistle, "We are a poor congregation that shouldn't for a technicality refuse a charitable donation." He calls the shamus back in to witness the ceremony and shrugs *nifter-shmifter* when the groom admits that he doesn't have a ring.

Both Deborah and Chaim know that a religious service has no legitimacy in the eyes of the state. But for the time being it's enough for the young woman, who takes to signing her name in letters home *Deborah Melnick Soutine*. (Her family, however, remain unreconciled.) She's purchased, with Chaim's money, a mahogany rocking cradle and a wicker bassinet, both of which she paints in festive colors with the artist's own imported oils. Her violin gathers dust while she knits (the flapper can knit) tiny booties and bonnets. She sits beside a frosted window with her clicking needles, having affected the Madonna smile of imminent maternity. Once she asks Chaim whether he might like to kneel at her feet and hold the spool of unwinding yarn, a request at which he can barely suppress a scream. The little solace he's taken in the unlawfulness of their marriage has evaporated in the face of the woman's preparatory measures for giving birth. He's forgotten there was ever a time when he liked to picture himself as begetter of a happy family.

Theirs is a charade of married life. When they sleep together, Chaim is nauseated by what he imagines to be the smell of milk souring in her breasts. He's revolted as well by her bizarre cravings for substances like soap and cigarette ash, which she swallows then disgorges into the toilet in the mornings. There's no question of his working in the apartment, suffocating as it is with the woman's distaff operations. Never mind the heat from the gas range, which—now that Chaim is once more paying his bills—she keeps blasting night and day. Perhaps he can paint again *en plein air*. He remembers doing impressions of the passage de Dantzig outside la Ruche and the impasse Falguière in his fledgling years. He's even taken a page from Utrillo and trekked up the butte to paint a streetscape of Montmartre. But the prospect of having his work exposed to the inspection of passersby, let alone the elements, gives him pause. Besides, even for Chaim Soutine, who's braved storms for the sake of a panoramic view, the weather is inclement.

A rare November snowstorm has enshrouded the whole of Paris. The boulevards are knee-deep in slush, the shop awnings sagging like—*kaynehoreh*—gravid bellies under their burden of snow. True, the city is quiet and spell-struck by the kind of beauty that would ordinarily be ripe for Chaim's subversions, if only he were equal to the task. The public urinals are furry with hoarfrost, the railings of balconies glazed in rime, the dragonfly ironwork at the entrances to the Métros fretted in ice. As are the nodding branches of the weeping beeches and yews in the Parc Montsouris, which Chaim trudges through in exile from himself.

If he were a trapped animal, he might have gnawed off his leg to get free. But how to extricate yourself from the nonnegotiable imperative of a woman carrying your child? At least she *says* it's your child. He asks his fellow émigré Marevna, with whom Deborah has become friendly, whether the woman—he refuses to call her his wife—has been unfaithful behind his back. But the libertine Marevna, whose cohabitations have included more than one man at a time, can only roll her eyes at such philistine jealousy. (Then he's too ashamed to pursue his follow-up inquiry: whether she knows some physician willing to dispose of the problem. Besides, for that you need the cooperation of the woman in question.) Displaced from the rue du Mont Saint-Gothard, Chaim attends a match at the Hippodrome between Carpentier "the Orchid Man" and the gruesome Georges Gardebois. Chaim's fists automatically duplicate their vicious jabs and uppercuts, and he thinks: "I might if I never paint again become a boxer," though he's remarkable for his lack of agility. He goes to the Cirque d'Hiver and laughs for the first time in months when the veteran clown Grock saws his fiddle in half with his bow. He goes to the Louvre and realizes he would swap any number of Deborah Melnicks for a single quince-yellow braid from Tintoretto's *Susanna*. So what if Modigliani, torn though he was, had rejoiced at the birth of his daughter. Dédo was hardly a model of principled behavior.

It's midwinter when Chaim explains to his counterfeit bride the urgency of his making a visit to the town of Auxerre. Why Auxerre? He's heard from Lipchitz, who had it from Max Jacob, that the Saint-Germain Abbey there contains murals in its crypt dating from before the time of Charlemagne. Chaim has suddenly developed a passionate interest in early Christian murals. If he'd heard there was a crypt full of mechanical toads, it would have been as good a reason as any for taking the trip. As they part, he avoids the sight of Deborah's protuberant belly. She utters something about "a missed honeymoon," but Chaim already has a foot out the door.

The murals are fine but the ancient Cathedral of Saint-Étienne, where the sun streaming through stained glass casts the Mass in a harlequin light, is enthralling. A similar light, prismed through a dirty window, would strike Chaim's crib in his infancy, and he fed on the colors as hungrily as on his mother's milk. That's anyway his conviction as he imagines how his canvases might drink up these colors: among them the cardinal of the choirboy's cassock, the foaming clotted cream of the first communicant's white gown. His senses are further quickened by the fact of his trespass in such a place. As a boy, he would shudder and spit against the evil eye when passing the threshold of a *christelakh* church. Now he sits, albeit uneasily, in a rear pew taking in the daunting spectacle. After the service, in one of his fevers, he forgets himself enough to approach a child and invite him to pose. This causes some agitation, and the roughcast stranger is surrounded by parents and clergy demanding to know his business. Realizing his error, Chaim is dumbfounded. Do they perhaps suspect him of plotting the ritual murder of gentile children? Jews have been charged before on such grounds, though usually around Passover time, when they're accused of wanting to siphon the blood of innocents for baking into their matzoh dough. Ultimately he gathers sufficient composure to try to placate his interrogators.

"I am Soutine, artist of note," he says, producing from his overcoat pockets press clippings in support of the claim.

But the culpability he feels at their questioning persists as if his intentions were in fact homicidal. This is no doubt due to the misplaced guilt he refuses to attach to the expectant woman he left behind—this time for good—in the Mont Saint-Gothard atelier. Shame and remorse are his constant companions throughout that late winter and early spring in his airy room with its cut-crystal lamps at the Hôtel Normandie. Shame and remorse, thinks Chaim, are my medium. He has nevertheless secured permission from the good parishioners of Saint-Étienne, mollified by fistfuls of silver, to paint their children, though they insist on overseeing the procedure. This is intolerable to the artist, who can no more suffer spectators to the performance of his art than to the workings of his bodily functions. Given no choice, however, he sets up his easel beneath the rose window in the cathedral vestibule. For the sake of the choirboy's red vestments and the communicant's confectionery white gown—which he striates with lashings of Prussian blues and greens—he submits to their parents' gawking. He even gloats over their horror at his ferocious assault on the canvas, and their distress at the transformation of their children into total strangers.

By June he's tired of watching the barge traffic on the turgid River Yonne outside his high hotel window. He travels by wagon-lit back to the Riviera. An habitué of hotels now, he is no longer intimidated by the guests and staff, having appropriated specimens of each for his art. He's become more at home among transients than among the settled residents of towns. A wandering Jew, you could call him, though that's a goyisheh legend about a man condemned by sin to remain a vagabond throughout all eternity. What does such a tall tale have to do with Chaim? He's still somewhat ill at ease in the lap of overmuch luxury though, and might have preferred the simpler lodgings provided by a country auberge or *chambre d'hôte*. But it's in the grand hotels that he enlists his subjects. He also enjoys a hotel's greater anonymity, though he's been waylaid once or twice when a guest, having gotten wind of his profession, requests a portrait. He has obliged them on occasion for a respectable commission, though they're generally disturbed by the results. (With the exception of a brittle Bulgarian woman who wept tears of gratitude over the depths of pity he'd dredged from her eyes. Chaim refrained from telling her the pity was his.)

Then the tiresome radiance of Cagnes, along with its sweltering heat, begins to wear on him, and he travels north again. He goes to the Beauce region in Brittany, the setting for Zola's tawdry *La terre*, which he's read with interest, but he soon grows bored with the unrelieved flatness of its russet plain. He goes to Touraine in the Loire Valley and is irritated at how the integrity of the natural landscape is so often spoiled by the excrescences of so many spun-sugar châteaux. He fetches up awhile in a farmhouse that Zbo has rented for his artists near the town of le Blanc on the River Creuse. It's a two-story fieldstone house built above a dirt-floored barnlike space in which the farmer keeps a threesome of cinnamon-colored Aubrac cows. They have velvety hides and lyre-shaped horns, these cows, and Chaim likes working in the barn beside them; he's comforted by the cadence of their chewing and belching and the pungency of their manure. He hangs his geese, pheasants, partridges, and hares from the rafters until the place looks like a zoological version of Jacques Callot's *Hanging Tree*. He dispenses with the chemical injections so that the stench is insufferable.

Paulette Jourdain is also there and he paints her. In an unusually relaxed moment he poses with her for a photograph, each of them holding the paw of an upstanding black-and-white dog, and both of them (marvelous in the case of Soutine) smiling. The dog, unaware of the artist's hot-tempered reputation, appears to be smiling too. He paints the Polish beauty Lunia Czechowska, who has taken refuge with the Zborowskis after her husband was executed by the Whites during the Russian Civil War. (Modi had painted and bedded her nearly a decade before, giving Chaim the illicit sense of taking liberties with his deceased friend's lover.) Both women complain of the hours of forced immobility they endure at the hands of the despotic artist, though both later acknowledge having felt ennobled by the abuse. Perilously close to satisfaction with his work, Chaim slashes most of his canvases. Zbo gives the nod to the seasoned Daneyrolle, who retrieves the shreds and takes them back to the city to be restored. By then Chaim has decamped once again. He goes here, goes there, remembering the towns he's visited only by the paintings he completed in them.

At some point in mid-September he returns to Paris, summoned by the promise of a one-man show at the prestigious Galerie Bing. Avoiding his old studio, from which he's long since had his belongings moved into storage, he takes a new apartment on the leafy rue de l'Aude. It's in the same arrondissement as the rue du Mont Saint-Gothard, if a little farther out on the fringes of the district, though finally not far enough. Derain, Braque, and Foujita are his neighbors, and the nearness of so many of his competitors prompts Chaim to move yet again, this time to the top floor of a building on the rue du Parc Montsouris. It's a smaller apartment than the previous, having the virtue of less room in which to accommodate guests. There's a file of horse chestnuts thankfully shielding his view of Corbusier's hideous custom-made house across the way.

Once installed, Chaim reestablishes his customary disorder. Ornament doesn't occur to him; he lives in the flat's few rooms as if squatting there, furnishing them only with the barest essentials.

He knows he'll probably relocate again soon, shifting addresses around the city much as he had traveled from town to town in the provinces. Put it down to restlessness, though some might call it a strategy of evasion. But whether he recognizes it or not, Paris is still for him a heady cordial, especially after his long bucolic retreat. Despite his solitariness, he's alert to the daily scandals, the news of which percolates through the piquant atmosphere: At a formal dinner hosted at his villa by the nefarious Count Harry Kessler, a naked Josephine Baker has sexually assaulted Aristide Maillol's *Crouching Woman* sculpture. The Surrealists, ubiquitous now in every café and music hall, have sparked riots at Diaghilev's *Romeo and Juliet* and again at George Antheil's fantastical *Ballet mécanique*. At the latter, dandies in silk foulards and tails battled outlandishly costumed artists and poets to the accompaniment of the whistles, hammers, car horns, xylophones, and electric bells onstage. The mayhem reached its crescendo with the whirring of a mounted airplane propeller, which blew the wig from the head of a man in the stalls to the back of the house.

"From a Dada point of view," Antheil himself is heard to say, "things could not have gone better."

Meanwhile the art market is booming, the collectors on a buying spree. The *Sleeping Gypsy* of the Douanier Rousseau, who died in poverty, sells for half a million francs. Anything by Picasso fetches prices through the roof. It's a bracing moment to be in Paris, the eye of a cultural hurricane, a fact not entirely lost on Chaim Soutine. Sometimes he feels he's viewing for the first time the river lights and arcade windows and rain-washed avenues dissonant with madcap citizenry. This fresh outlook is possibly the result of seeing the city from his late condition of solvency and a full stomach, squeamish as that stomach remains. He's energized, painting more still lifes, more portraits: one of his compatriot Jacques (né Chaim Jacob) Lipchitz, another of Émile Lejeune, a wealthy Swiss painter and admirer of his work. Lipchitz is cooperative but reliably critical, while Lejeune is not in the least disturbed by the giraffe neck and wide-apart eyes the painter has bestowed on him. Indeed, he applauds the distortions as his soul's own delineation and insists that the painter attend a concert of the composers' collaborative *Les Six* at his studio on rue Huyghens. Chaim tries out of habit to beg off but the Swiss won't take no for an answer.

The Surrealist contingent are there in force—as where are they not? They're dressed in idiotic getups, from a portable Arc de Triomphe to an assortment of unwieldy household appliances; they're accompanied by their current female muses, who are barely dressed at all. Chaim knows their names if not their faces: Breton, Éluard, Soupault, Max Ernst. They and their Dada precursors— who can distinguish between them?—make him squirm with their anarchic high jinks, their prescriptions for dragging their sick dreams into broad daylight. One of them, perhaps the polemical André Breton himself, a spruce-suited fellow wreathed in a crown of thorns, is declaiming a poem extempore: "My wife's tongue of rubbed amber and glass / My wife's sex of seaweed and platypus . . ." Another of their company, breaking ranks, seems to be making his way through the guests directly toward Chaim. This one's head is thrust through the center of a large round kapok clockface. It's quite a handsome head—Roman nose, upswept hair sleek as sealskin—in contrast to the absurd appendage that surrounds it. As always, Chaim feels diminished in the presence of handsome men. He smokes nervously, exhaling toward the skylight through which a mandarin orange moon is peering. The guest musicians are tuning their instruments inharmoniously in front of a hanging tapestry embroidered with a bird-headed woman.

The stranger asks the artist a question that, due to the noise of the gathering and the distance the clockface imposes between them, Chaim has to cup an ear to hear.

"Aren't you the sod that paints the strangled chickens?"

The question is not put antagonistically, but Chaim is nonetheless on his guard. The man doesn't wait for an answer but introduces himself as Louis Aragon, *poète d'automatisme*, then launches into an unsought analysis of Soutine's work. As usual, whenever his painting is discussed in public, Chaim feels his ears begin to burn. He hears only snatches of the poet's discourse, words like "atavistic," "primitive," "naïve," "innocent." The spongy kapok of the clock-face presses disagreeably against Chaim's chest as Monsieur Aragon leans forward.

"The purple stain of what's left of the chicken's wings," he exults, "the pearls of red ichor where the feathers were plucked! You're a vampire tipsy with blood, mon ami . . ."

Chaim has had enough already but the man is unstoppable.

". . . mouths agape, eyes protruding with fearful intensity. Their posthumous lives resolve the contradictory conditions of dream and reality. They achieve, in other words, a surreality. You're a maniac, Soutine. You're one of us!"

Chaim has no patience with such nonsense. He remembers Modigliani's reverence for Lautréamont, whom these meshuggeners have adopted for their godfather. "Beautiful as the chance meeting on a dissecting table of a sewing machine and an umbrella," his friend was fond of quoting. What's the point of such ridiculous juxtapositions? Chaim has seen them in the paintings of the Spaniard Dalí and the German Ernst, the prints reproduced in their propaganda rags. It seems to him that their glorification of the "unconscious" is a betrayal of what's real. He's never read their tin god Freud, but from what he's heard of his obsession with genitalia, he concludes that the guy is certainly not good for the Jews.

Monsieur Aragon is cracking wise: "A person has to be crazy," he's saying, "not to be insane in this world . . . ," but Chaim dislikes being included in such company.

"The difference between me and a madman," he truculently declares, "is that I'm not mad!" This sounds somehow amiss to his own ear, but the poet responds with enthusiasm.

"Oh, very good," he says, laughing, and turns to pass on the artist's accidental conceit to a comrade, who passes it along to another. Before the evening is out Chaim hears the line attributed to Dalí.

He tells himself he might have been at ringside watching the Orchid Man pulverize his opponent to jelly, but he has to admit that he enjoys the music. The distinguished fellowship of composer-musicians, brought together by Satie before his death, are also in fancy dress, and have begun playing the score of *L'éventail de Jeanne*. This is a children's ballet they've scored together and Chaim is captivated by its sweet-and-sour whimsicality. He's lulled into such a fugue state that he receives the blandishments of his neighbor, the Russian sculptress Chana Orloff, with a degree of grace. He even accepts her invitation to dinner. He returns to his flat with the impression, even without the influence of drink, that he has assumed his rightful place among the community of artists. Then he berates himself for such brazen audacity.

Along with his adherence to a strict diet of mostly garlic, sauerkraut, and green tea, Chaim has initiated a program of self-improvement. Out of sorts from a surfeit of Modi's transgressive authors, some of whom he thinks ought to be banned, he's begun dipping into the classical philosophers. He reads as well Montaigne and Rousseau late into the night. He has discovered the human Vesuvius Honoré de Balzac and is headlong into *Lost Illusions* when he hears a knock at the door. He's reached the scene where Mme. de Bargeton, having realized her mésalliance, breaks off her association with Lucien de Rubempré, thus abandoning him to penury. Brahms's Concerto in D Major conducted by the great Henri Büsser is playing on the phonograph and some moments pass before Chaim becomes aware of the persistent knocking. His recent spasm of sociability aside, he's annoyed by the intrusion.

He opens the door but doesn't recognize her at first, so utterly changed is she from the modish young woman from Vilna. Her plum purple cloche hat is faded, the stitching loose at the shoulder of her cocoon-wrap coat. Her excessive makeup, like a slipping mask, seems at variance with her oval face. The flesh beneath her chin has gone a little crepey and gravity tugs at the corners of her eyes. In her arms she holds a bundle, its puckered lobster-pink face squinting out of a billow of blue woolen blanket.

"I heard from Marevna you're here," she says.

Though he's yet to invite her in, she steps past him, leaving him standing open-mouthed in the doorway. A few seconds elapse during which he contemplates fleeing the apartment rather than having to confront her.

"Chaim," she says when at last he reluctantly closes the door, "I need your help."

He wishes he were anywhere else, and here I can be of some assistance. It's 1926 but it's also, remember, 1917, and the nine-kilogram boots with their cast-brass toes are kicking up sediment, which rises like smoke from the bed of the Seine. Somewhere above him old Babineaux is trundling forward with his rebreathing compressor and hoses along the towpath beneath the Austerlitz Rail Bridge. Having left the competition literally in his wake, Amedeo Modigliani reclines in his tub, creating the illusion that the honking ducks have done the work of conveying him across the finish line. Parties of Montparnassiers applaud him from the promenade, then wonder why he continues to sail on past the bridge. Meanwhile Chaim Soutine, despite his submersion, is aware that, the war notwithstanding, it's a perfect day for a boat race. He sidesteps a sunken dressmaker's dummy, between whose wire hoops swim a school of fish with rainbow scales; he wishes that he could as easily sidestep the woman whose circumstances he has reduced to privation.

"I try to make ends meet by giving violin lessons," she asserts, swaying a bit as she rocks the child in her arms, "but students are scarce and there's no end of the baby's demands on my time and energy." Moreover, her garret in a house on the odious place Maubert is not an academy the gentlefolk are eager to send their children to. "I owe three hundred francs in back rent," she states bluntly, "and then there are the doctor's bills; she's lately had the croup . . ."

The artist groans. "I gave you already my name. That's not enough?"

She has just enough dignity left to leave the question unanswered, but when the silence lingers, pleads with him, "It's not for me, Chaim, but the child . . ."

Resisting an impulse to glance at the infant, Chaim vehemently shakes his head. "Is not my child!" he bellows, clutching yet again at the straw of her imagined promiscuity. Her drowning eyes suffer the indictment without blinking. The baby has begun to cry. Under the river, Chaim sees the fishhooks dangling from the rods of anglers that line the embankment, and from every hook hangs a hobgoblin with a body like an inflated bladder with chicken feet. His anger at his inability to simply blot out the woman and the threat she represents has acquired a vindictiveness beyond his control. The knot in his intestines is as tight as a strangler's cord. He feels a fit coming on.

"I'd rather burn my money than give it to you!" he shouts.

Then, to prove he's in earnest, he pulls a wad of ten-franc notes from the pocket of his lounging jacket. He takes a box of matches from another pocket, stuffs the bills between his teeth, and strikes a match. He snatches the bills from his mouth, lights them, and thrusts the blazing cash toward the woman as one might brandish a torch to scare a shade. The flame burns his fingers and he howls as he waves away the ashes.

"Her name is Amélie," says the mother above the baby's piercing caterwaul.

Chaim claps his hands over his ears.

Exit Deborah Melnick with her bawling infant from his life.

His exhibition at the Galerie Bing is an unqualified success. The dignitaries of the art world, including assorted representatives from the School of Paris, are in attendance. Even Picasso and his mob put in an appearance. Also present are the wealthy collectors Madeleine and Marcellin Castaing, who have become devoted to the paintings of Modigliani and Chaim Soutine. (They have even offered to swap a Matisse for one of Chaim's vertiginous Gorges du Loup landscapes.) Substantial sales are made and eminent critics have begun to write about the Russian's frenetic work. Word has it that a monograph is forthcoming from the influential art historian Élie Faure. But Chaim has refused—and Zborowski has thought it impolitic to press him—to set foot in the gallery.

5

THERE IS A NIGHT, not long after they've made each other's acquaintance, when Chaim is conscripted by Modigliani to help him steal marble from a nearby construction site. It's 1915 and Modi is still carving his massive stone heads, an endeavor that to Chaim's mind has too much in common with idol making. They are tall, thin-necked, almond-eyed works inspired by the masks and statues the sculptor has seen in the Ethnic Art Museum at the Trocadéro. To them Modi ascribes talismanic powers that chill Chaim's blood.

"From magic you shouldn't muck about with it," he once admonished his new friend, who was no doubt ignorant of the frightful forces he dabbled in. Forces that Chaim himself naturally set no store by.

"Why, Chaim," Modi responded, "you sound almost like a believer."

"Feh!" spat Soutine.

"Sans blague," concurred Modigliani.

He will soon abandon sculpture in any event. His consumptive lungs will no longer allow him to grapple with the rose-marble and limestone blocks that, unable to afford their market price, he spirits away from building sites after dark. Moreover, breathing the noxious dust from the cut stones sends him into marathon bouts of

coughing. But here in this second year of the war he's still commit-
ted to carving his beloved sculptures, and after a few shared rounds
of chartreuse at the Rotonde, he convinces the Litvak to accompany
him on one of his foraging expeditions.

They arrive at an excavation on the rue de Rennes for one of the
new apartment blocks that are proliferating all over Montparnasse.
One day there's a row of condemned buildings old enough to have
witnessed the massacre of the Huguenots, the next day a great hole
in the ground. The full moon casts the site in a light like hammered
silver. A steam crane lifts its boom like the neck of a prehistoric
beast. The platform ladders, shoring beams, and cement mixers are
thrown into stark relief, as are the intruders themselves, making
their trespass all the more conspicuous. This increases the urgency
of their mission. As they tread down the inclined planks into the
dig, Chaim is, as ever, fraught with anxiety. He reserves an aspect
of his thrumming heart, however, for the exhilaration he feels in
the company of the intrepid Tuscan. The city, whose pulse he's
seldom in tune with, resounds in his vitals like a tolling bell when
he's at large in it with Amedeo—even more so when together as
now in the middle of the night. Which doesn't make him any the
less worried.

Modi makes a beeline toward a chest-high stack of masonry
on a wooden frame, and Chaim, anticipating his needs, hastens
forward to take hold of one of the topmost stones. He waits for
Modi to grab the other end—since aren't they all identical?—but
his friend only shakes his head and begins to examine alternatives.

"What are you," mutters Chaim, "Michelangelo at Carrara?"

Modigliani looks up. "Chaim, you made a joke!"

Chaim can feel the heat of his blushing.

Modi licks a finger and sweeps it over the fine grain of the marble. "The colors must be subtle and the veining subdued." He raps
on various stones with his knuckles as if expecting an answer from

within, then makes his decision. "This one," he says, and under-
takes to drag a large rectangular block out from under the others.

Chaim lets go a stagy sigh and pitches in. Together they
manage to wrestle the block from the heap—while others topple
to fill the space—and drop it in the dust with an earthshaking
thud. Then Modi looks about the subterranean area for . . . what?
"A wheelbarrow," he says. "There is always a wheelbarrow." But
though they scour the entire moonscape in search of one, none is
to be found. Modi makes a cavalier reference to building pyramids
and stoops to lift the stone again. Chaim grumbles but follows his
lead. Grunting, their muscles strained to the limit, they lug their
burden in stages as far as the ramp they'd descended into the site.
At the foot of the ramp they both give out, Modi from shortness
of breath and Chaim from the sour acid that's risen in his gorge
from an incipient bellyache. (These are the symptoms—Chaim's
ulcers and Modi's pulmonary ailment—that have scuttled their
attempts to volunteer for the army, much to the patriotic Italian's
disappointment and the Litvak's relief.) It's clear they will never
be able to hump the stone up the incline, let alone back to the
courtyard of la cité Falguière, where Modi performs his art before
an audience of peers. Chaim throws up his hands as a sign of defeat, but Amedeo, unflustered, exhorts him to help tip the smooth
pearl-gray block on its end. Then, with a gesture like a magician
producing rabbits, he pulls from either pocket of his once soigné
velvet jacket a chisel and mallet. He kneels and sets straightaway
to work.

Here Chaim utters the obvious: "Modigliani, tifshess! This is
craziness!"

"Bêtise, they call it in France," replies Modi, happy to own the
folly of his actions. As he begins chipping away at the upright stone,
he charges his friend to keep a lookout for *les flics* or whatever other
pests might be abroad in the small hours of a brisk October night.

But Chaim, for all his disquiet, can scarcely bring himself to look away from Amedeo's impassioned industry. It's an unholy task he's about and Modi is a very demon in his furious attack on the marble. There are other distractions: the screeching of the bats that dart and veer just above their heads, the soughing of the wind and the clanking of the chisel itself, which threatens to alert the district to their interloping. And there's Amedeo's own constant patter, his humming of songs whose Ladino lyrics burst from him in snatches that Chaim tries to shush with a periodic "Shveig!" But Modi is intractable and Chaim is too rapt by his performance to do anything other than surrender to simply watching him.

As he works, Modi ceases singing and begins to recite stanzas from *La vita nuova*. Then he repeats a legend he claims to have heard from Brancusi during the days when he and the Romanian sculpted together side by side. "In Transylvania," he says, the flying shards pelting his face, "to give strength and stability to a building, the laborers would capture a stranger and measure his shadow." Pausing to draw a ragged breath. "Then they would place the marked yardstick beneath the foundation stone as a good luck charm. But the man whose shadow they measured would always die within the year. "Chaim," implores Modi, "always keep your shadow close!"

"Where else I'm gonna keep it?" asks Chaim, though the senselessness of the warning still makes his hair stand on end.

Modi interrupts his carving to pull a slab bottle of rum from a bottomless pocket; he takes a slug, offers the bottle to his friend, and proceeds with his work. "I'm on the devil's merry-go-round, Chaim," he pants, "and sometimes it spins so fast I don't know if I'm the rider or the horse." *Chink*. "It tilts and spins until the earth looks to me like a landscape by Chaim Soutine." *Chink, chink*. "But the stone remains at the still center of the spinning earth. 'Luxe, calme, et volupté' as Baudelaire has it. What more should one desire? And you, mio amico?" *Chink*, a cough like a deracination of his ribs, *chink*. "What do *you* want?"

Chaim has been shushing him more insistently to no avail. He knows that Modi's questions are largely rhetorical and feels no compulsion to answer. But their present circumstance has made him intensely aware of the precariousness of their mutual existence, and as always Chaim is torn between his fondness for the Italian and his role as accessory to his self-destruction. Not to mention his own jeopardy in their helter-skelter blundering toward ruin.

"I would like," he replies, barely above his breath, "to be a ordinary person."

But Modi has heard him. "Fat chance!" he laughs hardily, then declares, "Porca puttana, where is Thérèse with her pram when I need her?" For it's Thérèse Laurier, his current paramour, who has helped him haul his stones in the baby buggy she hopes (vainly) will one day contain their child. This is the woman, it's bruited about in the Rotonde and the Dôme, that Modi makes love to between hiccups.

The platinum moon has traveled to the far rim of the sky. Chaim sits tired-eyed on a nail keg, alternating between an apprehensive vigilance and his fixation on the form emerging from the stone. The sculptor, blowing the stray curls from his brow, seems, as much with his manic talk as with his mallet, to be coaxing buxom contours from the block of marble; he has so far liberated from the marble an ovoid head with olive-shaped eyes and pendulous, duffel-sized breasts. All the while he hawks up the bloody phlegm he's tried to hide from all but his most intimate companions. After a time, which Chaim has entirely lost track of, the stone has become a caryatid crouching beneath a capital she endeavors to raise with powerful limbs. And given the Italian's penchant for trafficking in the necromantic arts, his friend doesn't put it past him to command the statue to shake off her frozen state. Then she will heave away the weight that oppresses her and stagger forth like—God forbid!—a goylem.

Chaim cringes at the thought, then abruptly sits up, starting at the sight of a gang of laborers skirting the edge of the dig. An incarnadine dawn is breaking over the mansard roofs that border the excavation as they stride single file down the shivering ramp. Chaim dismounts his keg, hisses a warning to Modi, and backs off a few paces as the men approach, though they ignore him. They instead form a ring around Amedeo, who continues his carving despite what must be a bone-weary fatigue. If anything, he works more frantically, perhaps somewhat revived by his expanded audience.

"Tiens!" exclaims a big fellow with a boxer's face, having apparently recognized the sculptor, "it's our friend, l'artiste le fou."

Others greet him, one or two in Italian: Modi, it seems, is a known curiosity. A stout character in a peaked cap and donkey coat, scratching his stubbled jaw, bends to inspect the statue. "She's one stacked broad, eh," he appraises, "but not my type."

"What do you mean, Batiste?" replies another in a leather vest. "Her backside's the shitting image of your wife's."

Unamused by the witticism, Batiste makes to strangle his comrade amid a chorus of more scabrous remarks. Chaim wants to flee but consoles himself that there's no real danger; the laborers are obviously aware that Modi has scrounged materials from the site before. They're seldom missed. Though since the war has begun, wood and stone have become scarce commodities. Every scrap, as the lantern-jawed chap in the sleeveless fleece reminds them, must be accounted for.

"Any missing property will be deducted from our wages," he reminds his fellows with an air of authority. This in case l'italien should lay claim to his labor.

At that the men nod in concert, almost wistfully, and step forward to intervene between the raging sculptor and his work.

Suddenly awake to the imminent separation from his oeuvre, Modi
drops his tools and throws his arms around the stone. The men tug
at his sleeves and collar, gently at first, before taking hold of him
with a purpose to pry him loose. Chaim worries that Modi will
assault them; he's seen his friend enter into brawls with much less
provocation. But he's clearly spent from his exertions, sodden from
draining the contents of the flask that's helped fuel them. He looks
ghostly due to the fine powder that cakes his face and silvers his
crow-black hair. Wilting after the confiscation of his unfinished
handiwork, he watches as the laborers haul the statue to a corner of
the site. There they dump it in a trench alongside other stones that
will form the foundation of the new edifice.

Modi shrugs off the efforts of his fretful friend to lead him
away. "Porca Madonna," he cries, shaking a fist, "one day they will
raze every structure in Montparnasse in search of Modigliani's lost
caryatid!"

✦

CHAIM IGNORES THE CONSTANT yanking on the rope that Gaston
Babineaux has wrapped for a safety line around his chest. This is
the signal that the *régate*, as Modi calls it, has reached its terminus
and the ruse has ended. The diver, his task accomplished, may now
be raised up from the deep. Régate, my tush! thinks Chaim. What
did we know from a boat race in Smilovitchi? A boat race you could
have in Paris, France; in Smilovitch you had the children of the
dimwit Chasids celebrating the *yahrzeit* of some dead rebbe. Then
they would float the cedar shingles with their masts of lit memorial
candles down the fog-bound Berezina. On the bank of the Berezina
they would chant their *niggunim*, while the fleet of flaming shingles
sailed from our miserable backwash toward the world, wherever
that was.

Chaim was told later on that the world was Paris, and a hundred landsmen wielding palettes and canvas stretchers would certainly attest to that judgment. But since his immersion in the silence of the river, he has come to understand that the world is not so much a place as a fluid expanse of time. So why, I ask, should he be confined to the dreary year of 1917? A year when the boulevards above him abound with the legless, sometimes faceless, survivors of Ypres and the Marne, and the alluring danseuse Mata Hari is at this very moment facing a firing squad in the moat of the Château de Vincennes. Food, sparse for Chaim at the best of times, has been rationed almost out of availability, and the platform of the Métro Pasteur, where he has taken shelter from the bomber squadrons flying over the city, is even harder on the spine than the flags in the courtyard of the cité Falguière. Why not, say, the summer of 1929, when he finds refuge after the Crash at the Elysian estate of Madeleine and Marcellin Castaing?

Though their first meeting in the spare days before the coming of Dr. Barnes is less than auspicious. The Castaings, highly cultured and filthy rich, are at their table at the Rotonde, where they've established a kind of regular Saturday evening salon. Ardent collectors, they have already acquired works by Matisse, Picasso, Utrillo, Rouault, Léger, Derain, and Juan Gris. They've purchased a Modigliani nude, which is mounted above their bed. But familiar as they are with the nascent School of Paris, they have yet to see work by the aberrant artist Chaim Soutine. They have, however, had a chance encounter at Paul Guillaume's gallery with the Russian sculptor Oscar Miestchaninoff. The amiable Oscar, in promoting his circle, has commended the painter whose eccentricity is equaled only by the prowess of his art. The couple requested the artist's presence at the café and Oscar assured them he would have him there at a more or less predetermined time.

He arrives wearing a flea market slouch hat pulled low over his brow, carrying the portrait of a garroted pheasant under one arm and a tormented landscape tucked under the other. He is more than two hours late. The Castaings' hobnobbers and sycophants have already departed, along with most of the other patrons of the Rotonde. It's that late hour when the motor traffic around the carrefour Vavin is diminished to a whispering oceanic sound. The sidewalks are deserted but for a few superannuated streetwalkers and a lone accordionist. Waiters are emptying ashtrays and removing glasses from the tables under the impatient eye of Père Libion, who is anxious to close. The author and swindler Maurice Sachs, chief flatterer of the Castaings, cups his mouth to inform Madeleine that the human flotsam standing on the pavement before them is Soutine. She invites the painter over to their table and he steps under the awning, looking for all the world like a street peddler come to hawk his wares. He makes a perfunctory excuse for his tardiness, something about a fit of dyspepsia. Marcellin glances at his watch and starts to complain, but Madeleine quiets him with a touch of her gloved hand to his sleeve. Twenty years her senior, he nevertheless defers to his elegant wife in all things. This is perhaps owing in part to his guilt over his extramarital indiscretions, which is not to say that he doesn't adore her.

Neglecting to take a seat, Chaim props the paintings against the backs of vacant chairs and takes up a curatorial position beside them. But the Castaings and their hanger-on are also on their feet, preparing to leave; it's well past time they returned to their hotel.

"The light is insufficient to properly view the canvases in any case," says Marcellin, buckling the belt of his Norfolk jacket.

Asterisks of light glinting from her choker necklace, Madeleine tenders their apologies. "Perhaps we can come round to your studio tomorrow," she says, while her husband drapes an evening wrap over her slender shoulders. She offers the disappointed painter a hand, which he does not take. Perceiving the slight to his wife, Marcellin stiffens, but Madeleine cautions him again with another touch. A diplomat, he removes his wallet from his pocket and plucks a hundred-franc note.

"Take this on account until we have an opportunity to perhaps purchase some of your work."

Chaim begins discernibly to tremble, possessed of a towering indignation. His cheeks are as hot as if they've been slapped, his left eyelid amok with fluttering. He snatches the bill from the plutocrat's hand and flings it back in his face.

"If you would have gave me for a painting five francs," he fumes, "I am the happiest of men. But to pay me for work you never seen is the basest insult!"

He takes up his canvases and stomps off in a temper down the avenue, wondering along the way whether the paintings are actually worth a hundred francs. Five years pass before he meets the Castaings again.

✦

IN THE MEANTIME, DR. Barnes arrives to inaugurate Chaim's annus mirabilis, and not long after the digression of the girl from Vilna comes his one-man show at the Galerie Bing. His work is esteemed, his merit affirmed; his name appears in the *bavardage* column of *L'Europe journal* with good-natured irony. There it's reported that he has refused to postpone painting the portrait of a woman with an abscessed tooth: the abscess, it says, has distorted her face after a fashion that especially appeals to the painter. He's observed in a café poring over the gift from Miestchaninoff of a book on personal grooming; and some swear—though who can believe it?—that the chap with the flapping forelock dancing alongside Kiki in an orgiastic scene from the film *Le lion des Mongols* is Chaim Soutine. The critic André Warnod has coined the phrase *École de Paris* and cites

Soutine in particular as an artist "carried away by a sort of delirium that makes his canvas surge with the jolt of a passionate world." Waldemar George, an arbiter of taste who will soon turn about in his regard for the artists of Montparnasse, writes: "His work looks to me like a hemorrhage; before rendering his soul, the artist spits up his blood, and each spurt gives birth to a new vision, singularly intense, tragic, and painful." The reviewers declare him instinctive, untutored and spontaneous, a *fauve pathétique*; frustrated, they judge him uncategorizable. They fall over themselves in the extremity of their rhetoric, struggling to explain the racial, biological, and geographical origins of his art.

Their zeal is also a source of the reaction and contrary voices begin to be heard. They're subtle at first: "In the Café de la Rotonde all the dialects on earth are spoken, sometimes even French." Then less circumspect: "A barbarian horde has rushed upon Montparnasse." The Dutch poet Fritz Vanderpyl asks in the *Mercure de France* where this sudden passion to paint comes from among the descendants of the Twelve Tribes, this passion for palettes and brushes. He concludes that it's greed, the avaricious Hebrews having realized there's money to be made in art. Maurice Raynal writes, with Soutine especially in mind, that these outsiders have "kicked over the tables of the Law, liberating an unbridled temperament and indulging in an orgy of the destruction of Nature—cursing the while, and cursing very copiously, its Creator . . ."

The flag-waving Camille Mauclair decries in *Le Figaro* that Montparnasse is inhabited by "the filth of Paris, 80 percent Semites and every one a loser." Vanderpyl adds the complaint that in the postwar salons the Lévys are now legion; and when asked which ten living artists should be represented in a new museum of modern French art, the puckish Kisling replies, "Simon Lévy, Léopold Lévy, Rudolf Lévy, Maxime Lévy, Irène Lévy, Flore Lévy, Isidore Lévy, Claude Lévy, Benoit Lévy, and Moïse Kisling."

Chaim oscillates as ever between shame and hubris. He paints more still lifes, reviving his old fear of hunger by fasting before attempting the carp or the dead duck. He paints the page boy at Maxim's, whose outstretched hand, coupled with his ebony eyes, makes it seem that his life (or yours) depends on the tip. The ferryman requesting his toll at the River Styx might strike such a pose. He paints a student in a blue jacket, who has six fingers and the pained expression of a boy on the verge of turning into a monkey. He's invited along with over fifty artists of renown—Bonnard, Matisse, and Chagall among them—to paint voluntarily "the famous silent film star" Maria Lani. It turns out, however, that the cadre of notables has been deceived; the woman is a total imposter, a secretary from Prague exploited by her husband and brother for the sake of amassing a fortune from the sale of the portraits. In Chaim's rendering you can see, albeit in hindsight, the pathos of ambition wed to nonentity. He paints a groom with legs like calipers, his uniform an exaltation of scarlet, his sensuous lips contradicting the desolation in his eyes. He paints yet another communicant whose gown reveals heretofore undiscovered moods of whiteness.

"A great painter thinks with his brushes," said Modigliani, quoting his sainted Baudelaire, and for Chaim every stroke is a visceral thought. After each he discards the brush until they lie like a heap of jackstraws at his feet, numerous as his cigarette butts. He continues his habit of painting only on secondhand canvases, scraping them first of their precious thatched roofs and water wheels. He destroys nine out of ten of his efforts and continues making the rounds of the galleries to buy up his Céret paintings and destroy them as well. Once or twice he has taken out his jackknife and slashed them on the spot, fleeing the scene like a crazed assassin, though he's been seen to relent and touch up a painting, also on the spot. (Gallery owners like Guillaume and Gimpel have learned to hang his work out of reach.) He goes to the Louvre and sits on a bench all day in front of Courbet's realist masterwork *A Burial at Ornans*. He travels once more overnight to Amsterdam to view *The Jewish Bride*. He takes the thermal waters again at Châtel-Guyon and paints the bathing women. He returns to Cagnes to paint the galloping horses (which do not gallop quite so fast), and to Vence farther up the coast, where he paints the ancient ash in the center of the town square. He disregards the gassy assertions of Dr. Barnes: this is no Axis Mundi, no Tree of Life, but merely a very old tree. For all its tentacular grotesquery, Chaim eliminates from its depiction what he might have included: the hair of Absalom tangled in its twisted branches, the unborn souls dangling like bloated teardrops from its limbs. He rejects the sensation, even as he paints it, that the tree has sprouted from his very loins. He detests every crotchet of the imagination that would divert him from le vrai, from the thing itself.

In the winter of 1927 the honorable Élie Faure, whose five-volume *History of Art* is considered definitive, publishes a monograph on Chaim Soutine. Unlike Warnod and Waldemar George, Faure is not a Jew writing for a largely Jewish audience. His stamp of approval leaves no doubt as to Chaim's standing in contemporary art. Chaim's old Vilna schoolmate Michel Kikoïne brings him the publication, an illustrated pamphlet in the series "Les artistes nouveaux."

"This is big, Chaim! The guy's a macher. And he likes Yids," alleges Kikoïne. "He stood with Zola in support of Dreyfus." He is also known to be an openhanded friend to artists, and was instrumental in advancing the careers of Cézanne and Rivera.

As with any praise of himself, Chaim reads it with a fugitive heart and mortified gut.

"Here," writes Faure, "the mystery of the greatest painting shines forth, flesh more like flesh than flesh itself, nerves more like nerves than nerves, even if they are painted with streams of rubies, with sulfur on fire, droplets of turquoise, emerald lakes crushed with sapphires, streaks of purple and pearl, a palpitation of silver that quivers and shines, a wondrous flame that wrings matter to its depths after having smelted all the jewels of its mines . . ."

"*Shtus!*" declares Chaim, dazzled by the extravagance of the prose. "Nonsense." But is it possible that the author feels with regard to his work some intimation of what the artist himself feels when painting it?

Faure goes on (for pages) to proclaim Soutine a "religious" artist and his vision fundamentally tragic. "Not because it shows, as is so often said of tragedy, the struggle between spirit and matter, but rather, in a flash of desperate lyricism, the indissoluble union of matter and spirit."

When he finishes reading, Chaim is conflicted. He can't decide whether to lock himself away in a closet or—a thing it's never before occurred to him to do—contact the author to say thank you. After much irresolution, he chooses the latter; he hasn't felt so indebted to anyone since Commissioner Zamaron deferred the removal of his ox carcass. But with his aversion to written expression, he entreats his neighbor Chana Orloff to pen some conventional message for him. In it, the indulgent sculptress ventures to ask, with the diffident consent of the artist, whether the writer would care to meet him at some mutually agreed upon location. "Say the Select," prompts Chaim. "It's less likely the chance we will run into old cronies there." He's amazed at the speed and enthusiasm with which the great man accepts his invitation.

Favorably disposed as he is, Chaim is unprepared for how quickly he begins to warm to Dr. Faure. Not since Modigliani has he come so soon to conceive a measure of trust in another human being. Of course, nothing incites his suspicions like trust.

The man is his elder by at least twenty years. He's shorter than Chaim (who is not tall) and stocky, with a broad face and a mustache whose ends display a halfhearted attempt at handlebars. His beard is neatly trimmed, his head bald but for a stubble of gray hair like frost. His eyes, for all their sharply glittering intelligence, are kind. He is somewhat formally attired in his tweeds and ruched-knot cravat, but his manner is easy as he lifts a glass of *vin ordinaire* to salute their imminent friendship. Chaim raises his licorice root tea.

They're seated at a table near a door opening onto the café's terrace. It's a fair afternoon in April; the empress trees along the avenue are in that early stage of bloom when the leaves resemble showers of confetti. The sidewalk is an unending procession of the chic and the threadbare: swells and clochards, porters, shopkeepers, peddlers of chestnuts, mincing facilitators of trysts. Chaim has the rare sense of being less a spectator than a player in this living tapestry. Dr. Faure has started right in extolling the virtues of Chaim's methods and technique, which the artist endures until he feels his colic coming on. He makes deprecating noises in an attempt to steer the conversation away from himself, and Dr. Faure, obligingly taking the cue, begins to speak openly of his personal history. Unlike Dr. Barnes, he is a practicing surgeon. He insists that, despite his prodigious critical output, he is still an amateur in the field of interpreting art.

"All of us who do not create are mere laymen," he protests without a detectable hint of false modesty. He confides that his inherent love of painting suffered a long hiatus after the death in infancy of one of his sons. "I couldn't even look at a Velázquez or Tintoretto for over two years. Then my old friend Émile Zola, *requiescat in pace*, enlisted me in the movement in defense of Captain Dreyfus. This was after Lieutenant Picquart's investigations had brought

Count Esterházy's guilt to light. Through Zola I met many artists whom I came to admire. And so the passion was rekindled."

Dr. Faure takes another sip of wine and nods toward Chaim as if to indicate it's now his turn to offer up some portion of his own biography. When Chaim remains evasively silent, the doctor is compelled to ask him outright, "Where was your original home?"

Chaim grows tense as he does whenever he's interrogated about the past. The word *home* has not figured greatly in his lexicon. But the learned doctor's sympathetic demeanor—his bedside manner?—encourages some minimal disclosure.

"I come from, you'll excuse me, the behind-end of nowhere. This is Smilovitchi, which it's a toilet that it would like to be a town." The doctor rests his elbows on the arms of his chair, his chin on his folded hands, awaiting more. "You wouldn't call it happy, my childhood," confesses Chaim. "One time when I drew a picture, my papa threatened to carve with his scissors the Second Commandment on my head." He lifts his forelock to show a scar from the aborted inscription. "He settled instead to beat me with the scuttle and lock me in the cellar without a . . . how do you say?" He stops, wondering whether he's divulged more than was warranted. His story could invite unwelcome pity or, worse, inspire disgust.

"Un pot à pisser?" suggests the smiling doctor. He leans closer and adds, "You may tutoyer me, Chaim."

Chaim feels a tremor of mixed sensations. He inhales the wine-fragrant air, smells the food from the neighboring tables: steamed mussels, escargots *á l'ail* with parsley and garlic butter—savory dishes his weak stomach, which wants to keep kosher despite him, forbids. He sees the ladies sauntering in their sleek dresses designed by the gamine Coco Chanel, and thinks it still above his station to desire them. Paris is a feast of which he's not invited to

partake, and unlike Modi he is no gate-crasher. Yet here he sits
in the Café Select at the center of the cultural universe with his
admirer, the celebrated physician and art historian. He believes he
could almost admire himself.

"Dr. Faure," he begins, and the other says, "Call me Élie." But
he can't, any more than he could call the Italian Dédo. "Dr. Faure,
what you said how I am a religious painter? This is not true. In my
work I am trying always to make it up for what God failed to do."

He waits for the doctor to call him out for his blasphemy; as
is his habit, he has alienated yet another potential friend. But the
good Dr. Faure only smiles and says, "That, Chaim, is the work of
saints."

Soon after, Chaim receives an invitation to dine with the doctor and his family at his town house on the île Saint-Louis. The
Second Empire facade of the house is imposing, though undiffer-
entiated from the others in their cul-de-sac near the river. Inside,
the furniture is heavy, overstuffed and claw-footed, the heirloom
sofa in the salon in need of reupholstering. A tin Blériot biplane
and a toy steam engine, over which the guest nearly trips, litter
the Oriental carpet. (Madame Faure shouts to her sons to take
them away.) There are touches of dusty grandeur: the high windows
and equally high mahogany bookshelves, the coffered ceilings and
trompe l'oeil foliage along the staircase. But such details only serve
to emphasize the interior's otherwise homely atmosphere. Even the
avant-garde paintings—a Picasso, a Matisse, a Paul Signac, and
one of Chaim's own Céret townscapes (which he restrains himself
from assaulting)—manage to complement rather than oppose the
prevailing warmth.

Dr. Faure introduces Soutine as "an artist without peer" to
his family, whom he presents to Soutine with the selfsame pride.
There is a coloring of cheeks all around. Madame Faure, despite

her beaded Etruscan tea gown and the tiny crucifix at her throat, has the large-bosomed robust nature of a shtetl *rebbetzin*. The boys, one a towheaded head taller than the fawn-haired other, step forward like little gentlemen to shake the painter's hand. The pretty daughter makes a slight curtsy, which Chaim examines for possible mockery, though her guileless umber eyes attest her earnestness. No fool, however, he suspects that the doctor may have tutored his brood in how to receive the Jewish bumpkin. "Don't be surprised," Chaim imagines them having been cautioned, "if he licks his plate like a hungry dog." Anticipating as much, he has spritzed himself with an eau de cologne called *Pour un Homme* and worn his serge suit with the lapels as wide as elephants' ears. He has reviewed the rules of etiquette Modigliani drilled him in—that is, when Modi wasn't himself violating every protocol of good taste.

But the dinner is a genial affair and Chaim chastises himself for his wariness. The table talk revolves mainly around the family's pet interests, but honest efforts are made to include the guest. Nor do they seem annoyed when Chaim's responses are mostly monosyllabic. The boys talk as freely as their parents; they're already looking forward to this summer's Tour de France. They ask Chaim his opinion of the Belgian cyclist Maurice de Waal, the only challenger in their view to the primacy of the Luxembourger Nicolas Frantz, and when he pleads ignorance, assail him with a bewildering barrage of statistics and figures. Dr. Faure, in his role as host and patriarch, tries to hush them and turn the conversation to higher matters. He begins to discourse without preface on the evolutionary element in art, a theory that, he owns, has stirred much controversy in scholarly circles. Gratified that the doctor deems him a worthy recipient of his deep-thinking ruminations, Chaim admits he has no special views on the subject. The doctor's wife, perhaps intuiting the artist's discomfort, sighs theatrically and asks Chaim over her husband's lecturing how he likes his egg noodle soup. She's been made aware of his intestinal troubles and has tried to ensure that there is nothing overly acidic in the meal. Chaim expresses his appreciation.

The middy-bloused daughter, Marie-Zéline, whom her parents call Zizou, has remained quiet thus far. Now she ventures, sheepishly, to inquire after the artist's acquaintances. "As a leading light of the city's artistic community," she begins (and Chaim squirms), "you must know many . . . personalities." Giving the last word a breathless significance. A graduate in design from the lycée founded by her father, the young woman has doubtless been exposed to much titillating hearsay concerning the current cultural scene. Apparently attributing to Chaim a measure of glamour he cannot lay claim to, she asks whether he has ever encountered, for instance, Rrose (with two r's) Sélavy, the mysterious woman whom the rogue artist Marcel Duchamp has designated his alter ego. No? Then perhaps Mina Loy? Nancy Cunard? All noted female figures of originality and dubious repute.

Not wanting to disappoint her, Chaim submits, "I know Kiki of Montparnasse."

His obvious pleasure in this contribution provokes laughter all around, and after a beat Chaim tentatively joins in. He is delighted to have made them laugh for whatever reason. Especially the unassuming Zizou, whose complexion has gone cameo-pink. The jovial mood persists as Dr. Faure, in an expansive humor, reflects on the madness of the present age. "What else can you expect from a decade that began on an evening when the president of the Republic turns up barefoot in his pajamas after falling off a train?"

Chaim remembers reading about the incident in the papers. It had coincided with a less comical inauguration of the subsequent years: Modi's agonizing final days in the charity hospital. But even that memory can't dampen Chaim's feeling of having been welcomed unreservedly into the bosom of a family. By evening's end he has become infatuated with them all.

✦

COMES SUMMER AND DR. Faure leaves town with his wife and daughter for their country house in the Dordogne. The boys are away at their *colonie de vacances*, learning to sail, so there's an extra room available in the cottage, and Chaim has an open invitation to visit whenever he likes. By now he has become an unofficial member of their family. For all his formidable learning, the venerable surgeon and art historian has adopted a paternal attitude toward the baseborn immigrant. Chaim is acutely aware that his own education, hardly begun before his arrival in Paris, has been catch-as-catch-can. Nevertheless, when Dr. Faure asks his opinion of a particular artist or of some fashionable dogma of the day, he knows his answer will be received and overcomes his self-doubt to offer a judgment. He makes observations concerning issues he's only half digested, and feels no shame. The doctor generally knits his brows and nods his assent at the artist's hypotheses, though sometimes he respectfully begs to differ and Chaim tingles at the word "respect." His devotion to the man is almost puppylike. It's a devotion that includes by extension the doctor's imperturbable wife, and his comely daughter Marie-Zéline—Zizou, eleven years Chaim's junior. Although they've exchanged only the most superficial courtesies, she has never condescended to him or shown an inkling of veiled repugnance. His fondness for her has become an article of faith.

Once again Chaim engages the reliable Daneyrolle to drive him into the provinces, his cargo of painting supplies rattling in the rumble seat. Instead of reading to him lugubrious passages from admired authors or delivering his customary *cris de cœur*, the painter is uncharacteristically cheerful. He looks forward to his visit with the Faures as to a homecoming. Nothing in his career, not the sales of his work nor the praise of the critics, has done so much for his self-esteem as his attachment to this splendid family. The chauffeur, however, is well acquainted with his passenger's extremes of temperament. Grown concerned for his charge over time, he worries that, having attained some precarious summit of gladness, the artist is soon due to plummet again. The chauffeur, his loyalty notwithstanding, would prefer not to be around when that happens.

But Monsieur Daneyrolle's apprehension is unfounded. The Dordogne is a pastoral idyll for Chaim. Never much of a fancier of the rustic, he is nonetheless charmed by the Faures' old farmhouse. Slate-roofed and vine-enveloped, it's like a cottage out of his cheder *Maaseh Book* where lost children are sheltered from danger by a benign sorcerer. Copper pots hang from hooks in the great stone fireplace; the brute armoire is stuffed with gilt-spined old books. A chandelier dangles its crown of candles from a raw wood ceiling beam. The casement windows open onto a valley through which a river meanders beneath a range of jade and carnelian cliffs. Here and there along the cliffs are little troglodyte villages, their compact abodes gouged into the steep rock face. These are structures built upon the footprints of habitations abandoned by cave dwellers untold eons ago. It is the essence of serenity, Dr. Faure's valley, and while the landscape refuses—unlike the forests and tarns around Céret—to give up the dark dream of itself, Chaim thinks he can do without that turbulence for a change.

He surrenders to a quietude like none in his experience. It's enough for now just to maintain the student-mentor relationship he's established with Dr. Faure, though the man has always insisted on treating him as an equal. The industrious doctor, whose interests are boundless, is writing an article about his friend the film director Abel Gance, who has begun to experiment with sound. Seated before the hearth in a Morris armchair on evenings when it's chilly enough to build a fire, he reads aloud what he's written during the day. Sometimes Chaim, acquainted only with Chaplin short subjects and two-reeler serials, dares to make suggestions for which the doctor heartily thanks him. While stomach disorders are not his host's area of expertise, Dr. Faure nevertheless oversees his wife's collaborations with the cook; he advises the addition of turmeric and honey to every dish their guest is served, in the hope that these ingredients will help to activate the artist's immune system. Chaim assures him his constitution is much improved. It's true that he hasn't been this idle since the bouts of enervation born of his civil union with the Melnick woman. But that was then, before he'd learned to be untroubled by the work he isn't doing. He takes long walks in the countryside, and sometimes, when she's not engaged in her designing projects (she's an aspiring fashion *modéliste*), Zizou might accompany him.

She seldom raises the frivolous topics she'd broached at their first meeting, perhaps having realized that Chaim cannot satisfy her appetite for café society gossip. It was clearly never that voracious an appetite. But the artist's lack of candor about his past discourages more intimate investigations on Zizou's part. On his, Chaim's abiding bashfulness inhibits him from pressing the girl regarding her tastes and predilections. So they stroll largely in silence. One or the other might remark on the weather or some arresting feature of the landscape. Once Chaim stoops to examine a crater-shaped fragment that Zizou identifies as a potsherd. The discovery prompts a dissertation on the various types of Ice Age artifacts to be found in the region; not for nothing is the girl her father's daughter. Despite their desultory communication, however, Chaim is convinced that there is a tacit understanding between them.

Sometimes other guests visit the cottage: a surgical colleague of the doctor's with an interest in the Dordogne's vernacular architecture; friends of Zizou's on a road trip, trim young women with their equally presentable male companions. They stay at an auberge in the nearby town of Castelnaud-la-Chapelle and invite the Faures on outings to scenic destinations. They are courteous enough to include the reticent artist in their invitations, but Chaim prefers to keep to himself until they've gone. He resents their intrusions, especially those of Zizou's chums—in particular one well-turned-out young man, a relation of some sort, who Chaim considers too familiar in his attentions to the girl. He tells himself, however, that his jealousy is misplaced. Like Modi, the doctor's daughter has seen his uniqueness, and upon that conviction Chaim has begun to construct a fantasy.

His visit is open-ended. No one seems to care how long he remains, and Chaim himself feels little anxiety about overstaying his welcome. He's that comfortable with his portion of the Faures' very rich hours. He walks, reads, joins the three of them on occasional afternoon excursions. They explore the medieval fortress overlooking Castelnaud, visit the vertical town of Rocamadour with its pilgrim church and black Madonna. They travel in Dr. Faure's racing-green Renault cabriolet with the top down, and on one occasion the doctor asks Chaim whether he would like to drive. Chaim has never before driven a motorcar, and despite the doctor's patient tutelage, he shows no aptitude whatever in handling the vehicle. But given his boyish enthusiasm ("Should see me now, Monsieur Daneyrolle!"), the family retain their good humor throughout the ride, give or take a few near brushes with death. If there is any trace of unease in the household, it's due to the family's awareness that Chaim Soutine, master portraitist and landscape painter, has yet to take up his brushes. But what most concerns his worthy host is that the artist himself doesn't seem to be concerned at all.

Thinking Chaim might require some goad to his creative instincts, Dr. Faure presumes to arrange an event for him. He is acquainted with a teacher at the local *école primaire*. The man has mentioned that during the upcoming weekend he will lead a cohort of students on their annual summer *randonnée*. The hike will take them practically across the doctor's doorstep. Dr. Faure promises to have refreshments prepared for the children. He also proposes that his guest, a modern artist of the first rank, might appreciate the opportunity to select one of the children to paint. He's painted striking portraits of children in the past. The teacher lifts a brow but is amenable, provided there will be proper supervision. On the following Saturday, the artist agrees, at the doctor's behest, to stand in the gravel drive before the house, reviewing a file of boys trooping past in their short pants and cricket caps. Their eyes are bright, cheeks taffy pink, dimpled knees like (thinks Chaim) piglet faces; their legs are strong. They offer well-mannered *mercis* for the lemonade and galettes that the Faure women serve them. They look as if they have never known an unkind word.

"These are for me no good!" Chaim suddenly erupts. Then, embarrassed by his outburst, he apologizes for his wholesale rejection of the youngsters. But he can't help resenting this violation of his hard-won complacency. Let their teacher lead them over a precipice for all he cares.

That night, to calm himself, he takes a walk before dinner. The air is cool, the moonlight spilling its mercury over the surface of the river. In the distance the silhouette of the Gratte-Bruyère escarpment resembles the hull of a capsized longboat. Chaim begins to feel again that he has finally achieved an identity independent of his painting. He turns back toward the cottage, its outline dim but for the saffron light pouring from the casement windows, their shutters flung open to release the overflow of luminescence. Drawn to a window, Chaim peers into the parlor where the doctor is reading. His daughter is at her drawing table, his wife in the kitchen conferring with the cook, a horse-faced local woman whose unsmiling husband brings her to work in a donkey cart. The scene might have been limned by Vermeer or de Hooch, and the astonishing thing is that Chaim can enter it as if he belongs.

He studies the young woman in her simple house frock bent over her patterns and sketches, tracing with his eye her delicate cheekbones, the slightly cambered arc of her nose. A strand of sorrel hair has fallen across her brow, which she brushes aside as if swatting a fly. What better position could one hope to attain in the world, thinks Chaim, than to become the son-in-law of Élie Faure? With such a tolerant family his ethnicity would not be at issue—though if it were, he would be willing to convert. Could baptism be any worse than circumcision? Naturally no whisper of matrimony has yet been approached between him and the girl. But so persuasive have become Chaim's intentions, at least in his own mind, that he's convinced Zizou must share them to some extent.

A few days later Dr. Faure leaves off his labors to announce a junket he's been at some pains to organize. What's more, he insists that their destination remain a surprise. Despite a sluggish morning, Chaim is roused by the doctor's abundant energy. His wife, however, tells him she's had enough of his surprises for one life, though she assures them a cassoulet (minus any gastrointestinally unfriendly ingredients) will be waiting for them on their return. Zizou is also infected by her father's animation, while her wry smile suggests she may have guessed the excursion's objective. Chaim is content to preserve the mystery.

The daughter's smile broadens as the doctor distributes pairs of Wellington boots to her and their guest. "I'm afraid yours belonged to Gargantua," he apologizes to Chaim, who stumbles haltingly out the door behind him in the overlarge boots.

The journey takes them upwards of an hour. The road winds along the river below villages hugging the high old-gold escarpment, one of them even straddling a waterfall. These are villages so fanciful in their cliff-hanging situations that Chaim supposes their inhabitants must be some exceptional order of humanity. People who dwell in their aeries like birds in their nests. Eventually the doctor turns off the paved road onto a narrow lane; the lane dwindles to a dirt track terminating in a stand of trees flanking a rude wooden lean-to open to the weather. A blast from the Renault's three-toned horn draws a stringy old man with a face like chipped flint out of the shed. He's holding a lantern and wearing a mackintosh as if, despite the temperate afternoon, prepared for a storm.

The doctor steps from the car to converse with him briefly, then signals to his daughter and Chaim to join them.

"This is our guide, Monsieur Lecroq," says Dr. Faure. The old man, tending the wick of his lantern, makes no effort to acknowledge the introduction.

Guide to what? wonders Chaim, who continues, if more uneasily, to hold his tongue. Meanwhile, without explanation, the old man has begun to crown each of the visitors with a tight-fitting canvas miner's cap. From a bracket at the front of the cap hangs a small carbide lamp whose weight causes the bill to slip down over the forehead. Monsieur Lecroq proceeds to light the lamps with a series of matches, the flames magnified by the reflecting discs behind them. Chaim has the unsettling sense of having been inducted without his consent into a tribe distinguished by their headdresses imitating miniature suns. The big sun retreats in deference behind a cloud. Monsieur Lecroq turns and, without ceremony, begins to walk down a weedy, pebble-strewn path into the woods. Unbeckoned by their guide, neither Dr. Faure nor his

daughter hesitate to follow. Chaim, however, feels a sharp, por-
tentous pang in his gut and, having had his fill of mystery, calls
out to his host for some explanation. The doctor and Zizou look
over their shoulders in tandem, Dr. Faure sharing his daughter's
quizzical smile. Chaim swallows with a mousy squeak, but more
fearful of being left behind than of following, he sets out after
them at a clodhopping pace. They tramp along the fern-bordered
footpath single file to where the path dead-ends beneath the lip of
a limestone overhang.

A nearly perpendicular flight of steps has been scooped out of
the mossy slope, leading down into a basin at the bottom of which a
metal door is fixed aslant in the bare rock. Modi has said that every
door may be a portal to the sublime, but this one, reinforced with
studded iron bands, looks more like a door to a catacomb. Once the
party has managed the descent to the foot of the steps, Monsieur
Lecroq sets down his bullseye lantern and produces from the pocket
of his waterproof a comically outsized key. The key to Gehenna,
thinks Chaim, who tries to eschew the thought while their guide
unlocks the door.

The opening in the rock exudes a wintry breath as the party
stoop to enter. They continue moving forward along a cramped
passage whose low ceiling prevents them from standing fully erect.
The incline is rather steep and slippery, and though there is a rope
railing attached to the wall, it is still treacherous to negotiate in
rubber galoshes. The beams from the lamps on their caps flit like
will-o'-the-wisps about the jagged walls. It's cold in the shaft and
Chaim, shivering in his light coatee (the one Lipchitz had glibly
dubbed *pet-en-plein-air*, a fart in wind), wants to cry out. He understands that his trust in these people is being tested, and tells
himself again that that trust is beyond dispute. So why is he on
the verge of turning round and beating it back toward the surface
of the earth?

From the head of their procession, their guide breaks his silence to inform them of what the doctor and his daughter must already have known. "This is the entrance to the cave of Peche Merle"—his voice is pedantic, stentorian, in disaccord with his gruff exterior—"carved by an underground river a million years ago. It was discovered in nineteen twenty-two by a pair of brothers, young boys who were encouraged to explore the cave by a local priest. It's a large cave with over three kilometers of tunnels and caverns, though only a third of them are available to the public . . ."

The words, though perhaps not his own, are pronounced in a proprietary tone lest visitors should get the idea that they're not intruding. Chaim is beset by the claustrophobia of his boyhood when locked in his family's cellar, his panic at first being confined to the scaphandre—circumstances to which he did finally adapt. Nevertheless, he believes he can feel this straitened passage actually contracting—"Like my sphincter," he thinks. He halts in his tracks, poised to reverse direction, when Zizou, just ahead of him, turns around. Something in the way the miner's cap with its carbide flame sits at a risible angle over her Psyche-knot is beguiling. Her illuminated face in that otherwise pitch darkness is pure Caravaggio. She comes back to where he's standing, takes his hand, and gently tugs him forward again. "Courage," she says.

The guide is nattering on, reciting for no comprehensible reason an inventory of animals. "Twenty-one woolly mammoths, twelve horses, seven bison, six aurochs, one bear, twelve human beings . . ." Chaim remains disconcerted, stunned now by an emotion both the equal to and opposite of his fear: for the girl has taken his hand. She's a good girl, Marie-Zéline, who might have taken the hand of any frightened child; the gesture may have no more significance than that. While on the other hand . . .

At this point the low ceiling suddenly lifts as the spelunkers emerge into an area the size of the dome of heaven. Or so it appears

to Chaim. While bracing, the air seems also thinner, as if insufficient to fill such a colossal space. Enormous columns rise like stone
geysers from the cave's rolling floor, reaching an impossible height
from which stone draperies hang in a diapason of colors. The walls
are a medley of rough-hewn organ pipes and frozen cataracts, tur-
rets, balustrades, and bays of iridescent stone. There are stalactites
as smooth as candlewax, others like the hide of pachyderms.

"This chamber is called the Basilica," announces Monsieur
Lecroq in his capacity as dragoman. He swings his lantern to indicate a curtain of dangling spectral cylinders. "These are what the
geologists call soda straws." Swinging the lantern again to high-
light formations like statuary niches in a cathedral apse: "And these
are your flowstones." The fissures and shadows themselves seem to
contain unknown depths that amplify the drama of the cavern's
stupendous beauty. The old man in his flapping mackintosh continues reciting his textbook commentary ("The flowstone consists
of sheetlike deposits of calcite formed where water flows . . ."), but
despite his unemphatic delivery, his countenance has taken on a
somewhat diabolical cast. No doubt perceiving as much, Dr. Faure
turns to his daughter and the shuddering artist.

"Welcome to the underworld," he says in a mock-spooky tone
that does little to relieve the uncanniness of the atmosphere.

Among the knobs and protrusions of the cavern walls, there are
those that have been carved by nature into resembling the features
of certain animals: here the accidental curve of a horse's back,
there a bison's hump. But look again, as Monsieur Lecroq holds his
lamp up to them, and a transformation occurs: the configurations
have acquired yet another dimension. Mere resemblances have
sharpened into specific images and the walls are revealed to
be thronged with a painted menagerie. Their guide allows the
visitors a few moments of slack-jawed silence before leading them
toward the farther end of the chamber. There he repeats again

with the sweep of his lantern the process of turning stone into semblance. The drawings possess an ineffable grace and fluency, and with the movement of the lantern along the adamantine walls, the animals—a herd of auroch, a flock of ibex—appear to be in motion themselves. Most of the creatures are identifiable from Monsieur Lecroq's stated catalog—the reindeer, the lion, the bear. Some, like the mammoth, have not been seen on earth for tens of thousands of years; others, with feathered limbs and crescent horns, have perhaps never been seen at all. They are rendered in dark, Rouault-thick outlines, painted in terra-cotta reds, goldenrod yellows, indigos—colors after Chaim's own heart. The artists have apparently let the contours of the rock determine what beasts they depict. Or is it that the rocks themselves, responding to the daubing of pigments, have released the creatures that lay dormant within them?

"Most of the paintings," their guide drones on, "date from the late Magdalanian period of around Sixteen Thousand B.C. But others, like these spotted horses, are said to be more than twenty-five thousand years old . . ."

The horses, even more than the other paintings, partake as much of sculpture as pictorial representation. The leopard pattern of their viridian spots gives them an preternatural aspect. Chaim can feel their heaviness and their heroic suspended energy in his bones. They are unspeakably beautiful.

Zizou still has hold of his hand, even as her father takes Chaim by his other arm, and together they advance into another chapel-sized chamber, which Monsieur Lecroq calls "the Combrel Gallery." Chaim begins to suspect he may be the object of a stratagem. Both father and daughter have expressed some anxiety concerning his lack of artistic activity. Perhaps this is a scheme to reintroduce him to the origins of art, the fountainhead, in the hope that the experience will awaken his slumbering powers. If such is the case, he resents their interference, though he has to admit that the strategy may in fact be working.

"The Hall of Discs . . . ," intones Monsieur Lecroq, "the Black Frieze . . ." Chaim questions whether he's even listening to himself. All this nomenclature and rote language is perhaps meant to keep them moored to a particular place in time, a useless effort. Here the millennia are condensed to a moment and history never happened. Chaim is near combusting with weak-kneed wonder, as over the old man's monologue Dr. Faure speaks in his ear.

"The paleontologist Abbé Breuil believes the paintings are examples of sympathetic magic. They're intended to conjure fertility, a good hunt, and so on. But I think the images represent a nostalgia for a state preceding consciousness, back before the species had eaten of the fruit of the Tree. Once consciousness has dawned, bringing with it an awareness of death, humans begin to long for the innocence of the creature condition from which they evolved. Thus are they compelled to capture these beasts and immure them in buried galleries where they can take their share in their deathlessness. Then begins the real evolution, from these murals to Giotto's and Tiepolo's, to the blue mares of Franz Marc and the butchered beef of Chaim Soutine . . ."

But Chaim can see no evolution at all. He remembers Picasso holding forth in his striped Breton sailor shirt at la Coupole. He had just returned from viewing the cave paintings in Spain to proclaim, "After Altamira, all is decadence!" *Shtus gemeyn*, Chaim had thought then, though now he might like to apologize to the Cubister bag of wind.

The doctor continues expounding his theories, while Chaim thinks, with all due respect: What currency do these fleas up his nose have here? Not that his host is right or wrong in his perceptions. It's just that they count for nothing here in the face of such mighty *mishegoss*; in the presence of that unreasoning impulse that supersedes all others, the one that inhabits you like, God forbid, a dybbuk. It replaces your soul with a chaos and hounds you into making a secret ceremony of drawing pictures in a hole in the ground. When it comes—and nobody knows when it will come— it blasts you loose, the impulse, from every other thing in existence that you might hope to hold on to.

Zizou has let go of Chaim's hand (though he's long since forgotten she was holding it) to inspect more closely a cluster of small handprints outlined in red on the stones. She starts to lay her own hand on one of the prints, as if to greet a primordial child.

"Don't touch it!" shouts Monsieur Lecroq, and Zizou's hand abruptly recoils. Their guide is the curmudgeon again, his unshaven jaw in coarse-grained harmony with the crags of the cavern wall. He grumbles that visitors have only to breathe to damage the legacy of the cave art, never mind the consequences of touching it. Clearly shaken by his rebuke, Zizou asks him politely whether he doesn't breathe himself. The old man hems and resumes his official demeanor: "The experts say the prints were made by children spraying red paint from their mouths . . ." But the spell is broken and the girl has already moved on.

Her father is meanwhile examining a prostrate figure etched beneath a knurled gypsum ledge. "The Wounded Man," Monsieur Lecroq has designated the figure, which looks to be impaled by spears. "Note how," maunders the doctor, possibly to himself, "the man is rendered with more complexity than the rudimentary depictions of the other humans around him. You can see in him an archetypal portrayal of suffering that will ripen over time into the Pietà . . ." Nearby, Zizou has spied the engraved image of a female reduced to only the convex triangle of her vulva. She observes it with a keen objectivity before redirecting her gaze toward another image, which she describes in a voice perhaps intended to get her father's attention: "This one appears to be a woman in the midst of metamorphosing into a four-footed bovid . . ." "A bovid?" asks Dr. Faure, interested, as Monsieur Lecroq advises the party that they've nearly exhausted the time allotted to visitors.

Chaim hears none of this, having once again been overtaken by dread. Despite the vaulting scale of the cavern, his claustrophobia has returned with a will and the brilliance of the paintings begun to scald his eyes. He's had his revelation: he understands that for these immemorial artists, even here in the bowels of the earth, especially here, there was no separation from the natural world. They and their subjects are identical. A man painting a mammoth is a mammoth, and painting a horse a horse—the images imply no more than what they are. And yet, to realize that fusion is everything. It's the same enterprise Chaim feels himself called upon to pursue even now, at the risk of losing all else; for when the urge is upon you, it tears you savagely away from whatever purchase you might have on ordinary happiness. He desperately misses the daylit houses and trees!

"I have to get out from here!" he blurts, and ashamed of having distressed the others, he snatches at the first excuse that comes to mind. "It's from nature the call," he explains. The words have a peculiar resonance in this environment.

✦

THAT VERY NIGHT, AFTER Zizou has retired early, complaining of fatigue, Chaim asks her parents for her hand. They've been sitting in the parlor, soft lamplight reflecting the cozy scene in the leaded windows—the doctor in his leather Morris chair reading his journals, Madame Faure on the adjacent settee with a ball of knitting in her lap. Chaim is sitting stiffly in a ladder-back chair, facing them both like a plaintiff in the dock. This is their typical arrangement of an evening, though tonight, sans book, Chaim has it in his head that he has in fact requested their presence. He thinks they must in some sense be aware of this. Never before has he wanted to import to these parts any aspect of Smilovitchi, and this night is no different; though he wonders whether there might have been some consolation in having the village matchmaker on hand as an advocate. Naftali the Nudzh he was called, the baggy-eyed *shadkhn*, for his relentless campaigns to find brides for even the least eligible of bachelors. In the absence of such an intermediary, and having no real knowledge of the protocol in such affairs, Chaim broaches the subject without prelude.

"I want to marry your daughter."

Dr. Faure and his wife, her needles no longer clicking, exchange looks of mutual consternation. Chaim thinks that perhaps they haven't heard him correctly.

"Marie-Zéline," he pronounces almost as a question should they need reminding. "I wish by you the honor that you will give to me her hand in marriage."

Though her turbaned head is turned partly toward Chaim, Madame Faure's eyes have yet to shift from her husband. The doctor shrugs almost imperceptibly, removes the nickel-rimmed spectacles from his fleshy nose, breathes on them, and wipes them slowly with a handkerchief. He replaces the glasses and for some reason pulls the railroad watch from his waistcoat pocket; he inspects it scrupulously as if he might have an appointment elsewhere. His wife's abundant bosom rises and falls in a long-suffering sigh. "Well, Chaim," says Dr. Faure at length, "this is rather sudden . . ." Chaim is on the edge of his seat, his fingers prayerfully entwined. It's clear that nothing will liberate him from his ramrod rigidity until he's been given an answer. "But I suppose," the good doctor continues, studiously avoiding the fretful gaze of his wife, "that if the girl is willing . . ."

The suitor screws up his face as if something has perhaps slipped his mind.

Dr. Faure is puzzled. "Have you not yet spoken to Zizou?"

In truth, so much forethought has Chaim devoted to anticipating this momentous conversation that it hasn't occurred to him another might have preceded it. Besides, given the close relations he already enjoys with the daughter, he holds a hope that the other conversation may hardly be necessary. In answer to the doctor's question the artist can only shake his head.

"Then," suggests his host, groping for the hand his wife has not offered him, "I suggest that at your earliest opportunity . . ."

It's unusual for the eloquent doctor not to finish his sentences, but Chaim tries to persuade himself that an ellipsis is as good as a blessing.

He approaches her the next morning at her drawing table and asks whether she would like to take a walk. She says maybe later, upon which his resolution begins to come apart. A shaft of sunlight swimming with motes is slanting through the open windows, striking the girl like, thinks Chaim, an Annunciation. The goyish association compounds his unrest. He watches her at her work while trying to control his facial tics. Her lustrous brown hair is pulled back in the strict spool of her topknot, her brow furrowed in concentration, her nostrils regally aflare. The girl, he realizes perhaps for the first time, is not a girl at all but a cultivated young woman, serious and modest if sometimes a little cheeky, sometimes alarmingly intelligent. What they call a bluestocking. Chaim summons his remaining molecule of courage.

"Marie-Zéline," he begins, and then, having captured her attention, "Zizou," in a lower register.

She invites him to forgodsake sit down.

Chaim appreciates the familiarity if not the untypical touch of impatience. He retrieves the ladder-back chair and sits in his buckram-stiff posture. "Zizou . . ."

She bobs her head slightly in an attempt to help tease the words from his tongue.

"Ziz . . ." The syllable rings a distant bell. "You know in Talmud . . . you don't know Talmud . . . why should you know Talmud? Is a giant bird, the Ziz, that with its wings can blot out the sun . . ." Elsewhere, the shadow of those wings darkens the water above him. Through his viewport he sees the bird dive into the Seine and ensnare from the silty bottom a sunken telephone kiosk in its beak.

"Chaim," the girl interrupts his babbling, "is there something you want to say to me?"

Facing him, she is more distinctly herself than the artist is prepared to absorb, and the speech he's rehearsed all night is stillborn on his lips. "Zizou," he finally manages, "will you, um, please to let me paint your picture?"

The portrait is by his standards mercifully accurate, but though he's promised it to the girl, he changes his mind and with apologies keeps it for himself.

This doesn't mean that Chaim has abandoned his suit. He has after all what he believes to be parental consent. But the whirl of activity surrounding the family's closing up of the cottage and departure for Paris interfere with his opportunities for being alone with the girl. Things remain no less unsettled during his visits to the house on the île de la Cité. Paris is not the Dordogne. The boys are back from their summer camp and they and their friends seem to occupy in their spirited pastimes several rooms at once. Dr. Faure divides his day between his surgical duties, lectures at the lycée, and work on his groundbreaking *Art of Cineplastics* (a term and science of his own coinage). In the evenings he's less inclined to entertain guests, and his *femme* tends to guard his leisure hours like a minotaur, though Chaim is always welcome. Zizou, however, is seldom at home. He's told that, a popular girl, she's out with

friends most evenings at the opera, the theater, the ballet. Chaim
has met some of her friends in the country, urbane and well-bred
young people, though he can't stop himself from imagining that
she runs with a fast set. He cannot miss a chance to salt his own
wounds.

It seems there may never be a convenient time to corner her,
but late one afternoon, having come at an unaccustomed hour,
he encounters her as she's descending the stairs. Outside, the
leads of the roof are being replaced and the chimneys repointed.
Scaffolding obscures the facade and laborers swarm all about,
shouting canards to one another over their hammering. The boys
are in and out of the house, upstairs and down, actively kibitzing
the work. The front door is ajar and Chaim has entered just as
Marie-Zéline steps into the foyer. Despite the cacophony he seizes
an opportunity he fears may not come again soon. He is anyway
unable to distinguish between the noise of the labor and the tu-
mult in his brain.

"Zizou," he says over the racket, quick before his nerve can fail,
"I want you should be my wife."

She cups an ear and asks him to please repeat what he said. He
does so at greater volume during a moment when, as luck would
have it, there's a sudden lull in the noise. His proposal resounds
throughout the house. The girl colors, then tenderly takes his hand
much as she had on that day in the cave. She leads him down a
hallway and out a door into a small back garden. There's a goldfish
pond and a border of asters and chrysanthemums making their late
summer flourish before flaming out. There's a wrought-iron bench
though neither of them seem to want to sit down.

"Chaim," says Zizou, smiling with humid eyes, "you're too
late. I'm very flattered," she assures him, subduing a nervous titter, "but just this week I became engaged to marry my cousin,
Pierre Matignon. He's an aviator who designs for the Aéronautique

Militaire. We've been friends since we were children. You might remember him from the cottage . . . ?"

Chaim has already begun to apologize for his presumption. A sweet girl, Zizou, she makes it sound as if he might indeed have been a candidate for her affections, though he's not deceived. He's become instantly aware of the magnitude of his folly. Whatever has he been thinking all these months? Did he really believe he could so seamlessly insinuate himself into the heart of such an estimable family? What was it that Modi's fancy woman, that Hastings baggage, had called him? Oh yes, a Jewish troll.

Back in his debris-appointed atelier, this one on the avenue d'Orléans, he rubs out with pumice the face in his portrait of a reclining Marie-Zéline. But, uncharacteristically, he refrains from destroying the canvas. In fact, he bears the girl no ill will. After all, an alliance with such as him would be for the like of her an indecency. It's her father that deserves the blame for Chaim's humiliation. Surely the man must have known her engagement was pending. Why was he not warned? Faure had as much as set him up for disappointment.

In his outrage over the perceived betrayal, Chaim, who detests the physical act of writing, prevails again upon Chana Orloff to function as his stenographer. Reluctantly, the matronly sculptress takes his dictation, pleading with him all the while to moderate the language of his rant. He remains inflexible. Almost by return post he receives an impassioned response from the doctor.

"You are atrociously unfair," writes Dr. Faure, "something you will regret—I hope so, for your sake—when calm has returned to your heart. No one in my home has made sport of you; we have both been victims of circumstance and of a common imprudence in which I see nothing that can diminish the respect in which I hold you and that you owe me as well . . ."He goes on for several pages lamenting the injustice of Soutine's accusations and professing his enduring admiration and affection. "You were, you still are, aside from my two sons, the only man I love . . ." In the end the doctor is left perplexed by the vitriol of Chaim's letter: "Yet you are not a base man. I know you better than you know yourself . . ."

"What do you know?" fumes Chaim. Once more he imposes on his neighbor Madame Orloff, who pens his reply, mending his broken sentences in the process, then vows never to play his amanuensis again.

"Monsieur, I have thought and reflected much on your letter and I prefer your daughter's making sport of me to all this admiration you throw in my face . . . As for your feelings of friendship, what can you mean by them at such a time? Future conversation no longer makes any sense. But rest assured," he is magnanimous enough to append, "I have memories of some good moments. C. Soutine."

More beseeching letters from the doctor follow, but Chaim remains unmoved. His answers, since he must write them himself, become terser until they cease altogether. Only after Élie Faure's death, seven years later, does the artist recognize his unpaid debt of gratitude to the man. But by then he's living dangerously in the eye of the storm with Gerda Groth.

◆

IN 1930 JULES PASCIN, né Julius Mordecai Pincas, returns to his large, glass-roofed studio in Montmartre. The night has been a typical round of cafés and soirées; he's had a dozen *pistes verte* and sat in on drums with a jazz band at Princess Marfa's. He has squeezed the bottoms of a bevy of ingénues as if testing them for ripeness at the bar of the Café Parnasse. But now he's unbearably tired, torn between his attachment to his wife, Hermine, from whom he's separated, and his mistress Lucy Krohg, who will not leave her husband. He is also sick with syphilis or cirrhosis or both. Beyond that, he's weary of painting the popular portraits of half-dressed little girls that his dealers have pressured him into producing en masse.

(These are the same little girls whom Chaim Soutine, one evening in le Select, confessed that he found exciting. "I forbid you to excite yourself in front of my women!" shouted Pascin.) The artist doffs his famous derby, takes a kitchen knife from a drawer, and slices his wrists. As he waits to die, he smears a message on the wall in blood: *Adieu Lucy*. But he does not die. Frustrated, he tears the cord from a console radio, ties one end around a lamp sconce, the other around his neck, and drops to his knees—which never reach the floor. Success. The galleries close for his funeral. Thousands walk in the procession of mourners—a goodly portion of them waiters and maître d's—from the boulevard de Clichy to the cimetière de Saint-Ouen. It is the event that marks the beginning of the end of les années folles.

Chaim receives the news of Pascin's death with mixed feelings. After all, this is the man who, once in his cups (when was he not in his cups?), declared himself the son of God, then promised that misfortune would befall anyone who didn't love him. Despite his contempt for superstition, Chaim, hedging his bets, had sworn aloud that he loved Pascin very much. Though he never really liked him. For one thing, he resented the well-fixed Bulgarian for having attained a status equal to his own in the canon of Dr. Barnes, and he resented him for having inherited the mantle, since Modi's passing, of Prince of Bohemia. His death seems in keeping with the change in the Parisian atmosphere, not that Chaim is especially sensitive to change. The Depression that has shattered the American economy has been slow in reaching the European continent, though the diminishing art market is an early victim of the stock market crash. Gallery sales have declined dramatically and collectors have started selling off paintings at rock-bottom prices for needed cash. Established artists such as Kisling and Chagall have had contracts annulled and scheduled shows canceled. There are the beginnings of an exodus from Montparnasse in search of cheaper rural retreats. Though for Chaim the city has long been only a part-time base of operations.

Meanwhile, Zborowski, with his marvelous talent for mismanaging his affairs, has lost the support of his Maecenas Joseph Netter. His debts have piled up and he's unable to keep his promises to his lineup of artists, though he hangs on to most by his fervent professions of loyalty. Ultimately he's forced to take a job as a waiter at le Dingo in order to keep his family afloat. Chaim, however, is unaffected by his embarrassed agent's reversals. He has taken a sabbatical from painting his eviscerated fish and fowl, whose entrails only ever augured ill, and returned to his default attitude of admiring women exclusively from afar. What's more, his new patrons have provided him with their unequivocal support.

Chaim Soutine is hardly the first artist whom Madeleine and Marcellin Castaing have cultivated. The most recent has been the one-armed writer Blaise Cendrars. The garrulous veteran had written a screenplay adapted from *Madame Bovary* and wanted the lovely Madeleine to star in the film. She would become, he claimed, the Mary Pickford of France. The Castaings were intrigued by the project until it fell through when Flaubert's surviving niece refused to give up the rights. Without breaking stride (or dropping Cendrars from their circle), the couple moved on in search of some new beneficiary for their largesse. It isn't long before they—if less enthusiastically on the part of Marcellin—have set their sights on the Russian Jew who had behaved so churlishly at their first meeting. While browsing in a gallery on the rue de la Boétie, Madeleine has come across Chaim's *Dead Chicken with Tomatoes* and is enraptured. All is forgiven. The painting, however, while on display, belongs to the novelist Francis Carco, who is not anxious to give it up. The Castaings, whose collection of modern art is quite extensive, offer an exchange, and the writer eventually succumbs to Madeleine's pretty pleas. He trades his dead chicken for a lady in a cornflower chemise by Derain.

After that the couple, largely due to Madeleine's persuasion, comb the galleries for more Soutines. Word of their interest bordering on obsession reaches Zborowski, who invites them to his flat with the promise of treasures. He asks an astronomically inflated amount for one of Chaim's choirboys and prepares himself to haggle, but to his astonishment Marcellin writes him a check at a stroke. Obsequious in his gratitude, Zbo, who ought by now to know better, offers to arrange an interview between them and the retiring artist. Recalling their previous encounter, Marcellin says that they've already had the pleasure, but talking over him, his wife leaps at the opportunity.

Though he's long forgotten their unfortunate interaction of five years earlier, Chaim is never keen on meeting the Lords and Ladies Bountiful of the consumer class. But when he hears the sum they have so readily forked over for a work of his, he condescends to make an exception. Zbo leaves the apartment soon after making the introductions. There's little love lost between him and the high-strung Litvak; their relationship, prickly from the start, has deteriorated further due to what Chaim correctly believes is the dealer's gross mishandling of his finances. (Of course, neither dealer nor artist has any real practical sense where business is concerned.) The rooms in Chaim's suite are cold. The ceilings are high with ornamental moldings and the windows are tall, opening onto Juliet balconies, but the place looks as usual as if it's been ravaged by Huns. It reeks from a potpourri of vile odors and, despite the respectable address, gives the impression that la Ruche has come to the avenue d'Orléans.

The artist himself, in his stained smock, corded trousers, and unshorn hair, is of a piece with his fetid surroundings. He greets his guests with the merest pretense to cordiality, inviting them to sit in what passes for a parlor. The once luxurious acquisitions that have survived from the post–Dr. Barnes days are in decline: the chairs crippled, the left-arm fainting couch giving up its stuffing. Marcellin has yet to remove his trench coat and trilby, having informed the painter that their stay must be brief. "Unfit for human habitation," he whispers to his wife while Chaim dispenses weak tea from a dented samovar. His wife, however, ignores the chill. She spreads her ocelot cape over the back of a club chair and lowers her silk-clad posterior into its concave cushion. Sunk too near to the floor, she raises herself to the edge of the seat, slightly arching the clef-note curve of her spine to accept a chipped teacup from their host. She doesn't seem to see the refuse or smell the spoiled paté Chaim has been eating since he left off watching his diet. She sees only a lonely man with an exceptional gift in urgent need of looking after, and has immediately conceived a calling.

For his part, Chaim feels his usual ambivalence in the presence of the affluent. On the one hand, he would like to consign them and their toffee-nosed pedigrees to oblivion, while on the other he must feel beholden for their patronage. Beholden to a degree that seems craven in his own eyes. Still, this couple strikes him as somehow different. They have an aura about them that seems almost incandescent, as if their cocoon of wealth and style has rendered them impervious to the world's wicked designs. Preoccupied as he is with self-pity, Chaim is not immune to their charm, or rather hers. The man, decades older than his wife, still retains the brilliantined good looks of a film idol, a John Gilbert or Ramon Novarro. His air of distinction is beyond even Chaim's capacity for envy. But the woman is of another order, a natural incarnation of refinement and grace, virtues the artist has only this moment begun to hold in regard. He feels almost sorry for afflicting them with his hapless person. And yet it is he to whom they have come to pay homage.

She's flattering him, alleging that his chefs d'oeuvre have altered forever how she looks at life—while her husband, having stationed himself behind the club chair, phlegmatically concurs. "Monsieur Soutine," she avows, no doubt observing the depth of his absorption in her dove-gray eyes, "someone has said that when color is rich . . ."(She knows quite well who said it: Cézanne; but she's been cautioned by Zbo not to mention names that Chaim might perceive as rivals.) "When color is rich, form is at its plenitude, and no painter is richer in color than you."

Her husband, a sometime drama critic, mutters his accord.

Chaim is ordinarily repelled by such eulogizing, and he's not unmindful of the irony of the word *rich* on the woman's crimson lips. So why does he feel so close to purring? He's been lost to himself these months since the Zizou debacle. His nights have been spent at catch-boxing matches in the Vél d'Hiv, imitating the jabs and kicks from his seat in the stands; or if not there, then alone in the louche music halls of Pigalle, listening to some shelf-worn chanteuse singing a song in adoration of her abusive lover. By day he prowls the bouquiniste stalls along the river, ferreting out more volumes of Balzac, for whom he's acquired an unhealthy addiction—although these days he's numb to the author's volcanic energies. He expects it can't be lost on his guests that, for all the disorder, there are no signs in these rooms of the working artist. No paint-spattered tarps or scattered brushes. The remaining canvases are turned to the walls like mirrors in a house of the dead. And if he's not painting, then he's not a painter. And if not a painter, neither is he a man. And if not a man . . . perhaps a bug?

The woman is interrogating him in a rush of questions. "Monsieur Soutine, your method . . . your palette . . . your revolutionary program . . . your iconoclastic sorties?" They are presumptuous questions, niggling and doctrinaire, intrusive enough to make the bug want to curl up in its shell. For all that, he finds himself receiving her third-degree in the nature of a lifeline lowered into the well of his solitude. ("Your solitude is my suffering," Élie Faure had written him toward the end of their correspondence, a sentiment Chaim had rejected out of hand.) This woman of fashion, with a tincture of chagrin in the corners of her eyes, has come down from her lofty sphere to rescue him. On the strength of her chatter and her heady vanilla scent, he feels himself being raised from an abyss, "evolving"—to use Dr. Faure's word—from bug to man along the way.

"What are colors for," she's asking, crossing her mauve-stockinged legs; she leans forward to prop an elbow on her knee, her perfect chin in the cup of her hand. "What are colors for if not to reveal the innermost life of objects?"

She's a shameless dilettante, Chaim reminds himself—so why is he suddenly possessed of an overpowering urge to confide in Madeleine Castaing?

"In my village," he volunteers apropos of nothing she's asked him, "I would gather for the barber the leeches from out of the marsh; I would grind on his hand mill the liver for the sausage maker. With the few coins they gave me, I would buy from a shop that it catered to sign painters the wax pastels. They would turn me, my brothers, *mit kop arop*—how do you say it?—upside down, and shake from my pockets the colors. 'A Jew must not paint,' they told me. Always they told me, but I don't listen . . ."

Bite already your mutinous tongue, he reproves himself, but all that matters to him now is that he hold her attention.

Madeleine's husband, with a barely audible moan, has scooted a chair to her side, and sits now with a cigarette in one hand and the other wrapped around his wife's spare shoulder. He supposes, does Monsieur Castaing, that this indecorous fellow is already in love with his wife. It's the price he must pay for his philandering.

At their country house at Lèves she has surrounded herself with a company of infatuated geniuses whom she collects along with her knickknacks and bibelots. Satie, Cendrars, the polemicist Drieu La Rochelle; even that invert Cocteau worships her after his fashion. Madeleine encourages their flirtations, which Marcellin views as essentially harmless. But this one seems different—too needy by half, he thinks. This poor soul looks like trouble.

But Marcellin has misjudged the painter (though not about the infatuation). Of course Chaim is in love with Madeleine Castaing, but he will never declare it. Not in their opulent town house on the rue de Grenelle, within striking distance of Montparnasse, or in their jewel box château near Chartres. True, he will be a difficult guest, but he has learned his lesson. From now on he will suffer his affectionate fixations in silence, as he did in the days before the Melnick and Marie-Zéline. The suffering will nourish his art. They talk, he and Madame Castaing, into the night. Chaim cannot remember ever having unburdened himself so willingly, or having wanted so much to prolong a visitor's stay. By the time his guests realize the late hour and prepare to leave, Madeleine has become his confessor and bosom friend. As he sees them to the door at their departure, he asks her:

"May I sometime to paint you?"

✦

THE CASTAINGS' DELIVERANCE OF the ill-groomed artist from his long despondency has little in common with the salvage diver Babineaux's efforts to haul Chaim up from beneath the Seine. In the one instance he readily acquiesces while in the other he continues by an act of sheer will to resist the old plongeur's tugging at his safety rope. His face mask has filled with water to a level that tickles his nostrils, resulting in a phenomenon known to frogmen as the mammalian dive response. This is the reflex that is activated

when the face is cooled by water during a dive. It is a clever physiological mechanism that enables the body to manage and tolerate a
lower level of oxygen. It's a vital reflex in dolphins and whales, and
in humans, though in the latter it may create the illusion of being
able to breathe underwater.

Chaim begins his portrait of Madeleine Castaing on the rue
de Grenelle and finishes it in the mansion at Lèves. This is unprecedented, accustomed as he is to completing his paintings in a
single lightning attack. But in Madeleine's company he has relaxed
his defenses; his headlong metabolism has slowed in its velocity.
Whatever prejudices he might have with regard to their privilege
and wealth have dissipated in the face of the Castaings' benevo-
lence and their disarmingly infectious savoir faire. Marcellin he
regards with equal portions of respect and disdain. For all his poses
and peccadillos, he is a serious devotee of the arts—or at least an
ardent advocate of his wife's enthusiasms. In this Chaim considers
him both praiseworthy and rather weak; he's uxorious in the license
he allows his wife to pursue her diverse passions, be they art or antiques or making a project out of nurturing the talent of a Russian
contrarian. (Though who would dare to stand in the way of those
passions?) So, with the understanding that his attachment to the
couple might compromise his integrity beyond retrieval, Chaim
has given himself permission to linger over Madeleine's portrait.

During the process he and Madame Castaing have become
thick as thieves. Not since Paulette Jourdain has Chaim known
such an uncomplicated connection with a member of the gentler
sex, and this one a virtual goddess. While there's no question that
he is utterly smitten with the woman, his feelings are finally more
fraternal than amorous. (He recalls that he does in fact have a sister
back in Smilovitchi, but there's only a foggy place in his memory
where her features should be.) Between sessions he and his "model"
stroll around the reflecting pool in the park that Madeleine has

reclaimed from previously fallow land behind the mansion. She speaks often of her ongoing romance with their neoclassical manor house, which she had admired from childhood. For this reason her husband had made it his wedding gift to her.

"It's been called by some a cabinet of curiosities, a flea-market Pandora's box," she says, "but really it's more a likeness of myself than any portrait could be." Chaim takes this as a direct challenge, though he doesn't say so. "In decorating a house," she continues with her patented blend of ingenuousness and hauteur, "you must be audacious, but with taste. It also doesn't hurt to have a little intuition, originality, and vigor." Chaim has never loved a house, but thinks he might learn to in this case.

She speaks too of her reverence for Proust, in whose honor she has taken to calling her husband Marcel. Chaim abandons his usual self-consciousness with regard to his hobbled French to relate the lumbering plots of Balzac novels, which she knows by heart but doesn't let on. He offers iniquitous tidbits about assassinations and beheadings from the Michelet histories he's been reading in the château's library. "Robespierre that he shoots himself before he is to be beheaded but manages only to blow away his jaw. The executioner has first to rip off his bandage to fit through the window of the guillotine his head." Playful and vivacious in conversation, Madeleine divulges how she once hired a detective to follow her husband on his extramarital forays. Having ascertained the address of a hotel where Marcellin had scheduled a rendezvous, she paid off the prostitute and took her place in the darkened room.

"When Marcel turned on the light, he soiled his peach silk boxers."

Chaim is frequently shocked by her unladylike candor, to say nothing of the blithe manner in which she relates her tales of matrimonial disharmony. But even more astonishing is that she apparently harbors no rancor toward her husband, who dotes on her despite his failings. She constantly makes unkind quips concerning his habits: "He never loses a minute to lie down and rest." But if Chaim attempts to join in the derision, she promptly silences him; she will not hear a discourteous word said about Marcel. By the same token, she has cautioned Marcellin, who tends to treat Soutine like an undomesticated house pet, to be tolerant of the painter's peculiarities. This is not always easy. Although Marcellin has a genuine admiration for the immigrant's maverick art, he's impatient at having to indulge the artist himself. You never knew what might set him off. Once he came upon Soutine painting a landscape in a hawthorn grove near the house and remarked that the work bore some resemblance to a Renoir he'd recently seen. Chaim pulled out his pocket knife and straightaway shredded the canvas. Marcellin groaned in exasperation but has begun to walk on eggs around the *fou furieux* ever since.

Although their relations are purely platonic, Chaim is persuaded that he and Madeleine have a special bond. This one, he's convinced, is not imaginary. They are after all nearly the same age, both perhaps twenty years younger than her husband. And her breezy air when she's with him seems to him much more congenial than the pragmatic bearing she reserves for Marcellin. Sometimes Chaim thinks her confidentiality might be better suited to a friendship with another woman; sometimes she makes him feel a bit like a eunuch. But to be the recipient of her winsome attentions is worth any amount of degradation he might have to endure. This dynamic, however, is reversed when he paints her. Then the artist is strictly in control. He does not allow her to move or speak, nor will he let her see his work in progress. He assures her, though, that she will live forever in his painting.

Forever? When he finally reveals the completed portrait, its subject looks as if almost at death's door. Madeleine winces at how he's advanced her age. He's injected into her sanguine countenance a

discordant melancholy; he's given her eyes a troubled cast, divested
of their typical levity, and stretched her round face into an unnatural attenuation. He's distorted her beauty and diminished her
authority. As she views the painting, she feels him scrutinizing her
for the least sign of disapproval, and concealing her injured vanity,
she declares the work a masterpiece. At any event the portrait bears
the stamp of his others. The harsh lineaments he's realized on that
recycled hemp surface, albeit not her own, appear to have . . . how
to describe it? They seem somehow to have simply happened there
on the canvas rather than to have been "made." She luxuriates in
the intensely cinnabar-red folds of the Patou gown.

They sit together before the fireplace in the salon, with its eclec-
tic furnishings of the type that will become known internation-
ally as *le style Castaing*. A freakishly padded Napoleon III armchair
and a chaise longue with dragon's head finials anchor the leopard
Ottoman carpet. There are wobbly mahogany fauteuils with ballerina legs acquired at a brothel's fire sale, brocade curtains in pale
aqua, poison green, and robin's-egg blue. The taxidermied heads of
ibex and antelope are mounted above the mantel; unframed paintings hang on the sgraffito-bordered walls. (Madame believes frames
"imprison" a painting.) But Chaim doesn't share Madeleine's love of
objects; objects require the artist's touch to complete their reality.
Only, reality is not what Madame Castaing is after. Her dizzy mixture of periods and trends, rather than collide, somehow manage to
balance each other, creating spaces complete unto themselves and
outside of time. Staggered by the effect, Chaim nevertheless de-
lights in the unique sensibility that has made Madeleine Castaing
a diva among decorators.

They walk together through the maze of box hedges in the garden and along the poplar allée in fair weather and foul. Madeleine
informs Chaim that she has planted all the trees herself, with the
exception of the great willow whose fronds invade the long French

windows of the southern gallery. He has known such peaceful inter-
ludes before; they never turn out well. His constitution is not built
for cosseting; he's afraid that, having lost the habits of bitterness
and hunger, he might also lose his edge. But he enjoys the sunny,
octagonal, pavilion-like outbuilding in which they've installed him.
Like, he thinks, a heavenly version of la Ruche. He appreciates
the smooth surfaces of the eighteenth-century canvases Madeleine
brings him from the regional bazaars, as well as the turkey, guinea
fowl, red mullet, sea devils, and pike she has her servants offer him
as potential subjects. Though lately Chaim is more interested in
living human models, and the Castaings also serve as procurers
for these.

There's the morose young laundress who complains of a charley
horse in her hip while posing and refuses to reassume the awkward
position she's been holding for hours. Chaim insists that she take
up the precise pose again, and when she still refuses, falls to his
knees to plead with her. The girl is frightened by his histrionics
and makes to flee but Chaim won't let go of her arm. Madame
Castaing, alerted to the fracas, rushes to the guesthouse. She presses
some extra francs into the girl's clammy hand to persuade her of the
paramount importance of holding the pose. Then there's the broad-
beamed shepherdess Madeleine assists Chaim in inducing into temporarily forsaking her flock. They coax her into miming a siesta
under a yew tree in the park, in an attitude reminiscent of the young
ladies in Courbet's *Demoiselles des bords de la Seine*. The woman,
though lacking any hint of the coy disposition of Courbet's ladies,
is compliant until it begins to rain. The rain turns into a downpour
and still the painter insists she resume her counterfeit nap. "C'est
dingue! He's mad!" cries the saturated woman, her pinafore clinging
immodestly to her ample frame. Without disagreeing, Madeleine,
holding a manteau over her head, slips the woman a few more francs.

There's the farmer's wife whom the artist importunes into wading in a braided channel of the River Eure with her shift hoisted above her knees, in an evocation of Rembrandt's *Hendrickje Bathing.* (Rumor has it Chaim once traveled overnight to London, as he had to Amsterdam, just to view the painting at the National Gallery.) This time he's unaccompanied by Madame Castaing, but no matter; he's able to offer his own pourboire, and besides, the jolly, apple-cheeked woman needs little persuasion. She can't cease chuckling as she lifts her petticoats and steps into the shallow water. Chaim can do without her hilarity, but he's satisfied with the mise-en-scène, until her yeoman husband shuffles into it with pitchfork in hand.

"Eulalie!" he shouts, unable for the moment to decide where to direct his ire, whether toward his wife or the painter. First his wife: "Pute écarlate, indecent woman!" But the painter is as offended by the interruption as is the husband by his wife's shameful display. "How dare you!" he challenges. "I am a professional artist!" Which means exactly nothing to the badger-faced little man, who has waded into the water to retrieve his wife. Chaim attempts to come between them, having dropped his high-handed manner in favor of imploring. He tries to assure the farmer that his wife is anyway long past the season of arousing impure thoughts. "Look on her legs like an elephant!" This is apparently the wrong tack to take. Having yanked Eulalie, who is laughing fit to burst, back onto the bank, the man turns again toward Chaim, still up to his ankles in the river, and commences to give chase. His pitchfork proceeds him like a fixed bayonet.

By the time a panicked servant has raised the alarm and the Castaings arrive at the scene, Chaim is floundering in the middle of the Eure where he'd fled the rusty prongs. The farmer and his hysterically giddy wife are standing on the bank, watching him drown.

There are the quiet days when Chaim provides no further fuel
for gossip in the nearby village. Then Madeleine is free to plan her
entertainments and Marcellin to concentrate on his tennis game
without fear of being called to defuse some impending scandal. But
between paintings the painter is prone to feeling debilitated and
depressed. He is naturally aware of his good fortune in being bil-
leted in such an Arcadia; one could do worse than to fetch up in a
place where your every whim is ministered to. The ambrosial estate
of Lèves is an eminently comfortable seat from which to launch his
flights and plumb his murky depths, with always the assurance of
a hospitable return to the quotidian. Witness the works these lush
surroundings have already fostered: his (fully clothed) *Femme au
bain*, the *Jeune servant au tablier bleu*, the bestial weariness in the
profile of *La concierge*. He's even painted, to their mutual morti-
fication, the single nude he's attempted since his student days—
a shrinking housemaid whose erysipelas flared during the sitting.
Some might say these paintings from his pampered period lack
the rapturous derangement of his earlier works. In particular, the
landscapes from Cagnes and Céret, which he still destroys whenever the chance arises—though these, some claim, are the vintage
Soutine. Perhaps. Certainly the palette has softened and his figures
become more formally resolved; the references to the art of the past
are more pervasive. But look at how the eyes of *La cuisinère* contain
the quintessence of a life defined by the forced marriage of cupidity
and a simmering despair.

Chaim understands that the château, with its museum-grade
kitsch and elaborate garden follies, affords no end of pleasures for
its guests and inhabitants. So why not him? The old melamed in
his slough of a cheder back in Smilovitchi would often invoke the
name of a sage for whom it was a sin to be without joy. The memory
reinforces the artist's stubborn conviction that it's a sin to be Chaim
Soutine. His moods irritate Marcellin, who complains to his wife

that it's like living with Raskolnikov. Madeleine reminds him of Chaim's hereditary disadvantages: "He's a Russian, a Jew, and a genius."

"Quite," replies her husband with a sigh.

She tries to cajole the artist out of his doldrums with compliments disguised as inquiry. "Chaim," asks his hostess on an indolent afternoon in her junglelike orangery, "Chaim, how did you come by your talent for making your pigments breathe light?" The observation is not original; she has overheard the remark from Jacques Lipchitz (who would never have said as much to the artist's face) at the Galerie Bing. The question succeeds in penetrating Chaim's languor.

"It's all in how you mix them," he tells her, and that's it; though the statement speaks volumes that the artist will never articulate. He lacks the wherewithal to describe the qualities his colors possess: how the whites that embody your garden-variety innocence can also reveal cowardice as well as stupefaction and ennui. There's the cerulean that denotes the dreamer, but also the prodigal and the lover of children. Emerald has only a single facet of envy, the other facets comprising sickness, beatitude, and a paralysis of the will. Red, blessed red!—aside from its standard expressions of lust and rage—can as readily command a steely forbearance when faced with the depredations of the Angel of Death. But mix the colors with the specific character of your subject, who may be anything— spiteful, complaisant, broken like a discarded toy—and the result is a whole new compound of emotions. Some of which have never before been expressed by the sitter, or anyone else for that matter.

Meanwhile, through the tchotchke-littered halls and hothouse galleries of Château Lèves, the luminaries come and go. Most have learned to keep a cautious distance from the resident artist, who seems to so easily take offense, often where none is intended. Cocteau sniffs a sprig of daphne in his buttonhole and ignores

Soutine but can't help making a show of his indifference. He takes swipes at him behind his back, though his supposedly biting bon mots—"Silence moves faster when it's going backward"—are often lost on his listeners. The poet Cendrars is too busy excoriating others for their mannered metaphysical anguish to take much notice of the lurking Russian, whose anguish is palpable. (When his diatribes grow heated, the stump of the veteran's blown-away arm begins to flap like a chicken wing.) Pierre Drieu La Rochelle, however, is somewhat more sinister in his active disregard of the painter. He has already begun his flirtation with the reactionary Parti Populaire, which will stand him in good stead with the enemy during the Occupation. For him Chaim is the very agent of a verminous infestation, and he likes to speculate (though never around Madeleine) that *le juif*'s distinctive odor is derived from drinking Christian blood. But Maurice Sachs, when not making obeisance to his idol Cocteau, finds the Litvak an object of fascination. A Jew himself, though barren of either principle or self-respect, the invertebrate Sachs has studied the paintings the Castaings have begun to hang alongside their Matisses and Cézannes. They stir him to the marrow, perhaps striking a long-unheeded chord in his breast. He has attempted to approach Soutine and been summarily snubbed, but is nonetheless undeterred in his admiration. To Madame Castaing, whom he worships just this side of Jean Cocteau, he reflects:

"I suppose what his native ghetto poured into his blood will never be taken from him—namely, his suffering. To the suffering of poverty and illness one must add that racial suffering of which one is never rid."

"Why, Maurice," says Madeleine, "one might almost believe you have a heart."

"Haven't you noticed," replies Sachs, flashing a gimcrack cuff link, "I wear it on my sleeve."

Chaim, who takes for granted the guests' disinterest, would be surprised at how often he is a topic of conversation. If he considers them at all, it's to resent them for the time they steal from his chaste assignations with Madeleine. But sensitive as is his hostess to his feelings, she is also not above savoring his jealousy.

In some remote cell of his brain, Chaim must be able to acknowledge how romantic a setting is the Castaing estate for his malaise. He broods in a reindeer-horn chair beside an opaline lamp, behind a Chinese folding screen and in front of a Byzantine stone hearth. He broods amid the ivy-clad herm sculptures hidden among the boxwood parterres and in an open, poppy-flecked meadow, where he spies a sad horse hitched to a painted Romani caravan. The wagon itself is striking, with its bow roof and sloping sides, its tin chimney and clerestory windows and brightly colored scrollwork under the eaves. But it's the horse—a woebegone piebald rackabones—that catches Chaim's eye.

"I have to paint it," he proclaims aloud.

Milling about outside the wagon are what Chaim assumes are a family of gypsies. They're removing pots and utensils from a still-smoldering campfire, carrying them along with various properties—ropes and Indian clubs—up the steps of the caravan. How, wonders Chaim, will they all fit into that wagon: the man and woman whom he takes for the father and mother, and their litter of children graduated in age from tykes to adolescents? All are outfitted in garments the hybrid of ordinary peasant attire and gala theatrical costumes. Beneath their smock-frocks and embroidered chemises, both sexes wear garish leggings of azure, lilac, and rose. While the parents exhort the older children to help with packing the van, the little ones turn somersaults and walk on their hands like the monkeys Chaim has seen in the Jardin des Plantes. The head of one hand-walking little girl is hidden by her inverted muslin skirt, her skinny legs twitching in the air like a rabbit's ears.

Chaim approaches them gingerly and explains to the tall, loose-jointed, mustachioed fellow he takes for the paterfamilias that he would like to paint his horse.

"He wants to paint Ethelinda!" the man exclaims in amusement, his fruity accent redolent of southern climes. "And what color would you like to paint her? Don't you think her current motley is becoming enough?" The last of the sunlight glints off the ring in his ear.

"I mean," says Chaim, trying to contain himself, "I want to paint her portrait."

The man tugs at the brim of his feathered hat in a gesture of thoughtfulness. "No," he concludes, "I don't like that you should encourage her vanity."

Chaim bristles; the man is making game of him. "I can pay you," he offers, though when he turns out his pockets he finds only biscuit crumbs.

The gypsy sniffs, having had his fun, then shouts to the others to get a move on; they're booked for tomorrow at a hall in Rambouillet. He squints above a line of trees toward a sky already streaked with red and grumbles to himself that they'll have to travel through the night. Then, remembering Chaim, he says rather off-handedly, "We are the Family Petulengro, acrobats, jugglers, and funambulists extraordinaire."

Chaim takes off running up the path to the château. He's not used to running, and by the time he finds Madame Castaing reclining in the library with a fashion magazine, the sweat is pouring off him in rills. "Come with me, I beg you!" he gasps without pausing to catch his breath. "I've found such a lovely horse that almost human it looks. Such a lovely animal I will never find again . . ." He snatches her hand, barely conscious of the liberty he takes in doing so, and tugs her stumbling in her pumps out the double doors. He drags her protesting through the French windows and across the marble terrace, through the garden and all the way down the hill into the turf-grass meadow. There, while she's still demanding to know his intent, he presents her with the sight of a downtrodden nag in its traces. Its coat is caked in mud, its visible ribs studded with weeping sores: a crime that, in lieu of a team to pull the ponderous wagon, this solitary, struggling animal must suffice.

"Her eyes are human eyes!" cries Chaim. "The strength she don't even have it to lie down for the merciful release." (Madeleine double-takes at his logic.)

The caravan is already in motion, Monsieur Petulengro seated on his box, holding the reins in one hand. In his other he holds a knotted stockwhip with which he switches Ethelinda's bony rump. The wagon sways from the weight of its many passengers, some of whom cling to the rear or perch on the roof. They wave to Madame Castaing, who they haven't yet realized is trying to flag them down.

"Wait!" calls Chaim, jogging alongside the wagon, which Monsieur Petulengro ultimately reins to a halt. He can see that the lady who's accompanied the artist is quality and so climbs down from his seat. Negotiations ensue, and though the gypsy adopts a gushingly ingratiating manner, he drives a hard bargain. They must be compensated for both their engagement at Lèves and for the one they will have to postpone on the following day. Madeleine ruefully agrees and Monsieur Petulengro enjoins his family to prepare for an evening performance. Ethelinda is unhitched and begins cropping grass with her few remaining teeth. Chaim hastens to fetch his brushes and oils.

On short notice the Castaings' servants have assembled a semi-circle of velvet-tufted bergère armchairs on the back terrace. They

have commandeered as many chamber lamps as can be found on
the premises and placed them at intervals along the window ledges
and balustrades. At no small risk to their persons they've hung
storm lanterns from the limbs of the enormous willow that sweeps
the terrace and looms over it. Fireflies are attracted to the lanterns
as if to their mothers. The mid-July night is sultry, the moon having emerged from behind the clouds like an egg from excelsior.
The breeze is a caress. It is all in all an ideal evening for a troupe of
traveling saltimbanques to present their skills before an audience
of the cultural elite.

The guests, an illustrious assortment of weekend pilgrims to
Lèves, whisper among themselves regarding the oddity of the entertainment. Nevertheless, they pay artful compliments to Madeleine
and Marcellin (who can't stop gazing askance at his wife) for
providing such an original surprise. The Family Petulengro have
meanwhile discarded the remnants of their common garb to reveal
the full splendor of their spangled costumes. Then, with operatic
gesticulations, they set about proving themselves the consummate
professionals that Père Petulengro's bombastic introduction has declared them to be. They commence performing feats of such physical virtuosity that even Cocteau is at a loss for his typically barbed
comments at their expense. The novelist Louise de Vilmorin, whose
Julietta is inspired by her much-publicized yearning for Madeleine
Castaing, finds it hard to maintain her signature boredom, while
the gallant young sculptor Iché laughs to the extent that his lungs,
seared by mustard gas at Belleau Wood, will allow. André Derain,
also up for the weekend, is similarly delighted. (He expresses his
glee by taking every occasion to utter lewd remarks in the ear of his
latest mistress—remarks principally concerning the budding anato-
mies of the young girls executing backbends.) All are in fact a little
embarrassed by the degree to which they are genuinely thrilled.

The Petulengros juggle balls, clubs, and lit Roman candles while dancing on a slack rope strung between a balcony and the garden pergola; they make cat leaps, turn handsprings and double back-flips over pyramids of their crouching siblings. They leap from the top of a stepladder onto a teeterboard, which catapults their brothers and sisters onto the shoulders of the ones who've gone before. In this way they erect a human tower that tapers as it rises from its foundation of strapping young men to the boys and lissome girls standing above them. When the tower has reached its penultimate height, Monsieur Petulengro himself—his gaunt frame supplemented by a fishing vest hung with lead sinkers—jumps from the ladder onto the board. At the other end stands a twig of a boy billed as "the infant prodigy," who is directly sent somersaulting skyward to the summit of the heap. Then comes the pièce de résistance: the tower topples, collapsing over the terrace steps and spilling the entire family onto mattresses spread there in preparation for their fall. All except the infant prodigy, who is left hanging from a star—or so the pickled Maurice Sachs, lamenting his long-lost innocence, will later insist.

After the event both guests and performers are directed to a buffet laid out on trestles in the glass-enclosed orangery. Cigarettes are crushed at the base of the potted citrus trees; the artist Derain plucks a priceless orchid to stick in his mistress's décolletage. All help themselves to charcuterie, cheese and onion tarts, foie gras duck au jus and dauphinois casserole, platters of escargots, Cognac shrimp, and chocolate cream crepes. Servants discreetly ensure the bottomlessness of the champagne flutes. Men make lecherous suggestions to the nubile acrobats while their ladies even the score by teasing the "ephebes," as Maurice Sachs calls them. (He offers one his birthright in exchange for a squeeze.) The troupe, however, has the last laugh; for after their departure, it's discovered that a number of precious household ornaments and utensils have gone missing from the château.

"Theirs will be the only Romani caravan," observes the blasé Cocteau, "whose interior is appointed in le style Castaing."

Small matter. The thefts are written off as included in the price of admission. The real regret, as Drieu La Rochelle avers, is that this banner evening has not been recorded for posterity. Where are Picasso, Dufy, or Chagall, who, like Lautrec and Degas before them, might have known how to do justice to such a spectacle? Where, incidentally, is the resident peintre?—though no one would expect him to concern himself with the kind of circus imagery that has so often captivated his counterparts. Maurice recommends that Soutine be left to his dead and disemboweled animals, or, in their absence, an animal nearly as good as dead.

To wit, Ethelinda, whom Chaim has surrounded by guttering beeswax candles in bronze candlesticks. Every available lantern has been enlisted for the presentation, so that he must rely on the candles he's placed strategically in the grass about the listless horse. Those and the candle he's stuck to his palette in its own melting wax (and an ivory moon) are his only source of light. But they're enough. He mixes into his oils the dusky shades the candlelight lends them, though God only knows what colors they will reveal at dawn. The wretched horse stands spindle-shanked in its ring of flames still munching grass, mashing it between ragged gums. Its tail has been docked to keep it from interfering with the driver's switch; its hooves are cracked, its back so swayed that its belly nearly grazes the ground. Midges halo its great, runny-eyed head and the semiliquid feces that dribble from its hindquarters. Chaim is not entirely deluded: he's aware that in painting the horse he's painting a self-portrait as well. Only instead of the wounded monstrosities he's reproduced from his own mirror image in the past, this one is conveyed with affection and a catch in the heart. He believes he can already hear the judgment of his critics: "Soutine's butchered birds and bunnies are more alive than this poor, depleted jade." And they will be right, although missing the point.

Once the gypsies have hitched Ethelinda back up to the wagon and goaded her into motion, Chaim wonders whether she even has the stamina to reach the next town. Or perhaps she will persevere a while longer in some mechanical lockstep beyond exhaustion before her bones give out and her carcass is sold for glue. *Makht nisht oys*, the artist will have no need to mourn her, having already rescued her from her appointed fate.

Elysium begins to take its toll on Chaim's internal organs and his ulcers send him back to the doctors in Paris. When he's had enough of Paris, he returns to the Château de Lèves. Then it's back to Paris, then Lèves again, with detours via Cagnes and the mineral baths of Châtel-Guyon along the way. This is the restless itinerant routine he will follow throughout the decade of the thirties, a restlessness that also informs his time in the city. Change your place and change your luck, goes the saying, but Chaim's constant movement seems more in the service of eluding the snares of good fortune. Toward that end he moves from the rue d'Orléans to the boulevard Edgar Quinet, then the passage d'Enfer, the rue de la Tombe Issoire, and finally la Villa Seurat—all addresses within the greater vicinity of the Parc Montsouris. (His friend Chana Orloff also has her custom-built atelier in la Villa Seurat, as do the tapestry artist Jean Lurçat, the young Surrealist upstart Dalí, and the American writer Henry Miller, all of whom, with the exception of Orloff, Chaim avoids.) Despite his migratory existence, however, good fortune dogs his heels and his reputation grows. There is a major Soutine exhibition in Chicago, gallery shows in New York and London, work included in *Les maîtres de l'art indépendant* at the Petit Palais. None of which the artist attends. His elusiveness stokes his legend and he's spoken of in the galleries and the cafés, though often unfavorably by envious compeers. They talk of a tempering: how his models sadly no longer appear as if in the throes of rigor mortis; the dolls his children clutch have lost their look of demonic fetishes, his dead animals less like murder victims than suicides. But the trademark madness they miss is the very stuff he continues to seek out and destroy.

On rare occasions Chaim succumbs to the loneliness he will not own. Then he might show himself at the Select or the Dôme, his once natty Burberry drooping from his shoulders like worn-out wings. He sips his chamomile, smokes his Gauloises, and remarks, without wondering why, that there's a scarcity of old acquaintances at the neighboring tables. He pays scant attention to the to-do about a poster being plastered over the masonry wall across the boulevard. Then even as the liberal supporters of Léon Blum's Popular Front are attempting to raise the poster, right-wing thugs from the Croix de Feu have gathered to tear it down. Never especially political, Chaim is deaf to the loosening of tongues long suppressed since the national disgrace of the Dreyfus affair. He's only vaguely aware that, since the worldwide economic collapse, all the ills of the French Republic are once again being blamed on the Jews. Having been the perpetual background noise throughout his Lithuanian years, such charges are a commonplace almost too familiar to detect.

Just as familiar are the growing attacks on the artists of Montparnasse. "When they speak about Poussin, do they know the master? Have they ever really looked at a Corot?" (With my eyes staring out of their sockets! thinks Chaim.) "These are people from 'somewhere else' who in the bottom of their hearts look down on what Renoir has called the gentleness of the French School—that is, our race's virtue of tact." This from Louis Vauxcelles, himself a Jew, and from that turncoat Waldemar George: "The School of Paris is a house of cards, a sterile movement not likely of any development.

The moment has come for France to turn in upon herself and to find on her own soil the seeds of her salvation." Of course, such condemnations are mild when compared to the uncoded Jew-baiting jeremiads of the gutter press. But in spite of the increasingly hostile climate, Chaim feels never so insulated. After all, only nominally can he be considered a "Jewish" artist, what with a body of work rife with choirboys and communicants. He's even done an indelible tableau of the cathedral at Chartres.

What's more, the Castaings have taken over the management of his oeuvre. They buy everything he paints and what they don't keep for themselves, they sell to friends and place in high-class galleries—much to the dismay of Zborowski and Paul Guillaume, who together attempt to sue the Castaings. But since no formal contract has ever been drawn up between themselves and the artist, there are no grounds for litigation. Zbo makes little effort to conceal his bitterness: "After all I've done for you . . . ," but Chaim remains adamant in the face of his pleas. Paulette Jourdain, whose loyalties are hopelessly split, is sick at heart. Only after Léopold Zborowski's premature death from a massive coronary a year later and his burial in a pauper's grave does Chaim express any remorse toward the impractical dealer: "He was nasty to me and I never liked him, but"—sparing a shallow sigh—"I would not without his help have accomplished my work." The gallery owner Guillaume was also dead soon after, ostensibly by his own hand, though some blame the chicanery of his greedy wife.

Late one autumn evening in 1937, on the terrace of the Café du Dôme, Chaim is introduced to a young German woman in a knit half-cloak. The introduction is made by Arbit Blatas, another Litvak painter and self-declared disciple of Soutine. It seems that Chaim has disciples. He is presented to the woman, whose name is Gerda Groth-Michaelis, as a "great artist." (Chaim resists his old impulse to spit against the evil eye.) The woman seems duly impressed, perhaps even a little starry-eyed—her eyes dark as black currants with a slight Tartar slant. She is delicate-boned, her nose arched and chin sharp, waves of marcelled auburn hair framing her face. It's a pleasant face, demure if a touch vulpine; what the French might call *belle laide*. But while the weather is mild and the avenue populated only with quiet strollers, she still has the look of a woman who's taken shelter under the terrace awning from a storm.

It's an expression Chaim has seen recently in the pinched faces of the elementals. The shretelekh, the trio of imps he'd thought himself well rid of, have found him again in his studio on la Villa Seurat. They've returned after sowing their oats amid the costume balls and riotous soirées of the crazy years. They have appeared again, shame-faced and penitent, with yet enough temerity to try to needle the artist into painting their individual portraits. They fear that their long-lived physical incorruptibility may at last be in jeopardy.

Remaining obstinate, he declares, "I won't paint what don't exist!"

He inveighs against them with a virulence similar to that with which the citizens of France have begun railing against the flood of refugees. Why must these bogies beset him now when he's that close to feeling a measure of self-possession? It's this aggravation that has caused Chaim to moon about for extended spells in the cafés, seizing any trifling excuse to keep away from his apartment. He accepts invitations he would otherwise have refused, such as Gerda Groth's to an afternoon tea at her apartment on the boulevard Raspail.

6

IN SEPTEMBER OF 1914 Amedeo Modigliani, good Italian that he is, is caught up in the wave of French patriotic fervor. His admiring friend Chaim Soutine is caught up in the fervor of Amedeo's ad hoc patriotism.

"Make no mistake, Chaim," Modi assures him, "it's a war brought about by the colonial, imperial, and protectionist aspirations of the European industrial class. But, buon amico, we're cowards if we try to hide from history." Besides, the inseparable Derain and Vlaminck, Moïse Kisling, and the saber-rattling Apollinaire are already in uniform, and Modi will not be thought a slacker.

Chaim doesn't mind being thought of as a slacker. Or even a coward, for that matter. He doesn't really follow Modigliani's reasoning and figures it's his fourth or fifth *fine à l'eau* at the Rotonde speaking; he'll think better of his resolution when he's sober. Though when is the Tuscan ever sober? But despite his better judgment, Chaim is susceptible as always to his friend's impetuosity; he is swayed as well by Modi's argument (however misguided) that citizenship will follow automatically upon their enlistment. So, with a world of misgivings, Chaim accompanies his comrade in penury to one of the induction centers that have cropped up all around the city. The nearest is in a Catholic hospital on the rue d'Assas. There they join the long queue of butchers, bakers, haberdashers, civil servants, pimps. There are besmirched sewer-men up from the tunnels, pudding-faced pigeon fatteners from les Halles, bookmakers, wrestlers, underage boys, and toothless old men. In short, every species of Parisian male is waiting to volunteer. The line winds around the building but moves swiftly, as the men are processed and dispatched into an infinitude of terrors.

In the vestibule, plastered with the propaganda posters featuring *le coq gaulois* that have appeared everywhere overnight, they are told to undress. They're given bicycle baskets in which to place their clothes. Some of the men are sinewy and hard from their labors; others waddle forward amid floes of adipose flesh. They are swag-bellied, stoop-shouldered, jaundiced, buttocks and backs dense with hair like animal fur. Among them, Modigliani's slim, alabaster physique practically glows, and no one is more conscious of his beauty than he. To further distinguish himself from the lumpen herd, he declaims aloud a phrase from his cherished Dante.

"'Hope not to see heaven, for I have come to lead you to the other shore.'"

In this way he provokes the animosity of all within his hearing.

Chaim feels guilt by association, a feeling that only intensifies the debasement his nakedness always inspires in him. He hides his circumcised schwantz as best he can behind the basket of clothes, which leaves the rest of him still exposed and vulnerable. He's ashamed of his shapeless body and the marks of his childhood punishments still visible over his shoulders and the backs of his thighs. The building is cold and the goose bumps make his skin resemble the rind of some albino fruit.

Having tucked his basket under an arm, Modi strides forward preceded by his conspicuously Yid genitalia. It's difficult to stride where others can only shuffle. At each station of the physical examination—eye, ear, and anal—he cites Dante's descent into another circle of the inferno. The overtaxed, white-jacketed physicians on their swiveling stools are not diverted. The only doctor to show even a flicker of humor is the one who puts a stethoscope to Amedeo's chest and declares, "Your lungs sound like a concrete mixer." After which a document is stamped, promptly disqualifying him from military service.

"You can't reject me!" cries the outraged Italian. "*Sans blague,*" he shouts, "don't you know the path to paradise begins in hell?" As if paradise was what he'd been denied admission to.

The officer in charge has had enough of him and summons a couple of husky subordinates to escort Modi from the building. As they hustle him out, Chaim can hear his parting shot to the enlisting men: "When you tell me your deity made you in his image, I reply he must be a very ugly deity!" Chaim hopes his extravagant friend remembers to put his clothes back on in the street.

Then, albeit unreasonably, Chaim is resentful at having been left to face the situation on his own. (Give or take the thirty thousand reservists who the papers claim have already been mobilized.) What, after all, does this war have to do with him? There's a saddleback goose back at la Ruche hanging from a hook in the corner of Pinchus Krémègne's studio, where he's sought sanctuary since Miestchaninoff gave him the boot. It's intolerable that the fate of the Republic should take precedence over his howling need to paint that goose. But Chaim's infirmities are not as detectable as Modi's. Regardless of the panic that sets his heart racing and his stomach secreting toxins, the gauntlet of examining doctors judge him fit.

Even before the physical is over, the threat to the nation has increased. Word has arrived from the *pis aller* front that both French and British troops have fallen back to the River Marne; the Boche are less than fifty kilometers from Paris. It's urgent that the city be protected. Without being formally inducted or even issued a uniform, Chaim is jolted into motion by a series of barked orders from the NCOs. He's marched into the street and stuffed along with a mob of frightened others into one of a fleet of Renault landaulet cabs. Blaring their horns, the taxis career along the avenues past monuments and over bridges—how much of this filigreed city Chaim has yet to see! They tear through the decaying banlieue known as the Zone and out into the provinces. Snug villages, smoke curling lazily from their chimneys, are cradled among rolling yellow-green pastures that make for an unlikely no-man's-land. But the thunder in the distance on this fair afternoon is not thunder.

Once he's been pried from the taxi, Chaim is handed a shovel, as is the befuddled phalanx of several hundred others, and told to dig a trench. They're given the precise measurements for the excavation in shouted instructions as confounding to the artist as those God gave to Noah. Chaim turns this way and that, sees himself as one segment of a millipede whose undulant spine stretches from horizon to horizon. He remarks the stillness of the earth between its spasms of trembling, smells the purple coneflowers and hears the birdsong. Then more shouts: *Poilus, bêchez!* and Chaim shakes off his stupor along with the rest of his detail; he begins to gouge the moist soil, opening what quickly becomes a long wound in the halcyon landscape. But soon the cramps begin, a familiar symptom of the ulcerative colitis whose diagnosis the military doctors have missed. Doubled over and groaning, he tries to persist in his task, convinced now that he's digging his own grave.

In consequence, he is mustered out before having been properly mustered in, and left to make his own way back to the city on foot. Along the road the troop trucks pass him, fresh soldiers gazing at the wretch staggering in the opposite direction with a combination of envy and contempt. He gets a lift in a wagon hauling pumpkins as far as the Marché Bastille, his innards jarred by every bump and pothole into exquisite pain. By the time he arrives at la Ruche he's less man than mortal remains. He lies in a fetal curl on the improvised plank bed in the corner of Pinchus's studio like refuse that's been swept there. Feeling guilty for having evicted him, Miestchaninoff brings him a bottle of buttermilk to help douse the flames in his gut (though the sculptor is not so guilty that he succumbs to Krémègne's pleas to take him back again). Days pass before he's visited by Modigliani.

"Take comfort, mon vieux," says Modi, "the Republic has decided to award you the Croix de Guerre."

"Funny person," breathes Chaim. He's feeling better but has yet to find a reason to leave his pallet. Krémègne complains to the Tuscan that his studio is in need of airing out: "Soutine is beginning to putrefy and his odor is peeling the paint on my enamels." Chaim himself supposes he ought to change out of his sour clothes and empty the contents of the chamber pot under his makeshift bed, but still he can't be bothered. He opens an eye to see that Modi, wearing his felt Borsalino and frayed strawberry cravat, has apparently recovered from his fiery indignation.

"The Battle of the Marne is won," he announces in a remarkably solicitous voice, "and all good patriots are obliged to celebrate." He grasps Chaim under the arms in an effort to force him to rise and, failing that, plunks himself down on the planks beside him.

But Chaim is perfectly capable of getting up on his own. Modi steps out on the landing to smoke under the cracked glass rotunda, while his *copain* exchanges his noisome garments for some less foul. Chaim wonders how he can be so glad to see his reprobate companion while at the same time decrying the plunge into degeneracy that his presence gives notice to. What is it about the Italian that so tempts him to take that plunge?

The fighting might be only miles away, the sky faintly droning with the sound of Gotha bombers, but from the mood at the Rotonde you'd have thought the war was nothing more than grist for the gossip mill. The mirrored walls advertise as ever their house apéritifs in gilded Belle Époque characters; the cane chairs are filled with ladies in shirtwaists and pearls, gentlemen in putty-colored plus fours. They sip their gin fizzes and speak of the craze for hypnosis and the loves of Mistinguett, turn their heads in unison at the klaxon of a flame-red Bugatti driven by the impresario Diaghilev. Unaccompanied women are prohibited, but who's to object if the likes of the monocled Violet Trefusis and Misia Sert, who rivals Madame Castaing as a "collector of geniuses," should choose to accompany each other? Max Jacob gives free play to his envenomed tongue at a farewell party the Delaunays have thrown for themselves before departing for Spain. Jean Cocteau (without whom no scene is complete) stares daggers at the willowy model his "protégé" Raymond Radiguet, alias Monsieur Bébé, is flirting with. ("Baby is depraved!" he cries in disbelief. "He likes girls!") Père Libion in his apron makes a mock pursuit after Kiki and her coltish friend Thérèse Treize, who've made off with a bottle of Pouilly-Fuissé, and a blue cloud of Lucky Strike smoke hangs over all.

Chaim and Modi have settled into a banquette in the café's less crowded interior. Chaim still fluctuates between adulation of his friend and resentment for the bad habits Modigliani has inveigled him into; though tonight he leans more toward allegiance, and finds himself perilously near to relaxing in the Italyaner's robust company. Neither of them, however, has the price of a drink. Modi has removed a charcoal pencil from an otherwise empty pocket and, securing a paper place mat with an elbow, has begun to sketch a lady at a neighboring table. Her face is equine, eyes querulous under the brim of an overlarge leghorn hat. The artist completes the drawing in a matter of minutes, then reaches across to show the woman his composition. "Only ten centimes," he says. "Cheap at twice the price." She receives the sketch with little interest and, after a passing glance, averts her eyes as if in pain. Her gentleman companion snatches it from her hand and takes a cursory look before crumpling the drawing in a fist and tossing it over his shoulder. A sport nonetheless, he throws some coins onto the artist's table.

Several sketches and snifters of Armagnac later, Chaim looks on in well-oiled admiration as Modi mounts a chair to recite a verse from Dante. " 'Amor, che ne la menti mi ragione' . . .," he declaims. "Love, with delight, courses in my mind . . ."There is a smattering of applause when he pauses to draw a breath, though it's unclear whether it's meant to encourage or conclude his performance. Still, the majority of the café's population is composed of bohemian brethren tending to be well disposed to the artist's impromptu exhibitions. This is not, however, the attitude of a patron at a nearby table. To his fellow topers the man observes in a voice clearly intended to be heard above Modi's recital, "Les métèques, foreign detritus."

Modi interrupts himself to bend an ear in the man's direction and, hearing further aspersions, steps down from the chair to confront his slanderer.

"Monsieur," he says, "I believe you're in the wrong place. The anti-Dreyfusard cafés are across the river and several years in the past." Though he knows that, on the contrary, there are diehards everywhere, who still believe that the honor of the French army supersedes the scapegoating of one inconsequential Israelite. To say nothing of the further defiling of the nation by a mongrel scourge that the curious can witness firsthand in such establishments as the Rotonde.

The heckler, obviously taken aback, endeavors to rise from his table. He's a large man, jowly and substantial of girth, and perhaps a little pot-valorous from too much chardonnay. With a helpful nudge from a comrade he's on his feet, his terraced chins at the level of Modi's fine nose. "Excuse me," he says a bit thickly, "but it's you and your kind that are in the wrong country altogether."

"My mistake," replies Modi, his flashing eyes giving away his enjoyment of the situation. "I was under the impression I was in France, but I seem to be in the Land of the Yahoos instead."

The reference may have been lost on the man, though he obviously intuits it isn't meant kindly. He puffs himself up beyond his already overfed avoirdupois to bluster accordingly, when Modi adds, "You don't matter enough to make me angry," and turns on his heel. Then, on second thought, he pivots back around and delivers a resounding slap to the man's beefy cheek.

"Amedeo Clemente Modigliani," he pronounces, "artist and Jew."

At that the habitués at the surrounding tables are brought to their feet, anticipating violence. A couple of Modi's partisans—André Salmon, the stroppy Manuel Ortiz de Zárate—are braced to come to his defense, if only by way of protecting the debts he owes them. But the injured party has his allies as well, prosperous-looking belligerents who have taken their positions on either side of him. In preparation for a possible dust-up Père Libion is seen to retrieve his cudgel from behind the bar. The struck man has placed a palm to his burning cheek, visibly rattled by the unexpected assault on his dignity. During the silence in which the café is suspended, he too offers his name:

"Hervé Charbonneau." And after another furtive prod from one of his companions: "At your service." That same companion whispers something in his ear, and Monsieur Charbonneau hands Modi his card and adds as if by rote, "It will be my distinct pleasure to reconvene with you, along with your second, at the Parc Montsouris at dawn."

Amazingly unruffled, Modi pipes, "Rapiers for two, coffee for one," saluting and clicking his heels like a music hall brigadier.

Monsieur Charbonneau's whispering comrade, whispering no longer, reminds the company, before he and his fellows vacate the premises, that his friend, as the insulted, will have the choice of weapons. The café remains in a state of agitation after their departure. Supporters of the artist have crowded round to commend him for calling out the xenophobe, while his more stalwart acquaintances plead his assurance that he has no intention of fighting a duel. "Je m'en fous," says Modi with a shrug. "Who fights a duel in nineteen-fourteen?" Modi's stalwarts heave a collective sigh of relief. Just then the artist's Litvak familiar, whose bowels were thrown into an uproar by the tense encounter, comes slouching out of the WC.

"Soutine," greets Modi, so that Chaim nearly turns back around to escape the attention, "you will be my second."

✦

SUNRISE AT LA RUCHE and the noises are already beginning to repeat those heard through its thin walls the night before: an accordion, a Spanish guitar, a voice denouncing di Chirico and the rage for *frottage* amid competing cries of erotic ecstasy. Provisionally awake in what so often feels like an alien body, Chaim hovers outside of himself, until he's tugged rudely back to his plank bed by a hand on his arm.

"Arise, Soutine!" chimes Modi. "It's time to fight the duel."

A duel? wonders Chaim, having forgotten the incident of the previous night. When memory returns, he feels his kishkes freeze. "You are not serious."

"Of course not," replies the Italian. "Nevertheless, I'm on my way to fight the duel. Get up!"

Chaim protests more fervently this morning than is his general custom: this is lunacy; though he knows he will surrender in the end to Modi's persuasion. Such fool's errands are a test of his loyalty, and besides, he should be present if, God forbid, things go awry. That said, the prospect of an actual duel remains wholly unreal. He rolls creakily from the planks still wearing the clothes he slept in and forgoes the ablutions he never performs in any case. He steps into his broken-backed espadrilles and swallows the wedge of congealed noodle pudding (not his own) from a dish on the windowsill; then he follows Modi down the stairs that spiral about the axis of a living laurel tree. They exit through the front door between stone caryatids, oblivious of their dotty founder, old Monsieur Boucher, talking to his pet donkey Solange among the hydrangeas.

Modigliani steps lively as if on the way to some festive event. He's in full feather this morning, sporting a cravat made from an apricot pompon tied to a piece of string, his corduroy coat brushed free of schmutz for the occasion. Slightly downwind from him in the passage de Dantzig, Chaim can smell the vapors from the spirits the artist has had for breakfast. They're met on the corner by a drinking companion of Modi's also grousing about having been roused from bed at such an hour. This is the cinematographer Achille Perret, a compact, poker-faced fellow carrying a tripod-mounted Pathé camera over his shoulder military-fashion. An acoustic megaphone swings from a loop at his hip.

On the long walk to the Parc Montsouris (since none have the fare for a hackney), Modi relates the tale of his last meeting with Paul Guillaume. The gallery owner had negotiated with him for a batch of drawings, forcing the price lower and lower still. When they'd settled on the bare minimum, Modi snatched up the drawings, poked a hole through them, and slipped a string through the hole. Then he took them to the washroom and hung them from the toilet chain.

"'They're yours,' I told him. 'Go wipe your ass with them.'"

Monsieur Perret is preoccupied, worrying aloud about the changing dawn light and the capacity of his camera lens to keep his figures within the frame. Chaim eyes him quizzically, then, coming at last to full consciousness of their destination, asks his friend, "You ain't afraid?"

"Who says I'm not?" replies an insouciant Amedeo. "But I take solace in the hallowed tradition of the duello among artists and poets." He recalls that their own Moïse Kisling has only recently fought a sword battle with Leopold Gottlieb, during which Kisling suffered a severed nostril. "He dubbed the scar the fourth partition of his Polish homeland." Then there are the legendary duels of the great Pushkin and Lermontov. "Of course," concedes Modigliani, "they died."

Chaim shudders. "You don't think you can too?"

"Chaim"—Modi's voice is infuriatingly composed—"my every third thought is of death."

Suddenly competitive, Chaim declares, "I don't think myself of nothing else!"

The streets are largely deserted, the tall houses still shuttered, leaves fallen from the plane trees skittering over the paving stones. A tattered citizen is spotted scurrying back—as Modi has it—to some convenient court of miracles. A draft horse with hooves the size of kettledrums hauls a cart piled high with cabbages and carrots toward the market of les Halles; a milk wagon deposits on doorsteps the bottles Chaim sometimes steals to relieve his stomach gripes. He knows these Paris mornings from his cockcrow excursions in search of work, though the business of survival has always precluded an appreciation of their singular spell.

Modi is quoting Baudelaire: "Here, hellcat! Come let us roll without remorse to celebrate a feud that never ends . . ."

Wonders Chaim: What can you do with such a man?

A chorus of starlings, numerous as the leaves of the yew tree they perch in, greets their entry into the park. The pale orange sky above the chimney pots and steeples is shading to blue. They ascend the hill to the monolithic Meridian Stone, which Modi claims marks the original site of Creation. There they are met by a small party showing marked signs of impatience. Monsieur Charbonneau, Modi's portly challenger, stands hatless in a silk brocade waistcoat, his thin hair, parted by the breeze, showing the rufous scalp beneath. His florid face is extremely grave. He's accompanied by his second, the stiff, whispering gentleman of the night before, and a sober-faced doctor with muttonchop whiskers gripping a hefty leather bag. The doctor, checking the hunter watch in his free hand, lets it be known that the arrival of Monsieur Modigliani and his associates is well past the appointed time.

"Please accept my humblest apologies," says Modi, adding quickly lest his words be construed as an apology for last night's altercation, "our driver took a wrong turn at the North Star." Meanwhile the cinematographer is busy spreading the legs of his tripod and threading film into his studio camera.

"What the devil?" Monsieur Charbonneau wants to know.

"It's the mechanism by which we may outlive our fate," replies Modi, eyes glassy from the morning's stimulant of choice. His adversary, whose own eyes are pink from broken capillaries, is not amused.

Calling the company's attention to the matter at hand, Monsieur Charbonneau's second has somewhat self-importantly begun recounting the basic tenets of the code duello: "In exercising his prerogative as the offended, His Honor Hervé Charbonneau, Sitting Magistrate to the Court of Petty Sessions, has selected as his weapon—" when he's interrupted by Monsieur Perret.

Having turned his flat cap around, the cinematographer is asking the group, needlessly through his megaphone, to please gather closer together, the better to balance what he calls his "establishing shot."

"Shut that fool up!" bellows the increasingly disconcerted Charbonneau, while Modi hides a smile behind his sleeve.

As no further concessions are asked for or offered, the officiating second has produced from a satchel a handsome morocco-bound case. He opens it with some ceremony to reveal a matching pair of walnut-stocked, brass-barreled, flintlock dueling pistols. At sight of the burnished weapons, Chaim feels his stomach turn over as on a spit. The kugel he bolted for breakfast makes a bid to return as Modi hands him for safekeeping his coat, a lit cigarette, and his pocket volume of *Les chants de Maldoror*. But what Chaim fails to realize in his distress is what Achille Perret's film will clearly show when it's later projected on the water-stained wall at Chez Rosalie: that Amedeo's opponent, unnerved by his antagonist's lighthearted demeanor, is easily as tremulous as Chaim himself.

✦

PRACTICALLY THE ENTIRE *CORPS d'elite* of Montparnasse turns out for it, or at least that portion whom the war has left in place. They are crammed into Madame Rosalie's narrow establishment in the rue Campagne-Première, having paid their six sous at the door to view the farce. (The community-minded Rosalie has ruled, over Modi's token objections, that the take be distributed among the neighborhood soup kitchens.) Jules Pascin is seated at a table with his wife and mistress, joined there by his eminence Pablo Picasso with his lynx-eyed gypsy consort Pâquerette. (She wears a necklace of gold coins and chews the stem of a rose.) Max Jacob, Blaise Cendrars, Mademoiselle Kiki and her current lover Gustav (his surname unpronounceable), and the omnipresent Jean Cocteau are also present, along with assorted shady denizens of the quarter. It's a rowdy assemblage made all the more restless by the poor quality of the picture's opening: The thirty-five-millimeter film flickers and stalls; the title, *Une affaire d'honneur*, judders beyond legibility; the dramatis personae, distorted by the irregular surface of the plaster wall, appear to be moving about in a storm of cinders. Then, as the film advances, the storm subsides.

The scrolled letters of the intertitle, "The Field of Honor," briefly obscure the action; then they vanish to reveal the moment that Monsieur Charbonneau's second displays the firearms. The audience snickers, then bursts into full-throated laughter as Modi inspects the single-shot flintlocks—about which he naturally knows nothing—like a connoisseur. His moonfaced challenger, looking on almost wistfully, is seen to be saying something for which another intertitle provides the tag.

"These are the pistols with which my father shot himself in the foot to avoid conscription."

The audience guffaws.

Modi is next seen handing the case containing the pistols to his own overwrought second, the Litvak paint-dauber Soutine, whose hands are already full. "It is the duty of the challenged man's second to load the firearms," reads the quotation. The film then reveals Chaim fumbling to hang on to his friend's belongings while attempting, without a clue of course, to distinguish between the priming pan and the business end of a gun. The challenger's man peevishly relieves him of the task, prompting another surge of hilarity from the spectators. But the merriment is subdued as Charbonneau's stilted confrere strides the lawn in his polished top boots, marking off the prescribed twenty-five paces; he then signals the duelists to take their places at either extremity of the field. They are instructed, as a new tag proclaims, to aim their weapons at each other's vital parts. At this point even Max Jacob suspends the irreverent commentary he's been mouthing into Cocteau's ear. The entire restaurant has fallen silent but for the snicker-snack of the limelight projector. All are respectful of the scoundrel Modigliani, who, often incapable of walking a straight line, stands firm and impassive in the face of his adversary's cocked firearm.

For his part, Monsieur Charbonneau on his opposing patch of grass appears to have been stricken with a palsy. At first you might have attributed his wavering arm and knocking knees to the jiggety nature of the film, but then it becomes apparent that he's suffering from a lily-livered funk. His head snaps toward the camera to bark a curse at the cinematographer ("Your mother should have swallowed you!" says the title), who has presumably shouted some further inscrutable instruction. When he turns back toward his foe, his arm is seen to recoil as a shower of sparks is released from the muzzle of his gun. Modi's brazen grin attests to the fact that the shot has gone wide of its mark. He lets drop the hand holding the pistol and slowly raises his other, aiming two fingers and a cocked thumb point-blank at his challenger. The tag, in sync with the movement of Modi's lips, reads, "Bang!" as flames shoot from his fingers. Monsieur Charbonneau—as does incidentally Chaim Soutine—drops to the ground in a dead faint.

The audience erupts again in gales of laughter.

But the film is not over. Monsieur Perret, master illusionist, has edited it to show the horizontal magistrate in the act of actually giving up the ghost. The ectoplasmic specter of Modi's fallen enemy rises out of the man's watch pocket to receive its harp and wings. The crowd at Chez Rosalie is transfixed, but the cinematographer's vanity won't allow him to leave it at that. He must explain the complex methods behind his effects: how the fireball emanating from Modi's fingers (which still remain singed) was produced from cotton paper soaked in nitro-cellulose; how the fallen man's ghost was created by the ingenious employment of a process invented by the German Eugen Schüfftan . . . But by now no one is listening, for this is a gathering that prefers illusion to truth. Then Amedeo Modigliani, who has yet to sell a single painting in his ill-starred career, is toasted by all as a hero among artists, while his sidekick Soutine is tolerated by virtue of their odd association.

The film is rumored to have survived to this day, though generations of postgraduates have combed the archives with no success.

7

GASTON BABINEAUX, LONGTIME VETERAN of the Brigade Fluvial, is bewildered as to why he's unable to haul the diver up from the bottom of the river. Ordinarily a tug at the safety line should bring him bobbing with relief to the surface. I could have told him, however, that added to the considerable weight of the diver's boots, belt, and copper breastplate is the burden of years Chaim is also schlepping along the bed of the Seine. Monsieur Babineaux scratches a whiskery cheek and checks the pressure gauge on the compressor case again; he worries that continued rebreathing of the same inert gas has depleted the oxygen to a level that may no longer support consciousness. Meanwhile, his birchwood and brass apparatus has drawn onlookers; children have gathered to watch him cranking the flywheel like the handle of a tuneless hurdy-gurdy. The old plongeur shoos them away, gives the cord another tug to no avail, and turns the crank again in sheer perplexity.

The diver is baffled as well, wondering why he has never been able to draw pictures other than from life itself. Why, for instance (circa 1907), has he lured the shtetl half-wit Dudl Harelip into the trees behind the ritual bath to sketch his portrait? Chaim baits him with a piece of sunflower halvah he pinched from a market barrel. The theft alone, never mind the disgrace of the drawing, could earn him a pitiless thrashing and internment in the cellar—which, notwithstanding the spiders, rats, and demidemons, has become over time a kind of second home. But why can he not make his portraits from memory and in secret, instead of exposing himself and his subjects to reviling eyes? Still, the risk is nothing when compared to the sweet celestial confusion he feels when depicting the thing itself.

Then it's thirty years later and he has yet to understand the compulsion. Just as he hadn't understood the impulse, twenty years before, to rehearse his own suicide at la Ruche: when he took the noose from the neck of the rabbit he'd hung up for a still life and placed it around his own. Krémègne found him like that under a rafter in his studio and never forgave him. But it's 1937 and he still persists and is still being derided for his painting, he and his kind. Where the School of Paris was once defended as a healthy cosmopolitanism, it is now attacked as pernicious cultural pollution. Phrases like "the Jewish question" and "the Jewish problem" appear frequently in the conservative press. *Le Figaro* has assembled an anthology of its chauvinistic articles in a volume entitled *Les métèques contre l'art français*. That Judas, Waldemar George, now a full-blown fascist apologist, writes of l'École de Paris: "The term is a conscious, premeditated conspiracy against the notion of a school of France. It is a hypocritical sign of the spirit of Francophobia and has no legitimacy. Shouldn't France repudiate the works that weaken her genius?" Such defamation is a complement to the voices denouncing the Jew Léon Blum and his Popular Front. The viperish Charles Maurras, who has picked up where he left off after his malevolent anti-Dreyfus crusade, calls in *Réaction* for alternately shooting, lynching, cutting the throat of, and guillotining Prime Minister Blum.

Chaim is not exactly indifferent to such noises; it's just that for him they're nothing new. Would that he could ignore the return of the shretelekh as easily as the burgeoning antipathy toward the Yids.

They roost in the rucks of his drop cloth, perch on his paint box, and materialize from the spout of his turpentine jug—Semangelof and his brothers, with their pigeon breasts and scaly rooster toes. Laila is back as well, though having had her kicks, she seems tempered, wanting only to be friends. They're nostalgic, expressing their longing for moonlit synagogue ruins and the maggoty outhouses they once called home; they miss the mystical books they originated from.

"I thought you came from the splendorish Upper Eden," taunts Chaim.

"The books," replies their spokesman Semangelof, "preceded Heaven."

"Then go already back in the books!"

"We can't," they croak in concert; then Semangelof: "The Nazis have burned them all, *a finster yor.*"

Chaim accuses them once more of nonexistence. "You're nothing but in my brain the bubbles from one time when I was underwater too long. You're a sick fancy that I can stick my hand clear through you." But when he pokes a forefinger toward the belly of one of the creatures, expecting ether, he's revolted by the contact with a spongelike solidity. Close to weeping, he asks again what he's never really wanted to know: "Why you pick on me?" and has his worst fears confirmed.

"You're like family."

To get away from them he heads out for the Vélodrome d'Hiver. The undefeated Marcel Cerdan, aka le Bombardier Marocain, is fighting the ferocious challenger Delannoit tonight. But doesn't Chaim have another engagement? Tahkeh, that German woman at the Dôme (what was her name?) had asked him to a tea party. He curls his lip at the prospect of a tea party. And hasn't he anyway misplaced the address? But this is only wishful thinking.

The little gathering in her small apartment on the boulevard Raspail was scheduled to convene at four thirty, but Chaim doesn't arrive until nearly seven o'clock. The hostess Gerda Groth-Michaelis has been warned by the artist Blatas, also one of her guests, that tardiness is often the case with Soutine. But Madame Groth—she was married to an architect and divorced before fleeing to Paris—has long since given up on his appearing. A pity, since she'd been somewhat intrigued by the hint of ironic gaiety she thought she'd detected in his eyes, and the gracefulness of his parchment-white hands. Then he knocks and is admitted, making no apologies, just as the party is beginning to break up. He's wearing one of his once stylish suits, unlaundered since the previous decade; his hair hangs over an eye like a sheepdog's and he reeks of the cologne he douses himself with in lieu of a bath. Though the other guests are saying their farewells, Madame Groth, too courteous to turn him away, invites the tactless artist to stay and have tea.

At his customary loss for words, Chaim compliments the spray of pansies in the bowl on the table adjacent to his chair, though in truth the spaniel faces of their petals make him uncomfortable. The Hôtel de la Paix is not a fashionable address, but Madame Groth has tried to cozy up her tiny flat as far as her meager housekeeper's salary will permit. Does he discern a note of self-pity in her voice as she gives a brief account of her situation? On second thought, no; it's just the regulation melancholy of the displaced. Chaim sips the tea, which he has liberally diluted with milk—for the sake of his stomach issues, he explains. He also declines her homemade *tarte tatin* for the same reason. They sit a while in an awkward silence, while Chaim wonders why he's come. The woman is pleasant enough, her ankles slender below the biased hem of her long wrap dress, and there is a warmth in her vixenish face. But the forced gentility of their circumstance makes him wish even more to be lost in the clamorous anonymity of the crowd at the Vél d'Hiv.

"Madame Groth," he begins, her German surname rankling a bit on his tongue; he's never been fond of Germans (even when they're Jews), and likes them less every day. "Madame Groth, I don't suppose you will like to attend with me a pugilistic event?" he asks, confident that she will refuse. But to his utter inexpectancy she shrugs her shoulders and says in her heavily accented French, "Pourquoi non?"

Right away he wants to disinvite her; she will no doubt be squeamish and intimidated by the raucous spectators and their savage cries for blood. But once they've arrived and taken their seats in the resounding vastness of the stadium, she maintains an almost prim composure; she behaves as if she has accompanied him to an opera or ballet rather than to a pitched gladiatorial combat. Satisfied with (if a bit daunted by) the woman's reserve, Chaim promptly forgets her and allows himself to become absorbed in the spectacle. He thrills to the sounds of leather punishing flesh, audible even at their height in the stands; he shouts his encouragement at each well-aimed blow. The Bombardier, dominant from the outset, seems at times to be holding up his staggering opponent in order to sustain a little longer the man's demolition. Delannoit's face is a gory pulp; he swings his arms wildly as if trying to find his assailant in the dark.

Meanwhile Madame Groth, having turned away from the battlers, studies the artist's profile instead. His response to the contest is nearly as disturbing as the contest itself. The glaring lights of the arena augment the sallowness of his complexion, the grime in his ears. She's been told that this Soutine is an original, a painter of the first order, yet here he is behaving like the grossest roughneck. He apes the punches and jabs, recoils from a haymaker so that you'd think he was in the ring himself. So completely does he identify with the fighters that he remains bent double after the Bombardier has delivered an especially powerful blow to the other man's solar plexus. It's a punch Chaim doesn't seem able to recover from, and he looks up in apparent agony to say that he must leave the stadium. Madame Groth is confused.

"It's my ulcers," he explains, attempting to rise from his seat and failing until the woman helps him to stand.

He leans against her as together they hobble out into the busy rue Nélaton. On the sidewalk Chaim feels as afflicted by the skirmishing carnival lights of the city as by the pain in his stomach. Everything both without and within burns and stabs. Ashamed of his helplessness, he manages, "I think I swallowed a dragon that in my belly breathes fire." The woman squeezes his hand, tells him she will take him home, and he surrenders to her care. She hails a cab and bundles him into the backseat, asks his address to give the driver. At 18 Villa Seurat she pays a fare she can ill afford and helps him up the stairs to his atelier. She dredges his pocket for a key and opens the door to an apartment that, once she locates a lamp, resembles less a domicile than a transient's encampment. Paint-stiffened garments hang from the open door of a wardrobe; unwashed dishes, inexplicably dispersed, fill the blackened maw of a hearth. The metal casters of the sleigh bed, perhaps jolted about in the night by a troubled sleeper, have left deep grooves in the wooden floor. Unearthly odors of an almost palpable density permeate the rooms.

"You live here like an abandoned cat," gasps Madame Groth, her tone somewhere between sympathy and reproof.

She sees him to the disarranged bed, loosens his tie, and removes his jacket and shoes, though decorum forbids her undressing him further. Then, decorum be damned, the man is suffering—so she lays him down and strips him of all but his grotty shorts and singlet. He brings his knobby knees to his chin as she covers him, and mutters the incantatory words "pink bismuth." Her heels crunch the carapaces of dead cockroaches as she inspects his arsenal of prescription physics on a shelf above the sink in the kitchenette. She warms some Vichy water on the stove for him to swallow after his spoonful of medicine. Then she returns to administer the palliative, tenderly lifting the back of his head to do so; she sits in a Windsor chair beside the bed until he shows signs that the intensest pain has passed. Content that he might now fall asleep, she's getting up to depart when she feels a hand grasp her wrist.

"Don't leave me," he pleads, scarcely recognizing the voice that would make such a request. He closes his eyes and is amazed when, after a dream that his sac was a coin purse, he wakes in the morning to find her still there. She's asleep in the chair next to the bed, the faintest sough of a snore issuing from her parted damson lips.

He feels better. What's more, he sees the place has been tidied, dishes washed, scattered clothes restored to hangers and drawers, the floor swept clean of cigarette butts and trash. There's a trace of camphor in the air. Then Chaim is seized with the anxious thought that her cleaning zeal might have extended to the adjoining studio. He wraps the blanket around his shoulders and shuffles into the east-facing room to find all still in its proper disarray. Missing, however (and good riddance), is any sign of the elemental creatures that have harassed him again of late. Has she swept them away as well? It occurs to him that, as a German from an assimilated family, she bore none of the superstitious baggage the uncultured Ashkenazim carried with them into the West. Perhaps the hobgoblins have vanished in the face of an incredulity that exceeded even his own. He approaches the woman again and stoops to better examine her features in slumber. Not beautiful, she is pleasingly *haimisheh* with perhaps a touch about her crows' feet and the slight circumflex of her eyebrows of the angelic. Then he observes that her blinking green eyes are open and staring back at him, and he abruptly straightens.

"You have been through the night my garde-malade," he announces, "and now I will name you Mademoiselle Garde."

She laughs a measured laugh at the unsought baptism and reminds him that she's not a mademoiselle, but he can see that she's
charmed by her new sobriquet. "I must go now," she says, "or I'll
be late to my employers, the Levasseurs. They live in the place de
Fürstenberg." She fusses self-consciously with her wavy auburn hair
and attempts to rise, but Chaim restrains her with a hand on her
shoulder. He ogles the hand, marveling at the colossal audacity he
has assumed in placing it there. But if so far, why not further?

"You took care of me," he says. "Now it is my turn to take care
of you." He who has barely managed to take care of himself.

But, beyond rhyme and reason, she stays, and so begins the
single fully functioning ménage of Chaim's life. The wonder is
that it isn't too late. He is forty-four and famous in certain circles,
for whatever that's worth, since his soul remains fundamentally
an open sore. She is twenty-three, a refugee from a broken marriage, a dispossessed family, and a blighted nation. Together they
may comprise a complete person, thinks Chaim, insensitive to how
that evaluation might offend his companion: in his defense there
are so few days when he's willing to acknowledge the veracity of
his own personhood. As for love, the word's only associations for
Chaim—forgive him, Madame Castaing—have been with frustration, humiliation, and depravity. He doesn't try to define his
feelings for Mademoiselle Garde beyond the fact that they seem to
be acute and unconditional. Feelings he's thus far believed himself
incapable of. And *mirabile dictu* (as Modi might say), the affection
appears to be mutual.

Chaim is not rich; these are no longer the boom years after
the coming of Dr. Barnes. But the Castaings have seen to it that
his paintings provide him with a living wage. His finances have
sometimes to be stretched to support the two of them, but Chaim's

needs are modest and Garde has long been accustomed to slender means. She prepares his bland meals—primarily boiled potatoes and milky vegetable soups—and shares them without complaint. (Later she will take him to a physician who, while issuing a grim prognosis and prescribing a more exacting pharmaceutical regimen, assures them he may resume eating meat, butter, and eggs—after which he begins to gain weight.) She keeps house for Chaim and is even allowed to straighten up his studio, where the paintings he hasn't locked away in a closet remain turned to the wall. If she feels the least bit constrained by his ascetic mode of living, she never shows it, though there's an extra buoyancy in her step when, from time to time, they go out together.

Chaim has no interest in theater and Garde draws the line at returning to the prizefights, but she happily accompanies him to the cinema, the first films he's seen since viewing Eisenstein's *Battleship Potemkin* with Dr. Faure. He avoids the grand movie palaces along the Champs-Élysées, preferring instead the smaller venues of the 14th arrondissement. (He misses the pratfalls of Chaplin and Keaton, replaced now by talkies reflecting the general mood of pessimism in circulation since the fall of the Popular Front.) They make the rounds in Chaim's compass: the marché aux puces at Clignancourt; the galleries along the rue de la Boétie, in search of more Céret paintings that Chaim can purchase and destroy. On a rare evening out they see Maurice Chevalier perform a number from the musical *Dédé* at the Casino de Paris, though neither is impressed by his mugging and pandering antics. Garde dons her one form-fitting gown with its metallic-thread trim and they go to the Palais Garnier to see Debussy's dolorous *Pelléas et Mélisande*. (Garde weeps buckets and Chaim, in an unwontedly endearing gesture, dips a finger in her tears and sucks the finger.) More sociable, if only for his companion's sake, Chaim accepts an invitation to dine at the posh atelier of his neighbor Chana Orloff, one of the few old acquaintances he hasn't antagonized. Once in a while they take a café crème on a crowded terrace, where Garde is delighted and Chaim annoyed by the younger artists who stop by to pay tribute to the maestro.

Remarkably, the woman does not seek to compete with his painting. She appears to be interested only in the man rather than his work. He has warned her never to look on an unfinished canvas, warnings as stern as those issued to Lot's wife; and though there's no door between parlor and studio, she compliantly averts her eyes. They have made picnic excursions by train to Garches in the Hauts-de-Seine and the bucolic old Impressionist resort of Bougival, out-ings that might almost qualify as romantic; but once Chaim erects his easel, he cautions Garde to keep her nose in her book. If he scolds her for allowing her woolgathering gaze to stray from the page, she considers herself well rebuked. Nor, when he's away from the apartment, does she presume to steal a peek at his art, which would constitute a betrayal. But while she honors his caveat with re-gard to spying on the paintings themselves, she has dared to glance at the artist in the act of creating them. She's seen him in his trans-ports brutally slapping and gouging the canvas, slinging paint from a dozen brushes—one for each nuance of color and magnitude of brushstroke; how he spends the brushes, then drops them into the growing mound at his feet. Like bodies slain in combat, she thinks. She has witnessed his paroxysms and wondered: What manner of man have I married my fortunes to?

Yet she tolerates his many tics and curious habits. She wishes he would keep his money in the bank but doesn't protest when told to cover her eyes as he fishes notes from his various hidey-holes. She observes with quiet desolation the damage incurred when he insists on cutting his own hair—the jet-black hair he's so afraid of losing that he goes once a week to a former nun who massages his scalp with an ointment made from goose fat and opium. Though his once fine clothes are worn to near obsolescence, he will not consent to buy new ones, but spends inordinate sums on his collection of gray fedoras. To her credit, Garde has cured him of his fear of bathing, sitting vigil over the hot water heater to assure him it's not leaking gas. Then he luxuriates in the enamel slipper tub while she scrubs his pallid shoulders with the diligence of a handmaid laving a warrior after a battle. She feathers their nest, places posies of pinks and forget-me-nots on every available surface. She finds frames for the cheap reproductions of Rembrandt and Courbet that he's tacked to the walls, purchases shelves for his volumes of Balzac and Dostoyevsky and the tabloid *Paris-soir* he refuses to throw away.

Their lovemaking is not passionate but neither are they shy with each other. This comes as an astonishment to them both. They discover that it's possible to express with one's naked body what cannot be articulated in a second language that neither is proficient in. Outside the bedroom Chaim is as tight-lipped as ever concerning the past, though the woman, with antenna-like fingers, believes she can read something of his history in the corrugation of his ribs and the moles on his back. In the wounds inflicted by others and the invisible wounds inflicted by himself. Schooled in pain herself, she is especially attuned to his. She seldom speaks of her idealist husband who was determined to become a martyr, or the hopeless family she left behind in Magdeburg, but Chaim thinks he can feel the contours of her *tsuris* in her small breasts and the clench of her womb. It's a new sensation, this reaching beyond his own hurt to touch another's, and it makes him want to handle her with extreme delicacy. There is of course no accounting for the bounty of her devotion; that he is undeserving of it is not in question. Stunted as is his capacity for trust, his affair with Garde requires no need for jealousy or fear of deceit. For all that, and not for want of desiring it, Chaim never summons the boldness to hold her as she sleeps.

Still, his habits of secrecy are inconsistent with his conjugal tenderness, which sometimes make Mademoiselle Garde feel like Bluebeard's wife. Her apprehension, however, is in large part dispelled by an unannounced visit from his *benefactrice* Madame Castaing.

Chaim, often idle in winter, is slouched in an armchair listening to a broadcast blaming the presidency of Léon Blum for everything from breadlines to stillbirths. The voice on the radio is prophesying a coming war for which the Jews will be responsible. But Garde has built a fire in the fireplace and is preparing a chicken for dinner—he eats chicken now, and Jägerschnitzel and rollmops with cheesy spätzle. He was impotent again last night, but she has assured him it's of no consequence; nor has she ever complained of his incurable naïveté with respect to the manipulation of the female anatomy. (He's conscientious enough for her, and besides, she's too restrained herself to offer instruction.) Chaim wonders whether this is what contentment looks like? He's begun to think there are worse things than feeling at one's ease. Still, he's deeply disturbed by the ringing of the downstairs bell heralding an uninvited visitor. Visitors are not welcome. But when Garde opens the door to receive the svelte lady in her fur stole and veiled turban, Chaim alights from his chair with uncommon exuberance.

Garde feels instantly sidelined by the vibrancy this glamorous guest has evoked in her man. So eager is Chaim to take her wrap and see her to a chair, while enjoining Garde to light the samovar, that he neglects to even introduce them. Seated, Madame Castaing lifts her veil, removes her gloves one finger at a time, and, her manners exquisite, introduces herself. She looks about the room and compliments—"Garde," supplies Chaim along with a hasty explanation of the nickname's provenance; she compliments Garde on her tasteful embellishment of the apartment. "I think I'm safe in assuming that Chaim has had no hand in the housekeeping," she says with a smile. Chaim grins and Garde wonders how it is that he's on such intimate terms with this grand lady. Jealous, she thanks Madame Castaing, who seems sincere when she asks her to "Please call me Madeleine. Chaim has told me so much about you." Garde suspects this is a lie, since when would he have had the opportunity to confide in her? But she is grateful nonetheless.

Madame Castaing begins to expand on the current Paris scene, of which she is wonderfully well informed. "We saw the revival of de Falla's *Three-Cornered Hat* with Massine's choreography at le Châtelet. Stravinsky and Coco Chanel were in the state box . . ." The more she recounts the goings-on about town, however, the plainer and more lacking in *joie de vivre* does Garde feel—even though the scene their guest describes is admittedly less scintillating than in former days. In fact, Madeleine has come like a bellwether to bring tidings of a creeping mirthlessness in the cafés. Some, like the Surrealists' Café Certa in the passage de l'Opéra, are virtually deserted, their patrons having dispersed into their respective political cells. The Cocaine Gang has disappeared from the Dingo Bar, leaving only the American refugees from Prohibition to carry on their tradition of lordly disdain. There is even talk that the venerable Sphinx brothel is auctioning off Edward VII's fabled stirrup chair. Django Reinhardt and Stéphane Grappelli are still playing their gypsy jazz at Bricktop's (though Sidney Bechet has been deported for attempted homicide), and Princess Santzo and her entourage can still be seen breakfasting on gin and strawberries at les Halles at dawn. But the party is essentially over.

"The party for me didn't never begin," says Chaim, sounding rather proud of the fact.

Madame Castaing sighs and appraises the couple with an al-most maternal concern. "Chaim," she says, all frivolity gone out of her voice, "even the Guignol puppet shows in the Luxembourg Gardens are anti-Jewish these days."

"You think I don't know this?" he replies. Hasn't he paid mind-
ful attention to the ill tidings purveyed in the newspapers and on
the radio? Isn't he well aware that, ever since they pulled Léon
Blum from his cab and beat him up, the hooligans of the Croix de
Feu rule the streets? He too has cringed over the case of Herschel
Grynszpan, the seventeen-year-old Polish Jew who assassinated the
diplomat vom Rath at the German embassy in the rue de Lille,
thereby triggering what the papers called the Night of Broken Glass
all over the Reich. Hasn't Chaim been, moreover, a student of the
future presaged by the offals of animals all these long years? He
knows what's going on, though as far as he's concerned such events
may as well be taking place in another galaxy.

Madame Castaing can see clearly the kind of inviolable air
castle the artist and his diffident mistress have been constructing
for themselves. She is also conscious of the fragility of such an edifice. She fixes Chaim with a stare to the exclusion of anyone else
in the room, an imperious stare to which she feels herself rightly or
wrongly entitled. "Chaim," she says, "do you love her?"

Angered by the sheer overweening cheek of the question,
Mademoiselle Garde feels the blood surge in her head. But Chaim
answers blithely without hesitation, "Mais oui."

Then Garde begins silently to cry. She starts from the touch of
the hand that Madame Castaing has risen to lay on her shoulder: Is
there no end to her sense of privilege? But later on, she will come to
believe that she and Chaim are living securely under the empyrean
protection of a guardian spirit and her spouse, and despite the dis-
parity of their characters, the two women become friends.

✦

SOMETIME IN FEBRUARY CHAIM gets word that Élie Faure has died.
Among the sage doctor's effects is the painting Soutine had sent
him in his ire of Marie-Zéline with her face viciously obliterated.

Chaim resents the way the news of Dr. Faure's death disturbs his domestic tranquility; he hates himself for the lukewarm condolences he sends to the good Madame Faure and wishes he could take the woman's pudgy hands in his. He adds the regret to a growing registry. In the meantime, through no intercession of his own, a retrospective of thirty-three of his works is held at the Leicester Galleries in London. There are one-man shows in New York along with his inclusion in several group shows in Europe and America. In response to the immigrant's growing renown, Waldemar George has written in *L'amour de l'art*: "The curse that weighs on Soutine's oeuvre extends to his whole race . . ." And then there's Chaim's disappointment upon learning that no Soutines are represented in the Nazis' Degenerate Art exhibition in Munich.

Moïse Kisling still roams the red sand floor of the Rotonde, sporting his Tom Mix shirt and Joan of Arc haircut. He still judges his famous farting competitions and calls the nationalist goons of the Camelots du Roi "untalented schlimazls" to their faces. But even though winter has passed, Chaim remains largely housebound. He continues to maintain the pact of denial that he and Garde have established in the face of the mounting hostility toward their kind, but he has no desire to push his luck. If he leaves the apartment, he pulls his hat brim down over his eyes. He spares no more than a nod to the neighbors in his building (such as Henry Miller) when passing them on the stairs. "Soutine is living quietly below me with his new, redheaded model," writes the venereal novelist in his diary. "He seems tame now, as if trying to recover from the wild life of other days. He hesitates to salute you in the open streets for fear you will get too close to him. When he opens his trap, it's to say how warm or cold it is—and does the neighbor's piano bother you as it does him?"

The quiet that Miller observes is due in part to his happy home, in part to Chaim's increasing frailty from his stomach complaints.

Never known for his stoicism, he nevertheless tries to put a good face on his suffering for the sake of Mademoiselle Garde. He makes an effort to be gallant, even gay, with her. Once, he tells her she is as beautiful as . . . Modigliani, which she doesn't know quite how to take; he pours his linden blossom tea into her shoe and quaffs it all despite the brackish taste. But the radio and the popular press have begun to break through his resistance and to cruelly aggravate his bellyache.

He reads in the scurrilous monthly *Je suis partout*—while Garde admonishes him against reading such garbage—that Maurras's Action Française has rehabilitated for a hero the old royalist fossil Henri Buronfosse. This is the man who claims to have fastened the sack over Émile Zola's chimney, causing the author's unnatural death by carbon monoxide poisoning. Chaim sees that the government has ruled that a balalaika orchestra performing in France must limit its Russian members to 15 percent of its instrumentalists and to 10 percent of its singers. He reads the flyer Garde has received from the *Comité d'assistance aux réfugiés,* advising alien Jews to:

1. Keep an eye on your outfit.
2. Be polite and discreet.
3. Be modest. Do not speak highly of the qualities of your country of origin that you think France lacks. ("Not bloody likely," thinks Chaim.)
4. Learn to express yourself quickly in French. Do not speak loudly. If you speak a foreign language, avoid using it in public.
5. Respect all our laws and customs. We want you to be useful and ask you to help us by following these suggestions, which are your duty to the French community that welcomes you.

On the Bakelite tube radio, Chaim hears the playwright Giraudoux calling for a Ministry of Race: "We are fully in accord with Monsieur Hitler for proclaiming that a policy attains its highest form only when it is racial." He hears the hate merchant Drieu La Rochelle indicting the flabby Third Republic for leaving France at the mercy of mongrelized foreigners—"the Jews, blacks, Arabs, and Annamites." (What are Annamites?) He hears Louis-Ferdinand Céline's rabid, if somewhat blithering, cri de cœur, "Kikes and half-niggers, you are our gods!"

The notable gastroenterologist to whom Madame Castaing has sent him counsels Chaim that some months of fresh country air might improve his condition. With encouragement from Garde the patient is persuaded. At dinner at Chana Orloff's, the art critic and collector Udi Einsild, another large-nosed Lithuanian compatriot, says he knows just the place. Civry-sur-Serein in Burgundy, about 150 kilometers south of Paris, is an unspoiled, picturesque little village, really no more than a hamlet, of under two hundred souls. "It's quite authentic and cheap," says Einsild, "and I guarantee you will never encounter there anyone that you know."

Having agreed on the expedient, the couple waste no time in packing their belongings, but there are shocks that must be absorbed before they can depart for Civry. There's the German Anschluss into Austria, the annexation of Czechoslovakia, the humiliation of the milquetoast Neville Chamberlain. There's the precautionary sandbagging of the Bourse and the Assemblée nationale and the removal of the stained glass windows of Sainte-Chapelle. It's summer before they arrive in the village, which gives every appearance of a place beyond the reach of the headlines—though its only shop still carries daily papers, along with stamps, cigarettes, and groceries. The whole of Civry consists of a single street, on either side of which shamble a row of centuries-old cottages with tilting stucco walls and roofs like tents atop camels' humps. Across from the shop of the voluble Madame Michel is the house of the dour Madame Galand, in which Chaim and Garde have rented a sparsely furnished room. There are electric lights and a coal-burning stove, but water must be fetched from a pump in the yard. They take their evening meals, for a reasonable fee, with Madame Galand and her son, a silent, sleepy-eyed boy apprenticed to a monument mason. She prepares good country fare, sometimes heavy on the sauterne marinade, but Chaim's digestion has thus far remained marvelously undistressed. As a refuge, Civry provides none of the comforts of Lèves or the Faures' idyllic cottage in the Dordogne, but for Chaim and his undemanding companion it is an ideal hideaway.

Germany delivers an ultimatum to Poland on the question of the status of the Free City of Danzig, Molotov shakes hands with Ribbentrop, and Chaim and Mademoiselle Garde cross an old stone bridge over the eddying River Serein. Garde carries a wicker basket with their lunch and Chaim his paint box and easel, a stretched canvas strapped to his back like a sandwich board. They ascend a gravelly trail that zigzags up a gentle slope to the top of a forested plateau, where they wander into the woods along a path carpeted in pine needles. The occasional rocky outcrops have smooth asymmetrical surfaces that prompt Chaim to cite "a Lipchitz" or "a Brancusi." They cross a meadow sprinkled with copper-red anemones and yellow sage. Around them the drowsy hum of the bumblebees, bright afternoon notwithstanding, is half a lullaby. But Chaim marches relentlessly forward in his hunched-over posture, seldom speaking, while Garde plods patiently behind him. She is inappropriately dressed, thistles clinging to her tea-length skirt, her square-heeled pumps threatening to turn her ankles at every declivity. She wonders whether the artist will ever halt but never complains. It's become a fundamental postulate, God help her, that wherever he is is where she belongs.

They arrive at a clearing where a narrow, unpaved road winds into a stand of balsam-scented aspens, and Chaim comes to a sudden stop, so abruptly in fact that Garde stumbles into him. He says nothing but she can see that he's found his vantage. To her the scene is no more arresting than any of the countless other prospects he's disregarded, but this one he seems to have recognized. She's correct in her judgment, though the recognition has nothing to do with anyplace he's looked on before. Unless, thinks Chaim, he's encountered it in a former life. But the notion of the gilgul, of reincarnation, with which the smelly old Smilovitchi melamed indoctrinated the cheder boys, he rejects outright. There is only this life, for better or worse. Nevertheless, here is a landscape that stands apart in its essence from all others, as if existing on the other side of the gauzy scrim of time. Thus, its stillness and clarity. But when he directs the full amperage of his concentration toward the butter-yellow road and the chartreuse trees, the sum of his years, and (so it seems) the years of myriad unknown others charge the scene, causing the winds of time to buffet the branches and scatter the clouds like spindrift.

Garde doesn't need to be told what's expected of her. She spreads her shawl over a clump of clover and seats herself on it; she lifts the lid of the basket with a show of appetite, and removes a baguette and a wedge of Camembert, which she offers to Chaim. He appears not to have heard her. With forbearing disappointment, she begins to nibble her lunch by herself while reading her book, alert nonetheless to the artist's rites of preparation. She can hear him mumbling to himself as he sets up the easel, hears his pacing back and forth and the throaty moan he emits before finally launching himself at the canvas. Now, she thinks, he will fling the brushes from his hand after every stroke like flamed-out torches used to illumine his vision, for the sun is not nearly radiant enough. Then the hours will pass. She smiles at the very idea of the once coddled Gerda Groth-Michaelis, apple of her father's eye, having thrown in her lot with a wild man.

It's twilight when he signals to her that he's finished. Stiff from sitting so long, she waits for him to help her to rise, but it's clear he hasn't entirely returned from wherever he's been. She worries that they'll have to retrace their steps in the dark, and with Chaim still the phantom captive of his art, she will have to lead him. (An omnivorous reader, she thinks of Lear on the heath.) Chaim neither shows her the painting nor makes an attempt to conceal it, and a chance glimpse reveals that he's included two small children on the untraveled road. Had she not noticed their passing while absorbed in her book or are they Chaim's own invention, though when has he ever drawn from his imagination? She only knows that, though the sky in the painting is a brilliant delft blue, it's for the beholder to decide whether the children have escaped the impending storm or are about to be overtaken by it. Later it will occur to her that she and Chaim are those children.

For a period thereafter he seems to believe that a landscape is incomplete unless populated with a couple of kids, don't ask why. He urges Garde to fill her pockets with hard candies with which to lure the little ones on their way home from school. Baiting them is one thing, but keeping them still quite another, and more than one posing child is frightened off by the artist's outbursts. If they so much as fidget or squirm, the artist cries, "Why can't I nail them in place!" and the terrified child takes to their heels. "Chaim, shah!" Garde pleads with him, since it's not prudent for a Jew ("Who knows we're Jews?") to be overheard threatening gentile children. Then she chases after them to coax them back with more horehounds. Their subsequent bouts of stomach cramps and regurgitation incur the wrath of their parents, so that Chaim has to look farther afield for his subjects. He and Garde take a bus as far as Champigny and the cathedral town of Auxerre, where he paints more children and trees: children sheltered under a nave of overarching branches, children in danger of being trampled by a stampede of elms.

All of which prompts Garde to wonder whether he might want a child of his own. She's had to instruct him in the use of the crepe-rubber condom and, distrusting his dexterity, has lovingly ensheathed him in the *capote anglaise* herself. There's never been any question of her getting pregnant; the often childish artist is enough of a handful. She approaches the subject with extreme caution, and is shocked when Chaim begins to writhe at her query as if he's been plunged in nettles. After some moments he blurts, "I got already a daughter." It's a fact he's seldom admitted even to himself and he's as stunned by the confession as Garde. When she delicately presses him for details, he becomes so evasive that she lets the matter drop, though she breaks the ensuing silence to ask, "Do you ever want to see her?"

"No!" he shouts emphatically, thereby closing the subject for good and all.

Garde thinks she understands: the girl belongs to a time and place that no longer figure in Chaim's eternal present. She believes, twisted reasoning aside, that it's up to her to assume a portion of the guilt the artist has waived.

The secluded village of Civry has never seen his like before. He's arrested twice. The first time is when the sober-sided parish priest, Father Souvestre, comes upon Chaim while he's painting a clutch of alders. Interested, he pauses to watch. When Chaim becomes aware of the eavesdropper in his sable skirts, he immediately shields the canvas with his body. The times are fraught with unreasonable fears and the priest lifts the skirts of his cassock and makes tracks for the local gendarmerie, which in Civry is no more than an office in the town hall. He reports the untoward activity; there is talk of a secret "fifth column," and while no one knows exactly what that is, an officer is dispatched to haul Chaim back to police headquarters. Before his interrogators Chaim teeters between petrified, as he generally is in the presence of authority, and irate.

"I am Soutine," he sputters at length, "painter of excellence. I got in high places important friends." (Somewhere he hears a teasing echo of Modigliani proclaiming, "I am Ozymandias, king of kings!")

The chief constable, Commissaire Gage, chuckles into his beard at the paint-smeared derelict's delusions of grandeur, and even Father Souvestre is unable to conceal his amusement. They share a barefaced laugh when Chaim insists they contact Albert Sarraut, Minister of the Interior, who will confirm his identity. Monsieur Sarraut is in fact an art collector who has acquired several Soutines and has even written the introduction to the catalog of an exhibition in which Chaim was included. If only to humor *le curieux*, the call is eventually made, and after a preliminary exchange with his secretary, the minister himself is put on the line. Chaim registers his doleful lament from his end, and Monsieur Sarraut, sensible to the impression the artist is likely to make on strangers, assures his captors that their prisoner is who he claims to be. Both priest and commissaire express sheepish regrets.

Some days later a young lieutenant from the Yonne prefecture, off duty but still in uniform, is visiting his mother in Civry when he sees an odd sight. An unkempt character is running back and forth for no obvious purpose between a squat village house and a large boulder in a field several dozen yards behind it. A beech tree is growing atop the boulder, its roots gripping the rock like the talons of an immense bird. The running man is of course Chaim, who has become enthralled by the vista of the rock and the tree, but must return to it again and yet again to test its freshness as a potential subject. Satisfied that he is witnessing the behavior of a certifiable lunatic, the lieutenant collars the artist and drags him back to police headquarters, where Chaim is received like a lost-and-found child.

In time Civry comes to accept the strangers with a minimum of suspicion. Some, like Madame Michel in her shop, even view them as wards of the village in need of looking after. The admirable woman tips a finger beneath the scales in their favor when they purchase provisions and sometimes tosses an extra bouillon cube into their basket; she invites them into a back room to listen to her tabletop radio, which they sit about as before a bier. (On it they hear a baying, haranguing voice from the Reichstag translated into limpid French: "If the international Jewish financiers should succeed in plunging the nations once more into a World War, then the result will not be the Bolshevizing of the earth and thus the victory of Jewry, but the annihilation of the Jewish race in Europe . . .") Money is short but the wants of Chaim and Garde are few. Besides, Chaim's superb paysages have been accumulating: *Les enfants sur route, Le retour de l'école,* the furious *La jour de vent á Auxerre*—paintings into which he's channeled all his immediate and anticipatory fears so that now, he believes, he can be brave. The Castaings have promised to buy them all sight unseen. As for the menacing events that the great world keeps trumpeting, they only make more precious the quotidian banalities of their tiny orbit. In this way their small pleasures and concerns eclipse the largeness of what's about to unfold.

For lack of a sofa they sit on their screeching brass bed and Chaim lays his head in Garde's lap. "Castaways I think is what we are here," he says. She strokes his hair, which has grown lank in the absence of his weekly baldness treatments, and reminds him that he is acclaimed both in France and overseas. "My paintings are a load of crap," he sighs, then, on second thought, "but better than Chagall and Krémègne." He inhales her overripe lilac scent, stronger than the mildew in Madame Galand's stone house, stronger even than the collective odors of the dead animals he's smuggled inside to paint on rainy days. (Those efforts have come to nothing, since it's livestock that holds his interest now—though painting the living always leaves him with a weird lingering sense of having betrayed the dead.) Garde kisses his forehead and tells him, "Madame Castaing has called you a saint of painting," then giggles. "This is funny?" he asks, sitting up, and although she tries to curb her laughter, he sees that, yes, it is funny, and together they cackle like children.

They laugh frequently. Such as the time Madame Galand serves them, swimming in a sauce like bogwater, what appear to be giant tadpoles trussed in swollen purple veins. "Couilles de mouton," Madame Galand proudly announces. Sheep testicles, a traditional dish of the region. Garde looks at Chaim, who's gone as pale as his shirt, and emits an un-Garde-like guffaw. She tries to undo the damage with an apology but it's too late; Chaim has already contracted her mirth. Laughter being a recent capability, he gives himself up to it wholesale, to the point of actually falling from his chair. Their landlady and her lymphatic son look on in bewilderment. Addicted now to hilarity, the couple leave the offended Madame Galand's lodgings and take up residence in a small rental house at the edge of the village. Its interior is not much larger than the room they've vacated, but here they can at least indulge their shared addiction without restraint.

They laugh. On an unusually nippy late August night they're seated in front of the soapstone stove, atop which perches the kettle they're waiting to boil. Garde sits on the floor leaning against the armchair in which Chaim is slouched, his legs stretched out before him. Suddenly the rope soles of his espadrilles, their glue melted by the heat of the stove, unfurl simultaneously like a pair of lolling tongues. It is a sight so obscene that Chaim feels compelled to ask Garde's forgiveness. "It's not your fault," she assures him, then succumbs to a wheeze. He surrenders as well to the contagion and they both convulse in peals of laughter. Such an excess of jocularity, however, can be hard on a gastric ulcer. Their merriment has the same corrosive effect on the walls of Chaim's stomach and small intestine as does Germany's invasion of Poland and the subsequent declaration of war by Britain, Australia, New Zealand, and, two days later, France.

Garde is scrupulous in seeing that he takes his medication daily. She keeps a food diary in order to eliminate any meals that have caused a flare-up of his symptoms. Skeptical but unstinting, she takes advice from Madame Michel and some of the peasant wives who gather in her shop: she serves Chaim cabbage juice and garlic cloves in honey. He tries to be a good patient but balks at the ground locust bark recommended by a local wise woman. "Next you will want like my mama I should put on my belly a poultice made from the unborn foal of a she-ass," he protests. His symptoms persist and he's often fatigued, especially after bouts of diarrhea, but his spirits are relatively good. Not that he isn't still prone to the odd temper tantrum, during which he complains that the Castaings are swindling him and rants about the spinelessness of his fellow artists: how they humor their detractors. He smacks his lips, spraying foam, and strokes his chin till it's raw, but the fits subside soon enough. For isn't each day a gift? The war is anyway a Phoney War, the Drôle de guerre, as the French have it. The lull after the Germans' Blitzkrieg into Scandinavia is dubbed the "Sitzkrieg" by the British press. Since France's failed Saar Offensive and the standoff at the Maginot Line, the aggression from either side appears to have stalled.

Not wanting to disturb the calm, Chaim and Garde begin to modulate their laughter. They're aware that to the villagers, who yesterday were so accustomed to their presence, they have become—a Russian and a German—strangers again. What was once a peaceful retreat has turned into an insecure bolt-hole. Meanwhile, the wireless clamors ceaselessly about hordes of refugees pouring over the border; stateless and refused asylum, they're turned back to the countries from which they departed, who no longer want them and turn them round again. Winter arrives and the countryside is a *tableau vivant* of Bruegel's *Hunters in the Snow*. The hills like powdered sugar, the trees as if wrapped in foil, spiderwebs like pendant brooches of ice. The air is invigorating but biting and neither Chaim nor Garde have proper attire, but they continue their walks, albeit more furtively. They inspect a snow-mantled Gallo-Roman arch, an icebound windmill with skeletal sails, sights that Chaim has not the slightest incentive to paint. When the pains grip his gut, he pretends it's only a stitch in his side, though Garde knows better. She curtails their walks and finds reasons they should keep indoors. Chaim doesn't argue; they have their books and a crank phonograph, some discs of Pierre Monteux conducting Bach, Josephine Baker singing "Si j'étais blanche." When she's not looking, Chaim sets himself the project of committing Garde's features to memory: the whisper of down on her upper lip, a beating turquoise artery at her neck, the brow that rises and falls like the spine of a silkworm. The scrutiny is not, however, with a view toward attempting her portrait; he will not subject her to that violation. He's merely obeying an instinct to retain her image for future reference.

With the thaw, what was suspended is released again into precipitous motion. German forces emerge from the forests of the Ardennes to create strategic bridgeheads along the River Meuse. Their Panzer Corps outflanks the French forces, penetrating with their Tiger tanks the "impregnable" Maginot Line. The Allies are repelled as far as the coast, where a vanquished multitude of British and French troops are evacuated in chaos from Dunkirk. They're ferried across the Channel in a ragtag flotilla of vessels from destroyers to paddle steamers and fishing boats. The German army is then able to march into Paris unopposed—which cannot have happened. The occupation is in its way as inconceivable as, say, an unending storybook holiday in Civry. Of course Chaim has known all along that happiness, even to the extent that one such as he can bear it, is finally not sustainable. In defiance of his own judgment, however, he volunteers to Garde in a moment of unguarded gratitude, "Is not my life charmed!" More nurse now than lover, she bestows on him a look of such inconsolable sorrow that it frightens him. It's apparent that what he feels for her is as impossible as the surrender of France, as the Second Armistice signed by Maréchal Pétain in the railway car at Compiègne, site of the German surrender of World War I. Their love affair is as impossible as the half-demons that Garde, sensible Mitteleuropean lady that she is, has kept at bay. (Chaim has seen them pressing their bent parsnip snouts against the windowpanes.) Reading the headlines is like putting his intestines through a sausage grinder; he cries out and Garde says it's time for him to return to Paris and consult his physicians.

He's surprised at how ready he is to go. His attitude toward Paris has always been steeped in ambivalence. While his immigrant cohort were seduced by the city and have since become its staunch partisans, Chaim has remained conflicted. The hunger and hardship of la Ruche and the cité Falguière years still color his memories. Then there are the grudges he holds, well-founded or not, against contemporaries who've set up shop in every café. But weighed against the adversity is his recollection of his first dazzled encounter with the lights of the Parisian boulevards, his first breathless visit to the Louvre, to which he habitually returns to revitalize his flagging energies. There are the mysteries of the city's unsung quarters as he's seen them through Modigliani's eyes. Not to mention the apartment in la Villa Seurat—more spacious than their cramped cottage in Civry—that has been his base these several years. (To say nothing of the *objets* and antiquities Chaim recalled from his tour of the bottom of the Seine.) So they prepare to leave the village, but there are obstacles. New laws are issued weekly by the recently established Vichy government: As aliens (an enemy alien in the case of Garde), the couple are required to register with the mairie, and are forbidden to leave the town or village where they reside.

But Chaim has his connections. Once more he appeals to Minister Sarraut, who is himself on the way out, but includes among his parting directives a *laissez-passer* for the immigrant artist. Unfortunately, no such document can be obtained for Garde. Chaim refuses to leave her and is somewhat ashamed at how quickly he submits to her urging that, for his health's sake, he must go. But on the eve of their separation, he's seized by a depth of emotion that rivals even the sublimity he feels schmearing paint.

"You are my wife," he tells her. "I will come back for you."

An opera buff in her youth—she forgets that she's still young— Garde thinks mournfully of Gluck's *Orfeo ed Euridice*.

Sadness aside, Chaim's heart throbs percussively when he sets eyes on Montparnasse again. The painted streetlamps are no more than blue bruises in the evening mist, but splashes of neon still adorn the cabarets. Granted, there is a stomach-churning proliferation of German uniforms in the streets and Nazi pennants hanging outside of the municipal buildings, but at first glance the city still gives a fair impression of normalcy. Look again, however, and you see the lines outside the shops waiting to buy rationed goods, the stealthy exchanges in the cafés and arcades of cash for meat, tobacco, and clothes. The avenues, nearly vacant of motor vehicles other than troop convoys, are swarming with bicycle cabs. (A few cars have strapped tanks to their roofs to power their engines with coal gas and methane in the absence of gasoline.) Since the great *exode* from the city following the lost Battle of Sedan, most of its citizens have returned, but they repeatedly look over their shoulders when strolling the thoroughfares. They are right to: the French constabulary, zealous to curry favor with their German overlords, often lack discrimination with regard to whom they arrest. Meanwhile gangs of homegrown fascists, having designated themselves an unofficial arm of the Gestapo, harass the citizenry at the least perceived hint of provocation. Sirens are frequently heard.

The sense of well-being Chaim has acquired since his alliance with Mademoiselle Garde soon starts to erode now that he's on his own again. He's been previously treated by a pair of specialists in digestive disorders, but Dr. Guttman, the more coolheaded of the two, has fled to Montpellier. This leaves Dr. Abramy, who leans toward more experimental remedies. He prescribes the usual cocktail of astringents, antiseptics, and sedatives, but also administers a trial course of raw mammal small bowel physics. He calls this "organotherapy," which smacks for Chaim (retching from the vile taste) of ghetto sorcery. Abramy insists as well on irrigating the artist's intestines with a zinc solution through which he runs an electrical current. Chaim howls from the voltage, imagining his bones illuminated like an electrified character he's seen in a Disney cartoon. The only benefit he gains from these treatments is the relief he feels when he stumbles away from the clinic.

Throughout the following weeks, Chaim runs from pillar to post in his attempt to attain traveling papers for Garde. Civry has in his mind become an airless place, a closed chapter in their lives, and it's imperative that he bring his partner back to Paris. Monsieur Sarraut has been transferred from his bureau but his chief of staff Dubois remains, an unctuously sympathetic type who nevertheless claims his hands are tied. "We must defer to wiser heads," he says, inclining his vapid own. Chaim cables Garde not to be discouraged; he's yet to have exhausted all options. But he himself has begun to lose heart. Still, he refuses to believe, despite all evidence to the contrary, that Paris is no longer Paris. Though when he visits the Louvre, he finds that the Tintorettos and El Grecos are absent, having been wrapped in paperboard and sent to châteaux in the Loire for safekeeping. There's an enormous pale rectangular space on the damask wall where Géricault's *Raft of the Medusa* once hung.

His neighbor Chana Orloff tells him, "This is not 1914. You never heard from the *Ordonnance d'Aryanisation*?" It seems that, while Chaim was navel-gazing in the Yonne, draconian measures have been put in place against the Jews. The perfidious Vichy regime, needing little encouragement from the conquerors, has instituted the *Statut des Juifs*. This is a blanket policy limiting Jews from holding public office or any position that might allow them influence over the general populace. Since the compulsory registration of the Jews in both the Occupied and Unoccupied Zones, the government may now confiscate their property at a whim. The Rothschild château at Laversine has already been sacked of its Rembrandts and Vermeers, and Pétain himself has seized their Sert frescoes to present to Generalissimo Franco as a gift.

"*Gib a keek* in the bistros and the brothels," continues Madame Orloff, ample as a gazebo in her floral apron-smock. "The field-gray tunics outnumber already your double-breast Schiaparellis. They're replacing with the Luftwaffe and the SS the human beings."

Nu, thinks Chaim, so I'm a Yid again. The tribe he thought he'd left so far behind has caught up with him once more and claims him for one of their own. It's overtaken him here in Paris, a place from which much of the Hebrew nation is on its way to scattering far and wide.

"Everyone's gone," whispers Kisling, whom he finds still a holdout at an unlit table in the back of the Rotonde. The flamboyant artist has trimmed his bangs and is wearing a nondescript worker's boiler suit. The Delaunays, he says, have made off to the Auvergne, Halicka and Marcoussis along with Marevna to the Free Zone, Lipsi and Indenbaum to God knows where. Miestchaninoff, Zadkine, and Mané-Katz have fled to America, where Moïse himself plans to follow. Others have been interned. A Légion d'honneur recipient after the last war, Kisling had rejoined the French forces until their swift defeat. Now it's every man for himself.

"The authorities, they got screwy ideas about how you determine who's a Jew," he repines. "They use calipers to measure your skull. I gave the census guy this line about how I wasn't purebred Hebe but an Alsatian descended from the Celts who were converted to the Mosaic Law before the arrival of the Catholic apostles in Gaul. But that didn't wash." He spits. "I'll never eat vichyssoise again."

Chaim confides in Moïse his own dilemma and Kisling tells him of a man called Varian Fry, a bureaucrat turned saint, who's holed up in the Hotel Splendide. He heads a committee from there that provides refugees with visas, passage money, and escape routes to the United States. "He's got a list of all the artists he thinks are worth saving," says Moïse. "Lipchitz and Chagall are on it, even Max Ernst and Duchamp for God's sake! When he offered Chagall free passage to New York, the schmuck wanted to know if there were cows there . . ."

"What about you and me?" Chaim asks impatiently.

"We didn't make the cut."

By degrees, however, Chaim's persistence begins to pay off. He has never been so assertive in approaching public officials, all the while struggling to overcome his timidity and dread. Eventually he has gathered written references from the Castaings and a few of their friends whose arms they've twisted. He has needled Chana Orloff into drawing up a petition and appealed to some leading lights among the gentile artists to sign it. Dufy and Jacques Émile-Blanche reluctantly agree, but the momzers Derain and Vlaminck, about to embark on a tour of Nazi Germany at the invitation of the Reich Minister of Culture, decline. In the end, if only to rid

themselves of his nuisance, the petty tyrants at the Ministry of the
Interior issue papers allowing Madame Gerda Groth-Michaelis to
leave her confinement in the Yonne. Over a month has passed since
Chaim's separation from her and their reunion in Civry is nearly
hysterical. They hold on to each other at the station, mingling hot
tears for close to an hour, each unwilling to be the first to let go.
They celebrate their triumph with the extravagance of a plate of
Madame Michel's profiteroles and cups of dandelion tea. But in the
morning, when they present the documents to Monsieur Sébillotte,
the mayor, he refuses to recognize their legality.

He is a bald, freckle-pated man in an outmoded frock coat
with a medal from the prior war on its lapel. His eyes peer guard-
edly from beneath the half-drawn shades of their lids and the car-
roty hair at his temples is swept outward like wings. He has been
quite friendly before the occupation but now seems to have become
cognizant of an authority he has not previously enjoyed. Or is he
simply afraid of unknowingly transgressing some ordinance from
the Vichy administration's tangled web of newly imposed laws? In
either case, he remains adamant in the face of Chaim's increasingly
intemperate arguments.

Boiling with frustration, Chaim returns to Paris and resumes
his campaign of hounding functionaries at the Ministry of the
Interior. They drive him away though not before one of them, distracted by some personal headache, reinforces the officialdom of his
papers with another perfunctory stamp. Back in Civry he submits
the documents to Monsieur Sébillotte with renewed confidence,
only to be met with the same unbending obstinacy. This time the
mayor puts it in writing.

"I, Georges Sébillotte, mayor of Civry, by virtue of my discre-
tionary power, have allowed Monsieur Soutine to travel for reasons
of health. As for Madame Groth, who is in good health but whose

nationality calls her allegiance into question, I cannot allow her to depart."

Allegiance to what? To France, or to the occupiers—whose nation she has fled after the persecution and disenfranchisement of her entire family? Chaim questions the soundness of the man's reasoning, and when the mayor declines to reverse his decision, throws a fit.

"You are like in Egypt the Pharoah!" he explodes. Then he's as aggrieved by the way the shtetl has lately come to inform his thoughts as he is by his uncontrollable temper. Garde leads him still frothing from the mairie.

When his anger refuses to subside, he vows to parlay it into action. Emboldened by his lover's distress, he will be more than himself. He resolves to spirit her out of the village that very night. Garde smiles covertly at his posturing; she has no wish to deflate his novel show of bravado; it will fizzle soon enough on its own. Only this time it doesn't. "But why go to Paris at all?" she wonders. Aren't they safe enough there in Civry, a place so insignificant that the Germans seem to have overlooked it? Chaim reminds her of their neighbors' prying eyes. Besides, his doctors are in Paris (though little good they've done him) as well as their friends (though who are their friends?). Of course Garde knows that, rail against it as he might, Paris has always been Chaim's touchstone and the seat of his operations; despite his need of the natural world for his epiphanies, he remains in many ways habituated to the city's restive intensity. He's worked himself up into a fever against which common sense cannot prevail.

She sighs and begins to gather up what she can carry, stuffs everything into a cardboard suitcase, then plumps herself down on the lid to snap it shut. In truth, there's little in their two-by-four cottage she minds leaving. Their plan, such as it is, is to steal away from Civry on foot after midnight, thus avoiding the mayor and his minions; then, bona fide fugitives, they will walk the dozen kilometers to the station at the village of l'Isle-sur-Serein. From there they can catch a train to la Roche, where they must change for the express to Paris. Once their decision is made, each tries to subdue the trembling they hope to conceal from the other.

They're used to walking in these hornbeam woods by day; the path is familiar and the wildlife they've encountered—a deer or a snuffling hedgehog, the occasional fox—are not threatening. But in the dark without a flashlight—a flashlight could give them away—they have entered an altogether different domain. Some of the animal sounds are recognizable: the owl's hoot, the Jew's harp twang of the bullfrogs; but others are strident and keening, as if emanating from things other than ordinary animals. Bats flitter insanely in the moonless sky; a creature Chaim could swear is the size of an ottoman scuttles across their path, causing his hair to stand on end. Though the night is chilly, Garde can feel how the artist's palm has become slippery with sweat. He's squeezing her hand so tightly that she tells him, "Please, not so hard," but when he releases her, she takes hold of his hand again. She says they are like Hansel and Gretel, and as Chaim is unfamiliar with the reference, she begins to tell him the story. There's a squealing like ancient hinges as the trees graze one another in the wind, and Chaim starts; but though he ordinarily has little patience with fairy tales, he clings to the distraction of the outcast childrens' predicament. When Garde gets to the part about the witch tossing the kids into an oven, he laughs a nervous laugh at the preposterousness of it all. In this way they divert themselves from the real dangers with imaginary ones, until they emerge from the woods into the next village.

They spend the remainder of the night huddled on a bench in the open kiosk that serves as the l'Isle-sur-Serein depot. It's too cold to sleep, so they sit shivering on the platform, sharing Garde's ratty fur-trimmed overcoat pulled round both their shoulders. "The cloak of invisibility," Garde murmurs, wanting to further distract the artist. But the allusion to Siegfried's magic garment from Wagner's Ring Cycle has such sinister teutonic connotations that she doesn't pursue the thought. She senses correctly that Chaim has spent his quota of recklessness in initiating their flight; he's worn himself out in his efforts on her behalf. It has now fallen to her to reassure him of their inconspicuousness and, at the conductor's call, to nudge him gently on board the early morning train. The sun has hardly risen and the other passengers are as groggy as they are; no one's curiosity is aroused in the least by the outlaw couple. The journey is blessedly uneventful. They make their connection at la Roche and arrive in Paris at midday, exiting the Gare de Bercy into a city of downcast faces. They take the Métro to Porte d'Orléans and walk from there to la Villa Seurat, toiling up the stairs to the apartment in mild triumph and utter exhaustion.

The rooms have reverted to their pre–Gerda Groth shambles, but weary as she is, the woman begins to reimpose order before even removing her coat. "You see, Garde . . .," says Chaim, sunk in the recess of his wing chair, where she plumps a pillow behind his back; she opens the shutters, sweeps butts and pistachio shells from the carpet, then, having determined that the gas range is inoperative, stoops to stoke the hearth with the legs from a broken table. "You see," proclaims the artist, "how I am guarding you. Now we will never anymore to be apart." And satisfied that they belong in these hermetic rooms if nowhere else, he falls abruptly asleep.

In the succeeding days Chaim lowers the volume on his radio until it's barely perceptible but still can't bring himself to turn it off. A small, distant voice from deep inside it informs them that the German Blitz of England has begun. There are air raids in London, Southampton, Bristol, Cardiff, and Liverpool. Meanwhile the État français, in compliance with its Nazi puppet masters, is effectively banishing the Jewish presence from every arena of cultural and commercial life. Every Jewish business must post a sign in both German and French: JÜDISCHES GESCHÄFT and ENTREPRISE JUIVE; after which their windows are invariably smashed and their contents looted by hoodlums of the Milice or the Croix de Feu or the Action Française—they're interchangeable. The streets of the Pletzl and Belleville are virtually empty, though on Saturdays—in unprecedented numbers—their synagogues are full. Chaim's neighbor Chana O has told them this among other items that the radio ignores.

Jewish gallery owners such as Wildenstein and Kahnweiler, after hiding their collections in bank vaults and mausoleum crypts, have gone abroad or retired to the provinces. Jewish artists are no longer allowed to sell their works, which—according to the Ministry of Culture—disrupt the tradition of harmony and balance that has given French art its superiority. As Xavier Vallat, Commissioner-General for Jewish Questions and literal fragment of a man—he lost his left leg and right eye in the Great War—declares, "The Jews are only bearable in homeopathic doses."

"The Jews, the Jews!" moans Chaim. "Why it is that it's always the Jews?" As if the people themselves were complicit in their own victimhood.

He and Garde are in the drawing room of the luxurious studio-house built by the architect Auguste Perret for Madame Orloff. Her attachment to it is why she remains one of the last of the old École de Paris crowd yet to leave the city. "Hymie," she croons, relishing the diminutive; she's a big woman with a bust like a filled carpetbag; "after they murdered the Czar, a government official says to a rabbi, 'I bet *you* know who's responsible.' 'I have no idea,' says the rabbi, 'but the Duma will conclude the same as it always does: they'll blame it on the Jews and the button-makers.'"

Chaim knits his brow. "Why the button-makers?"

Chana shrugs. "Why the Jews?" She delivers herself of a horse laugh that no one shares.

The stentorian voice of Charles de Gaulle over Radio Londres has dwindled to crackling static; only the anti-Allied propaganda of the Vichy stations is still audible. But it's early spring and, as Chaim and Garde step out for a stroll, there's a cat perched on every balcony. Daffodils encircle the plane trees whose budding branches arc over the boulevards like the spray from uncorked champagne. The horse-drawn fiacres that have replaced the mothballed taxis add a quaint touch to the seasonal allure. The café terraces are crowded, though the homburgs have had to make way for the gray-green peaked caps with death's-head insignias; the rugby collars are being supplanted by those bearing lightning runes. A woman in a knitted "madcap," eyelashes like Venus flytraps, leans toward a thin-lipped Junker in a black leather trench coat lighting her cigarette. A fat, linen-suited plutocrat whispers in the ear of an equally porcine field marshal, who spews his beer over the salacious remark. Here is a different breed of flâneur and flâneuse.

An enormous swastika billows from the Arc de Triomphe. Goose-stepping jackboots fill the square in front of the Hôtel de Ville. The Berlin Philharmonic is performing at the Opéra, Schiller's *Wallenstein* is at the Théâtre de Champs-Élysées. All the rooms at the Hôtel Ritz are reserved for high-ranking officers of the Reich, who have also booked Maxim's to overflowing; they flood the Casino and sniff about the Jeu de Paume, viewing the art that Hermann Göring has not yet commandeered for himself. They walk four and five abreast along the sidewalks, forcing pedestrians to step from the curb to avoid them—though there are those who hang on to offer their services and ingratiate themselves by report-ing the infractions of their neighbors. Dazed citizens watch as con-scripts for the labor battalions are transported in their truckloads through the streets. Their wives have been recruited as well and

are shuttled via the Métro to the Renault factory—since converted
to manufacturing German armaments—on the outskirts of Paris.
Left behind with no one to look after them, their children have
begun to exhibit feral behavior in their never-ending quest for food.

Chaim and Garde have been thus far "passed over"—like,
thinks Chaim, the Israelites who smeared lamb's blood on their
doorposts to ward off the avenging angel. He pictures himself doing as much with a bucket of blood fetched from the abattoirs he
frequented in the old days. He no longer chastises himself for entertaining such notions of Old World mumbo jumbo. The times won't
allow him to forswear his origins anymore. Still he insists, somewhat fanatically, that he and Garde are special; they're protected
by his illustrious associations, if not by the insuperable nature of
their affection for each other. Of course there are more prosaic reasons for their extended impunity. Although they're included in the
Vichy census, they've yet to register their presence with the Paris
police. Registration is mandatory for all Jews, especially resident
aliens, and Chana warns them that if their delinquency is discovered, it will not go well for them. "And it will go for us well when
they got us on their books?" asks a liverish Chaim. Nevertheless,
they visit the commissariat on the avenue du Maine the next day to
have their names inscribed in the rolls of the expendable. They pray
that Garde's unlawful departure from the Yonne has not caught
up with her, and exhale when they're mechanically processed by
a clock-watching minor official. Then they return home and wait,
without knowing exactly what they're waiting for.

They seldom have occasion to leave the apartment together anymore, since Garde has taken it upon herself to do the foraging for
necessities. Several times a week she goes from butcher to baker to
crèmerie, enduring interminable lines full of bad-tempered women.
There are particular coupons for particular items that can only be
obtained on certain days of the month. Often she waits hours for

a pound of butter that turns out to be a beef tallow substitute or the coffee that's nine-tenths chicory. It's not unusual to find, after an eternity of anticipation, that the eggs or dried peas or that slice of charcuterie has already vanished from the shelves. The enforced austerity is as cruel to Chaim's system as is overindulgence. His new doctor (he's lost faith in all the previous) prescribes alternate courses of mecamylamine and sulfasalazine in suppository form. These Garde administers with such seraphic tenderness that Chaim releases sighs like a squeezed concertina during the procedure. Afterward he declares that his considerable improvement is cause for celebration.

Despite Garde's protests against such imprudence, he insists on taking her out for a night on the town. "You deserve from such humdrum a *bisl* fun."

She teases him, "Since when are you a *maven* of fun?" But she remains ill at ease and can see that he's not really so sanguine about the notion himself. Previously "a night out" for Chaim meant the catch-boxing (which Garde abhors) or a film, activities that have lost their luster in the current climate—as what activities have not? Still, he will not relinquish his idée fixe: he is determined to show her a good time. And as it's the first enthusiasm of any kind he's evinced since their midnight escape from Civry, Garde cannot find it in her heart to discourage him.

Together they navigate the gauntlet of tension and mistrust that the city streets have become. Chaim has set his mind on the Brasserie Lipp in the boulevard Saint-Germain, where he once dined with Zborowski after the Dr. Barnes bonanza. This is a classic old Parisian bistro: mosaic floors, bentwood chairs, maroon banquettes, and a syrupy imitation Watteau on the ceiling. There is also, around a single table, a small party of German officers, one of whom looks up to give the couple a baleful once-over as they enter. Chaim ignores Garde's tug at his sleeve and steels himself to return the maître d's formal greeting. He remembers Zbo touting the place for its boeuf bourguignon and *cuisses de grenouilles*, and these items are still on the menu. But once seated at their white-clothed table, the couple are informed by the smug young waiter that today is not a "meat day"; the house can offer nothing this evening but noodles and something called "chops."

"Chops?" inquires Chaim.

The waiter somewhat too cheerily describes how the cold oatmeal is molded into the shape of pork chops, then sprinkled with bread crumbs and fried. Clearly accustomed to the disappointment of his patrons, the waiter bends to state sotto voce that, for a few extra francs, he might be able to provide them with something more toothsome. Without his Polak dealer on hand to bargain with the waiter, the unworldly artist is out of his depth. A drop of perspiration glistens on his brow.

"Hmph," says Chaim, and "hmph" before asking, "How many more francs?"

"Five hundred," replies the waiter with maddening serenity.

Garde makes to get up and leave; they have no business in such an establishment, what with the sore thumbs of their Semitic features and their dowdy apparel, but Chaim grabs her arm. He produces his wallet, snatches out all but one of the bills, and hands them to the waiter, who bows in sham deference. Garde becomes deathly pale and asks whether he's lost his mind, but Chaim declares, "Tonight we are *apikorsim,* which it means epicures!" He grins in his awareness that the word's Yiddish implication is closer to "heretic."

Garde bites her lip; she understands that Chaim's good spirits are his incautious attempt to fly in the face of unrelenting gloom. It's all she can do not to remind him, as the performance is for her benefit, that he's making his flight on wax wings. The waiter delivers their meal in covered dishes, which, uncovered, turn out to be odorous plates of boiled cabbage. Abashed, the couple look toward the waiter, who is now standing behind the bar. He winks theatrically. They look to each other for an interpretation of the gesture, then back toward the waiter, who winks again and nods in the direction of a table of well-heeled gourmands in a frenzy of stuffing themselves. Garde experimentally lifts a cabbage leaf with her fork and discovers underneath, compliments of the black market, a juicy *pavé de rumsteck* with asparagus and hollandaise. Chaim makes a similar discovery and they exchange wan smiles: all pleasure in the Paris of 1940 must be had on the sly. All pleasure is guilty.

As they eat, the waiter brings an unlabeled bottle to their table. Their affable benefactor now, he whispers that this might be the only undiluted bottle of Beaujolais in France. Chaim samples it—again against Garde's protestations—and approves. He clinks Garde's glass, toasts her valor. Outside the restaurant, flushed from the success of their dinner, the artist empties the contents of his stomach into a potted hibiscus. Garde steadies him as they direct their steps toward the Odéon Métro; they must make haste in order to get home before curfew. On the corner of the rue de Condé and the carrefour de l'Odéon, they see a citizen, face hidden by the bill of his flatcap, halted by a pair of Wehrmacht soldiers. The soldiers are shouting at the man and shoving him, and when he raises his arms to fend off their slaps, a cascade of leaflets fall to the pavement from beneath his jacket. One of the soldiers blows a shrill whistle while the other reaches for his rifle strap, but before he can unshoulder his weapon, the citizen has drawn a revolver from his waist. Instead of aiming it at the Boche, however, he places the pistol under his chin. The soldiers freeze as he lifts his chin with the gun barrel—the streetlamp revealing a beardless youth of no discernible gender—and pulls the trigger.

What the couple have witnessed is unseen as soon as it's seen, though it will reappear at chance moments: while listening to a phrase of music on the rackety Victrola or losing a filling after biting into a crust of stale bread. At the time, had either Garde or Chaim spoken a word to each other, neither would have heard; so loud did the metallic report of the pistol reverberate round their skulls. Only when they arrived back at 18 Villa Seurat was Chaim able to make out the voice of his companion over the ringing in his ears. "Oh, Chaim," she cried, "how we have tempted fate this night!" It's the first time he can remember hearing her speak out of unalloyed fear.

✦

YET THEY KNOW THAT what they've seen and can't unsee is not an unusual event. Word of some new outrage is their daily fare. Hardly a day passes without news of hostages taken in retaliation for the murder of this German gauleiter, the attempted assassination of that diplomat. "Judeo-Bolshevik terrorists," randomly selected from among ordinary citizens, are routinely rounded up in these reprisals, then transported to a suburban parade ground where they're summarily shot. But the majority of arrests among the Jews are made on even more arbitrary grounds: they're Communists, immigrants, they have no correct identification, no families—reasons the solid Yid citizens point out in order to convince themselves that *they* are exempt from harm. The detainees are dispatched in droves to the transit camp at Drancy just outside Paris, from which they're sent east in cattle cars to places—says Chana Orloff bleakly— "somewhere to the north of God." In their wake are left plundered apartments, rifled strongboxes, and abandoned children.

Every week more anti-Semitic edicts are issued with the frequency of czarist ukases. "You can almost from the pogroms of Mother Russia be homesick," says Chaim in a labored attempt at humor, but who's laughing?

The native-born French Jews can still not believe that what is happening is happening, and often blame their foreign coreligionists. They're incredulous when forced, along with the immigrants, to have their identity cards stamped *Juif* at a local prefecture. (Chaim's is smudged in the process, and in showing it to Garde he remarks, "Look, they botched my 'Jew.' ") They're made to sit only in the last car of the Métro and prohibited from entering parks and public gardens. Soon after comes their exclusion from restaurants, theaters, cinemas, museums, and concert halls. Quotas have reduced them to a phantom presence in the liberal professions and schools, and their complete exclusion from commerce and industry is nearly complete. When the police still complain of the difficulty of identifying them (this is before the imposition of the yellow star), the flics are themselves sent by their superiors to the Palais Berlitz in the 2nd arrondissement. There they can study the exhibition entitled *Le Juif et la France*, which graphically catalogs the racial characteristics of the Hebrew. The rococo facade of the Palais is itself draped in a gigantic banner depicting a monstrous Jew devouring the globe.

Radios are confiscated, telephones disconnected, news limited to rumor and the Vichy press. The latter is devoted almost exclusively to touting Axis victories and mocking the sheenies in cartoons and screeds. The rumors reach Chaim and Garde primarily through Madame Orloff, who has her sources: she tells them of *le rafle du billet vert*, when loudspeakers in the streets of the Marais called for all Jews to come out from wherever they were hiding. Thousands are swept up and sent to the camps at Compiègne in the Oise department and Beaune-la-Rolande in the Loiret. Chana informs them of the bombing of a Paris synagogue (and of Pearl Harbor) and informs them of the epidemics of suicide in the occupied towns. She also alerts them to her own imminent departure for the Swiss border, the means for which her well-placed son is pulling strings to provide. They must make their own plans, she counsels, for "the city of light has become the city of dreadful night."

"Such a way you got of saying things," replies Chaim, but Garde observes his left eyelid flickering like a leaf in a gale. They're both painfully aware of the urgency. Perhaps they should have stayed in the village after all. But it's clear to his companion that their escape from Civry had exhausted Chaim's capacity for forward motion, and perilous as Paris has become, he's in the grip of an inertia that precludes any further travel.

The season turns and the knock at the door has yet to come. But the remittances from the Castaings are more irregular than ever. In their letters they remind the ever more desolate couple that no gallery can accept the work of Jewish artists, not that anyone is buying art in any case.

"What's it got to do, their buying and selling, with the price of a lump of coal?" grouses Chaim, coal being as scarce as diamonds these days. "They're rich as Rothschilds!"

"Chaim," Garde tries to placate him, "we don't want charity."

They exchange looks that seem to say: Who says we don't want?

Winter is upon them again and the fitfully functioning radiators seem permanently defunct. They complain to the stone-faced concierge, who gives them some bunkum about a defective boiler; she's been waiting weeks for the thing to be replaced. So why, they wonder, is her own apartment so toasty? (Garde has seen the woman talking with the police and suspects she might be a *collabo*—it's best, in fact, to suspect everyone.) Having burnt in the fireplace what sticks of furniture they can spare, the couple wrap themselves in blankets and sit on the floor like red Indians. The monotony of their days is punishing. Garde has her daily expeditions in search of sustenance, but Chaim can scarcely be bothered to blow the dust from his Balzac and *Arsène Lupin*. It seldom occurs to him to put a disc on the Victrola. He never sets foot outside the apartment, hardly even looks out a window. Instead he spends his time— a man for whom Lindbergh's flight and the advent of women's suffrage had gone practically unnoticed—combing through the state-sanctioned distortions of the *Paris-soir*. You never knew when you might stumble upon some morsel of truth.

Which is how Garde finds him this afternoon on her return from a shopping foray. She drops an armload of scrounged items on a surviving end table—a powdered milk substitute, a handful of cigarettes, a wrapped fish of no identifiable species—and sighs.

"Chaim," she says, with the modicum of exasperation she allows herself, "why don't you paint?"

It's been her gentle plea throughout the months of their Paris cohabitation. His excuses are always the same: he has no desire to paint still lifes, having had enough of dead animals for all time, and the cold weather (it was the heat in summer) is not favorable for the plein air. Then there's his stomach. But there's another reason that he doesn't tell her. When it comes upon him now, the itch, he resists scratching with every fiber of his will. For when he paints, the woman no longer exists for him, and he cannot leave her again; that Chaim can never do. He sets great store by the magnitude of his sacrifice, though his immobility is putting both of them in jeopardy. For all their anxiety and the stifling tedium, however, they still have the small moments when their feelings for each other open up a vast interior space, which they inhabit awhile in a peace beyond reason.

Spring again and the Allies bomb the Renault factory in its Paris suburb. Nonaggression Pact aside, the Germans invade the USSR. More Wehrmacht officers are murdered in public places, more hostages (frequently Jews) taken and shot. Le Maréchal Pétain meets with Hitler at Montoire and an exhibition of the works of Arno Breker, state sculptor of the Nazi party, is mounted at l'Orangerie. Jewish bank accounts have been seized and safe-deposit boxes opened, thus confirming Chaim's wisdom in hiding his money in his socks. In making her rounds of the *magasins* and markets,

Garde has worn out her shoes. There are ration coupons you can use for purchasing dry goods, but all available leather has been requisitioned by the occupiers for the manufacture of soldiers' boots. Improvising, the shoemakers have begun making a kind of clog with a vamp of woven raffia and a wooden sole. They're cheap and Garde buys a pair but finds it hard to walk in them. She says it's as if her feet have turned to hooves. She hobbles about and ultimately falls down a flight of stairs in the apartment and, though she doesn't like to complain, is afraid she's broken her left arm. Chaim sees the inflamed and swollen limb and immediately snaps out of his torpor. He insists on taking her to the hospital in the nearby rue de Sèvres, where they wait for hours in a corridor among figures that might have stepped out of Goya's black paintings. When they finally see the rumpled, put-upon doctor, the man assures Garde rather dismissively that it's only a sprain, albeit a bad one; he wraps the arm in a surgical bandage, places it in a sling, and gives her a prescription for painkillers that no pharmacy has in stock. The couple return to number 18, where they find a notice slipped under the door.

Madame Gerda Groth-Michaelis is advised by order of the prefect of the Departement Seine to report to the Vélodrome d'Hiver by noon of Thursday, May 16. The official purpose of the order is stated in a paragraph couched in an impenetrable bureaucratese. If there is any hope that the directive is merely routine, it is undermined by the instructions that she bring with her a blanket, a change of underwear, a blouse, a sweater, a toothbrush, and no more. Transport will be provided. The injunction is made further alarming by a second shoved under the door a few days later. This one exhorts the Jews "not to wait for these bandits in your home . . . Barricade the doors, call for help, fight the police. You have nothing to lose!"

"Why you and not also me?" stammers Chaim, sounding almost jealous. He argues with some cogency that the specific targeting of German nationals has happened already before they arrived in Paris—so why now? Though they both know that the collaborationist state has since cast a much wider net.

All in a lather, Chaim drags his companion through a fine spring rain back to the dusty warren of the Ministry of the Interior, from whose offices all sympathy has been purged. Chaim presses her case to a starched official behind an immaculate desk that she surely cannot be detained in her injured condition; he lifts her arm in its sling as evidence, causing Garde to cry out from the pain.

"No one is exempt," says the official, unimpressed: case closed.

Chaim frowns, considering. "*I'm* exempt," he replies.

"Chaim, shah!" cautions Garde, tugging him toward an exit. She reminds him he should be thankful that he's yet to be caught up in their snares. "You are fortunate, *meine Geliebte.*"

"That's right," he acknowledges bitterly, "fortunate, untouchable even, like I was in Smilovitchi."

He resolves to save her: they must hide. But when he contemplates their escape, he thinks more in terms of fleeing into some nebulous pipe dream—the kind that emanated from Modigliani's hookah—than of any earthly asylum. He proposes options, all of which are impracticable; they're both aware that the time when they might have slipped away from the city undetected has come and gone. He asserts, with diminishing ardor, that they still have well-wishers who can give them shelter; they can move from house to house, keeping always one step ahead of the Gestapo. But Garde has become ruefully resigned, even fatalistic. She tells him he must save himself. She consoles him, without much conviction, that the few belongings she's been told to bring with her suggests that she won't be gone for long. She cups his bristly cheek in the palm of her hand. "You will wait for me," she says, the statement just shy of a question.

The knock when it comes early on the morning of the sixteenth is almost solicitous, not the thunderous pounding one might have expected. But it is accompanied by the doorbell, which doesn't stop ringing. The sound makes for a rude transition to consciousness from the dream Chaim is having about the tree in the square at Vence. In the dream Dr. Faure is trying to explain to the tree the value of art in time of war, while the tree, with a face like a fist, yawns disrespectfully. When his eyes fly open, Chaim sees Garde already out of bed, awkwardly hastening to put on her clothes without the help of her left arm. She glances in a mirror, licks a finger to smooth a stray curl, then takes up the drawstring bag she's folded her allotted garments into the night before.

She heads quickly for the parlor and opens the door to a pair of blue-suited gendarmes, one fat and one thin, waiting on the landing. The thin one turns to dismiss the walrus-faced chap standing behind them with a toolbox strapped over his shoulder: the locksmith they've brought along in case she had refused to let them in. Before leaving the locksmith leans forward to remove a matchstick from the doorbell, and in the absence of its ringing you could now hear the bullhorn-enhanced shouts from the street.

There is some relief in the fact that the officers are French rather than German, and that they are somewhat foolish in their uneven appearance. But they are no less officious than the occupiers. Still, Garde believes she can discern the merest hint of shame in their puffed-up faces. She's mistaken in this but nevertheless summons the courage to ask their permission to say goodbye to her man. They neither give their consent nor prevent her from turning, but follow her as far as the door to the bedroom, where Chaim has practically slid under the bedclothes in his fright. Garde leans over to kiss him, her dark eyes liquid, her expression fixed in a sorrow with no horizon. It's the expression that has so often informed her features of late, as if she were already looking back from an impossible distance. Chaim's heart is in his throat, caught there along with the cry he's never been able to release, the one that rose up in him the first time he saw the butcher kill a goose. Then, to the shock of all present, he ducks out of his companion's embrace and springs from the bed in his underwear.

"I'm coming with you!" he declares, searching for his pants.

The fat flic shouts a warning as the thin one unholsters his weapon. They close ranks around their captive, who gives Chaim a look like "*Meine Liebsten*, you don't really mean what you say." With one foot in and one foot out of his pants legs, he watches as they escort her from the apartment, the sparrowlike, redheaded Jewish girl with the wounded wing.

Chaim lurches for the open windows, trousers still clinging to his ankle. Indifferent to whatever devilish spirits may have wandered into the apartment upon her exit, he leans out over the box of geraniums Garde has hung from the faux balcony. The sky over Montparnasse is lapis and salmon pink, the beryl-green butte of the Parc Montsouris just visible above the rooftops, the morning air cool. Below, the cops are hustling his beloved across the street to a waiting motorcoach. A score of others, mostly women and children, are also being herded from their houses by barking gendarmes. Who knew there were so many Jews in la Villa Seurat? Chaim reminds himself they're being taken to the Vél d'Hiv, a place he associates solely with sport and recreation. What harm—notwithstanding the blood of the combatants he's cheered time and again in its arena—what harm can come to one there? Then he wonders how long before a world gone *gantz kapoyer*, gone topsy-turvy, is set aright again by some hidden hand?

As if a small kindness can mitigate a great evil, a flic helps Garde onto the cream-colored coach, and Chaim leans a little further out the window. Another finger's width farther and he will tumble over the iron railing.

"I didn't never deserve you!" he shouts, and lowering his voice, "Don't leave me," in a tone more accusatory than imploring.

Behind her a young mother with her roan-brown hair in a snood is boarding the bus with her little girl. The child is clutching a doll, which the helpful gendarme snatches from her hands and tosses onto a heap of other confiscated toys.

8

IN APRIL OF 1917, during the fourth year of the Great War, Amedeo Modigliani got the cockeyed idea of staging an artists' regatta in the Seine. Esteemed artists of the day would throw together improvised boats from available scraps and race them from the pont Louis-Philippe to the viaduc d'Austerlitz. That the course was upstream occurred to no one but Modi, who had a plan. He talked his friend and protégé Chaim Soutine into donning a deep-sea diver's equipage and hauling the bathtub that doubled as his boat from underwater. Then it would appear from above that the ducks Modi had harnessed to his tub were the cause of his victory.

Chaim protested as he always stubbornly protested before submitting to the realization that he would do anything for the Italian, though not without bearing an eternal grudge. Hadn't he, only weeks before, agreed to play Punch to Modi's puppeteer? He allowed himself to be got up in a two-tone waistcoat, sugar-loaf hat, and one of Modigliani's abominable African masks. Strings were attached to his arms and legs, which Modi, mounted on stilts, would manipulate, all for the purpose of making an (uninvited) entrance at a Dada soirée. The effect was a good one, at least for the two or three steps during which the squiffy Amedeo was able to maintain his balance before toppling from the stilts. Falling in fact upon the head of the Litvak. Chaim resolved never again to subject himself to the Tuscan's humiliations, then awoke that very night from bad dreams to find himself in the throes of one of his *petit mal* seizures—and Modi holding him tightly till the tremors subsided.

After getting over the initial panic and confusion of finding himself at the bottom of the river, Chaim began to take note of the curiosities he encountered. There are schools of fish with somber faces and artifacts of archaeological interest, objects trailing milfoil and fronds like horses' manes. He trudges the kilometer and a half along the riverbed in his cumbersome gear, pulling Modi's tub until he's passed beneath the Austerlitz bridge and the race is won. Unaware of the hoopla erupting on the embankment above him, however, Chaim continues his forward slog. The veteran salvage diver Gaston Babineaux, who has manned the respirator and monitored Chaim's progress from the riverbank, is confounded as to why he's unable to haul him back aloft. Modi himself shouts from the water to *per l'amor di Dio!* pull the Litvak out of the river; he's released the ducks and is ready to row his tub to shore. Still the old plongeur cannot manage to draw the Italian's friend up from the depths. I have suggested this was due to the accumulated weight of the episodes from his past and future that Chaim has amassed during his underwater promenade, and no one has yet offered a better explanation.

As for the "delusions" suffered by Soutine in his submersion, historians of art have attributed them to decidedly physiological causes: namely, the buildup of pressure and the toxicity of the recycled air inside his copper helmet. Personally, I think they should have also taken into account the pliancy of subaqueous time. Whatever the case, Chaim persists in forging ahead in his clumsy boots toward the wavering figure that beckons him.

Between him and the figure is a volume of water imbued with sunlight like cloth-of-gold draperies, and through their shimmering swim dozens of refugee creatures. Some are *lilin*, an aerial species who have recently adapted themselves to the submarine element, their bodies like huge spermatozoa with squinty eyes. They are out-numbered by the *farfir lichter* and the *kesilim*, whose wispy anato-mies have developed, for the sake of their new environment, webbed feet. More at home beneath the river than these is Tanin'iver, the blind dragon from *The Book of Enoch*, astride which a number of horned *mazikim* are riding. All are beings that have once inhabited the privies and moldering synagogues of the old Russian Empire; they have resided in these places after venturing forth from volumes such as the *Pirkei de-Rabbi Eliezer* and the *Midrash Tanhuma*, the lot of which have since been burnt by barbarian invaders. Bereft of heritage, they have fled west seeking sanctuary, some of them having come to feel less vulnerable underwater than on dry land.

Chaim tries his best to disregard them as he plods forward, having no tolerance for the existence of such beings in the first place. More difficult to ignore is the figure—its features beginning to clarify themselves through the haze—who sits on a three-legged stool athwart his path. It is a very old man in a billowing white caftan of the type pious Jews wear on Yom Kippur, the Day of Atonement. He has streaming silvery hair and an undulant beard twined in flotsam, and upon his hoary head is perched a skull-cap embossed with snails and fairy shrimp. The wings of his large nostrils fluctuate like gills. In his lap is a great open tome that completes his countenance of a scholar or sage, an aquatic tzaddik if you will.

The sight of such a character at the bottom of the river is un-nerving enough, but even more disturbing is the fact that, as the momentum of his heavy-footers draws him irresistibly nearer the old man, Chaim finds himself unable to breathe. The demand valve between his teeth has thus far functioned as reliably as a heartbeat, filling his lungs with the oxygen-helium mix that keeps him vital. But now, though he bites down on the rubber regulator for all he's

worth, the thing refuses to deliver the breathing gas. His chest collapses like a trod-upon bagpipe, while his mouth stretches open
as if to invite in the air he cannot swallow. He gulps, gasps, and
chokes in the throes of his imminent asphyxiation. Then it's only
logical that Chaim should conclude in his agony that the ancient
gentleman hovering now in front of him is *malach hamovess*, the
Angel of Death.

There's nothing of a supernatural nature, however, going on
above with the plongeur's compressed-air gadgetry. All that has
happened is that old Babineaux has fallen asleep over his portable
respirator. He's exhausted from the effort of coordinating the place-
ment of his bulky compressor in its hardwood cabinet with Chaim's
dogged march along the riverbed. His shoulders are in torment
from operating the rotary pump and from trying without success to
haul the diver back to the surface. Kneeling on the embankment in
that late April afternoon, he has laid his cheek against his rig, closed
his yellow eyes, and wondered what it would hurt if he rested a moment. Meanwhile the tzaddik, with spindly fingers, has taken hold
of the handle fixed to Chaim's copper bonnet and forced his viewport toward the open book. Then, in the midst of his struggling,
Chaim hears a sound—as sound travels well underwater—like a
burbling yodel, and raises his eyes to see that the ancient is speaking. But while his speech is unintelligible, bubbles emanate from
his lips and each bubble contains a word or phrase in Yiddish script.

"If you can . . . read . . . you can breathe."

But under these circumstances Chaim cannot read. His burst-
ing lungs are an impediment to concentration, and besides, the
pages are rippling like fishtails and the words themselves seem to
float from the page. He proceeds to suffocate. With dimming eyes
he sees the tzaddik's pronouncement in a string of bubbles, which
burst as soon as they're observed—though the message somehow
penetrates the artist's delirious brain:

"In paradise . . . every soul of Israel . . . reads Torah . . . according to his lights."

With what he feels must be his final gasp, Chaim mouths the words: "This is paradise?"

The tzaddik releases more bubbles, most merely the result of laughter though the last few include his reply: "This is . . . the bottom of a river." Upon saying which he redirects Chaim's helmet back toward the book.

Then Chaim is able to comprehend what was previously indecipherable. One reason is that the sage keeps the pages from fluttering and turns them for Chaim as he reads; he even pins down with his thumb the words that would otherwise have floated free. Another reason is that, to his rhapsodically light-headed relief, Chaim's lungs are again inflated with air. This is either a miraculous occurrence or else Monsieur Babineaux has simply woken up and begun to crank the respirator again. In either event, Chaim is afraid to stop reading. The text, he finds, is not holy writ but rather a volume of stories: they are bubbeh maysehs, brief household tales of the kind he'd heard from his mama and the old melamed in his tumbledown study house. Stories Chaim has disdained all his life, though in this instance he thinks it best to keep reading. One tale is about a hidden saint for whose sake God refrains from destroying the world. Another is about the Baal Shem Tov, Master of the Name, who liberates a soul from a tree. Another is about a cave that leads from Chelm, the town of fools, to Jerusalem, and another about an infant snatched from its cradle by a tribe of half-demons called shretelekh. They replace the stolen child with one of their own. The poor *bane-man*, the changeling, scorned by its foster family, is further cursed with a morbid passion for painting pictures, and each portrait it paints possesses the misbegotten features of its own kind.

Narishkeit! thinks Chaim. Everyone knows that when goblins steal babies, they substitute them with dolls of wood and straw. "I

am the wretched son of the wretched Reb Zalman Sütin!" he would
have cried out was he not still sucking air from the rubber valve
that filled his mouth.

But the source of the itch still resists all rational explanation.
Why, for instance, should a boy on a back bench in a village shul
risk a whipping and confinement by drawing a portrait of the rabbi
Leyzer-Eyzik at his prayers? This is on the Great Sabbath before
the Passover of Chaim's sixteenth year. All the Jews are gathered
in the old timber synagogue, which was built—like the temple in
Jerusalem—without using a single nail. Which is no doubt why
the structure is falling apart. Mushrooms sprout from its decaying
joints, birds' nests colonize the rafters. The wind whistles through
its cracks to rival the cantor's warbling and the skirling of the ram's
horn; it competes, the wind, with the male congregation's wor-
shipful *davening*, as well as their bargaining and airing of petty
squabbles, let alone the scandal-mongering rampant in the women's
gallery. In the midst of the cacophony the old rabbi, wrapped in
the shawl that will serve soon enough as his shroud, sways on his
canopied *bima*. Then the anomaly of his face in its exalted devotion
arouses in Chaim the forbidden impulse to make a sketch. The image will blister his brain if he doesn't do it.

There are blank pages at the end of his well-thumbed *machzor*,
a lead pencil burning a hole in his pocket. While the congregation
is immersed in their prayer and palaver, Chaim cautiously slides
the pencil from his pocket and makes a hasty rough study of the
holy man: his eyes like craters half-obscured by briary brows; his
nose is a rudder, the spidery veins of his cheeks like roots spreading
from his ocher shrub of a beard. With a cough to cover the sound,
Chaim tears the page from the book and stuffs it into his pocket
along with the offending pencil. He looks both ways to make sure
the congregants are preoccupied with either their dickering or God,
then steals out of the synagogue.

Truth is, Chaim is never content with a sketch; a drawing is bare bones until it's quickened with color, and he'd prefer to dispense with the preliminary outline altogether. He crosses the muddy market platz, empty on Shabbos but for a peasant and his arthritic goat at the town pump. He turns into an unpaved lane, wooden hovels staggering on either side of him, their roofs missing shingles that have flown off in blizzards like shuffled cards. There's a stench of raw sewage that has kept the boy's eyes watering since birth, a keen stench from the tannery whose waste has turned the Berezina into a river of boiling putrescence. A benighted rural slum, this Smilovitchi. Chaim ambles down the slope where the women, with kilted skirts, spread their laundry, and crosses the soggy plank bridge to the old cemetery, dense with burdock and ferns. Today even old Issachar, the hunchbacked mourner for hire, is absent, and Chaim will have the place to himself.

Alone is his standard condition. His father and his bullying brothers have seen to that: they've advertised his misdeeds until his standing in the village is no better than that of Dudl, the *dorf idyot*. The "mislooked" one. It's a station he's begun to assume with an odd defiance. If the village avoids and derides him, he will avoid and deride it in turn. Loneliness, he's learned, is sometimes a stimulating companion.

Chaim feels as well a rare sense of fraternity among the lichen-studded headstones leaning toward one another in the posture of Jews spreading rumors. Some of the stones predate the Chmielnicki pogroms, some even the Black Death. Some are topped with rocks to the height of a cairn. But the graveyard is too frequently visited to be a safe place to practice his . . . art? Chaim knows the word only as a proscribed activity. He's vaguely aware that the word has a timeworn history about which he is ignorant, and that everything in his experience conspires to keep him so. He has of course seen illustrations of people and events in newspapers; he's even glimpsed

through the open doors of the Russian church the icons that the
christelakh claim were made by no human hand. But what do they
have in common with the thing his instinct compels him to do?
A thing he would never dignify, nor denigrate, with the word *art*.

He stoops to remove a boxboard panel he's wedged between
the stones of the cemetery wall; then he wanders into the trees
beyond the Sabbath boundary, where he's stashed his materials in
the hollow of a rotten birch. Here are the wax pastels and the jars
of paint he's purchased with the kopecks he's earned from odd jobs,
money he managed to squirrel away despite his brothers' regular
shakedowns. He sits on the ground with his back against the birch,
the panel propped against his bent knees, and makes a quick copy
from his original sketch; then he rises again and unbuttons his
pants to moisten the dried paint pots with his pee. Some contain
colors—magenta, old gold—that he's mixed himself from powdered pigments, diluting them with the poppyseed oil he filched
from his mother's pantry. He stirs them now with the handle of
a commercial brush from which he's plucked all the bristles until
only a fine point remains.

He leans the panel against the tree, kneels in the weeds before
it, and begins to stipple, daub, slather, and smear. When the brush
is not a tactile enough agent of expression, he places the handle
between his teeth and strokes the paint with his fingers. He sculpts
the contours of the rabbi's craggy features until the face behind
his face starts to emerge. The beating heart and burning brain that
Chaim has brought with him from the synagogue have reached a
pitch of hectic agitation. Then the picture he's attempting to em-
blazon upon this neutral surface must also continue to beat and
burn. If it doesn't (and few do) he will smash it to pieces, as if the
image itself has betrayed him rather than the reverse. Momentarily
out of breath, he pauses to take stock: the colors are too muted,
the texture less granular than intended (he knows these things

with his spleen), but the face, the face is the one that has belonged to Rabbi Leyzer-Eyzik since maybe even before he was born. This one he will keep.

The boy tucks his creation into his pants under his loose-knit jumper, heedless of the still-damp paint, then rises and starts for home. It's dusk and the family will have returned from shul. They will be gathered for the Shabbos meal, which includes on a good night a dollop of pot cheese in his mama's cornmeal mamaliga. But he must first hide the rabbi's portrait among his cache of others: along with Sonye the *opshpreker* and Zusman the wedding jester and Blume the Byelo-blue cow—all of them sharing a ledge in the dry well behind the outhouse. Three of his brothers, however, are milling about in the barren yard in front of their crippled abode. One of them (is it Kalman or Borukh?—they're all of a thick-necked piece to Chaim) remarks on the rectangular configuration beneath his jumper, to say nothing of the paint bleeding through the coarse fabric.

"What are you trying to smuggle there, *gruber yung?*" he asks, as one of them grabs his arms from behind. Then Borukh (or is it Yosl-Zisl?—it's getting dark) lifts his jumper and yanks the portrait out of his pants. Another pulls the bill of his cap down over his eyes.

"Give it back!" shouts Chaim, breaking free of his captor. He raises his cap and makes a leap for the picture, which the brother holds just beyond his reach.

They're laborers, Chaim's older brothers—loutish porters, rope spinners, and woodcutters. Not religiously observant, neither are they political; they're mostly impervious to the Zionist and revolutionary enthusiasms that are sweeping the Pale. But they're of one mind in berating the *pisher* for his artistic pretensions. They also enjoy poking fun at his blubber lips and shifty eyes, though they are themselves not much prettier. They cluck their tongues at the double sin of making painted images on Shabbos and begin to confer over the portrait, leaving fingerprints in the wet oils as they pass it around. They elbow their nebbish little brother out of the way as he tries to retrieve it. Several candidates, some of them animals, are offered as possible subjects of the portrait before it's concluded that it bears a vague resemblance to Rabbi Leyzer-Eyzik, the spiritual leader of their backward-looking community.

"I don't see the likeness," says Yosl (or is it the bullet-headed Gershon?), but he's overruled. Chaim feels an instant's gratification at their correct identification of the picture, until one or another of them suggests, "Reb Gdalye might like to see this."

Gdalye is a *shoychet*, a ritual slaughterer, a hulking type whose ruddy cheeks reprise the gore of the beasts he butchers according to the strict laws of kashrut. He is also Rabbi Leyzer-Eyzik's only son. Always quick to assist their father in punishing the apostate, the brothers Sütin have not previously had the habit of farming the task out to others. Not so long out of cheder, their threat recalls for Chaim the tale of Joseph and his vengeful brethren. It's flattering to feel himself akin to the dreamer, though his own dreams have brought nothing but monsters. He thinks it a good idea to steer clear of the butcher's open-air stall in the market square.

Several days pass without consequence, and while Chaim is never able to recover his painting, he begins to believe he might escape retribution after all. This doesn't mean he relaxes his wariness; he never relaxes. But on the next Friday morning his mama assigns him the chore of carrying her pot of meatless cholent to the baker's, where it will simmer in his oven overnight. The errand takes him past the sooty shop windows of Menke One-Crutch the tailor and Henoch Hernia the watchmaker, past the foul-mouthed Libitchke's matchbox grocery and Feyvish Freethinker's apothecary and Reb Gdalye's journeyman meat carver's stall. Chaim has not forgotten that the man might still be a menace, but he's clearly preoccupied with the business of slicing briskets from shanks of beef at his butcher's block. Nevertheless, Chaim hurries past the shambles, though he can't resist giving the red-bearded butcher with his rope-veined forearms a sidelong glance. What he sees is that the man in his blood-smeared apron has buried his cleaver in a cut of meat and fixed Chaim in his turn with a gimlet stare. The stare stops the boy in his tracks, hesitating long enough to allow the butcher to leave his stall and fall upon him raining curses and blows.

Knocked from his feet, Chaim goes sprawling in the mess spilled on the ground from his mother's stewpot. He curls into the knees-to-chin tuck he assumes during his father's drubbings, a position that has always provided a minimum of protection. But the butcher is no raw-boned clothes mender, and his stunning blows acquaint the boy with a whole new order of pain.

"*Kholyerah*," shouts Reb Gdalye, leaving off with his fists in favor of his boots, "don't bother to get up alive!"

If it seems to Chaim that the butcher has more than two feet, it's because he's being aided (not that he needs it) by a pair of apprentices eager to show themselves in accord with their boss. Merchants and vendors, the glazier, the blacksmith, a bookkeeper, a scribe, have all abandoned their commerce to look on; Menke One-Crutch comes out from behind his sewing machine, Szymen Zlotnik from behind his last. Froy Shvager the fishwife at first emits a volley of braying laughter from her booth, then falls silent. No one makes a move to interfere but watch in a hush like witnesses at some solemn rite. Crows caw, a shaft horse whinnies, and the boy suffers an immensity of pain too great for his meager frame to accommodate. Then comes a kick to the back of his head that completes the job of his ouster from himself and transports him to a garden-like tranquility free from all hurt.

A return to consciousness means banishment from the garden where Chaim wants so badly to remain, but his swarming head has awakened him to a dim awareness of his situation: he is dead and disembodied, having been retired to the *Otzar*, the repository of souls, where you await a second birth. This conclusion, however, is contradicted by the perception that he's still in possession of his arms and legs. Naked souls don't have limbs and his, where they aren't wholly numb, are suffused with a sensation of simultaneous burning and cold. His teeth are chattering. He's still in the world, which stinks of rank straw saturated in blood. With the single eye he's able to open, he can see that he's been confined to an enclosed compartment hung with sackcloth curtains. Its walls are lined with shelves supporting bins containing casket-sized slabs of ice. Sides of beef are arrayed atop the slabs, as is the supine boy himself. More carcasses dangle from hooks in the ceiling, their splayed ribs resembling the jaws of opened traps. When he tries to stir, Chaim is seized by such stupefying pain that he resigns himself to lying still until he freezes. The prospect is not without consolation. But after an indefinite time the heavy door groans open and the sackcloth is parted to admit Chaim's mama, Toyvah-Freydl, into the meat locker. The tatty woolen shawl pulled over her clotted wig frames an expression alternating between sympathy and disgust.

"Put in the wheelbarrow, my son," she tells the two dull-witted apprentices who have shown her in.

As her broad bulk commands a certain authority, they grab the boy by his arms and legs and drag him howling from the block of ice. They deposit him unceremoniously in the wheelbarrow amid some discarded tripes but do not offer to conduct the vehicle any further. Then it's left to Toyvah-Freydl to take up the handles and guide the barrow up a short ramp out of the locker. She wheels her broken offspring through the shambles under the nose of the implacable butcher himself, who turns his head away. Not so the rest of the market population, who have formed files of gawkers between which mother and son must pass along the length of Zabludeve Street. They mutter, the good people of Smilovitchi, that the Sütin

kid has finally got what he's been asking for all these years. By the
time Toyvah-Freydl has reached the tar-papered shanty that passes
for the village infirmary with her burden, Chaim's disgrace and
comeuppance are a general cause célèbre.

There's no space for convalescence at his home, so he's left to his
misery in the flyblown infirmary for fifteen days. Its single room
reeks from the necrotic bodies, both gentile and Jew, that have
preceded him—and from his own neglected hygiene and fevered
wounds. His concussed head is swathed in bandages, as is his torso,
an adhesive corset binding the cracked ribs in place. There's a cen-
tipede's worth of stitches above his right eye and across his scalp
where the hair has been shaved. The unseen damage to his internal
organs, already contorted from chronic hunger, will plague him all
his days. His father, humiliated, refuses to see him, maintaining
like his fellow *prosteh yidn* that his son has gotten what he deserved.
His brothers, who had so vindictively shown Gdalye the rabbi's
portrait, may feel some degree of shame, though they too refrain
from visiting the boy. His only visitors, other than a moonlighting
horse doctor and the woman who ladles the turbid soup, are the
unclean spirits Chaim is too weak to disbelieve in.

Toyvah-Freydl herself is of a mind to let him languish; the boy
has been a trial and an embarrassment to his family all his life. But
at length an untapped residue of affection prompts her change of
heart. Surprised by the acuity of her anger toward her people, she
determines without confiding in her husband to seek redress for
her son's inhumane treatment. She might travel to Minsk to petition the authorities, though the authorities are seldom concerned
with what torments the zhids inflict on each other. Besides, a Jew
who reports her own would be subject to an ostracism beyond that
which her family already endures. Instead, she summons from some
forsaken recess of her nature the chutzpah to attend the weekly *beit
din*, the court, at the home of the rabbi.

Because he supplements his negligible stipend by arbitrating civil litigations, the rabbi can afford a larger house than most, though it is no less decrepit than any other in their penurious backwater, and like the others it appears to be sinking into its foundation. The stolid Toyvah-Freydl waits her turn on a bench in the crowded vestibule. She's seated next to a woman holding a live chicken with a milky eye, which she hopes to get certified as kosher by the holy man. Next to her is a tinsmith complaining aloud of the barrenness of his wife, whom he wishes to divorce. (The wife sits in listless patience beside him.) A pair of mop-headed water carriers are involved in the vocal feud they've been called to the rabbi's court to resolve. It's nearly sundown when Chaim's mama is finally admitted into the stuffy little room that Rabbi Leyzer-Eyzik calls his "chambers." The old man sits slumped in a straight-backed chair, while a member of the *kahal*, the shtetl's executive committee, seated beside him in his four-cornered yarmulke, plumps him back up when he begins to slide toward the floor.

"Froy Sütin," says the rabbi, whose high-pitched voice sounds to Toyveh-Freydl almost to be veiling a threat, "what is your business here?"

Her first impulse is to beg his pardon for imposing on his time and make a hasty retreat: she has no business here. But the memory of her child's grievous ill-usage restores her firmness of purpose.

"I want for my son *compensatzieh*," she declares. She has rehearsed the word innumerable times while waiting.

The rabbi cups an ear: has he heard her correctly? There is of course no reason to review the issue; by now the whole town is acquainted with it. Many have even seen the evidence, which the butcher has brandished about to vindicate his actions. (One or two of the viewers, uninformed as to the severity of Chaim's trespass, confessed that the painting failed to do justice to its subject—upon which the incensed butcher barked, "That's not the point!") So the old rabbi merely cites again the letter of the law and asks the woman, "Has he not been justly punished, your son?"

Toyvah-Freydl hasn't come to defend the boy: right and wrong are categories for the men to decide. Her appeal has a more pragmatic bias. "Twenty-five rubles," she stammers, "would be for my Chaim enough to leave from this place."

The rabbi blanches, sputtering into his beard. "How is this reasonable? You want that the boy should be rewarded for his crime?"

But the deputy of the kahal—duly elected by virtue of his goods and chattels if lacking any real credentials to judge—leans over to whisper in the old man's tufted ear. Toyvah-Freydl, with her mite of intuition, can guess that the wry-faced deputy is speaking to the general nuisance the boy represents. She knows too that beyond his nuisance there's a deeper concern. Hasn't she heard more than once the complaints of her neighbors who've discovered themselves the subject of Chaim's portraiture—that they feel themselves in danger of having their *neshomah*, their soul's essence, compromised by his studies from life? And those who have thus far escaped them live in fear of falling victim to the Sütin kid's charcoals and paints. His mama, who acknowledges there might indeed be a diabolical component to her son's obsession, suspects that the rabbi himself is not immune to the prevailing unease.

This is her gambit: that if the rabbi's lowering *bulvan* of a son is unwilling to pay the full amount, a collection might be taken up to augment the fund and facilitate her boy's exodus from Smilovitchi. Then the village will be rid of him and, thinks his mother, he will be safely beyond the range of its knocks and venomous tongues.

The wintry old man lifts a sere finger: their conference is ended. "So be it," he pronounces. "Does not Mishnah tell us that the highest form of wisdom is compassion?" But he continues his sputtering as if the words have left a bad taste.

The rabbi has to repeat her dismissal before Toyvah-Freydl realizes that she has succeeded in her suit. It is the only victory she can lay claim to in her entire self-abasing existence, though she lacks the artfulness to gloat. On Pesach donations are solicited in shul to which even the poorest congregants contribute. Toyvah-Freydl pockets their fair share for the family and gives Chaim the rest. She gives him also some black bread and onions, which he tosses into a tow sack along with his scant belongings. Only his mama and his demented sister, Ertl, with her wandering ashen eye come into the yard to see him off—though the girl is more concerned with the shriveled rhododendron she's tried and failed to coax into blossom than her brother's leave-taking. He's wearing his workman's jacket and the pants that barely reach his ankles, a dried speck of weeks'-old blood still visible below an ear. His flat *muzhik*'s face shows no emotion. In an unusually maternal gesture his mother places a cloth cap of his father's on his head (his own was lost in the melee). If her husband discovers her part in its disappearance, he may murder her.

The cap slides to Chaim's ears and practically covers his eyes. "It's too big," he says.

"The cap is fine," replies Toyvah-Freydl, "but the head is too small."

Chaim lifts the bill to see whether his mother is joking with him, but the Family Sütin seldom make jokes. He flings the sack over his shoulder, cringing from the residual pain, then, without the least inclination to spare his home a backward glance, exits the yard and begins to hobble down the rutted road toward Minsk.

9

ON THE EVE OF her backdoor departure from Paris, Chana Orloff offers to sew on Chaim's yellow star. He reminds her it's not for nothing that he's a clothes mender's son. He stitches the star onto the left breast of his old serge suit jacket, "at the level of the heart" as prescribed by the government decree. There is the predictable talk among the Jews that one should wear the star as a badge of honor and so forth: some merely stick it on with pins for easy removal; one impenitent woman hangs hers about the neck of her dog. But such mutinous gestures invariably result in the arrest of their perpetrators. It's true that the odd Parisian might offer a wink or a furtive salute as a sign of solidarity, but no one really has any illusions anymore: they know that the star is both a target and a brand. When Chaim removes the jacket he can still feel the imprint of the Magen David seared upon his breast.

The cupboard in his apartment is bare, but the artist is reluctant to leave the building; he must be there in case Garde returns. He has received a note from her, improbably delivered by a reverent young pompier. The man is a member of a brigade sent to the Vélodrome to attend to the threat of fire hazards. There he and his fellows were entreated by a desperate multitude to carry messages to the outside world. Garde's hastily scrawled note urges Chaim not to worry; she's all right—though she wasn't. The glass roof of the Vél d'Hiv, painted blue to deceive the bombers, caused the voluminous arena to retain the heat of the day to an infernal degree. The heat intensified the mephitic odor of frightened humanity and the clogged toilets that forced the internees to relieve themselves in the stands in full view of others. There was no food save the few loaves a party of Quakers were permitted to distribute. Children cried inconsolably, their mothers helpless to calm them. The doors were sealed and anyone trying to escape was in peril of being shot on the spot. When it became clear they had not been gathered for the purpose of merely taking names, their panic took the form of a general paralysis. One elderly gentleman in a kippah and sidelocks invoked the *kiddush hashem* at Masada and called upon others to follow his lead by cutting their throats.

More letters from Garde are forthcoming, many in fact, but they remain stillborn in sacks that won't be discovered till after the war. Chaim will never know that she has been, uncannily, one of the lucky ones: that thanks to an outdated ordinance pertaining to German nationals, she is sent not to Drancy and the netherworld beyond but to the internment camp of Gurs at the foot of the Pyrénées. After some months, a further bureaucratic snafu—this one reinforced by forged papers provided by a friend, a cunning woman she's met in the camp—allows her to leave Gurs for the unoccupied zone. (It is occupied soon after.) Garde (now Marie Dupas) and her friend find safe harbor in the medieval fortress town of Carcassonne, from where she continues her futile attempts to contact Chaim. She manages to communicate with Madame Castaing, who by then has reasons for concealing from her the artist's whereabouts. Madame does, however, relent upon word of Chaim's final illness, though Garde will be notified too late. She and Chaim will never see each other again.

He loses weight, neglects to take his medications; it naturally doesn't occur to him to bathe. The one time he bothers to shave, he's fascinated and appalled by the greenish tinge of his woeful face. He remembers the night before they took Mademoiselle Garde away, the single tear she'd allowed herself to shed: how when it coursed down her cheek, he caught it on the tip of his tongue. He's done this before but this time the taste reminded him of the salt water you dip the karpas in at the Passover seder. Such unbidden associations have lately begun to throng his brain. They invade his thoughts like the spectral refugees from the cesspools and burnt books of the Pale, who have bivouacked in his studio since Garde went away. It seems that the more Jews they deport, the more these implausible creatures emigrate from the East. They claim that, as their near relation, Chaim owes them asylum. They appear, however, as chastened as is Chaim himself, no longer up to the kinds of funny business that made them such pests in the Old Country. Instead, they content themselves with recalling the tales of their heyday. Chaim clamps his hands over his ears.

"Life is not a story!" he insists. It's a storm.

He worries that the reason he's yet to be detained is because he is, as they intimate, one of them. To prove he isn't he decides to put himself in harm's way. His arrest will kill two birds at once: it will demonstrate on the one hand that he's perfectly human, and on the other help him to atone for not having yet been taken himself. It should have been him instead of her. The guilt gnaws at his ulcers with filed teeth. But in some cloistered compartment of his mind, Chaim knows that such unsound reasoning is a function of Garde's absence, just as is his inability to forgive her for having left him alone.

He goes down into the streets, which are eerily quiet though not for want of pedestrians. The crowds, democratized now by circumstance, are still regularly swallowed up and spat out of the Métro; they're still standing in tense resignation in endless queues, sitting warily on the terrace of la Coupole, their ranks everywhere interspersed with the *feldgrau* and black uniforms. They're largely taciturn, these citizens, though their ears are alert for whispers: someone may be even now reporting you for that indiscreet remark about Ambassador Abetz or Maréchal Pétain, or for having been overheard listening to the BBC. Breaking into line at a boulangerie can get you labeled a Freemason or Communist. Claustrophobia drives the people from their apartments and agoraphobia sends them scuttling back again, while their silence seems somehow to thrust the city's grandeur into an even bolder relief: the Beaux Arts houses along the river, the redbrick and blue slate facades of the place des Vosges, the gilded figures atop the Opéra Garnier, all put forward their best faces as if to remind its population that Paris is still the capital of brilliance. But the population is much too distraught to pay heed.

Nothing happens to Chaim. Police, common soldiers, and officers alike ignore him, until he begins to think that he's either transparent or simply regarded (if at all) as a sick Jew unworthy of even being abused. In a café, while sipping his lime tea, he meets Per Krohg, the Norwegian painter and melodeonist who had shared his wife, Lucy, with Jules Pascin. He's a friend of the École de Paris, considered by critics an honorary member.

"Moishe Kogan, Henri Epstein, Adolphe Féder, Jacques Gotko, Rudolf Lévy, to name only a few," he confides to Chaim under his breath (the walls have ears), "have all been sent east. Max Jacob thinks his conversion and his Legion d'Honneur will save him, but he's sporting the yellow star as well." He leans close enough that Chaim is a little dizzied by his odor of anisette. "What makes you think *your* days are not numbered, mon ami?"

For weeks Chaim continues to alternate between staying holed up among the phantasms in his atelier and offering himself as potential quarry in the streets. His clothes hang from his bones like washing on a line and even his shadow is ragged. The canteens that catered to artists during the Great War no longer exist and the ration tickets obtained by Garde have all been perforated and stamped. He makes do with a bowl of gray bilge in the Crémerie Leduc, where his credit is still good. This is his only meal of the day. He tugs down his hat brim and scours the quarter for a bootleg cigarette or a pint of milk. At the place Denfert-Rochereau, near the Lion of Belfort statue, he spies an SS officer approaching him, the sheen of whose boots reflect the primrose flags of the square. Chaim swallows and prepares to be halted, expecting a reckoning, but the German accosts another man before him, this one also a Jew.

Chaim hears him ask with surprising courtesy, "Où est la place de l'Étoile?"

The Jew is in his middle years, hatless but well dressed, with deeply creased cheeks and a pince-nez perched on his downturned nose. Instead of answering the officer, he raises his chin to look the man in the eye, a dangerous gesture in itself, then points to the star, *l'étoile*, on the breast pocket of his suitcoat. Chaim wants to walk on but is riveted by the scene. The officer's taut features redden after a fashion that might almost be interpreted as shame. Then he slaps the man's face, causing his eyeglasses to fly from his nose. Passersby look the other way. Finding the single gesture insufficient, however, the officer slaps him again, and again, with the flat of his palm on one cheek and the back of his hand on the other. The man's head is whipped from side to side with every cuff, but he makes no effort to protect himself. Apparently satisfied, the Nazi walks abruptly away, though he pauses soon after to ask directions from another random pedestrian.

Chaim stoops to retrieve the shattered glasses but the man makes no movement to take them back. His damp eyes are unfocused, and though Chaim is standing right in front of him, he doesn't seem to see him at all. Chaim grasps the man's hand and folds his fingers about the spectacles, then feels a shudder of contagion in the touch so that he experiences the man's humiliation as his own—so much his own that it's as if, in that moment, they have traded places, and looking at himself through the man's myopic eyes, he sees, rather than Chaim Soutine, artist and genius, no one at all.

Tahkeh, he thinks, may the beasts of prey remain as blind.

Meanwhile, the Arts Club of Chicago has been looking for Chaim. Its board had mounted a show of his work in 1937, and having since discovered his exclusion from Varian Fry's august list, they've tried to contact him via the post. A series of letters has arrived at 18 la Villa Seurat offering to provide the cash and necessary documents to bring him to America. There is even mention of a possible academic position. But Chaim is not in residence. Having ultimately read the writing on the wall (in both its modern and Gothic calligraphy), he has begun to move from place to place. He checks into various rundown hôtels particuliers in far-flung corners of the city: a couple of nights in a fleabag in the back streets of the Latin Quarter, a couple in a kip around the Porte de Clignancourt, the neighborhood where the plague had broken out during the year of Modigliani's death. On occasion a concierge is unwilling to rent a room to a Jew, but the more squalid the accommodations the more welcome are his few sous. There's a certain familiarity to these rooms, their cracked walls seething with vermin that emerge at night to crawl over the sleeper. It's as if Dr. Barnes and Élie Faure and Mademoiselle Garde have never happened: he's back in la Ruche again—a portable la Ruche. And as he'd done in la Ruche, Chaim contemplates *zelbstmord*; he pictures himself hanging (pace Pascin) from a light fixture, as the fixtures in these rooms seem designed for that purpose. Then he realizes he would lose the chance to paint that image—so consistent with his tradition of still lifes—if he were dead. Not that he thinks much about painting these days.

He hopes his perpetual motion will also give him some respite from his parasitic bugbears and bogies, though they're even more at home in his sordid lodgings than he. No matter, Chaim has made his peace with them: they're *mishpocha*, he's conceded, next of kin, despite their bird beaks and bodies like gaseous carafes. (The hypocrites, they've taken in their apprehension to wearing skullcaps and prayer shawls, and reciting psalms.) So when he returns sub rosa to his apartment to check his mail, he's not surprised to find that his followers have already preceded him there. He also finds the letters from the arts club.

His heart is buoyed a moment before plummeting all over again: he has neither the wish nor the wherewithal to go to America. The obstacle course of negotiating such a journey, with its entrance and exit visas, its waivers and affidavits, is frankly unimaginable, the logistics overwhelming. The hugeness of such an undertaking with no Garde to assist him dwarfs in his mind even the menace of the war. Besides, America is a barbarous nation, where the only means of conveyance—so says Lipchitz—is by bucking bronco, and the landscapes are all flatlands and mesas without trees. Ill-fated as he may be, he belongs in France, especially now that every Jew is as much a pariah as was Hayim Sütin in Smilovitchi. *A sheynim dank*; thank you but no thank you. For the time being he'll continue his hole-in-corner existence.

He runs into Kisling, who informs him before making off for Marseille and Portugal, then on to California, "A new decree they got: A Jew may draw only one breath for every three inhaled by your good-faith human person."

But Chaim, who once learned to breathe underwater, wonders whether he can perhaps hold his breath for the duration.

✦

MADAME CASTAING IS SEARCHING for him as well. She knows he's alone and incapable of properly looking after himself. Despite the invasion, she and her husband have reoccupied their apartment on the rue de Grenelle. Marcellin's investments have suffered severe reversals and the upkeep of Lèves has become too costly. So they've closed up the estate and moved back to Paris, where Madeleine has opened a soon-to-be-celebrated shop on the Left Bank selling high-end antiques. She has visited Chaim only once since Mademoiselle Garde's seizure and before he went on the lam. She found him surly and reproachful, complaining (not without some reason) that she and Marcellin have exploited him. Since then they have not communicated. Still she worries about his health and safety, worries more than ever now that he seems to have disappeared. Dismayed, she tries contacting some of his old comrades like Krémègne and Kikoïne, who have also vanished. Though even if she were able to locate him, how can she help? She and Marcellin might hide him in some forgotten corner of their capacious flat, but it would only be a matter of time until the Gestapo came sniffing around, aware as they must be of her friendship with the *jüdische Künstler*. Then she has an idea.

She employs a resource she's used before in confirming her husband's infidelities. She hires a private investigator: Monsieur Hervé Duluc of the Duluc Detective Agency to be precise. His sleuthing procedure is cut-and-dried: the man has only to stake out 18 la Villa Seurat and wait for a person of Chaim's description to appear. (Madeleine has given him a photograph.) Chaim has meanwhile gone to what he thinks of as some lengths to disguise himself. He's allowed his scruffy beard to grow out, concealing his weak chin, and as always pulls down his hat brim. And that's it. His faith in his nonentity aside, the distinguishing slouch, along with the yellow star he doesn't dare to remove, are an instant giveaway. For his part, the pear-shaped, tortoise-faced Monsieur Duluc is hardly an intimidating figure, but any stranger lingering at the threshold of his building is for Chaim a cause for alarm. As the man starts to approach him, Chaim is poised to bolt but stalls upon hearing in an unaccented voice, "I was sent by Madame Castaing." Then the detective hands him a message in a scented envelope, gives him a gentlemanly salute, and departs.

Madeleine has asked him to meet her at the Café de Flore, the old haunt of the Surrealists, and of Huysmans and Remy de Gourmont before them, in the 6th arrondissement. It is still popular among those (Germans included) looking to absorb what's left of its legendary atmosphere. But Madeleine has suggested that they convene on a Friday evening at eight o'clock. This is the hour just before curfew when—she explains in a postscript—the SS and their staff are most likely to be garrisoned in the theme rooms of the notorious luxury brothel One-Two-Two.

For once Chaim is early. His self-destructive impulse temporarily in abeyance, he is left with nothing but raw nerves. Paranoia is not paranoia but common sense: the message from Madeleine might be some kind of a setup. Though why would his pursuers, whoever or whatever they are, need to resort to a ruse? He no longer expects his thoughts to follow a logical course; knows only that, in the vacuum left by Garde's absence, he has a need of seeing someone who was once kind to him. To compensate for that weakness, he has adopted a hard-boiled demeanor—Jean Gabin, he imagines, in *Pépé le Moko*. He throws back his tea as if from a shot glass and stuffs a poorly rolled cigarette between his thick lips; his narrowed eyes shift in the shadow of his fedora. This is his ludicrous posture when he and Marie-Berthe first clap eyes on each other.

Her comeliness outshines even that of Madame Castaing, whom she accompanies. She's wearing a tailored, rustic tweed suit as voguish as Madeleine's, and just as flattering to her slender figure, though the fabric appears a little shelf-worn—as does, on closer inspection, the woman herself. Her large hazel eyes have a startled look that persists even as she takes her seat, suggesting that the expression may be changeless. Her skin is as smooth as a porcelain doll's, with a fragility you could imagine becoming one day fretted, like porcelain, with cracks. She wears her amber-brown hair in a fringe over her forehead, the rest swept into a pompadour mostly hidden by a claret beret. Though indisputably lovely, her features leave Chaim with a blurred impression, as if viewed through a cloudy lens.

He's more glad to see Madeleine than he can even admit to himself, though the unexpected presence of her prepossessing companion causes his spine to stiffen.

"Chaim," says Madeleine, hiding her shock at his pitiable countenance, "this is Marie-Berthe."

The woman offers her hand and Chaim realizes he's heard her name and seen her face before: she was the subject of a much admired portrait of Foujita's and an equally memorable photograph by Man Ray. She is a *ci-devant* celebrity from the world on whose margins—since the days of Amedeo—he has preferred to remain. Its center has been lost to him for years.

He takes her white hand but avoids her eyes, which might possibly hypnotize or annihilate the unvigilant. In days to come he will learn more of her pedigree: She is Marie-Berthe Aurenche, the ex-wife of Max Ernst, a painter whose bughouse enigmatic visions Chaim has never had much use for. She has been a model for the Chanel fashion house, a bit player in a Luis Buñuel film, and has posed as a range of (mostly nude) mythical figures in her former husband's paintings. She likes her aperitifs at all hours and the occasional opium pipe, and has survived two suicide attempts: once by jumping out a hospital window and again by leaping from a bridge over the Seine. Her mother, a die-hard royalist, has traced their lineage back to Louis XVIII and believes that, when the error of the French Revolution is finally corrected, her daughter will be in line to be Queen of France. Her father, mortified by her reputation, has disowned her. She is kittenish, temperamental, spiteful, and nurturing by turns. When Madeleine confided in Maurice Sachs her plan to throw Marie-Berthe and Chaim together, the skeptical old pederast declared, "You have signed Soutine's death warrant."

But Maurice's warning is not entirely fair. Madeleine knows that Marie-Berthe, unmoored since her breakup with Ernst, is in the market for a new genius to be muse to. And if the genius happens to be ailing and half-mad, then so much the better. The less refined the material, the more challenging the project.

"Monsieur Soutine," says Marie-Berthe without preamble, her flutey voice as penetrating as the glare of her eyes, "they say you're a barbarian. Are you a barbarian?"

Rigid, Chaim looks to Madame Castaing for an explanation of her friend's impertinence. She laughs: "Marie-Berthe is quite irrepressible."

The woman persists, "You don't look like a barbarian. An *apache* perhaps, but not a barbarian. Have you a light?"

Chaim flinches: one may deny an enemy every courtesy but a match. He pulls a pack from his pocket and lights her cigarette. She takes a deep drag and exhales arabesques of blue smoke, which wreathe her face and enhance its dreamy, ill-defined cast. Chaim's annoyance makes room for a glimmer of fascination.

"Marie-Berthe is a great admirer of your work, Chaim," says Madeleine, the conciliator. "She insisted I bring her along to meet you."

"So what is it," the woman asks with genuine interest, "what is it with you and all your scrawny fowl with their broken necks? Is this a Jewish thing?"

Chaim stiffens again: Does she really expect an answer?

"Personally," she goes on, "I don't believe in the current rage for racial mysticism. Leave all that folksy bêtise to Chagall. You're beyond all that, Maestro, like Kokoschka or that divine Nazi Emil Nolde . . ."

"Who?" asks Chaim, unheard.

". . . Only, they *superimpose* their feelings on their chosen motifs, no? Whereas your work boasts a blood connection to your subjects. Matisse says that the tomato he paints is not the tomato he eats, but I can sense your mouth watering over your tomatoes and even your uncooked chickens. You want to gobble them up along with your bellboys and pastry chefs, don't you? You're a cannibal, Soutine!"

Chaim's jaw is hanging: never has he heard such a combination of claptrap and, for all he knows, authentic insight. Now she's begun to sing in an off-key trill a children's song about a little pastry cook: *"Ayez pitié d'un p'tit pâtissier dont l'amour se perd . . ."*

Who is this woman?

Madeleine breaks the spell by calling over the waiter. He comes to their table, hesitates when he sees the artist's star, but is snapped to attention by Madame Castaing's authoritative tone. "A grenache for me, and what for you, Marie-Berthe?"

"A gin and tonic with angostura and dripped absinthe, if you please."

"More tea for you, Chaim?"

He doesn't seem to hear her at first, then unthinkingly shakes his head. Then, in the shrill whisper that has become the preferred means of communication among Parisians, he says, "Why you asked me here?"

Madeleine tilts her head as if the answer is obvious. "I was worried about you."

Chaim feels a trapdoor drop open beneath his heart. "You goddam right you should worry," he rasps. "I got on my back the eye from the bull!"

"Hush," says Madeleine as if to a child.

Then Marie-Berthe chimes back in, "Is this hand-wringer the ferocious Soutine you told me about?"

Chaim is speechless, riven with conflicting emotions: he's chafed and insulted, while at the same time ashamed at having shown himself less than the undaunted virtuoso he's always aspired to be in Madeleine's eyes. Unforgiving of the backhanded validity of this presumptuous shiksa's indictment, he stares daggers at the woman—which she suffers unperturbed. Her expression softens, however, as the drinks are delivered.

"What is it you need, Maestro?" she asks him in a stagy undertone. "I've got a friend who's a wizard forger. I've got also a stack of counterfeit *cartes de rationnement* and"—producing a wad from her purse as if flashing a dowry—"Métro tickets that I filled in the punched holes with bits of bread . . ." Madeleine signals her to put them away, which she does with a smile that suggests she still has more to offer.

At that point Madame Castaing begins to talk finances. She assures Chaim that she and Marcellin can continue to buy his paintings through intermediaries, and that she's found a young dealer, Louis Carré by name, who's willing to sell his work to a private market. "So stop your grumbling," she scolds him affectionately, though Chaim has yet to say a word, "the money will come. Just keep us posted as to your current address." Her eyes are moist as she suddenly stands to excuse herself; she has an appointment at her shop with an estate auction agent. She leans over to kiss the artist on both hollow cheeks and is gone, an attar of Shalimar slowly dissipating in her wake. Then Chaim is left alone and uneasy in the company of the decorative Marie-Berthe.

She smokes, drinks, speaks without prompting of her various strategies for making ends meet since the occupation: She's done some modeling for a few of the remaining state-certified

artists—Othon Friesz, Dunoyer de Segonzac, names at which
Chaim pulls a face; she's taken on proofreading work for—lowering her voice again—the underground press *Les Éditions de Minuit*.
In that capacity she has doctored the seditious manuscripts of intimates from her old circle of acquaintances, such as Louis Aragon,
André Breton, and Paul Éluard. Chaim is unimpressed with (if
not distrustful of) her ostentatious name-dropping. Why does she
feel so compelled to advertise her avant-garde credentials? It's as
if she's auditioning for his approval. Then it dawns on him why
Madeleine has summoned him to this rendezvous: she has as much
as volunteered this mercurial young woman as a candidate for the
replacement of his lost companion. Chaim bristles at the thought;
no one can take the place of Mademoiselle Garde.

He looks past Marie-Berthe across the dark boulevard to the
elegant stone statue of the Goddess of Flowers, on whose head some
scamp has placed a Phrygian cap. A German soldier is angrily removing the treasonous symbol with his bayonet. The soldier is not
one of your spit-and-polished "blond warriors" who had originally
taken possession of the city; *they* have all been sent to the Russian
Front. This one is among the lubberly substitutes lately deployed
to police the population, though they have little enough control
of themselves. These prefer to preface their interrogations with a
rifle butt.

Chaim slouches in his chair, tries to cover his breast pocket with
a lapel. He's heard that Picasso roams the rue des Grands-Augustins
as if he were invincible. ("Are you the creator of *Guernica*?" it's said
he was asked by a Nazi with respect to his great painted invective.
"No," replied the artist, "*you* are.") But the stinking-rich Pablo can
afford to feel invincible, whereas Chaim Soutine doesn't dare to
sleep twice in the same bed. This woman, this Marie-Berthe, she is
clearly *meshugah ahf toit*; but she is also a *shainkeit*, a most fetching

lady who seems willing, after her fashion, to make herself available. Of course her interest is in the preeminent artist rather than the sick and desperate Jew, but if she's inclined to waive the distinction between the two of them . . . ? Chaim squeezes shut his eyes and asks Garde's forgiveness: *What am I thinking?* It's just that he's so frightened and alone.

"Soutine," begins Marie-Berthe—such liberties she takes with his name. "Soutine"—leaning close enough that he can count the flecks of gold in her hazel eyes—"why haven't you quit this city?"

"Because," he replies gruffly, "milk I couldn't get in the provinces."

She laughs—has he said something funny? "Imbécile," she declares, "there's no milk left in Paris either."

He nods reflectively and has to concede, "This is true."

He neither invites her to accompany him nor discourages her from walking back with him to la Villa Seurat, though at every corner he half expects her to say farewell. Nor does he remember asking her to follow him up to his apartment, where he has briefly lit before pulling up stakes again. But there she is, casually nosing about his sullied quarters. Fatigued from all that has transpired this evening, he collapses into the grease-stained wing chair and leerily watches her movements. Unlike the intrusive Melnick or Garde with her tender mercies, this one makes no pretense of going through domestic motions. In fact, who can tell if she even takes notice of the unsightly state of his suite? She keeps up her idle talk of better days without troubling to pinch her nostrils against the rancid odor; nor does she seem to observe the sideshow contingent of *lutin* and *fae* and their other more distant relations encamped in the apartment's far corners. (They haven't bothered, Chaim's creatures, to make themselves scarce as they had for Gerda Groth.) She lifts a pair of mole-gray underpants from a doorknob, makes a face, and lets them drop; she blows a plume of dust from the mantel. She follows a spoor of mouse droppings into the studio, where she starts to inspect a rolled canvas leaning against the wall.

"Don't touch!" shouts Chaim from his chair, and she instantly lets it go, waving her fingers facetiously as if they've been burnt.

Returning to the parlor, she asks him, "What are you afraid of, Chaim?" This is the first time she's used his given name, which comforts him not at all.

"Ask better what I ain't afraid of," he replies. Then he says that if she wants to make herself useful—though she's shown no such inclination—she can warm on the stove some of the bottled water that no one will call Vichy anymore. She saunters into the kitchen alcove, no doubt accentuating the sway of her hips, and complies; then she serves him his hot-water cordial in an unwashed cup with a slice of lemon she'd pocketed in the café. As he sips, she settles herself on the squashed leather hassock opposite his armchair, crossing her legs so that the susurrus of her silk stockings reverberates disturbingly in Chaim's loins. He recalls the proverb: "A wife shall be for her husband a footstool in heaven," and thinks how little that would apply in this case. But she's some kind of French bonbon, this Marie-Berthe, who continues to offer up unsolicited bits of her past.

"*L'ange noir*, they used to call me among the Surrealists," she submits, as if that baleful byname were a term of endearment.

It's a one-sided conversation, the continuance of an interview Chaim never requested. Yet he marvels that any woman could aspire to the unenviable position of his caretaker, especially given how little she can expect in return. Shouldn't such a person be counted as a blessing? But whenever Chaim counts his blessings he weighs them against the sum of his lifelong curses, and he wonders whether Marie-Berthe might perhaps figure among the latter.

The hour is getting late but it's become clear the woman has no intention of leaving. Finally Chaim interrupts the recital of her résumé to complain of his tiredness.

She takes no offense. "Come," she says, standing and taking hold of his hand, "let me tuck you in."

She pulls him to his feet and begins to lead him in the direction of the bedroom when he digs in his heels. Who is this woman? But she gives him a good-humored tug and he stumbles after, surrendering to the habit of passivity he had acquired during the benevolent dispensation of Mademoiselle Garde. He allows her to lay him down across the dirty sheets and unlace his shoes, then detach the celluloid collar. Her fingers are deft as she removes the cuff links and shirt studs, deft and gentle; he wouldn't have thought she could be so gentle. She understands that I'm *krankeit*, he thinks appreciatively, a sick and enfeebled man. Then, not so gently, she begins yanking at the buttons of his fly.

Chaim tries to sit up but she shoves him back against the mattress and pins his shoulders there. "Please, I'm feeling a little bilious," is his fainthearted excuse, but the woman is undeterred.

"I'm feeling a little *libidineux* myself," she breathes, hoisting her skirt to her waist and throwing a leg over his hips. It's a slender leg, as shapely as if turned on a lathe, the thigh pale as crème fraîche above her stocking top.

He lacks the strength to push her off but is in no condition to respond to her advances. Even if he were so disposed, he would not betray in this very bed the fidelity he still owes to Garde. But the woman has begun to grind her hips against his; she has pulled aside an intimate garment to give access to her magnetic heat, and Chaim feels a stirring in that part of himself that has no regard for his conscience or decrepitude. She rides him with the predatory appetite with which he's been ridden in former times by

Laila, who is herself looking on from among the gallery of spectators. These include the triplets, the archdemon Ketev Meriri, and
a barnacle goose with an elastic umbilical stem.

Chaim sleeps restfully and in the morning concludes that he
must have been bewitched. Hab rachmones! Hasn't he got enough
on his plate already with the Nazis and his family of vaporous
squatters? Who needs the further intrusion of a flesh-and-blood
siren? Her misuse of his person, let alone the violation of his sac-
rosanct solitude (frightful as it's lately become), is insupportable,
and he determines to rid himself of the creature at his earliest opportunity. But meanwhile his intestines are enjoying a moment of
unusual complacency, which attests to some fundamental shift in
the order of things.

The Aurenche woman, Marie-Berthe (such a goyisheh name),
is up and chirping about something or nothing as she brews a pot
of coffee in the kitchenette. Semangelof whispers duplicitously in
his ear: "It says in Talmud he who indulges in intercourse ages
quickly; his strength ebbs, vision dims, breath becomes foul . . . ,"
and Chaim rolls his eyes at the cant. Marie-Berthe brings the coffee on a tray to the artist, who refuses it: the caffeine is bad for his
digestion.

"There's no caffeine in this, you ninny," she says, and laughs.
"It's made with flax seeds."

"I knew that," he mutters, and seizes the cup. She pours.

She's wearing only a flimsy slip, which highlights her sleek
contours, though the torn hem gives her a touch of the slattern.
Yesterday's cloudy features have sharpened, however, and the flighti-
ness seems somewhat subdued. She appears to be taking it for granted
that some compact has been resolved between them. But rather than
relaxed, she appears a bit brittle, even anxious. Not quite the Marie-
Berthe of the day before. She straddles the wooden chair next to
the bed, leans her arms and chin against its high back. Chaim tries

to avoid looking between her carelessly spread legs. But the siren is no longer in evidence and today's young enchantress has assumed a matter-of-fact tone as she asks Chaim to produce his identity papers.

He sits bolt upright in the bed, spilling the ersatz coffee. "Are you Gestapo?"

She replies with forced patience, "I can only secure you a phony ID if you give me your original document to take to the forger."

Thinks Chaim: this is all happening too fast. One day he's invisible, the next marked for extinction, and the next thrust willy-nilly into a ménage with a nymphomaniac. "Why I'm going to trust you?" he asks.

She glowers at him, then thoughtfully sucks a tooth. "I don't know. Because I went to a convent school? Or maybe because I have your Madame Castaing's seal of approval and it's in my horoscope that we're already a *fait accompli.*"

"In such hokey-pokey you believe?" asks Chaim.

"Not really," she sighs, "but I believe in providence."

He swings his broomstick legs from under the sheet and sits on the edge of the bed, mops his oily face with the palm of his hand. "From superstition I don't believe," he states, adding, "kaynehoreh." The goblins titter.

"That's good, Soutine"—it's *Soutine* again—"a good strategy: fear everything and believe in nothing." She shakes her head, her pretty head, the fair amber hair still tousled in elflocks from her sleep. Her girlish anatomy appears nearly weightless as she rises from the chair and begins to gather up her scattered clothes. But for all her darting and dipping, you can detect a slight lethargy in her limbs. Maybe, thinks Chaim, it's from the strain of keeping such beauty afloat despite the ballast of a heavy heart, or maybe—go figure—she's actually worried about the peril he's in.

A Catholic schoolgirl yet, her unheralded presence in his life is finally beyond comprehension. "You know that by me," he says, obliged to put her on notice, "it's nothing but leavings you get. Have fled already all your blue-chip artists."

She shrugs. "In these times a girl must settle for what she can find." Then she snickers, coquettish again, and tells him not to run himself down; he is after all an undisputed master.

Chaim grunts indecisively, then takes his time setting down the coffee cup and getting to his feet. With the sheet wrapped toga-style round his naked body, he pads to the otherwise empty icebox and fetches from among his trove of important documents the identity paper with its haunted photograph.

Then she's gone for a couple of days and Chaim's instinct is to flee before she returns. It is anyway unsafe to remain in one place for long; no one but Garde can make him wait and he's given up waiting for her. But he doesn't dare leave the building without the proper credentials. When at last she turns up, he's astonished at how relieved he is to see her. She enters in a rush of businesslike efficiency and wastes no time in presenting him with his new designation. The document is at first glance indistinguishable from the original; the counterfeiter's job has been that professional. Only on closer examination does Chaim observe that the previous information has been altered to create a stranger. He is now Karl Sutin, refugee from Soviet oppression and an adherent of the Russian Orthodox Church.

"Congratulations," says Marie-Berthe, proud of her success, "you are no longer a Jew."

She stands before him with folded arms, awaiting some acknowledgment of her yeoman service on his behalf. But rather than feeling liberated, Chaim experiences a head-swimming nausea: so abruptly has he been deprived of his old identity—though hasn't that identity been the real oppressor of his days? Then why does he not feel more disencumbered by its loss? While he frowns, Marie-Berthe has removed his jacket from the wardrobe and is in the process of ripping off the yellow star. Watching her, Chaim has the sensation of a plaster being prematurely torn from a festering wound. When she takes the piece of cloth to the gas range in order to burn it, he snaps out of his vacancy and lurches forward to snatch it from her hand.

"It's all that's left from what I was," is his pathetic plea.

"The more reason to destroy it and be born again," replies an exuberant Marie-Berthe.

"Was bad enough to be born already one time," broods Chaim.

The young woman charges him to show a little gratitude, then proposes they go out and celebrate. "Celebrate?" wonders Chaim, as if asking her to define the word. No vestige remains in him of the audacity that Mademoiselle Garde had once inspired, and he has no desire to put his precarious new deception to the test. But Marie-Berthe now has a claim on him. Moreover, she seems to have recovered the verve she displayed at their first meeting and he supposes that, vey iz mir, he owes her some tithe of indulgence.

Outside, the sky is unblemished and powder blue, the terraced houses along the avenue du Maine a dazzling pearl-white; wine-purple berries infest the ivy climbing the walls of the brasseries, but no one is fooled. This Paris is no more authentic than Karl Sutin is Chaim Soutine. It's a cheap mise-en-scène of the authentic city, which is disassembled after curfew and warehoused overnight when not in use. The citizens are not citizens but hired extras, caricature sneaks and spies, *mouchards*. The only real persons are the ones in black uniforms with lightning-bolt insignia, and the ones wearing yellow stars. Those last look questioningly at Chaim, as if to ask why one whose face resembles the topography of the Holy Land should have dispensed with his own badge.

Marie-Berthe drags him from one venue to another in what is perhaps a vain attempt to re-create the fervor of the Crazy Years. She assures him the occupiers are seldom suspicious of couples, and besides, when they're together, all eyes will be on her. They see, despite Chaim's bootless protests, Sacha Guitry in *N'écoutez pas, mesdames* at le Théâtre de la Madeleine; they see Arletty in *Bolero* at le Grand Rex. (Both performers will be tried for collaboration after the war—Arletty, who's had an affair with a high-ranking German officer, famously stating at her trial, "My heart belongs to France but my ass is international.") They take café crèmes (and sidecars in the case of Marie-Berthe) at les Deux Magots and the Closerie des Lilas, where Chaim tries to hide his face in his collar. "If you sink any lower you'll be headless," chides Marie-Berthe, who can't resist the urge to flaunt her latest conquest. She greets every stray artist she recognizes and invites them over to pay their respects to Soutine, who grinds his teeth.

Among the café notables is of course Jean Cocteau; there is no smart scene or gala where he fails to make an appearance, regardless of its political taint, though his naïveté is judged by many as more willful than innocent. He drops by their table just long enough to flash his wit: "Poetry is indispensable at such times, *chères âmes*—if only I knew what for." In Cocteau's train is also the clubbable Max Jacob, who is appalled to see Chaim still in the city.

"Why haven't you gotten the hell out of Paris?" he gasps.

"Why haven't *you*?"

Max's expression is untroubled. "I'm a Roman Catholic," he says, tipping the high hat riding the glossy dome of his head. "It's been yonks since I was a Jew."

And Chaim: "Yonks it's been since I am a painter." He raises his collar again.

"You will always be a painter," Max assures him, then is chilled upon realizing the irony in the artist's reply.

Kiki, who's been entertaining the café with a medley of bawdy songs, slides off the grand piano and begins moving from table to table selling matches and safety pins. Her tigerish cosmetic mask, designed by Man Ray, is runneled with perspiration and her voluptuous curves have become obscured by fat.

Marie-Berthe's headlong endeavor to kick up her heels soon begins to have diminishing returns. In the end she seems no more stimulated by the evenings' entertainments than her skittish companion, whom she blames (rather than the Nazis) for the general heaviness of heart. But while she might often pause to wonder what kind of burden she's saddled herself with, she gives no sign of wanting to quit him. For this Chaim feels genuinely beholden—that is, when he doesn't wish she would leave him alone. It's wiser to alternate lodgings, so they return at night to either la Villa Seurat or to Marie-Berthe's place on the rue Littré, a one-room, mezzanine flat as unhygienic as Chaim's own. Every night she makes another effort to seduce and ravish him, but the postcoital holiday of his stomach troubles proves to have been short-lived.

There is some good news: the Wehrmacht have surrendered at Stalingrad, Rommel is defeated in North Africa, and the Allies are bombing factories and railyards on the outskirts of Paris. But mostly bad: In retaliation, the occupiers have increased exponentially the number of arrests, confiscations, and hangings. Tales of bone breaking, blinding, and castration during Gestapo interrogations are legion. On every wall you see plastered *affiches rouges*, the posters displaying the names and photos of the executed so-called terrorists, many of them no more than children. Three hundred and fifty thousand French men and women have been requisitioned to work in German industries. Thirteen thousand Jews are apprehended in the roundup that becomes known as the *grande rafle* and sent *east*, a word that has acquired plutonian connotations. Those who remain are forbidden every public space and facility, including phone booths. Tensions in the city have reached the critical stage.

Chaim and Marie-Berthe return to 18 la Villa Seurat after an unrewarding evening out to find that the apartment has been violated in their absence.

"How can you tell?" asks Marie-Berthe, because at first glance the disorder is no greater than usual. But Chaim is tearing his hair. The front door lock has been jimmied, the doors to the icebox and cabinets left open, letters and documents scattered, canvases unrolled and trod upon in the studio. The Zenith radio is missing. What's more, the shretelekh and *shovavim* appear to have absconded, leaving Chaim surprisingly heartsick, like someone whose pets have been stolen—though even in his distress he would wager they haven't traveled far.

Marie-Berthe resents being infected by his fear. She takes it amiss that, having wed her fortunes to his, the party should thus be over for her as well. How many times in one's life can the party be over? "Maybe it was just vandals," she offers, affecting hopefulness. Chaim shuns the suggestion with a forlorn look: they both know it's likely the secret police. Then the woman is forced to acknowledge that, like it or not, his danger is hers. "We need to get out of here," she insists.

They assume her apartment is also no longer safe. Hasn't she made it known all over Montparnasse that she and the Yid artist are now paired? Rue Littré may be under surveillance as they speak. Marie-Berthe decides they should go to her parents' house across the river in the exclusive 8th arrondissement. This is a decidedly bad idea. Marie-Berthe herself has not been welcome there since her marriage to Ernst, who was despised by her family as both a foreigner and an indecently older man. So, to bring home a Jew, badge or no, is unpardonable on at least three counts. Nevertheless, that's precisely what she does, only to be met at the door by her affectless father. A sturdy gentleman in a silk dressing gown, auger-eyed, lips tight as a coin slot, he orders his weeping wife, who apparently still has a heart, to go to bed. Then he informs his wayward daughter of what he's often assured her over the years: that she is no longer his daughter.

"Him I know already," mutters Chaim, as the porch light is switched off.

He's beside himself now, making hysterical suggestions: they should hide in the Catacombs, beg sanctuary in the cathedral— until Marie-Berthe tells him to give it a rest. From a booth she phones Marcel Laloë, a friend of her former husband who had always treated her with respect and consideration. He is a mildly successful painter of mediocre talent who lives in a rambling apartment on the rue des Plantes with his wife, Anne, a well-known soprano who goes by the stage name of Olga Lucher. Marie-Berthe is pleading with him to take them in for the night when Marcel interrupts her to ask, "Did you say Chaim Soutine?" It happens that he is an avid devotee of the artist's work.

As they trudge up the stairs to the Laloës' fifth-floor landing, Chaim and Marie-Berthe can hear Marcel's wife singing a Bach cantata through the door. "From *Wachet auf*, I recognize this," breathes Chaim, adding, though seldom given to optimism: "A good omen."

But meeting their hosts, who receive the couple with a warmth they might have extended to long-lost cousins, Chaim is immediately on his guard. So gracious are the Laloës, in fact, that Chaim wonders whether they might be attempting to lull their guests into a state of ease before springing some kind of a trap. But after tea and compliments and a morsel of scarce Cantal cheese, he begins to recognize the unreasonableness of his thinking and allows himself to unclench a bit.

Marcel is a tall man with thinning sandy hair and a perpetual stoop, as if in deference to those shorter than himself. Despite the lackluster quality of his painting (which is nonetheless bankable), he has a discriminating eye for the work of others, and his appreciation of Chaim's oeuvre is earnest and discerning. His wife, Anne, is a stately, reed-thin woman, at once high-bred and unpretentious, a versatility of nature that has given her a dual standing in the opposing spheres of both opera and cabaret. She flutters about her guests as if they might be recently eloped newlyweds rather than refugees on the run. They have an adult son, the Laloës, who's been sent to work in Germany, but his letters home—they contend—are encouraging. They also have an absurd-looking dog.

Their apartment is a combination of lavishness (ornate furnishings, framed Japanese landscapes) and bohemian bric-a-brac, like a Bonnard interior. The guests are offered the absent son's room or, if they prefer, and since the late September nights are still moderate, the outdoor loggia. Madame Laloë recommends the "romantic ambience" of the latter, and Marie-Berthe, who still reserves the right to believe that theirs is an amorous liaison, persuades Chaim to sleep with her on the balcony. Madame Laloë prepares a pallet for them, and the couple, having peeled respectively to their skivvies and chemise, settle down under a thick blanket in the refreshing open air. Since the lights of Paris are dimmed (now against Allied attacks), the stars of the Milky Way are visible in their glittering infinitude. Both the artist and his young mistress, lying beside each other, inhale the night's soft deliverance.

"When I was a little girl," whispers Marie-Berthe, "I was scared of the stars. I thought the night sky was black gauze and the light that shined through all those pinholes was as much of the light of heaven as we could stand. I was afraid that, if God got mad, he would tear aside the material and his blazing face would blind us all."

"When I was a little boy," replies Chaim, "I don't remember when God wasn't mad."

Marie-Berthe sighs. "Were you ever happy, Soutine?"

"I am always happy."

During the brief time that they've been together, Chaim has tried and failed to find some quality of Mademoiselle Garde in Marie-Berthe's disposition. But tonight, comforted by the nearness of her body *en déshabillé* and becalmed by the respite the Laloës have provided, he thinks he can maybe trust her erratic affection. He's further soothed (even somewhat aroused) when he feels the warmth of her tongue begin to tickle the lobe of his left ear. Then the tickling graduates to an ardent licking, as if she wants to lap up the ear from his head. This alerts him to the fact that the rough tongue belongs not to the woman but to the Laloës' demonstrative dog, Jonquille. She had yelped ecstatically upon their arrival and tried to nestle into Chaim's lap while he was still standing.

Jonquille belongs to some nameless breed of canine resembling a matted, stump-legged, rust-brown rag mop. Her peculiar pungency might explain her attraction to Chaim, with his not dissimilar scent, and as it turns out the affinity is mutual. In the coming weeks his preoccupation with the dog will spark several instances of jealousy in Marie-Berthe, to which Chaim turns a mostly deaf ear. He views Jonquille's preference for him as a mark of distinction. With an uncharacteristic fondness he cradles the animal in his arms; he returns her nuzzling nose to nose, sneaks her table scraps, and takes issue with Marie-Berthe when she refers to the dog as "it."

"Does the thing even have eyes?" asks an annoyed Marie-Berthe.

"Bien sûr," says Chaim, parting the shaggy hair of her brow to reveal a pair of opaque black buttons. "And she's not a thing."

The Laloës' generosity is bolstered in part by their militant opposition to the accommodations the Vichy regime has made to the enemy, and in the spirit of resistance they have invited their guests to stay as long as they like. Chaim has never subscribed to the myth of "the righteous gentile," but he is learning to believe in his hosts' genuineness. There are certainly worse places to spend a war.

Here they've been given an interlude during which the prevailing
unpleasantness remains, like a mirage, at an ever elusive remove.
Although he keeps to the apartment during the day, Chaim insists
on venturing out with Marcel after dinner when he walks the dog.
Their quiet quarter on the outer edge of Montparnasse has been
mostly ignored by the Boche, which is not to imply that it's safe;
but the peace of the Laloës' domicile has had the effect of salving
Chaim's frayed nerves, and Marcel is too desirous of his company
to discourage him from coming along. How can he deny *le maître*
his need for stretching his legs? Of course it's an open question as
to whether Chaim is motivated more by his pleasure in Marcel's
company or in Jonquille's. In any case he owes his host his attention, since the man and his wife are after all risking their lives to
save his. He indulges Marcel's obtrusive interrogations about his
methods and habits, even as he only has eyes for the dog, which he
watches in amusement as she skitters along the pavement, looking
with her feet concealed under her shag like a fugitive hairpiece.

At the outset of their strolls Chaim's responses to his host's
questions are fairly noncommittal and brusque: "It depends, everything, on how you mix the color, how you capture and put it in its
place." Then silence. But when pressed the artist might remember
that he owes Marcel more than crumbs and even begin to warm to
their conversation: he offers typically disparaging opinions about
his colleagues; about, say, Cézanne ("Too stiff and mental") and
Cubism ("Incapable of giving joy"). In his memoirs Monsieur Laloë
will confess that he had never thought of Soutine as a joyful artist,
though some might argue that the judgment attests to Marcel's
own shortcomings. Somewhere he quotes Chaim expressing, in his
tortured syntax, his particular frustrations:

"To do a portrait, is necessary you should take your time. But
tires the model, who assumes a stupid expression. Then I have to
hurry up, which it irritates me. I become unnerved and begin to

see flames that they burn my eyes and I have to scream. I slash the canvas then goes everything kaplooey and I find myself on the floor . . ." Marcel describes how Chaim had worked himself into a near delirium in the telling, how the dog barked and passersby turned their heads. Then Chaim had paused and asked ingenuously, "How happens this, I wonder?" The author here admits he hasn't a clue.

Another reason Chaim admires Jonquille is for her tolerance of the skeleton crew of elementals that have clandestinely invaded the Laloës' apartment. The triplets are naturally represented as is the now virtuous Laila and the reformed devil Ketev Meriri. Why bother, wonder these uprooted oddities, why bother pursuing their penny-ante discord when men have so far usurped and exceeded any mischief they might instigate? At first hostile toward the freak-ish intruders, the dog soon ceases her whimpering and growling, having realized that they are perhaps more afraid of her than she of them. Then she welcomes them, the genial creature, into her own fellowship of not-quite-human beings, and even allows the dwarfish triplets to ride her low-slung spine.

Chaim, for his part, has become more or less reconciled to the fact that wherever he goes the sheydim will follow. At least they no longer sneer at his portraits in progress (since he's not making any) only to demand that he paint theirs. Instead, with bodies visible and voices audible only to Chaim and Jonquille, they reminisce; they recount the pranks and practical jokes they initiated during the salad days of the destruction of the Second Temple, the exile from Spain, the Chmielnicki massacres, and the Cossack pogroms. A captive audience, Chaim is given an earful of their bedtime tales, and on the edge of sleep their memories sometimes mingle with his own.

The Laloës have made sacrifices in the interest of their guests' se-curity. They have, for instance, suspended entertaining their rather

broad circle of friends—not an unusual deprivation given how
the occupation has put so many friendships on hold. Otherwise,
Götterdämmerung aside, the couple have largely managed to maintain the appearance of an ordinary life. Their complaisance gives
Chaim and Marie-Berthe an opportunity to share in the make-
believe, though the guests are not always capable of taking their
part. Unaccustomed yet to each other, they're forced to play out
their tentative give-and-take in front of onlookers. Their position
as asylum-seekers compels them to try to suppress the tensions that
often erupt in regrettable scenes, embarrassing to themselves and
their hosts. Still, for the sake of civility, they make an effort—more
material on the part of Marie-Berthe—to integrate themselves into
the Laloës' daily routine. Marie-Berthe accompanies the distin-
gué Anne on her early-afternoon shopping odysseys—afternoons
because Madame Laloë sleeps in after her late-night engagements.
The two women divvy up the ration cards and separate, one for the
greengrocer's, one for the *poissonnerie*. They stand in line sometimes
for hours to purchase items that are often unavailable, then trade
on their wit and good looks to tease a little something extra from
the cheese or the tobacco monger. On their return Anne produces
wondrous stews and bouillabaisses with mostly illusory ingredients,
while Marie-Berthe, a dreadful cook, peels potatoes and washes up.
She drinks numberless glasses of watery wine to aid the process.

Lying low, Chaim tries to keep out from underfoot. When not
petting the dog or studiously pulling a thread from the sleeve of a tattered sweater, he spends a good deal of time looking out the window.
He watches the two women as they commence their circuit, then
looks past them over the lead roofs to the spires of Saint-Eustache
and Notre-Dame and beyond to the hill of Montmartre—all still
in place. So why do they no longer seem to announce themselves
as landmarks of the city of Paris? *Ayn klaynikeit*, he sniffs, no big
deal; it's not as if Paris ever belonged to him.

They dine together at night before Madame Laloë, ornamental in a velvet Vionnet creation, is picked up by limousine. She's driven to the Palais Garnier, where she performs as Sophie in *Der Rosenkavalier*, and afterward, in her Olga persona, sings "Parlez-moi d'amour" at the famed Folies-Belleville. Her audiences are mainly composed of German officers and their mistresses *du soir*, whom she detests (though she enjoys universally spurning would-be suitors); she deplores this compromise of her Gaullist sympathies, but one must survive. Mornings, she sleeps late while Marcel works in his studio. His canvases are painterly landscapes limned from previous sketches, large-scale productions of the type often labeled "regional naturalism." With only a superficial nod to the Fauves, they retain enough of the nationalistic flavor to pass muster with the critics of the day. Chaim loathes them but must not say so, his situation having necessarily tamped down his arrogance. Marcel's studio is well supplied and north-facing, its sliding windows giving onto sun-suffused cauliflower clouds, but only once has he invited Chaim to paint alongside him. "It would be an honor," he had tendered, but Chaim's refusal was so emphatic—"I will only fuck everything up!"—that he never asked again.

Marie-Berthe urges Chaim to paint as well, a line of persuasion in which even Garde had failed. But why doesn't he? For one thing, there's the fear, and the intermittent wrenchings of his intestines that leave him prostrate for hours and would have handicapped the most resolute artist. But I would respectfully submit that Chaim Soutine's dormancy has more to do with the way the world has stolen his fire; the savagery with which he once charged his canvases has been hijacked by these merciless times. He knows, however, that his inaction weighs on everyone; it smells of ingratitude and makes him feel guilty. These people have stuck their necks out to save his because they regard him as an artist of value, but an artist who doesn't make art is nothing and not worth saving.

(Goes the old Jewish joke: "I'm nothing, Lord!" cries the rabbi beating his breast on Yom Kippur. "*I'm* nothing!" cries the rich banker; "God forgive me for thinking I was something." Then Velvel the synagogue beadle falls to his knees and cries, "I also am nothing!" The rabbi elbows the banker and says, "Look who thinks he's nothing.")

But loaded as the sentiment is for him, Chaim does feel a significant measure of gratitude toward the Laloës, as well as toward the woman who sometimes behaves as if she's been sentenced to care for him. Depending on her mood, Marie-Berthe will coddle or abuse him. She might massage his temples, debone his mackerel, and mince his *choucroute* to ease his digestion; she attempts to darn his socks, though he shows her how to do it more skillfully. She strikes provocative poses in a print kimono for a portrait he may never paint, stands in long queues at the pharmacy for his medications, now seldom in stock. At the same time, impatient with his lassitude, she refers to him at table as "the Jew," prefacing the word with coarse modifiers. She needles him over his bonding with the dozy dog: "I thought you only liked your animals dead and nailed to the wall." Madame Laloë, ever the peacemaker, tries to mitigate Marie-Berthe's sniping. "I think Chaim and Jonquille make an adorable pair," she croons, then laments how no amount of scrubbing can succeed in ridding the dog of her disagreeable odor. Which only gives Marie-Berthe the occasion to make a similar complaint about Chaim, who has decided that no one but Garde should ever bathe him again. The *no one* apparently includes himself.

But she is a beauty, Marie-Berthe, which Chaim never quite loses sight of; an autumnal beauty to be sure but more stunning for being on the brink of decline. And sometimes their moods coincide in a kind of shared quiescence. Sometimes the woman strikes a balance, and treats him equally as invalid and lover. In bed (with the coming of winter they've moved into the absent son's bedroom), Marie-Berthe no longer mauls him with her voracious assaults but gently fellates him and, when she's enabled his putz to stand on its own, climbs on board.

Over the months they've spent in the Laloës' apartment, Chaim and Marie-Berthe have begun to forget the jeopardy they've placed their hosts in. As have their hosts. Their coexistence has achieved its own diurnal rhythm. Then Marcel is confronted by Monsieur Jouhandeau, the beetle-browed concierge, who has seen him out walking nights with a male companion. He asks whether the friend is a guest and whether there are others; the municipality requires an official list of any unauthorized occupants in a building. Marcel concocts a faltering excuse for their guests' protracted visit, but the concierge can't be trusted not to denounce them to the prefecture. The jumpy fellow has himself been under observation since a former tenant (and neighbor of the Laloës), one Jean Moulin, has become infamous as a leader of the Résistance. Moreover, to be caught hiding a Jew can mean death for all concerned.

"We've been living in a fool's paradise," concedes Marcel, reaching for his wife's likewise trembling hand. It's time for their visitors to leave.

Shaken as they are, the Laloës are still not prepared to relinquish the responsibility they've accepted for the welfare of Soutine and Marie-Berthe. Are there really such people? But despite the colossal killjoy that Chaim has so often shown himself to be, Marcel's admiration for the better artist remains undiminished; and though the women are not distant in age, his wife has acquired a motherly concern for the changeful Marie-Berthe. Marcel books a trunk call with an acquaintance, Fernand Moulin, no relation to Jean but antifascist all the same. He is also, along with his occupation of veterinarian, an art collector and mayor of the commune of Richelieu near the tourist destination of Chinon in the Loire Valley. The area is a part of Vichy France but its chiefly agricultural landscape has been of little interest to the occupiers. When he hangs up, Marcel jubilantly reports that the mayor has said, "Send your protégé. I'll find him and his lady a place to stay."

Chaim winces at the word *protégé* but Marcel explains that it might be unwise to reveal the artist's true identity.

The guests pack the belongings that Marie-Berthe had retrieved from their two apartments soon after their flight. It is an act that should be second nature to Chaim by now, but while his garments are few, the heft of his baggage seems to contain the added weight of centuries. At the moment of their departure Jonquille begins whimpering plaintively and tries despite her short legs to leap into Chaim's arms. He drops his bag (the building quakes) and stoops to pick up the dog, who licks his cheeks as if his tears are nectar.

"You're not alive," she babbles huskily in his ear, "unless you know you're living."

Puzzled, Chaim holds the wriggling creature at arm's length, trying to remember where he's heard the words before. He gives up and settles for squeezing Jonquille to his chest.

"*Mayn ziskeit!*" he cries.

Marie-Berthe makes a face as much over the Yiddish syllables that infect Chaim's speech more frequently these days as at the mawkish display of affection. They say their thanks and goodbyes, then totter down the stairs followed by a short train of spirits and ghouls.

◆

IN THE GARE MONTPARNASSE a patrolling Wehrmacht officer releases a falcon from his sleeve; it darts aloft to bring down a chimney swift wheeling under the high glass ceiling and returns to the man's arm with the dead bird in its beak. A coterie of his subordinates zealously cheer their captain. Chaim and Marie-Berthe look to each other for reassurance, finding none, then duck on board a passenger carriage of the southbound train; they travel to Chinon without incident. We are strange bedfellows, reflects Chaim en route, thrown together by circumstance. He does not love the woman, has indeed resolved not to love her; that would be disloyal. But he remains spellbound by the fact that this sylphlike *maideleh* has chosen as her mission maintaining the damaged poor bet of a hunted Jew. He wonders whether she is as intrigued by their *mariage de convenance* as he.

The mayor meets them at the station; he has no trouble identifying them since they're the only passengers to disembark the train. Introductions are exchanged: he's Fernand Moulin "at your service," they are Karl Sutin and wife. Chaim's previous experience of mayors has not been auspicious and this one, a squat, nervous fellow in a porkpie hat, doesn't inspire much confidence either. His cheeks are puffed as if filled like a squirrel's with chestnuts, his imperial mustache waxed in a horizontal defiance of gravity. He greets the couple as if they are ordinary tourists, and after cursorily asking after the Laloës' health, begins to cite local history in a voice meant to be overheard: Chinon is François Rabelais's birthplace, the town where Joan of Arc's voices told her to go and meet the Dauphin; the region boasts many troglodyte dwellings, frequent *brocantes*, and of course a castle. Then, looking both ways, he drops the cicerone act and lowers his voice.

"There's a troop of Germans garrisoned in the town, so I took the liberty of securing you more isolated lodgings."

He drives them in his leek-green Fiat, surgical instruments rattling in the bag at his side, to the village of Champigny-sur-Veude. It's a charmless place of staid cement and slate-shingled houses surrounded by flat yellow sorghum fields. The only citizens in sight are a few householders and shopkeepers with hard-bitten, mistrustful faces, the only trees a nearby plantation of gaunt poplar saplings. There's nothing for miles around to arrest the imagination, not that Chaim's is active in any case. Monsieur Moulin assures the couple they'll be safe here; he sees them installed in rooms above the Hôtel-Restaurant Commerce, whose combined clerk, cook, and chambermaid is the redoubtable Madame Coquerit. She's a hatchet-faced, choleric woman in whose bad graces Chaim wastes no time in finding himself. Having made no secret of his vocation, he has proposed paying their rent in original paintings, an idea she promptly rebuffs. Chaim feels an unexpected relief.

Their rooms are small but clean, a condition that Chaim and Marie-Berthe, easily as slovenly as her companion, proceed to alter for the worse. He spills tobacco and scatters ashes over the area rugs, while she, consuming cheap brandy by the quart, leaves the empty bottles to gather on the windowsill and in dresser drawers. Though she tries her best to conserve it, she loses precious particles of the mysterious powder she's brought with her from Paris and snuffs through a rolled franc note. The ensigns of her unwashed step-ins are draped over lampshades and chairs, and it occurs to neither of them to make the bed or sweep up a clafouti crumb. Madame Coquerit, after one or two visits, refuses to clean their rooms again, and after some weeks threatens to evict them if they don't clean the suite themselves. The villagers are in large part unreceptive to more Parisian refugees; tiny Champigny cannot absorb them, and this new pair, whom some local wag has dubbed *Beauté et la Bête*, are especially dubious. All the more reason for Madame Coquerit to get rid of them.

Still, she needs the rent—though the couple's inconsistent payments are hardly worth the aggravation. And while the stuck-up *tartelette* has a healthy enough appetite, the "artist" (when does he ever paint?) turns his nose up at the crepes and confits in which Madame takes such pride. He complains of a queasy stomach and does in fact look quite green about the gills. Marie-Berthe sees this too and frets accordingly; she's dutiful in her attendance, spoon-feeding him his milk of bismuth, applying the warm compresses to his brow—that is, when she's not otherwise distracted with indulging her own bad habits. Then she's not averse to letting him know that she never signed on to be his nursemaid, which for Chaim begs the question as to why she's there at all.

"Did you think I'm maybe the Sheik from Araby?"

Left to his own devices during the periods of neglect, Chaim pursues his inveterate occupation of languishing. Given the lay of the land, what else can he do? Marie-Berthe scowls at him for his sloth, then relents, invites him to come with her to the street bazaar that reminds her of the place des Fêtes; come with her to—God forbid—church. She has found a sweet little chapel that looks like Saint-Chapelle, "where I go to pray for your miserable soul, Soutine." The thought of her uttering his name in such inimical quarters gives him gas. "Don't do for me no favors," he grumbles, then has second thoughts in case the prayers might actually have some influence. The woman abandons him for hours on end; she drinks the schnapps that makes her intrepid, sniffs the dust that makes her think she can fly, and dashes out into the broad day. Then she returns, having heard rumors of an assassination and hostages taken in a nearby village, of Germans combing the vicinity. She hurries back to the hotel to hunker timorously in their rooms and is good to Chaim again.

To his chagrin, it's his demidemons that show him the steadier concern. How often has he heard their reasons, all insipid, for seeking him out? They're drawn to him by their kinship; they're his comrades in the confederacy of the homeless, and *bubkes-bobkes*. But for all their assurances that they want only to share his shelter, he can't get free of the notion that they've come to take him back again. Back to *where*? The creatures, they're nothing but maggots from the brains of the ancient rabbis. Grown bored with the legalistic tenor of their religion, they snatched these entities from dreams and secreted them within the pages of their holy books. But words could not confine them and they escaped the books, taking to the quagmires and root cellars of the Russian Pale, from which they have since been driven. The books that were their original abodes have all been destroyed. So there is no *back* to which they could carry Chaim, who reminds himself that he was not spawned from a story, and that this line of thinking might be a symptom of looming insanity.

✦

THEY COME TO HIS bedside, even as the woman sleeps beside him: the mazikim and their relations—Poteh, the demon of forgetfulness; Igrat, the daughter of Mahalath, who commands her myriad of angels of destruction, one of which is the angel Duma, who conducts souls on their weekend furloughs from hell. Also present is the Golem of Prague, who fled the attic of the Altneushul during an air raid and arrived in Champigny via the power of the *kefitzat haderech*. (This is the prayer the monster was taught by the sorcerer-rabbi who created him, and enables him to leap seven leagues at a stretch. The hope was that he might use the faculty in future to aid him in trouncing the enemies of Israel, but instead he elected for flight.) They come not to taunt but to recite for Chaim the Psalms and Torah verses that defend one against both pursuers and affliction; they recommend remedies: thorny saffron mixed with head lice and menstrual blood; pennyroyal and fenugreek blended with the embryo of a she-ass; or in lieu of the embryo, the fat of a scarab beetle; or in the absence of the beetle, the gall of a white stork in beer. "To give health to your navel and marrow to your bones," they say.

Chaim dismisses their suggestions out of hand, then sometimes thinks contrarily, What can it hurt? He asks Marie-Berthe if she can maybe bring from the market some eggs and perhaps the spleen of a hairless goat. When she squints at him mordantly, he explains that it's a traditional remedy for stomachache, then summons an ounce of mirth: "But only if it's in season, the spleen."

"*Bien entendu*," she replies, "and shall I administer it to you by enema?"

The farm radio in Madame Coquerit's lounge broadcasts only Axis victories—the retaking of Kharkov, the rout of the Allies in Tunisia; the only newspapers on the rack in the hotel are the Vichy-controlled *Paris-soir* and *Je suis partout*, which has taken to serializing *The Protocols of the Elders of Zion*. Chaim reads the latter scrupulously, while Marie-Berthe asks why he wastes his time with that fascist rag. "It comforts me," he tells her, "that it says in it is owned and operated everything in the world by the Jews." His fatalistic brand of humor grates on Marie-Berthe's nerves until practically every kindness she renders him is grudging. They're at odds over the slightest issues: he tells her to close the window, it's cold outside, and she caustically replies, "If I close it, will it be warm outside?" She upbraids him for failing to pull the chain on the toilet down the hall, "or are you too weak to flush your own shit?" He replies, simpering, "I leave it so you can see how I did a good job."

"*Sale juif!*" she exclaims to the ceiling. "How did I, the ange noir that inspired a thousand portraits, end up with this sickly Yid?"

Mutters Chaim: "I think that l'ange noir for the Surrealist is a bête noir by Chaim Soutine," and grins, clearly pleased with his conceit. Marie-Berthe flings a bottle at his head, which shatters beneath the crucifix she's hung on the wall. He tries to continue calmly sipping his tea but the bitter taste makes him wonder whether she's maybe poisoned it.

At dusk the lamp flickers mothlike and dies. The madder-red glow from the twilit window finds Marie-Berthe once again reciting the litany of Chaim's precursors, men whose creative energies and sexual prowess leave Chaim's in the shade. "*Bel hommes* with impressive parts who knew how to satisfy a woman. Ernst's phallus was twice the length of yours and Breton's twice as long as his. Of course, Soutine, I can't remember the last time I saw yours at full salute."

When she tires of biting her thumb at him, she takes pity and begs his forgiveness; she clings to him again and sits on his knees so that Chaim's head reels from her inconstancy. He only knows that their ongoing conflicts exhaust him. His gut yowls, the Nazis lurk, and he confesses, like Modi identifying with Bacchus, that he and his limp putz are one.

"Maybe I am better off dead."

Then the woman suddenly springs from his lap and strikes a pose with a hand on her hip, the open bodice of her kimono revealing the peekaboo nipple of a snow-white breast. "Paint me, Soutine," she requests.

"You got on you too *shaineh* a *ponim*, a pretty face," he repines, and she frowns. "You're too pretty. I don't do pretty."

"Paint me!" The entreaty becoming a command.

He refuses and another bout of mutual antagonism commences.

After months of their stormy rows, about which the other guests have never ceased complaining, and the insupportable trashing of their quarters, Madame Coquerit has finally had enough. She escorts the couple, clamoring of injustice, into the street. Feeling exposed to unsympathetic eyes, Chaim turns appealingly to Marie-Berthe, whom he credits with having at the least kept him hidden until now. "Don't look at *me*," she snaps, and for good measure, "*I'm* not a Jew." But neither does she show herself prepared to leave him. They are yoked together by their common plight. Accommodations, however, are scarce in the village and Madame Coquerit has not been sparing in her back-fence chatter about the troublesome pair. As a consequence, they find the doors of the few local auberges closed to them.

Madame Pichoreaux, proprietor of a local café—the women run everything in the village, the only remaining men being too old or hors de combat—Madame P overhears the couple debating their dilemma at a corner table. An agreeable busybody, she recommends a farmhouse on the road to Chinon that may take in boarders. They drag themselves there on foot and are met by the Xaviers, a childless farmer and wife, poor but hospitable, who for a reasonable fee agree to make room for the refugees. They feed them from their depleted store and give them their single bedroom while they sleep in a dormer loft. But lean as are the times and straitened as is the family, they find their guests, on balance, intolerable. Quarrels aside, Chaim's sullen fastidiousness at meals and Marie-Berthe's fuddled monologues, let alone their general lack of hygiene, their public spats, their self-indulgence, are beyond enduring. The same pattern of reception and eviction is repeated at the next house that admits them. Only there the husband and wife and their bulbous-headed children are not so amiable: the rent is increased and this time the tenants made to sleep in the loft. As they shuttle from one lodging to another throughout that heartless winter, their reputations have spread and their profiles risen, as has their level of fear.

By late March, having run out of funds and exhausted the generosity of strangers, Chaim and Marie-Berthe throw themselves on the mercy of the mayor. They have been thus far reluctant to take advantage of his limited protection, but finally resort to contacting him by phone. An open-handed man within his means, Monsieur Moulin had thought to have done his duty by the Laloës with his initial aid of the artist and his paramour; their acquaintance has since become something of a liability. He asks them why they have not come to see him sooner in a tone that suggests they should not come again. But he intercedes for them nonetheless at the Hôtel Saint-Louis, an eyesore of an establishment on the village's northern edge, and pays their first month's rent. The ramshackle pension, patronized primarily by the transient and destitute, is viewed in ordinary times as merely dispiriting. Now its dodgy residents invite the suspicions of all and sundry. Chaim and Marie-Berthe resolve to quit the place as soon as they can accumulate a little capital, though just how that will be accomplished is anyone's guess.

Goaded by Marie-Berthe acting as both editor and stenographer, Chaim dictates a letter to Madame Castaing, asking for an advance on work he's yet to even begin. Instead of responding by post, the concerned Madeleine makes the trip in her chauffeured Delage to visit in person. She is appalled by what she finds. The current Soutine has reverted to the same beggarly specimen she and Marcellin had first encountered on the terrace of the Café de la Rotonde. Nor have the artist's reduced circumstances dampened his entitled attitude. But there is, as always, a fragility to his bluster, and Madeleine suspects the Aurenche woman has put him up to his present demands. Marie-Berthe, who has been obviously derelict in her caretaker duties, sits beside him on the bed with folded arms in their pigpen of a room. Her wide, gold-flecked eyes are rimmed in red, the Botticelli features somewhat bloated, her agitation implying a deficiency of the stimulants she's accustomed to. Madeleine remembers Maurice Sachs's bleak prophecy and realizes she's made a terrible mistake in foisting this volatile woman on Chaim. Of course, she's only half-right, but on first impression the couple's situation appears irredeemable.

"Chaim," she chides him by way of reassurance, "you're not a charity case." Though that's precisely what he has been these past few years. "Louis Carré is eager to buy all the Soutines he can get his hands on despite the interdict, but I have nothing new to sell him."

Marie-Berthe pokes a furtive finger in Chaim's ribs. "You didn't from the earlier sales give me a big enough percent," he argues, discounting—give or take the healthy profits they've claimed for themselves—a decade of the Castaings' liberality. He can see that he's hurt the feelings of his benefactress, who's come all the way from Paris despite the risks, but holds his ground as Marie-Berthe has enjoined him to do.

"This is unfair, Chaim," says Madeleine, thrusting forward her sharp chin. "When have we ever let you down?"

Never, but just now Chaim finds himself beyond any sense of indebtedness. This is in part the result of Marie-Berthe's suggestion that he's been played for a patsy, in part due to the calamitous predicament that is his life. All of which is exacerbated by the feeling that the *sympathique* Madame Castaing represents an Eden from which he is forever cast out. Her only real fault, he knows, is that she is present, which today is cause enough for his resentment.

"You are cheating me!" he accuses her.

Familiar as she is with his moods, Madeleine realizes there's nothing for it but to bid him adieu. Standing, she takes a wallet from her purse, snatches a fistful of bills, and shoves them into Marie-Berthe's hands. "Take good care of him," she says, which sounds less like solicitation than threat.

"Well," observes Marie-Berthe when she's gone, "you've burnt that bridge, Soutine."

He looks at her with the outrage he had not fully expended on their visitor. Can she really be reproaching him for doing what she asked? "I can't by you do nothing right!" he exclaims, causing Marie-Berthe to scoot away from the ferocity of his response. Frightened, she begins to speak when Chaim interrupts her, "Why you don't leave me?" Why indeed? he expects her to reply, or some barbed retort to that effect. After all, both of them know the way things stand is unsustainable. But instead of offering more repartee, she appears to be honestly considering the question; then she rises, facing him, and runs her fingers through his hair, which he fears is receding. He imagines it falling like plucked feathers about his shoulders.

"Because, Chaim," she says at length, pressing his face against the ruffles at her breast, "you are my man."

This is too much, the commiseration somehow worse than her callousness. The woman is impossible! Chaim gives a strangled cry, wrestles out of her embrace, and launches himself from the bed. Then he's out the door of that lousy suite and down the stairs into the unshaded courtyard. He ducks beneath an arch only to realize how much he's become over time a stranger to the out-of-doors.

Neither woman nor figments have followed him. He's alone in the village street, an uncommon spectacle in his soiled pea jacket, torn pajama bottoms, and jute-soled espadrilles. But before he can arouse curiosity, he turns a corner into a narrow passage between a post office and a *confiserie*. He emerges into an area flanked by a kitchen garden and a potting shed, crosses a gravel path, and enters an unplowed field of purple fountain grass dotted with black-eyed Susans. To try to still the tattooing of his heart, he begins to do mechanically what Mademoiselle Garde had done during the hours when he painted: he looks for four-leafed clovers. That she never found one didn't seem to discourage her, resigned as she was to the fact that luck should remain elusive; the search was everything. But Chaim cannot be satisfied with looking and not finding. Where is she, his beloved Garde? He continues looking.

Lately he suffers, even at the best of times, from low-grade stomach cramps, and is always weary from sleeplessness—the insomnia induced by his chimerical voices and the insomnia that comes from lying awake listening for the voices to come. Though he keeps his eyes to the ground, he takes no notice of the freshly planted spring wheat he's trampling over; he wastes no glance at the vineyard on its flinty clay slope to the west. The rolling agrarian landscapes of the Loire Valley hold no interest for him. The cow pasture beyond the stile is a riot of color—violet hyacinths, burgundy lavender, orange and red nasturtiums, the bravura pink blossoms of cherry trees at the borders; they all fall into the category of tchotchkes for Chaim, who never even knew the name of the gladioluses he so loved to paint. He climbs another wooden stile over a mossy stone wall and steps off the other side onto the shoulder of a tarmac road.

The road winds past a number of old and more recent houses toward a bridge in the distance, which passes over a moat and under a monumental stone gate. Turreted ramparts extend from the gate to enclose the spires and domed pavilions of the town. This must be Richelieu, thinks Chaim, the eponymous walled borough of which Monsieur Moulin is mayor and about which he had spoken so proprietarily in his Baedeker vein. It was built from scratch, he'd had them know, in the seventeenth century at the direction of the powerful cardinal as a complement to his resplendent château. The château was plundered during the Revolution and demolished soon after, but the model town, which La Fontaine once called "the most beautiful village in the universe," has its postcard allure after the dullness of Champigny.

Chaim's legs are a bit tottery from long disuse, and he's left behind the shepherd's crook cane that Marie-Berthe bought him. Still, he plods on over the cobbled bridge, drawn forward if only by the need to put increasing distance between himself and the Hôtel Saint-Louis. It's Sunday and the town is quiet, with few citizens abroad. The nearly empty streets in their symmetrical grid, the spotless freestone facades of the row houses, even the burbling fountain in the central square leave the artist with the impression of a bone-dry necropolis. Heightening Chaim's discomfort is the sight, among the handful of strollers admiring the architect's heavy hand, of a pair of German soldiers with shoulder-slung arms. Though they're sharing a guidebook and don't seem to pose any immediate threat, Chaim loses no time in shrinking away from the scene. He hastens several blocks down an avenue that ends at the privet-bounded entrance to a public park. The park is what remains of the cardinal's estate, and while only a few weathered fragments of the palace have survived, the original gardens are

still preserved, with a broad pleasure ground sloping down to the
River Vienne.

Chaim arrives winded at the bottom of the slope, where a grove
of woodland borders the slow-flowing river. He rests his hands on
his knees, imbibing great lungfuls of air; then he looks up at the
trees. What he sees he has no words to describe. Neither do I, at
least not through his eyes. But I can suppose it's like coming upon
a herd of creatures whose existence predates the world. They're a
species that, unlike the human tribe he belongs to or the mar-
ginally human that claim him, have no relation to time. Chaim
dwells in time after a fashion that has precluded his occupying any
fixed place for very long. But the trees—he doesn't even know their
names—they writhe, twist, and bow to one another, rooted to the
earth but still involved in a perennial dance. Not known for his
nimbleness of foot, Chaim would nevertheless like to join them.
He'd like to step into their midst, where no one else—not even his
bogies—may follow, though they can imagine the places he goes.
(Then his adventures become the tales they tell to each other.) They
can picture him shepherding the trees, for a brief eternal moment,
into his own dark climate, and corralling them there as if they belonged to him. He will release them in due course to return to their
natural habitat, but not before he's gathered—and for this he may
never be forgiven—irrefutable evidence of what he's seen.

In his mind he's sprinting, albeit he's only hobbling and limp-
ing, all the way back to Champigny. He bursts into their rooms,
and while Marie-Berthe wrings her hands and demands to know
where he's been, snatches up his palette and paint box and slings
the strap of his field easel over his shoulder. Then his knees give
out and, utterly spent, he drops like a marionette whose strings
have been cut onto a rickety chair. But he's up the next morning
at dawn. He takes his painting materials and slips out of the suite,
leaving the woman still sleeping. From the hotel kitchen he grabs

yesterday's croissant and pours the dregs from a jug of cold coffee into his flask; then he sets off without stopping for the grove by the river. He returns at sunset so sweat-sodden and in such complete disarray that Marie-Berthe bites her fist to keep from crying out loud. His work smock is so splattered with paint that he looks as if he's been standing in a parti-colored rain. But when he unloads his gear, which includes a finished canvas, he's smiling. True, it's the grin of an imbecile or a madman, but it has a certain luminous quality that Marie-Berthe has not witnessed before. Seeing it, she's reduced to a fit of laughter during which she opens her arms to the artist. He steps into their circle and is enfolded.

✦

HE PAINTS FOR EIGHT to ten hours at a stretch, and returns each day more debilitated than the previous. He leans his latest painting against a growing stack of others facing the wall, then, close to collapsing, begins preparing tomorrow's canvas: he stretches the cloth taut with his pliers and tacks the corners to the frame, sometimes falling asleep in the process. He arranges his oils—the linseed, the poppy, the Flemish siccative; then the brushes—brights and filberts, stroking their bristles as if they were still attached to the horse's mane. He grips the trowel-shaped palette knife like an Excalibur. Most nights he abstains from dining with Marie-Berthe in the tenth-rate restaurant downstairs, but instead heats a pan of broth on a hotplate; he sucks a piece of sourdough after dunking it in the broth, winces from the pain of digestion, and goes to bed.

It's his unusual lack of complaining that both intrigues and troubles Marie-Berthe. "I think you might be killing yourself, Chaim," she remarks. She calls him Chaim now. Of course she's not faring so much better herself. She's used up her reserve of fairy dust and there's little money left for drink. Her moods alternate radically between extreme foreboding and a vigorous denial that there's anything to fear. She frequently addresses Jesus and voices her life-or-death need of a good hair salon.

In response to her concern for his welfare, Chaim replies, "This is for you wishful thinking?" which wounds her. Because his behavior of late, monomaniacal as it is, is in fact the kind Marie-Berthe most respects; it's more in line with the quixotic idea she had of the artist before they met. What she can't endure, however, is being left behind for a grass widow while he goes off to paint.

Against his admonitions she inspects the canvases when he's gone. With Ernst and his cronies, it was always the "romance of the artist." They entered, often with the aid of narcotics, dream states from which they retrieved the oddball visions they transmitted to their canvases. But this Soutine is different. Like them he travels for his visions—geographically rather than psychically—but his destination is not some other order of reality. He arrives where he began, at a familiar scene—a landscape, for instance, that may perhaps include a reclining figure, the paint ablaze and layered thick as frosting—which he views as strange and new. He sees the subject as if it has never before been observed with mortal eyes. How do you suppose he does that? she wonders.

She follows him early one morning before the first light. She keeps a healthy distance between herself and the artist as he clatters with his paraphernalia through gentian-dappled sheep meadows and over the cultivated fields, skirting the walled town before finally reaching his sacred grove. She makes no effort to conceal herself, content that Chaim is oblivious of her shadowing, just as he seems indifferent to the attention a character such as himself might draw from the wary villagers. *Ça ne fait rien,* the two of them still have the protection of the mayor, don't they? And the document declaring Soutine a refugee of Russian Orthodox affiliation. Besides, the Vichy government is not likely to worry much about having arrested their quota of Jews in a hamlet as remote as Champigny-sur-Veude.

He has erected his easel before a stand of trees by the river but has yet to remove his tubes of oils from their box. Instead, he sticks his hands in his pockets and appears to be listening to the dawn chorus of birds in the imbroglio of branches overhead; he watches the fog lifting like a veil of cobweb from the river, the sky changing from cobalt to smoke blue with the rising sun—while Marie-Berthe, having seated herself on a rock wall a dozen or so yards behind the artist, watches him. Wearing only the thin housedress she's worn all week, she rubs her bare arms against the morning chill; she grows quickly bored but still doesn't move. If she can't see things as Soutine sees them, she can at least see him seeing them. Then comes the insurgent moment when he begins to paint and she's captivated.

She's surprised to observe him later that morning, and on the morning after that, abandoning his easel to accost some local person happening by on the nearby road. Dire circumstance has if anything amplified his timidity, so how is it, wonders Marie-Berthe, that Chaim has found the nerve to approach them? His bashfulness seems to have been superseded by his desire to include human details in his paysages. The road is not well traveled and the few passersby tend to give the artist as wide a berth as they might have a supplicant leper. Eventually, however, he is obliged in his appeal (and offer of monetary reward) by a farmer on a wagon drawn by a blinkered mare, who appears in no more of a hurry than her master. Fanning himself with his rattan hat, the farmer seems more amused than frightened when Chaim's reserve dissolves into a bullying outburst at his failure to hold a pose. There are others in the following days—a saucer-eyed child climbing a fence, a young girl intently reading in the shade—whom Chaim manages to capture without their knowledge.

Such scenes are not unusual in Soutine's oeuvre, but Marie-Berthe, shrewd for all her contradictions, believes she can detect a difference. She's seen some of the Céret works in a gallery where the owner kept them out of reach of Chaim's pocketknife. She knows how the artist can perceive a tumultuousness in the most peaceful of environs. But here he seems to be attempting, conversely, to wrest from a tumultuous season oases of repose. Still, he can't help it: the figures in his foreground, unaware of the menace, appear as if stalked by a band of bodeful trees.

Menace aside, Marie-Berthe is jealous of the figures in his paintings. She envies the lonely woman with the umbrella, the mother with the marrowless child in her lap, the little calf lifting its credulous head as if to question the slaughterer. She's even jealous of the wallowing hogs. Who is Marie-Berthe Aurenche if not the muse?

"Paint *me*, Chaim!" she insists when he returns from his working day.

He can hardly stand. He was caught in a thunderstorm and his clothes are drenched, hair streaming rivulets, shoes caked in the mud he tracks across the floor. Mademoiselle Garde would have swaddled him in warm towels and tucked him into bed, but this one . . . the Black Angel they called her, though her looks are distinctly fair. But her nature, when not lighter than air, can be black as her limp leather Bible. Still, who can deny her heart-stopping beauty, the more intense as it's on the threshold of flaming out?

"I don't do beauty," he says more to himself than to her. Then, due perhaps from fatigue or remorse, and more out of pity than passion, he relents; he succumbs to the idea of capturing what's left of the woman's luster before it's extinguished. He will paint her and bestow on her the portrait as a keepsake to make her happy—and to shut her up. "Put on your dress that it matches the color of your lips," he tells her, and she excitedly throws on a scarlet frock. He hasn't the heart to tell her he meant the Alice blue.

No sooner has he set up his easel and mounted a fresh canvas, however, than he groans and drops his brushes in exhaustion. Marie-Berthe is all attentiveness. She undresses him and puts him to bed, prepares the bouillon and spoon-feeds him, cooling the hot broth with her vinous breath. At daybreak she brings him a tartine slathered in lard and tea with condensed milk. Then she helps him out of bed and stands him upright, still in his long johns, behind his easel. She places the brushes and palette in his hands. He scolds her for continuing to fuss with her dress, which shows signs of having been worn overnight. Away now from the ardency bestirred by the open air, the artist takes his time.

In light of Chaim's conviction that the Castaings have misused him, Marie-Berthe has begun a correspondence with the Laloës. Chaim at first has his qualms: their account with the large-hearted couple is already beyond settling. Marie-Berthe reminds him that beggars can't be choosers and asks Marcel whether he might be willing to play the role of middleman: For a commission acceptable to both parties, he could transport Chaim's new paintings to the dealer Carré in Paris, thus bypassing the Castaings. Marcel waives the commission, viewing the task as an act of partisan resistance as well as yet another opportunity to demonstrate his allegiance to Maître Soutine. He and Anne arrive on a summerish afternoon in May in their mustard-colored Voisin Aérodyne, which, old and rust-cankered as it is, causes a stir in the village. They apologize for having caused a stir. But despite the hazardous state of affairs, they still manage to give the impression of an energetic couple on an outing in the country.

Like Madame Castaing before them, the Laloës are stunned by the condition in which they find the artist and his mistress. Chaim and Marie-Berthe in their shabby suite appear less like *comme il faut* hotel residents than the distressed survivors of a shipwreck. Which makes it all the more jarring that they should greet their guests with such ebullience—but it's been so long since either has seen a friendly face. Marie-Berthe, overdressed for the occasion in one of her back-numbered gowns, is trying too hard to play hostess; she assures them the rubbery oysters she's offering from an open tin are the rarest delicacies the wartime economy can provide. Chaim had at first expressed his disappointment that the Laloës had not brought with them the dog Jonquille, but assured that she is prospering and well looked after, he is instantly cheerful again. Meanwhile Chaim, so often defensive at the mere mention of his work, shows himself eager to display to the Laloës his most recent paintings. Marcel and Anne steal glances at each other, both wondering whether the couple are in the grip of some shared febrile infirmity. They nevertheless take the cue to join their inimitable friends in making a pretense of normality.

Anne gives Marie-Berthe the gift of a hand-painted scarf, which the delighted Marie-Berthe ties with a dashing gesture Romany-style round her head. Marcel nods his approval at the canvases Chaim has begun to show him. In truth he is wildly enthusiastic, the paintings are sublime; but there's danger in overpraising them, which can backfire with an artist of Chaim's thin-skinned temperament. Still, he can't suppress his admiration and begins to wax grandiloquent, invoking "Daumier's inner strength coupled with Corot's vivacity . . ." Then he holds his breath, waiting for Soutine to take issue, but Chaim only beams until a hint of color is seen to return to his pasty cheeks. Anne seconds her husband's esteem for the paintings, and Marie-Berthe takes quiet pride in her association with such an accomplished master. She swells with the Laloës' unleashed encomiums: "The headstrong lyricism . . . the waves of space and light . . ."; though if she's honest, she remains a little

bothered by an element in his compositions that she can only identify as "Jewy." This includes the pigs.

Chaim requests a song from Madame Laloë, and after the
obligatory modest protests she gives them a soul-stirring rendition
of a Bach chorale. "By you sounds good even the German," asserts
Chaim, and for once an atmosphere approaching festivity invades
those seedy rooms.

Then Marcel proposes they take the party on the road, parlous
times be damned! They can drive to Chinon, see the sights and later
visit Mayor Moulin. Since his days of being chauffeured about by
Daneyrolle, Chaim has never been able to refuse an excursion in
an automobile. All are in a mood to call a moratorium on trepida-
tion. But on their way out the door Marcel pauses, having spied
the covered easel in the corner, and, curious, takes the unexampled
license of asking Chaim what he's currently working on. Under the
influence of the moment's good cheer, Chaim removes the sheet
with a matador's panache from the unfinished portrait of Marie-
Berthe. "Voilà!" More fulsome praise ensues, but Marie-Berthe,
whom Chaim has not yet allowed to look at the painting, remains
silent. She begs off the junket, complaining of a sudden headache,
and no amount of insisting that the ride will do her good can persuade her to come.

They return that evening with their high spirits much subdued.
The fortified town was dreary and on edge owing to the invaders,
and it was imprudent to leave the car. Their attempt to visit the
mayor was also disappointing, as the principled little man was feeling besieged; recent bureaucratic demands weighed heavily on his
conscience and he was in no mood to renew old acquaintances. Then
too, gaiety has always been as hard on Chaim's system as despair.

As they reenter the suite, the artist notes that his work in progress has been covered over again. Funny but he doesn't remember

having replaced the linen sheet, and since when has Marie-Berthe ever lifted a finger toward keeping house? Besides, she's been advised to stay clear of his easel. Chaim approaches the *chevalet*, raises the cloth, and is instantly apoplectic. This is not his painting. Gone is the mouth's pouting thoughtfulness, maimed by the upturned corners of the lips forcing a phony smile; gone the gold-flecked depths of the eyes, whose mystery has been squelched by a vapid apple green. Careless sepia strokes conceal the polychrome highlights of her hair, and the virulent lust-red of her dress has faded to a pallid carnation pink. Even the questioning attitude of her head seems to have been rotated into a more forthright position.

"I fixed it," says Marie-Berthe, having appeared in the bedroom doorway in her tacky robe de chambre. She looks even muzzier than usual, as if just emerged from a nap or a bottle.

Chaim emits a growl that slowly evolves into words. "You defiled it."

"You made me old."

"I made you ageless!" Frantic, he begins rummaging among his materials until he locates his scissors.

Marie-Berthe screams and tries to place herself between the canvas and the artist, but when he raises the scissors murderously above his head, she steps aside. He stabs the painting, ripping a long incision down the middle, then proceeds to snip the whole composition into irregular pieces. Marie-Berthe is in hysterics, the Laloës horrified. Marcel gathers up the paintings designated for the market and makes some inane attempt at a seemly departure. ("Well, I guess we'll leave you two to your . . .") Still wielding his scissors like the beak of a predatory bird, Chaim spares them a dismissive wave, while Marie-Berthe, on her knees and sobbing disconsolately, scrambles to collect the torn fragments of herself. She's still weeping and trying in vain to reassemble the portrait with a needle and thread when Chaim walks out the door.

Leaning on his cane, he directs his flat-footed steps toward the homestead of Ambroise Crochard. Monsieur Crochard is a cabinetmaker, with a shop and a low-lying cottage just beyond the walls of Richelieu. He also does a little farming and has given Chaim unrestricted permission to paint his forlorn pony (shades of Ethelinda), his purblind dog (shades of Jonquille), and his pigs (the pigs being a late unsanctified addition to Chaim's petting zoo of subjects). A mutual respect for each other's artistry has resulted in an unexpressed accord between the two men, a rare sort of fellow feeling in Chaim's experience. He likes the smell of sawdust in Monsieur Crochard's shop, likes watching the gristly old man stain a red oak veneer; he takes pleasure in the way the planing tool leaves a wake of curled shavings like lovelocks when the carpenter bevels a beechwood plank. By the same token, Monsieur Crochard—whom Chaim has not discouraged from watching him work—marvels at the Russian's technique of creating surfaces as swirling and thick as meringues. He might puzzle over the deformities of the resulting images, but he views with favor the artist who suffers so to conceive them.

The old artisan, whose chiseled features give him the look of eroded statuary, is an odd duck in these parts. His politics lean far to the left and he's sometimes carelessly outspoken in his views. This tendency, along with his rabid anticlericalism, has made him something of an outcast among his neighbors, who nevertheless seek him out for his expert craftsmanship. Another reason for the cabinetmaker's solitariness is his desolation over the absence of his apprentice and only son, Lothaire, who was captured by Germans at the Battle of Arras. The old man keeps a chair and a place setting waiting for him at his table. Chaim, who has been invited on occasion to this table, is made uneasy by the empty chair: it puts him too much in mind of the chair appointed during the seders of his youth for the visitation of the prophet Elijah, whose advent he has always feared. He's thankful the prophet has yet to have seen fit to join the crew of bugaboos that have pestered him all his days.

The cabinetmaker is surprised by the painter's unannounced visit. He can see that the man is upset but asks him no questions. Instead, he gives him a glass of the weak tea that Chaim prefers to his briny homemade vintage and cranks up his relic of a wireless. The device, whose possession is grounds for arrest and even execution, is a complicated arrangement of naked copper coils and vacuum tubes. Since the curtains are drawn and the lamps dimmed by order of the occupiers, the tubes are the only source of light in the cluttered room. Their topaz glow gives the exposed ceiling beams and the unplumb tufa-stone walls a hallowed quality. Monsieur Crochard twists the dials through various frequencies, producing kazoo-like noises until he's able to access the crackling voice of Charles de Gaulle broadcasting from London. The news is not all bad: the Germans are finally defeated at Stalingrad; there's the Palm Sunday massacre of an Axis troop-transport aircraft over Tunisia, the Allied bombings of Hamburg and Sicily—though Chaim cringes as much at announcements of victory as defeat; the tremors of the battlefield are that far-reaching. Monsieur Crochard is diverted by Chaim's responses, since other than their shared hatred of the Germans, the artist has never expressed any political convictions at all. The man's taciturnity aside, the cabinetmaker doesn't subscribe to his Karl Sutin fiction. He's seen how Chaim shuddered at the news of the Warsaw Ghetto uprising and the rumors that the Jews are being gassed. Not that his identity matters a wit to his host; no one is who they are anymore. But this misfit, this poor *deraciné*—it's not so much that he doesn't belong here in this particular place as that he doesn't seem even to belong to this moment in time. And yet, events have conspired to drag him into history.

Monsieur Crochard has tried to interest Sutin (or whoever he is) in the game of chess, but the man has no aptitude for it. He has no aptitude for anything that the cabinetmaker can see other than hurling colors like a swarm of Gadarene butterflies at a blank canvas. So they sit in silence, two eccentrics, listening to staticky voices telling them what they already know: the planet is burning, the flames lapping as far as the door of a cottage in a valley of the Indre-et-Loire.

By now the regional curfew is in effect; the Richelieu regiment will be on the lookout for violators and it's too risky for Chaim to return to Champigny. He had not wanted to return anyway and is grateful when Crochard asks him whether he would like to stay the night. He says the artist can have his bed (there is no sofa), but Chaim will not hear of it. "Is good for my spine, to sleep on the floor." The old man shrugs. "Suit yourself," he says, then brings him a pillow and blanket and starts to turn off the radio, but Chaim asks him please not yet; the Voice of America is broadcasting a show featuring the musician Louis Armstrong performing with the band from the Hot Club de France in exile. The carpenter retires and Chaim listens alone to the brassy music that takes him back to the sonorous boulevards of Montparnasse. He's astonished as always to find that he should want to go back. After the concert there comes on a voice that he recognizes. It's the poet André Breton, also in America, leaving off his psychic automatism long enough to exhort his fellow Frenchmen to be brave.

Is easy, thinks Chaim, to utter such platitudes from the security of New York, America. "I know this man," he says aloud to the cabinetmaker, whose stertorous snoring can be heard from behind the curtain of his bedroom alcove. "A bigmouth." Nevertheless, it soothes him, this familiar voice from across the sea, and he listens, nodding, until the station signs off.

He is curled on the oiled timber floor in front of the wood-stove. It's a gentle spring night so Crochard has allowed the fire to burn to embers. Nestled in the lingering warmth, Chaim is reminded all the same of the floor of la Ruche, which was always cold. I've come back where I started from, he thinks, which isn't true; the truth is that he has never left. He's still the same lowborn artist eaten up with yearning, and it's still that lean year during the Great War when Amedeo Modigliani talked him into donning the scaphandre.

He's in it yet, having labored more than one and a half kilometers along the bed of the Seine. Enthralled with all he's seen at the bottom of the river, he continues trudging forward past the bridge that marks the finish line of the artists' boat race. Eventually he encounters a sort of merman in rabbinical garb, an aquatic tzaddik with a book in his lap. He's surrounded, this glimmering sage, by swimming entities of the type that Chaim has always attracted, much the way he attracts the fleas at la cité Falguière. Such occult creatures may or may not be a product of oxygen toxicity, nitrogen narcosis, gas bubbles in the bloodstream, or a variety of other effects one can suffer from overlong submersion underwater; though these particular symptoms (if indeed Chaim has them) have resulted not from the malfunctioning of his surface air supply but rather due to the supplier himself, who has fallen asleep. Gasping for air, Chaim is assured by the merman that reading his open book will temporarily restore his breathing. It does. But frenziedly turning the pages of the far-fetched narrative, which purports to be the story of his life, he finds little that is familiar. He rifles the volume in search of a chapter in which the character designated as himself perhaps finds redemption, but settles instead for a recognizable episode—the one wherein Chaim Soutine has accompanied his friend Amedeo to a dinner at the apartment of the occasional poet and art dealer Léopold Zborowski.

The war has yet to begin and the city still sparkles like a net of jewels, none of which its artists can afford. But they can feast their eyes, and that somehow sustains them. Modi is fresh from his affair with the seductress Anna Akhmatova, the very slope of whose Roman nose is a legend. The alliance of their physical beauty and Olympian talents has been enough to make their beholders shield their eyes from the combined brilliance. Chaim has arrived from Lithuania too late to witness their liaison, but he's still in time to experience its afterglow. He has quit his lessons at Cormon's academy for want of tuition and lack of faith. His real teachers are anyway the Old Masters in the Louvre, and his head never ceases spinning from his recurrent visits to its measureless galleries. It spins as well, Chaim's head, from Haussmann's broad avenues and the labyrinthine streets that the baron has overlooked, and the palaces and church towers and the fantastical domes atop the butte of Montmartre. He supposes his own work is in some way an antidote to that profusion of splendor, but in the absence of proper nutrition, he's not above consuming a bit of that splendor to fuel his art.

Chaim's head is also addled from the brandies that he and Modi have cadged at the Rotonde on their way to Zborowski's. Keeping up with Modigliani has done no end of damage to Chaim's already sensitive stomach, which is further aggravated by his irregular meals (though when were his meals ever regular?), to say nothing of the deliberate fasts he imposes on himself to heighten the intensity of his still life compositions. But he can't fight it; Modi's tameless personality has an attraction to rival gravity itself, and Chaim is helpless to resist his overtures of friendship. Tonight they've been stood drinks by the Creole model Aicha, daughter of an African prince, who is always good for a touch. (She's propped up many a penniless Montparnassier, including that Russian bluffer Lenin, whose tirades on the café terrace give Chaim a pain.)

Outside the door of the Zborowskis' apartment at 3 rue
Joseph Bara, Modi takes another whiff from his vial of ether.
Now he's suitably convivial. Despite his vainglorious manner
and dissolute habits, the dealer and his wife adore him, and have
given him a standing invitation to dinner. Zbo has even stocked
a guestroom with artists' supplies so that Modi can paint there
at his leisure. (This also allows the dealer to keep an eye on his
investment, encourage his production, and spy on the undraped
models he imports.) Zborowski's belief in the Italian's talent
is categorical. Soutine, however, is an unknown quantity, and
though Modigliani has sung his praises ad nauseam, Zbo and
his wife have yet to meet him. Nor has he been invited on this
particular evening.

So they're surprised, and not happily, when they open the
door to see that Modi has brought along his pot companion. The
man appears to have been fished out of a bog. His face is that of a
common muzhik and his foul clothes hang on him like a suit of
dead leaves; his velour hat has the shape of a battered bell buoy.
Plus, he has an aroma that threatens to overwhelm the fragrance of
Madame Zborowski's cuisine.

"Here's the paragon that will make your fortune," announces
Modi, "*il meraviglioso* Soutine!"

The dealer has a certain tolerance for the unscrubbed denizens
of *la vie bohème*, some of whom have proved to be virtuosi. His wife,
Hanka, however, has no such predilection. Born into a Polish family whose aristocratic ancestry she never lets her husband forget, she
greets the uninvited guest with the stiffest civility. She knows her
husband's livelihood depends to some extent on these *youpin* immigrants, but this one is beyond salvation. Like all women she has a
weakness for Modi and has attired herself in a clinging black gown
with a sequined bodice in anticipation of his coming. But upon
sight of the company he keeps, she already considers the evening

a disappointment. She turns to march into the dining room to set another place at the table.

But Modi is at his irrepressible best. He flirts with the *domestique* Paulette Jourdain as she serves the first course, thus arousing Hanka's jealousy. He placates his hostess by appealing to her discreet craving for talk of scandal, carrying tales from the salons and cafés, spicy gossip concerning his many illustrious acquaintances. He tells her that the artist Marie Laurencin, Apollinaire's current inamorata, is withering away from a deficiency of sexual satisfaction. "Some attribute this to Apollinaire's staunch refusal to remove his clothes while making love." He tells her that Max Jacob has lately developed a taste for sergeants of the Republican Guard with chevron mustaches. He tells her, with undisguised pride, how he disarmed a gun-wielding Alfredo Piña at Marie Vassilieff's soirée for Georges Braque (neglecting to say that it was he who provoked the skirmish in the first place by insulting Alfredo's lover, who was formerly his own). Madame Zborowski covers her mouth with a hand to conceal a smile, but her blush betrays the pleasure she takes in such reports. Slightly uncomfortable with this line of table talk, her husband attempts to turn the conversation to more pressing concerns; he mentions some potential buyers of Modi's work but delicately repeats their common complaint about his portraits.

"They wonder why you never put pupils in the eyes."

Modi replies with his customary hauteur, "When I know their souls, I will paint their eyes."

"Of course," submits Hanka, as if such an attitude were self-evident, "but do you never feel obliged to defer to the tastes of your patrons?" This from a wifely anxiety over her husband's failure to sell the work of his protégé.

Modi assumes an injured expression. "The function of art, *mia gentildonna*," he asserts with increased disdain, "is to struggle against obligation."

Hanka makes an insincere apology.

"What I'm seeking," says Modigliani in one of those lofty pronouncements he has ready for every occasion, "is not the real or the unreal but rather the mystery of the instinctive in the human race."

Zbo and his lady smile feebly, both perhaps thinking that instinct has a poor rate of exchange in the marketplace.

But for his slurping and gobbling while devouring his dinner, Chaim has thus far been silent. Modi has tried to instruct him in the fundamentals of table manners, but he has apparently forgotten it all in his voracity over what for him is a veritable banquet. He has dribbled a goodly portion of the sour rye soup down his front, saturating the napkin he'd tucked into his collar to protect his peasant shirt. He's eaten the herring in aspic with his fingers, licking the jelly from them with a doggishly greedy tongue. Just now he has pitched into his goulash with a gusto that promises to soil the tablecloth if not the wallpaper behind him. In past weeks, with Chaim's uncertain sanction, Modi has shown Zborowski some of his paintings, which the dealer thought barbaric but agreed to try to sell if only to please his principal artist. But the bargain had never included eating with the man.

Still singing for his supper, Modigliani has commenced one of his impromptu lectures—this one tracing the literary lineage of the Comte de Lautréamont through Rimbaud to Alfred Jarry, all of which Zbo has heard before. He looks to his wife, who is watching Soutine with a look vacillating between fascination and disgust, settling on disgust. In fact, she's holding her napkin to her lips as if she's about to be sick. In the hope that the Litvak might cease for a moment his gluttony, the dealer interrupts Modi's discourse to address Chaim:

"Monsieur Soutine, what about you? What was it compelled you to take up painting? We lay folk are always curious."

It's the old unanswerable question, which Chaim, still chewing his food with an open mouth, answers in standard Yid style with another question. "Because I couldn't be a boxer?"

Neither husband nor wife seems to know whether or not he expects a reply, and in the interim Chaim proceeds with making a mess. He's not entirely unaware of the impression his boorishness has on his hosts, but good student that he is of Amedeo's program of *épater le bourgeois*, he is perhaps a little more reckless with his utensils than usual.

Clearly enjoying the Zborowskis' mounting repugnance, Modi recites from Villon: "'We love filth and filth pursues us; we love honor but honor flees from us, in this brothel where we ply our trade . . .'" Then he stands abruptly and, without excusing himself, exits the *salle à manger*, only to return seconds later having fetched his palette and brushes from the guest room. He closes the door behind him and bids Soutine to rise. Chaim is confused but does as he's told; after all, Modigliani is nine years his senior and has his involuntary respect. He stands, picking his teeth with a fingernail as long as the one the mohel uses to pry the prepuce from an infant's *schmeckel*.

Modi stares hard at his friend, spits on his palette and stirs his brush in the egg tempera, then turns to face the knotty pine door. The Zborowskis sit dumbfounded as the artist begins to paint an outline of what appears to be the Litvak on their door. He has painted Chaim before in his mannered style, with a boy-ish forelock, his signature elongated neck, and an uncharacteristic composure—paintings that give the Russian immigrant an almost waiflike quality. But this version, which Amedeo is now render-ing slapdash without looking again at his subject, is different; it's rougher by necessity and full-length, and perhaps, by virtue of the unprimed wooden surface, somewhat iconic. Even despite Modi's inclusion of the dirty duffel and preposterous hat, both of which Chaim had removed, the portrait has begun to take on the gravitas of a saint's panel in a cathedral.

"Zborowski, make him stop!" entreats Hanka, but far be it from her dewy-eyed spouse to interfere with a genius at work.

"One day," he assures her, "that door will be worth its weight in gold."

"But until then we'll have to live with it," she despairs.

As he nears completion of his project, Modi teases Hanka that she should admit it: Soutine's bee-stung lips and bedroom eyes drive her wild with desire. At the same time Zbo tries to further appease her, appealing to her Catholic upbringing by suggesting that the portrait bears a distinct resemblance to the Shroud of Turin.

✦

CHAIM WAKES WITH THE sun, feeling awful. His joints are stiff, his guts wound tight about the crucible of his belly. The seething crucible has come close to boiling over from his anger at Marie-Berthe and his abiding sense of dread. His condition is not helped by Monsieur Crochard's sulfuric coffee, which he sips lest he insult his host. Otherwise, he has a flaming itch to be painting again. He thanks Crochard and, leaving the cottage, is reminded of the roll of charitable souls who have given him shelter over the years. Sadly, his gratitude flickers out before it's properly set alight. Still, Chaim remembers that Garde once called him fortunate, and Garde was never wrong. "I am a fortunate man," he says aloud, catechizing himself as he steps out into the bright new morning, but saying doesn't make it so.

What is truly fortunate is that Chaim has left his materials for the sake of convenience in Monsieur Crochard's hay barn. He sets up his easel outside a fold wherein the cabinetmaker has penned his single lamb, Desirée. Chaim has never understood the French habit of naming animals you plan to eat. He has also left unanswered the question as to when and why his own preference in beasts has shifted from the dead to the quick. In any case, by offering her a succession of the dried butter beans he scooped from a jar in the barn, he induces Desirée to hold an approximate pose throughout the morning and well into the afternoon. When the painting is finished he realizes, to his dismay, that he has transferred his anger and fear to the bleating lamb behind the fence—"like on Yom Kippur the Jews will put on the kapparot chicken their sins." Can you scapegoat a sheep? he wonders. But this is unfair; this poor walking soap foam of an animal does not deserve to be a vehicle for his *schmerz*. Art is not an exorcism and Chaim Soutine does not paint allegories. He takes out his jackknife, opens its blade, and is about to lacerate the canvas when, like Abraham on the verge of murdering his son, an angel (or is it an imp, or maybe the presence of that oafish kid spying on him from behind the garden wall?) stays his hand. Then it's sunset, and having stored his accessories once again in the barn, he carries the picture with him on the grueling walk back over the fields to Champigny.

He asks himself why he should return to Marie-Berthe at all. The word *destiny* enters his head, which makes him laugh, the laughter causing an agonizing contraction of his gut. "Sometimes," considers Chaim, struggling to straighten himself, "I think I am maybe giving birth." He arrives in the village leaning on his cane, too toilworn to worry about stealth. Crossing the little postage stamp of a village square, he totters into a circle of light from the single lamppost, where he is met by a tall figure coming toward him from the opposite direction. It's a German soldier and at his martial. "Monsieur!" Chaim abruptly halts. He can see by his high boots, peaked cap, and beribboned tunic that this is an officer of some rank. It's unusual to encounter German military in tiny Champigny-sur-Veude, though its trifling black market has warranted the occasional investigation; then the inquiring officer will freely select his portion of swag before shutting the operation down. Judging from the bulging haversack this one is carrying, he has most certainly done just that.

Chaim is too bone-tired to experience the appropriate terror. He waits to be asked for his papers, which he has neglected to keep on his person, and expects that their absence will likely result in his brutalization and probable arrest. "Do your worst," he moans to himself. But instead of demanding his documents, the courtly *daytshlander* asks him in a serviceable French, "Monsieur, you are an artist?"

Chaim looks down at his paint-besmirched garments, notes the picture under his arm, as if only just realizing that he is what the German has perceived him to be. "Oui," he says, blanching at how the French affirmative still sounds like "Oy" on his lips.

The officer lowers his sack to the cobbles and unsnaps a pouch at his duty belt to withdraw . . . But rather than the weapon that Chaim has anticipated, he produces a wallet, and from the wallet a well-thumbed photograph. Though his brow is largely obscured by the shadow of his visor, Chaim can see that, despite his high station, the German has a youthful face seemingly free of malevolence. He holds out the snapshot for Chaim to examine, tilting it a little so that it's spotlit by the streetlamp.

"*Ma fille chérie*," he says, "mayn Liesl."

It's a photo of a pretty six- or seven-year-old daughter of the Master Race, her blond braids encircling her ears in the style of Jeanne Hébuterne. Even in black-and-white one can tell that her eyes are a pellucid china blue. "Make me a portrait of her," says the officer, "and if I like it, I will pay you well."

Assuming he has no choice, Chaim nods and takes the photo. He agrees at the German's direction to meet him on the square under the awning of Madame Pichoreaux's café in three days' time.

Some minutes later he enters the wreckage of their hotel suite and sees on the floor, among the dust devils, empty bottles, strewn clothes, and broken-spined books, the ghastly tapestry that Marie-Berthe has created from the stitched-together bits of her portrait. It is the handiwork of a madwoman. The subject of the patchwork portrait is sitting on the floor beside it looking undone and in tatters herself. She's still wearing the dingy nightgown, her back leaning against the gutted divan, her legs splayed open like a discarded rag doll. She seems, with her washed-out features and livid-pink eyes, to have turned the corner overnight from femme fatale to aging frump. But if Chaim is alarmed by her appearance, she is just as shocked by his. His ordinarily sallow complexion is the blue-green of verdigris, and when did he get so thin? Consumed with sorrow for herself during his absence, she's been poised to lay into him on his return. But all she can manage at the fearful sight of him is, "Soutine, you're a ghost!"

"This makes of us two," he replies.

She rises awkwardly from the floor, but instead of attacking him, she sets about preparing his bismuth cocktail, adding a splash of *marché-noir* vanilla for flavor. She brings it to him and Chaim acknowledges the kindness by squeezing her wrist.

Then it's a coin toss as to which is the source of his greater pain: the time wasted on a portrait whose facile aspect amounts to a lie of the soul, or the pain in his abdomen that has spread to his shoulders and back? Plus the chronic nausea and the heaving into the toilet of what looks like coffee grounds mixed with blood. He employs a soft palette—beige, peach, honey yellow, water blue—and finishes the portrait of the little girl long before the allotted three days. The results are no better than the academic exercises he'd been made to produce in Vilna and later at Cormon's. No better nor worse than what any street artist might execute, and thereby inoffensive. After completing it, Chaim takes to his bed and refuses to leave it until the appointed hour of his meeting with the German. He is visited in his inanition by shretelekh and the levitating shade of the rebbe Tsvi Poupko of Ger.

Punctual for a change, Chaim finds the officer already seated at a table outside the café. There's a gunmetal pocket watch on the table beside his demitasse, a lit cigarette in the saucer, but he gives no indication of impatience. His pleasant demeanor remains at odds with a uniform that ought by rights to exclude him from all humane sensibility. It's a fine afternoon and Madame Pichoreaux has emerged from the interior of her café to hobnob with the pork butcher and the pockmarked stationer sunning themselves in front of their shops. Chaim notices as well the armored car with its waiting driver parked in the street. He can see—his eyesight remains acute even as the rest of him is failing—beyond the car and driver to the hills and valleys of dry bones that the insignia of the smiling man before him has engendered. At an encouraging nod from the officer he unrolls the painting and holds it in front of him like a shield.

The officer is instantly on his feet and leaning close to examine the portrait. "Wunderschön!" he exclaims. Chaim peeks over the top of the painting to observe the man wiping an eye with the back of a chamois-gloved hand. Then, affably, he offers the same hand to the artist: "Sturmführer Dieter Vogt, and you?"

Were it not for the pain that wrings his gut like a wet rag, Chaim might have clamped the canvas with his teeth; he might have twisted his head to tear the portrait, then pulled it apart and flung the two halves to the ground. He might have stomped the halves in a vicious clog dance under his heels. As it is, he passes the painting respectfully to the German's extended hand, and in response to his introduction says, "Karl . . . ," then clears his throat of some blockage. "Chaim," he states, "I am Chaim Soutine, degenerate artist and Jew."

The Sturmführer's spine stiffens, his gallant jaw twitches. The sudden annulment of his sham cordiality has the effect of removing a mask to reveal a skull. Then, by degrees, the smile returns, this time tinged with bile. Rolling up the canvas, he clicks his heels sharply, pivots, and returns to his car.

Madame Pichoreaux, alert to a change in the atmosphere, spares Chaim a melancholy glance before retreating into her establishment. The other shopkeepers follow suit. Left standing alone beneath the café awning, the artist gives himself up to a convulsive quaking; he lets loose a sepulchral sob at the realization that he has suffered what is politely called "an accident" in his pants.

Back at the hotel Marie-Berthe ignores his admission that he has sentenced himself to death and tells him to for God's sake clean himself up and change his clothes. Only gradually does she come to understand that he has done what he has done.

"Chaim, we have to get out of here!" she insists, uttering the phrase that has been a frequent refrain of their shared days. It has an urgency now like never before. Chaim doesn't argue but is too drained from his recent encounter, the spasming of his gut, and his general hopelessness to budge from his chair.

The woman has begun haphazardly throwing garments into a pair of suitcases. She sits on the bags in order to close them, though sleeves and flounced hems hang out of them like bunting. Her frantic activity appears to Chaim to include at least three actions for every one that is necessary. He bites his tongue to keep from calling aloud for Garde to come to his rescue.

"Marie," he says, while she actively disregards his paralysis, "you should leave me."

She drags their bags to the door and turns around to retrieve a forgotten corselet from under the bed. "I should have left you months ago," she replies without stopping.

"It's not too late."

This time she pauses to consider. She presses a forefinger to her temple as an aid to contemplation or in mimicry of a gun. "Yes it is," she concludes, and continues making ready for their departure.

The problem is, they have nowhere else to go. In the course of their peripatetic existence, they have long since worn out their welcome in the village. (They still have the remnants of chilblains from two frigid nights spent in an open field between lodgings.) They have exhausted the patience of Mayor Moulin, who is too preoccupied with unthinkable compromises and an epidemic of anthrax in the region to worry about a single sick Jew—for who hasn't guessed by now that Chaim is a Jew? As a consequence, this scratch house of a hotel has become their last resort. Marie-Berthe sits on the bags as if waiting at a depot. They've often talked of escaping Champigny, perhaps finding sanctuary in the Unoccupied Zone, in Montpellier, where Chaim's former physician Dr. Guttman has settled. Marie-Berthe has written him, floating such a plan, only to receive unasked-for dietary advice and prescriptions that have been little help to the patient. She has also corresponded with Guttman's assistant, Dr. Lannegrace, who is still practicing in Paris, asking whether she might visit Chaim in the Loire—so far have Marie-Berthe's good intentions strayed from the feasible. The lady doctor assured her that was impracticable, inviting her instead to bring Soutine to Paris for consultation, an undertaking she must know could be ruinous for everyone involved.

Marie-Berthe gazes at the sapless artist and seems finally to grasp that he's unfit for travel. His jaundiced flesh appears nearly translucent, and hugging his abdomen, he sways in his chair like an old Jew at prayer. What do they call it, their ritual of mourning? Sitting shiva. It's like he's sitting shiva for himself. She might once have walked away from him but now it seems the only vocation left to her is to try to keep him alive—and to participate with him in the vigil that Yids are everywhere observing: that is, waiting for either the Messiah or the sound of boots on the stairs, whichever comes first.

But days pass and neither comes. What does arrive is the concierge Monsieur Galipeau, who doesn't bother to knock. He barges in, a heavy-set, putty-nosed party accompanied by a fresh-faced village policeman, so young he looks to be just out of short pants. Galipeau directs the young flic in his ill-fitting uniform to deliver the piece of paper he's holding, which he seems almost embarrassed to do. It's a document bearing an official oath to the effect that the undersigned is not a Jew. In this way the concierge clearly hopes to cover his *postérieur*. (The wily Pippin Galipeau employs a variety of unofficial devices for keeping the authorities off his back but avails himself of legitimate resources when he must.) Before the cop can hand over the paper to the artist, however, Marie-Berthe lunges forward to intercept it and rip it in two.

Why, wonders Chaim, has she done this, after all the trouble she'd gone to to attain his false identity? Is it a gesture in solidarity with his own suicidal impulses? Or is it just that, now that he's so incapacitated, she feels obliged to carry on his custom of tearing things to shreds? Whatever the case, she has left the practically apologetic youth no recourse but to issue Chaim the yellow star.

"I got one already," says Chaim, rising shakily to his feet in order to produce from the pocket of his hanging jacket the souvenir from his Paris days.

The boy gendarme and the concierge depart, though not before Monsieur Galipeau has demanded that the couple leave the premises by nightfall. In the silence following their exit Marie-Berthe begins to clutch at straws. She says they needn't worry about Galipeau; they have the check that Marcel Laloë (Marcel has been as good as his word) has forwarded from the Carré gallery as an advance on future sales. It's more than enough to buy additional time from the mercenary concierge.

"Time for what?" broods Chaim.

Marie-Berthe persists in her magical thinking, observing that a callow village flic is neither Schutzstaffel nor Gestapo; every minute the Germans cease to come is another minute in which some twist of fate may defer their arrival. Perhaps the Sturmführer—didn't Chaim say he believed the man had a conscience?—perhaps he's so satisfied with his daughter's portrait that he is willing to forgive its creator for being a Jew. Perhaps the German division stationed at Chinon has been suddenly mobilized and sent to the lost cause of the Russian Front? Such things happen.

"Maybe will open the earth and swallow the momzers all up," says Chaim, squirming in his chair as he gives vent to a threnody of strident groans. Once Marie-Berthe believes that she hears him murmur the name of that milk-and-water forerunner of hers, Mademoiselle Garde, and thinks, I'd like to see her stick it out with him now.

At some point Chaim hauls himself to his feet and staggers out the door, on his way to the water closet down the hall. He doesn't make it, pausing on the landing to spew his black vomit. That's when it dawns on Marie-Berthe that—Holy Mother of God!—the poor man is in critical need of a doctor.

Crossing herself, she sees him to bed and hurries out into the high street looking for a local *médecin*. She's told by the postmistress that there are no practicing doctors in the village, but there is a retired old bonesetter living above the tobacconist's shop. Marie-Berthe climbs a flight, pounds on a door, and is eventually admitted by a sour-smelling old duffer with a head like a big baked apple, still in his nightshirt. She coaxes the man—who complains all the while that he knows nothing of your tummy distempers—into his trousers and shoes, and hustles him to the end of the street and into the hotel. They climb the stairs, step over the puke, and enter rooms that appear to have reaped the whirlwind, but the invalid is not there.

While she was away, Chaim has taken a powder. With an act of will practically beyond his ability to imagine it, he had strapped on the easel with a stretched canvas lashed in place; he took up the paint box and the crook-handled cane and set out once again, aiming his unsteady steps over the fields toward the river. He is trailed by a procession of followers. There's Semangelof and his brothers stumbling over the plowed furrows on chicken feet, and Laila escorting her fiendish mama as faithfully as Ruth supported her mother-in-law in the Five Scrolls. There are the disgraced seraphim Azrael and Shemhazai, banished from heaven for fornicating with the daughters of men. A host of the misshapen progeny spawned by their miscegenation follow them, holding hands like feebleminded schoolchildren. There's Moses's broad-bottomed second cousin Serah bat Asher, the woman who refuses to die, and circling above her the third dove that Noah released from the ark, who has yet to find a friendly place to land. They kick through patches of bluebells and scatter the heads of dandelions in starburst detonations, some shrinking from the warm daylight but advancing nonetheless. They've come from as far as *Alma d'Shikra*, the World of Illusion, and *Sitra Achra*, the Other Side, by way of a number of incinerated texts—the *Sefer Ma'assiyot*, *The Fountain of Israel*, *The Lost Book of Raziel*, the Torah. They have crawled from under kitchen middens and out of quicksand to travel incognito through realms of slaughter dating back to Creation.

They seem to believe, thinks Chaim, that he's leading them somewhere. This he finds (though he's careful not to laugh) almost laughable, since all these years he's been afraid that they'd come to take *him* back to wherever they hailed from. Isn't that finally their errand as inscribed in the open book in the lap of the gossamer-bearded merman?—the book Chaim is compelled to keep reading in order to save himself from drowning at the bottom of the Seine. But that's only a story, a legend if you will, and Chaim's life is no legend. It's not even a dream.

He aches, sweats, every step a shock to his system, but he's strangely unafraid. Or rather, the fear is confined to the knot of pain in his gut. "The fire in your belly is no metaphor, Chaim," he remembers Amedeo affirming. But it's never been so fierce, the pain, nearly a match for his longing to look again at his trees.

It's a still summer afternoon. Only the merest exhalation of a breeze stirs the thistledown clouds in an otherwise pastel-blue sky. A woodpecker hammers, a ruddy duck yammers, a wood thrush trills; a willow dips its fronds into the water at the river's edge like a woman letting down her hair to rinse it in a basin. *Et in Arcadia ego*, as Modi used to say, or as they said in Smilovitchi: "Since dying is all the fashion, living's become dangerous." But the day is a tonic and Chaim is content, after blenching from another intestinal cramp, that no one and nothing—neither the woman nor the elementals—can touch him here. He prepares his materials and begins to paint his trees. He feels at once, despite the prevailing calm, like that Englisher artist Turner who had himself tied to a mast to better witness the storm; at the same time he feels as if he's looking out from Jehovah's watch pocket, from where he can view with impunity the march of the tall trees: how one by one they break ranks and plunge into a marauding charge.

What distracts him is not the crowd of memories pressing him from behind—the past is powerless here—or even the ache, but the boy peering over his shoulder from a short distance away. He knows this boy, a nuisance. He belongs to the widow Charlot, the termagant neighbor of Monsieur Crochard. She keeps honeybees and a few wasted sheep and goats, and treats her mooncalf of a son—Eustache, is it?—no better than her livestock. And why not?

His unfortunate features—a shoulderless torso and ponderous head too heavy for the stem of his neck—have more in common with some kind of nonnative fauna than an authentic human being. His hair is a rooster's comb, nose a thimble, doughy face seeded with blackheads; a couple of his mother's bees seem always to be orbiting his skull, and the air around him is acrid from the urine stink of his knee pants. The painter has shooed him away with curses more than once.

Though in truth, Chaim, the most secretive of artists, has not really minded the boy's silent kibitzing, no more than he does Crochard's stick-legged lamb nuzzling his thigh. Moreover, the kid's eyes are not unlike those of the mournful farm animals Chaim has been so attracted to in these *shreklekh* years. He might even have done the abject boy's portrait if he thought he could be persuaded to stand still. But he's forever hopping from one foot to the other like some wading bird, then taking flight when the artist shows any sign of displeasure. Today, however, perhaps under the spell of these tranquil surroundings (notwithstanding the scrum of poplars and hemlocks and ash), he remains motionless. Chaim slowly adjusts his easel so as not to scare him off and begins to include Eustache as a detail in his landscape. But the boy's needful presence soon takes dominion over the composition, his face eclipsing the trees and obscuring the blue of the sky. Yet somehow trees, sky, the hemorrhage of red poppies in the foreground, the sound like a cat's purr or a hummingbird's wings, are all absorbed by Eustache's face, without in the least diminishing his ugliness. It's an ugliness the companion to Chaim's own, Chaim's very own sum and substance. Then, for a moment—I'd contend an exquisite moment—the only self left standing in Chaim's broken shoes is the one whose pain wrenches from his heart's core a shattering cry.

The boy runs for it and Chaim manages to gather up his gear and shuffle off in the direction of the cabinetmaker's cottage. He leaves the painting on the standing easel near the river. Along the way he encounters the ill-humored Charlot woman at her clothesline, with her son cowering behind her hessian skirts. The artist in his agony unhooks the oil-encrusted palette from his paint box and hands it to the widow.

"Keep for your son," he says; "it may one day be worth even more than Modigliani his door."

Nonplussed, the woman squirts a stream of tobacco juice through her teeth at his departing heels.

✦

THE ALLIES HAVE THEIR successes: they bomb Sicily and Sardinia, bomb Hamburg in Operation Gomorrah, creating a firestorm that leaves the city in ashes. But the Warsaw Ghetto Uprising has ended regrettably in the deaths of fourteen thousand Jews, and the rest, around forty thousand, sent to the camps. In London the citizens of Whitechapel listen for the double-crack that signals the incoming of the V-2 rockets, and in Bialystok the Jews mount a futile resistance, then kill themselves when they run out of ammunition. In Champigny-sur-Veude the Schutzstaffel raid the Hôtel Saint-Louis, rounding up random undesirables, but by then Chaim Soutine is in a hospital in Chinon.

After his collapse the cabinetmaker, borrowing a neighbor's telephone, notified the artist's mistress, who once again roused the creaky old sawbones from his nap. She dragooned the man into driving her in his hiccupping four-cylinder Berliet to the Crochard homestead, where he takes one look at the foundered artist and pronounces him advanced in illness far beyond his humble proficiency.

At the hospital Marie-Berthe hangs her Saint Christopher medal around Chaim's neck and has him admitted as the Russian émigré Karl Sutin. (Gone is the defiance that had laid hold of her only a day before.) The patient, docile in his misery, is made to undergo a battery of tests over the course of several days. During that time Marie-Berthe is harried by questions from interns: Are his stools black and tarry? Does his vomit resemble fish roe? Panicked by their interrogations, she presses the ministering nurse, a Franciscan nun, to try to find her some water from the spring at Lourdes. To conciliate her, the nurse procures an acid-yellow vial of holy water from a local church, which Marie-Berthe pours down Chaim's gullet, then waits for a miracle. When the miracle fails to happen, she considers calling in a priest for a bedside conversion that Chaim will be too weak to resist, but on second thought, recalling their steadfast support, she contacts the Laloës by trunk call. Madame Anne has her engagements and Marcel, truth be told, is not as eager to prove his loyalty to the couple as in former days. But pressured by Marie-Berthe's plangent reminders of his past devotion, and moved by a genuine concern for Soutine, he eventually rises to the occasion; he braves a series of stressful checkpoints to drive down from Paris to Chinon, where he arrives in an enervated state. Entering the hospital room, Marcel hardly recognizes the artist—a waxen figure twisting in his torment like an insect trying to wriggle out of a chrysalis.

When it comes, the diagnosis is grim. It's delivered by a Dr. Renvoysé, whose center-parted hair and toothbrush mustache give him the look of a headwaiter in an opéra bouffe. He informs Marie-Berthe, who he's been led to believe is the patient's wife, that Chaim is suffering from a perforated ulcer complicated by an infection of the stomach lining and bloodstream. His fever is high and anemia has also set in. The doctor seems to savor his pronunciation of the word *proctocolectomy*, an operation by which the colon and rectum are removed in order to save the patient. "Immediate surgery is necessary," he unequivocally insists. He adds that the procedure cannot be performed without the written consent of a responsible party. But Marie-Berthe has no faith in this self-satisfied doctor's authority nor in the competence of such a backwater facility. She's been on the phone with Dr. Lannegrace, who has again invited her to bring Chaim to her private clinic in Paris. There he can be treated by skilled physicians employing the most up-to-date methods. With gentle diplomacy, Marcel suggests that the risk of transporting the artist to the city might be greater than the risk of having the operation performed at Chinon.

The conversation takes place at the foot of Chaim's sickbed, though it's assumed he's too stuporous from the morphine injections to have a say in his own affairs. Nevertheless, raising her voice as if he were hard of hearing, Marie-Berthe asks him, "Chaim, what do *you* want?"

He hears the question through an opalescent fog, though it may as well have come from a cloud. "A painting studio I want," he says thickly, "with a north-light window like in the submarine *Nautilus* of the captain Nemo." Sometime after his long immersion in the Seine, he had been moved to read Jules Verne's *Twenty Thousand Leagues Under the Sea*.

Despite Marcel's cautions and the doctor's strenuous objections, Marie-Berthe signs Chaim out of the hospital on a form specifying that the patient has been discharged "Against Medical Advice." (Later, Renvoysé and his colleagues will claim that, had they known Marie-Berthe was not Soutine's legal spouse, they would never have released him to her care.) Marie-Berthe prevails upon Marcel to hire a vehicle suitable for conveying the sufferer. He reluctantly complies—the Aurenche woman, he allows, is a force of nature, if sometimes an ill wind. He leaves his own too-compact motor in the care of a shifty mechanic for an exorbitant fee, wondering whether he'll ever see it again. Then, at his own expense, he manages after much negotiation to lease from the hospital itself an Avions Voisin ambulance. (Its ebony finish and landau-style tasseled windows allow it also to double as a funeral coach.) Unfortunately, no driver is available.

Mounted on the *voiture*'s hood is the black-and-white banner denoting a vehicle used for medical emergencies. Regardless of the flag, however, and of their papers, which are more or less in order, Marie-Berthe worries about German roadblocks; she recommends they take an indirect route back to Paris. Marcel argues that such a detour might lengthen their trip beyond what Chaim, in extremis, can endure. But Marie-Berthe counters that the checkpoints could themselves result in interminable delays, and with the fresh memory of his white-knuckled drive down from the city, Marcel concedes to her will. He's a little afraid of Marie-Berthe.

With the help of hospital staff Chaim is settled as comfortably as is possible on a folding cot in the rear of the ambulance. Marie-Berthe tells Marcel, seated anxiously behind the wheel, that they must first stop at Champigny to collect Chaim's paintings; their sale can go toward defraying his medical expenses. Here Marcel protests: the pictures can be sent for. But from behind them they hear a cracked voice: "And don't forget please my easels and oils!" The patient's last morphine dosage has largely worn off, leaving him groggily conscious of his situation. The doctor has given him some analgesic tablets for the journey, but without the numbing effects of the strong narcotic, the pain has come roaring back. It's a pain like a refining fire purging his vitals as it ravages them, until everything that's recognizably himself is cast out. Then there's another Soutine, outside himself and free of pain, viewing his tortured body from the vantage of ogres and imps and disgraced angels. They huddle about him in the back of the ambulance, telling tales of their glory days.

In the village square at Champigny, a clump of men and women hang from a newly constructed gallows flocked by crows.

German soldiers are posted at the splintered door of the Hôtel Saint-Louis, and so the ambulance drives on. The paintings can wait to be retrieved another day. They take to the narrow back roads that are sometimes no more than country lanes, dodging potholes and jouncing over gravel where the pavement has worn thin. Sometimes the pavement gives out entirely. The *malade*, having thrown off his blanket, cries out from the jostling, the cot slides to and fro with every curve, and Marcel looks askance at Marie-Berthe, whom he blames for this rocky ride. Marie-Berthe, for her part, sits rigidly, suffering Chaim's incoherent babble in silence, though she recoils whenever he calls out the name "Garde!" She discovers a road map in the glove box, but due to her trembling hands cannot pinpoint the little towns they pass through—Thiaville, Bazoches, Ducquesne—on the jittering page. The Loire landscape is familiar enough: the orchards and vineyards and villages on their slopes above the flood terrace, the hunting parks with their holm oaks and hidden châteaux—they're the setting Marie-Berthe has become accustomed to over these many months. So why does she feel as if they've strayed into a part of France that has yet to have been explored by the automobile? Still, she offers the conviction that they are outwitting the Germans, while Marcel, fretfully grinding gears, mutters that they've perhaps outwitted themselves.

Meanwhile Semangelof, always the chatty one, is recalling the time he guided the hand of the great sage Rashi in inscribing an obscenity in his commentary on a tractate of the Babylonian Talmud; not to mention the changes he and his brothers made to the parchments stuffed in the mezuzahs of the *shteteleh* Slutsk, thus inviting demonic intrusion. Sansenoy whispers in Semangelof's ear to remind him of when they kidnapped the mohel at the circumcision of the Mezhbizh Rebbe's son and replaced him with the bloodsucking Broxa bird; and of when they rubbed a powder made from a black cat's afterbirth in the eyes of every sleeper in Hrubeshov, causing them to interfere with one another somnambulistically. Then there was the time they swapped an ill-featured child of their own, the one who liked to make crude pictures, for Reb Zalman Sutin's beautiful baby boy . . . which is when Chaim shouts, "Shveig! I never belonged to you."

"Why not?" asks Semangelof.

"Because," he sighs, "I'm not like you. I didn't never learn how to play."

The shretelekh beg to differ.

"Who does he think he's talking to?" asks Marie-Berthe, not really expecting an answer.

The direct journey from Chinon to Paris by motorcar ordinarily takes no more than five or six hours. Even with having to pass through the dense traffic of Tours and Orléans, the trip is not difficult. But Marcel and Marie-Berthe have been on the road all day and through the length of a nerve-racking night. Though thankful for the absence of barriers and spot checks, Marcel has become increasingly annoyed with his headstrong "partner in crime," as he's begun to think of the woman responsible for this misadventure. From the outset she's behaved as if their cargo was not an ebbing artist of international renown but some type of contraband. Her attitude has infected his, for which he's heartily ashamed; but for all his admiration of the sick man's oeuvre, in all honesty it's always been hard to square the uncouth immigrant with the modern master. At any rate, this pointlessly roundabout itinerary is making him certifiable. He doesn't think Marie-Berthe wants to kill Soutine—she chews her lip, bites her nails to the quick; her apprehension is surely unfeigned. Perhaps she believes that by taking such a circuitous route she can prolong the inevitable? Finally, the woman is beyond comprehending, though Marcel is nevertheless of her mind in refusing to admit that they're lost.

Chaim's bogies continue arguing in favor of his antic nature. They remind him of the times he and his pal Modigliani terrorized the slumming sightseers of Montparnasse, the times he performed (albeit back in his drinking days) a spontaneous *bezem tants* in the streets. They remind him of his zany works of art. And Laila, who has become sentimental about their past intimacy, recalls the colossal hoax he participated in with Modi, when he walked the floor of the river in a clunking scaphandre.

Sometime the next morning, though God knows how, they reach the *banlieues* of the chapfallen city. They drive through the Paris streets between rows of unpruned locusts and swan-white houses embarrassed by their own gleaming exteriors to an address in the 16th arrondissement: the Maison Santé at 10 rue Lyautey. There's some consolation in the building's hulking classical facade, and in the concern with which they're greeted by a severely coiffed Dr. Lannegrace and her colleague, the surgeon Ghislain Olivier. It's a concern worthy of the importance of their patient. As the orderlies scramble to lift Chaim from the ambulance onto a gurney, an exhausted Marcel Laloë, having acquitted himself of his part, fears that Marie-Berthe will set him yet another task. Instead, she wilts upon leaving the vehicle, so that Marcel comes round to help hold her erect. She shrugs off his assistance, thanks him bluntly for services rendered, and follows the orderlies as they wheel the flailing artist up a ramp into the clinic. Thus dismissed, Marcel assures Marie-Berthe, who shows no sign of having heard him, that he will be in touch, then staggers out of her life forever.

Once she's consigned Chaim to the hands of the physicians, Marie-Berthe crumples onto a hard bench in the vaulted corridor. She feels she has been forgotten and so is surprised when Dr. Olivier, a fussy man whose spectacles have slid to the tip of his needle nose, reappears to confirm the Chinon diagnosis. He questions aloud, perhaps rhetorically, why the doctors there did not immediately operate, then affirms that a radical—and here he uses that very long word again—must be performed without delay. Marie-Berthe fails, however, to detect the note of grave necessity in his voice, which makes her wonder (though she dare not ask it) whether by now the operation is a mere formality. Left alone again and overwrought, she imagines the doctors performing an autopsy on Chaim's living body. She wavers awhile between guilt and self-pity, then tries to remember occasions when her own and Chaim's singularities seemed to rhyme. That's the word that comes to mind: *rhyme*, and it somehow soothes her. Eventually she sinks into a fathomless sleep, and dreams that Man Ray has photographed her as the Queen of the Night.

In the operating theater the elementals are trying to convince the incorporeal Soutine, floating above his violated body on the table, that there's no point in hanging about *olam ha-tohu*, the world of confusion, any longer. They reassure him that separating the soul from the body is no more troublesome than "plucking a hair from a glass of milk." They even offer written instructions for negotiating the afterlife torn from the pages of an underwater volume that Chaim happens to be currently reading.

"I only just begun," he complains, while they assure him that that's what everyone says.

Marie-Berthe is awakened by *le docteur* Lannegrace in her surgical gown, whose standard professional face has slipped into a disclosure of genuine sympathy. "It's over," she says, placing a hand on the seated woman's shoulder. It takes the groggy Marie-Berthe some moments to realize that she's not simply referring to the procedure itself.

Marie-Berthe's emotions are no longer mixed. When she's able to rise, she stumbles through a Chaim-shaped hole in the fabric of her days, from the far side of which she cannot bring herself to view his remains. Instead, she locates a telephone and, with perhaps a touch of spite, calls Madame Castaing at her shop in the rue du Cherche-Midi. Madeleine reels at her end as from a battering ram to the heart; her sobs bruise her ribs. Later, having yet to forgive herself for what she has concluded was a disastrous matchmaking scheme, she sends a telegram to Mademoiselle Garde in Carcassonne. Garde, traveling under her new alias, catches the next train to Paris. Madeleine meets her at the Gare Montparnasse and the two women fling themselves into each other's arms with a fervor as befitting to combatants as comforters. The Castaings believe that, owing to their objectionable art world associations, their town house is being watched; so Madeleine arranges for Garde's accommodation in the Right Bank apartment of her brother Gérard. She gives his address to Marie-Berthe, who is medicating herself with Cointreau in a cheap Latin Quarter pension, then washes her hands of the woman ever after. Garde receives an invitation to the funeral signed by M-B Aurenche-Soutine.

It's as desultory an affair as one would expect of a funeral or-chestrated by Marie-Berthe. Jews are forbidden to be buried in Paris (their bodies disposed of who knows where), and while Chaim's forged documents might have passed as official in the one-horse provinces where he'd resided, in the city the name of Soutine would likely be recognizable to the prefecture. To throw the authorities off the scent, Marie-Berthe circulates a public notification announcing the site of the interment as Père Lachaise. This also sows confusion among the prospective mourners, only a few of whom are informed of the actual site: le cimetière Montparnasse, where Marie-Berthe's family, who have fled to the Free Zone, own a plot. As a conse-quence, no more than a handful are assembled by the gate on the appointed day. Among them is Pablo Picasso, who views his role since the occupation as a kind of elder statesman (he's sixty-two) of the arts. He believes, as do most others, that his presence gives the imprimatur to events of cultural significance, and the untimely death of the bedeviled Litvak certainly qualifies as such. Cocteau is also on hand, because when has Cocteau missed an opportunity to see and be seen? And Max Jacob, who goes where Cocteau goes, is there as well. Max is wearing the yellow star, from which he thought his conversion would protect him, and is only weeks away from being sent to the deportation camp at Drancy, where he will perish of pneumonia.

The humidity is oppressive, the sky heavy with leaden clouds intermittently lit by lightning from within, but the rain holds off. Cocteau whispers to Picasso that, given the atmosphere of the dead man's paintings, the Aurenche woman might have at least arranged a storm. Some of the absent are more conspicuous than those in attendance: Madeleine Castaing has apologized for her phobia of graveyards (and perhaps of Marie-Berthe?); the School of Paris, having closed its doors, has dispersed its graduates far and wide. But Jules Pascin is there, if only under a slab down an avenue of lindens past Baudelaire's cenotaph and Dreyfus's rock-strewn tomb. Thankfully there will be no priest; Marie-Berthe has spared Chaim that. No pallbearers or service, no pious eulogies, which he would have detested. The casket will simply be lowered by anonymous laborers into an as-yet-unmarked grave. Later on, with money from the sale of the Champigny paintings, Marie-Berthe will purchase him a stone. The stone will bear a large cross and an inscription with his name curiously misspelled as "Chaïme" and his date of birth wrongly given as 1894. She will soldier on in virtual seclusion until 1960, then kill herself after leaving word of her wish to be buried next to Soutine.

But at the burial this afternoon Marie-Berthe steals the show, though her histrionics come as no surprise to those who know her. An abundance of tears stream from beneath her veil, dripping from her chin into the bodice of the thin silk gown that serves as her widow's weeds. The bodice itself has been deepened since she's torn it in a misguided nod to Jewish ritual, thus revealing an expanse of damp, ghost-white flesh. The stickiness of the afternoon has caused the black gown to adhere to her bust and hips, showing her still-slender contours to good advantage. Her repeated lamentation before the plain pine casket—"Did you have to die!"—is what the gathered are treated to in place of proper solemnities. It's a cry that contains as much of recrimination as bereavement. The graveside onlookers perhaps try to discern where her performance leaves off and authenticity begins; they may wonder whether Marie-Berthe knows herself. A couple of mourners restrain her as if she might throw herself upon the bier.

Only Max Jacob, flush with compassion from his days in the monastery, comes forward to console her. "I think there's still more of Chaim here on earth than in heaven," he offers, and Marie-Berthe turns toward him a face full of frightened bewilderment. Mademoiselle Garde hangs back from the assembled beside a moss-grown monument in the shade of an elm, content to let the other woman take center stage. Grateful to have missed the sight of the artist's final suffering, she's free to recall his poorly aimed, overly moist kisses. There was the time he painted her belly when he thought she was sleeping, making her navel the eye of a bluebird in flight; and the time she was stung by a hornet and he prepared for her a poultice out of tobacco and a cow turd "dropped in the mystical month of Nisan," swearing all the while he was the least superstitious person she would ever meet. Who says you can't sustain yourself on memories alone? The hired men are removing the planks from over the grave and beginning to lower the casket into the ground. One or two of the mourners—a small gallery owner, a journalist from the defunct *L'art vivant*—come forward to toss in clods of dirt. Max Jacob, despite a tongue grown accustomed to reciting the Magnificat, mumbles a swift Kaddish under his breath. There's a crackle of lightning that illumines a cloud like a momentary firefly lantern, but the rain still refuses to come.

✦

IN THE MEANTIME, GASTON Babineaux, formerly of the Brigade Fluvial, is awakened from his catnap by an exercised Amedeo Modigliani forcefully shaking his shoulder. Seated at the edge of the embankment, the old man stirs from his drowsiness and begins to get the gist of what the Italian is shouting.

"*Pazzo stupratore,* pull him up!"

Jarred back to his senses, Monsieur Babineaux takes a quick slug from the bottle in his vest pocket and becomes all business. "Turn the crank!" he barks at Modigliani, as if it had been the painter rather than himself who was sleeping on the job. Then the old fellow immediately sets to work hauling on the braided security rope once again.

Seven and a half meters below the river's glittering surface, Chaim Soutine is still reading the waterlogged book. Its waving pages are turned for him by what he takes to be some ancient species of rabbinical merman. Though he's been at times a great reader, Chaim has lost interest in this particular story. He only continues reading because he has been advised to do so in order to perpetuate his breathing. All temptation to the contrary aside, he desperately wants to keep breathing.

But he's heard the story before, the one about the changeling he's been fed in snippets over the years by creatures who were themselves born out of fables. They're reading the tale over his shoulder even now, his familiars, having assumed forms more suited to the subaquatic realm: jellyfish and seahorse adaptations that might have been more fitting in the deep ocean than in an inland waterway. Then suddenly there comes again the rush of what passes for air in the confines of his ungainly helmet, which makes redundant any further perusal of the book. At the same time Chaim feels the tug of the lifeline wrapped around his chest, pulling him slowly upward. His head throbs and his lungs are raw and scalded from deprivation and abuse; cold water seeps into the supposedly impermeable diving suit. A resident tapeworm turns over in his gut. But he's mortally relieved to be finally ascending, having spent what feels like a lifetime underwater.

As he rises, the surrounding manifestations, part demon and part sea urchin, angel and electric eel, begin to fade and dissolve. Words wriggle from the page like a school of fish and swim away. They dart through the woven wicker of the sunken gondola from a balloon shot down in the Franco-Prussian War, then turn sharply like windblown silver leaves when the turbulence begins. A whirlpool has commenced to spiral about the merman, whose fleshless hand reaches toward Chaim from inside its vortex. The hand pinches the air hose—what Babineaux calls "your umbilical"—which is connected to the top of the copper bonnet. Again Chaim feels his windpipe constricted, his breath abruptly lost along with the memory of all he's witnessed below. He gulps an aching emptiness, trying to swallow some last molecule of the air that is as vital as color and light. He struggles there at the end of his tether, a goose choked by a butcher until its eyes roll back and are sightless. He fights with every cord and tendon against his expiration.

"Come back to us, Chaim!"

It's Modi's voice calling him from somewhere on the other side of his eyelids, which snap open to the grizzled sight of Gaston Babineaux, his leathery head coronaed in sunlight. Next to him lies the sloughed scaphandre from which Chaim has at last been delivered. The old plongeur is perched astride his chest, pumping his ribs like a baker's bellows in his effort to restore air to his lungs. Chaim coughs explosively, drool dribbling from his lips, then feels himself as if inflating after an immense inhalation. Shoving the old man off him, he sits up in his muggy underwear and rubs his smarting eyes to see more clearly the shayneh punim of Modigliani. His friend is seated before him on the oyster shell towpath hugging his knees, the coal-black curls dangling over his forehead. His grin is as glaring as the day, his red cravat floating in the breeze.

"You've survived, amico mio," he says, laughing, and offers Chaim a swig from the prize bottle of Château Lafite. "The race is won and Paris is ours." He makes a gesture that takes in the tree-lined embankment, the striped awnings and balconied windows and the whole of the enchanted city beyond. "And as Max says," adds Amedeo, "it's the most glorious afternoon in the history of the world."

ACKNOWLEDGMENTS

CHAIM SOUTINE WAS CLEVER at erasing his tracks; he left no written records of his life. And while there's substantial writing about his art in various *catalogues raisonnés*, there's little biographical writing about him outside of his mention in the biographies and memoirs of acquaintances. The book that sparked my interest in Soutine—beyond the paintings themselves—was Stanley Meisler's marvelous *Shocking Paris*, which details the history of the School of Paris and its more outstanding members. My gratitude to that book for revealing a world. For Modigliani's picaresque exploits there was Jeffrey Meyers' *Modigliani: A Life*, and for the very rich background of the period, Dan Franck's *Bohemian Paris* and Michael Marrus and Robert Paxton's *Vichy France and the Jews*. A shout-out to those who found the artist before me: Rick Mullin's book-length narrative poem *Soutine*, and Ed Ifkovic's novel *Soutine in Exile*. I hope I haven't stepped on your toes. I'd also like to thank the good guardians of Melville House, Dennis Johnson and Valerie Merians, my very talented editor Carl Bromley, and as always my stalwart agent and dear friend Liz Darhansoff.